D1280810

Secret Talents

Secret Talents

by

Anonymous

Grove Press, Inc./New York

First Black Cat Edition 1983
First Printing 1983
ISBN: 0-394-62483-1
Library of Congress Catalog Card Number: 83-081369

Manufactured in the United States of America

GROVE PRESS, INC., 196 West Houston Street,
New York, N.Y. 10014

5 4 3 2 1

PUBLISHER'S NOTE

The history of erotic literature is long and distinguished. It holds valuable lessons and insights for the general reader, the sociologist, the student of sexual behavior, and the literary specialist interested in knowing how people of different cultures and different times acted and how these actions relate to the present.

Because of the inherent value to all students of the human condition of these classic erotic works, we have chosen not to alter this book in any way, shape, or form. It is presented to the reader exactly as it first appeared in print. Thus, all of the subtleties are exposed to our view—the haste or extreme care taken by the author and the original publisher, the manner of speech and communication, the colloquialisms of the time, the means of expression, and the concepts of erotic stimulation—both real and imaginary—used by the writer who was, in every sense, representative of his time.

Introduction

Secret Talents is a rare gem among the erotic novels of the Victorian and Edwardian age. Unlike such earlier classics as *The Romance of Lust,* it belongs to a period when the new ideas of Krafft-Ebing and Havelock Ellis had stimulated a great exploration of sexual excitement, in fact and fantasy alike. The story which "Madame Borgia" has to tell is imbued with an eroticism which is often decadent and sometimes perverse.

The truth to life of the novel lies in its reflection of these new, "modern" enthusiasms. Yet its story is carefully detailed and plausible enough. Who was the prima dona, the narrator of this bizarre sexual career?

Both the action and the publication of the book can be dated with some precision. For instance, we learn that the heroine's first proper theatrical engagement was at the opera of Frankfurt-am-Main. While there, she learns of the more unusual lecheries which men like to practise on women. There are men who enjoy whipping a girl and sodomising her, as their favorite lusts. The author gathers this from reading a book, *Opus Sadicum,* a version of Sade's *Justine.* This particular adaptation of Sade was first published in 1889, so that the heroine's operatic career seems to have begun somewhere in the 1890s.

Soon after this, the prima donna is informed that the use of women in this unnatural manner is "an art practised since the days of the Caesars." This remark seems to come directly from Forberg's *Manual of Classical Erotology.* The first English version of this, with a false date and title-page, was published by Charles Carrington in Paris in 1899. Finally there is the reference to the heroine's triumph in the part of Juliette. This may have been a revival of Gouonod's *Romeo and Juliet.* If, however, it was the newly fashionable *Village Romeo and Juliet,* by Delius it gives a precise date of 1907. These clues, plus the reference to England's monarch as Prince of Wales and Edward VII, define the story as taking place in about 1895-1910.

Who published it? To judge from the way in which *Secret Talents* updates *Pauline: The Memoirs of a Singer* (1898) and from the reference to Forgerg's *Manual,* it was probably Charles Carrington, who published both the earlier books. He continued in business until just after World War I. Madame Borgia's story seems to date from then. There is, for instance, a new American resonance in the use of such a word as "pussy" for "vagina." Moreover, the novel uses terms not known in English until after the war. The heroine likes to dress in tight black crape for her lovers and she calls the material "georgette." The first use of this term, according to the Oxford English Dictionary, was in 1920, when it became something of a vogue-word.

But such details count for nothing beside the true modernism of the book. The author confesses, for example, to having a "fetish," meaning a sexual obsession. The word would have meant nothing, in this sense, to Fanny Hill or to those who were innocent of Krafft-Ebing.

The fetish is mild enough. The author likes to go into water with some clothes on, so that when she comes out her panties, bodice or dress will be tight and translucent, "my thin clothing clinging to me....every line and curve of my body standing out in bold relief."

It was Carrington's achievement to take such sexual obsessions out of the medical textbooks and put them into popular fiction. In this case, the "wet look" became an accepted fashion. After the age of Krafft-Ebing and Ellis, it was even possible for such costumes to seem more erotic than nudity itself.

Among the earlier novels which Carrington published, *Pauline* has a remarkable instance of this. A girl is to be brought into a prison yard and birched. She is stripped to her underwear, its tight silk stretched smooth over her buttocks. The implication is that it has been sponged over so that it will outline the hangman's target more easily.

For the most part, Carrington's publications make such fetishes a sport or a game. In *Beatrice* (c.1895) there is a charming scene involving a couple of girls and their mistress. Caroline and Beatrice are made to sit naked astride their horses on velvet saddles. The horses are tethered to canter in circles, causing the two equestriennes the most exquisite thrills by the movement on the velvet saddles between their spread thighs. Then, the girls are commanded to lie forward on their horses' necks and raise their backsides high. The canter continues but with the whip of the mistress cracking across the two pairs of female buttocks. After that the two girls are taken to the stables and, by use of chains and restraints, are fastened bending in a pair of stalls. A groom with a sponge and a bucket of stable-water comes round and washes them intimately between their thighs and buttocks until the water runs down to soak their silk stockings.

The wet look was also exemplified in another charming scene, in a Carrington novel of 1908, *The Amorous Adventures of Captain De Vane,* also published at some stage as *Venus in Tight Trousers.* The scene is a room in an English country house on a fine summer afternoon. Two young women are teaching an adolescent dancing pupil to perform a lascivious harem dance. Jane, the pupil, is an appealing *ingenue* with lank brown hair and a short fringe, firm pale features and steady brown eyes.

Pretty Jane, her arms twining above her head practises her writhing dance of hips, belly, and thighs. She is dressed in a breast-halter of translucent silk and matching panties. "As she turned, showing the seat of her tight silk pants, a childish tautness and a feminine allure were mingled in the shape of Jane's agile young bottom." Then ends of the dark brown hair sweep her bare shoulders, the glances darted back at the onlookers are half teasing and half apprehensive. With her flat young belly arched in and taut buttocks rounded out, she performs her lascivious seat-squirming dance. The pale translucent green of her tight panties is like a last veil.

A shallow bowl of liquid soap stands close by. Edging her rump towards it, the youngster tilts the rim so that the viscous liquid soaks the seat of her thin silk panties. She becomes teasingly young and playful. "Can you imagine a woman of twenty-five or even a proud beauty of sixteen soaping the seat of the knickers she wore to amuse her lover? Jane looked adorably haughty...The slippery wet silk of her pants clung in silhouette to the cheek-swellings of her young bottom." As her taut young buttocks arch and squirm in the harem dance, it is predictable that the thin punishment strap keeps time across the cheeks of Jane Mitchener's bottom. Soon after this she learns to sleep with her head pillowed on her admirer's bare thighs each night, having sucked his penis to exhaustion but with its limpness still held gently in her mouth.

Secret Talents goes further still when the young heroine is required to release the flood from her belly before the eyes and even over the face of the man who covets her.

This diversion is a reflection of the *fin de siecle* sexuality, the pleasures of jaded European desire.

A more common fashion of the day, described by the author is the eating of food from upon or within the female body. In *Secret Talents,* Ferry enjoys three young women whose vaginas are filled with candy, the soft sweets also being spread between their buttocks. This was no mere fantasy. There was a famous occasion in Paris when four flunkeys wheeled in a huge silver platter under a dome at a dinner of wealthy bon viveurs. The dome was whisked away to reveal the nude beauty of young Cora Pearl, bathed in pink sauce and with parsely tucked between her thighs. With whoops of delight, the young patricians began to scoop off the sauce with their spoons and to seek the last dollops in the most unlikely places. Iwan Bloch also records the passion of one European nobleman who made a tall and beautiful girl straddle naked so that he might eat strawberries from her vagina.

Fiction, of course, seized upon such scandals long before the Victorian age. In Sade's *Julliette,* Minski's dining-table and plates consist of the living flesh of young women. Upon their breasts or buttocks an hors d'oeuvres and the hot omelettes are served. *Birch in the Boudoir* has a banquet scene where the platter is Jackie, a plumpish, sluttish blonde of twenty-five. The hors d'oeuvres are served on her breasts with her nipples as the cherry-tops, the main course on her belly, and the pancakes on her bottom. The surface of the table is conventional enough. Yet it supports at either end are two girls kneeling naked on all fours, the table supported on their backs.

The possibilities are innumerable. One of the supports is Maggie, a shopgirl of about twenty with a pale slightly stocky figure, hard young features and long blonde hair on her shoulders. To the man on one side of the table Maggie must offer her tongue, to lick his fingers as the alternative to a finger-bowl. To the man behind her, she presents her vagina as the place to warm and ripen his dessert banana. The receptacle for olive-pips and an inconsiderately large number of plum stones is provided by Maggie's behind. Like Sade, this account belongs to the world of surreal humour rather than actuality.

Yet in Carrington's novels the universal sexual obsessions, whether acted in reality or not, are never long absent. The equestrienne or pony-girl fetish is there in *Beatrice, Dolly Morton, Birch in the Boudoir,* and *Pleasure Bound.* In the first of these the girls are the riders, in the second they are harnessed or driven as ponies or mares. *Birch in the Boudoir* has its "carriage outing," as well as Jackie and Mandy harnessed and under discipline at the winding-wheel. *Pleasure Bound* marks a distinct advance into the twentieth century by placing a naked girl, Marsuma (presumably the Persian *Massoumeh*) on a bicycle. A trailer is attached behind the bicycle so that the man and woman in it can admire Marsuma on her saddle, the movements of her naked thighs, hips, and buttocks as she labours to pull them. After this "hot cycling," there is "a taste of leather" between her thighs and in her rear cleavage.

Charles Carrington spent much of his life one step ahead of the law, as represented by Chief Inspector Drew of Scotland Yard. It is not surprising that many of his novels—some of which he adapted or even wrote—should have a strong vein of subversion. Scotland Yard complained bitterly to the French authorities for allowing Carrington to include female pubic hair in his Paris printed erotica. Yet no action was taken about books like *Studies in Flagellation.* These described scenes in which English reformatory girls like Sarah Barnes, Elaine Cox and Sally Fenton—or young women like Phyllis Blake, Susan Webb, and Ann Turner—were stripped of their skirts and pants, strapped down over a block and their bare buttocks birched or caned. Such punishments were "normally improving" and there could be no objection to describing them.

As if in derision, *Secret Talents* shows us what Carrington and his authors really thought. We are taken into a prison run by a Russian ogre who might almost be Sade's Minski in *Juliette* again. One of his sidelines is to supply girls, on parole from prison, to Countess Marie Rossenloff in Budapest. The judicial whippings which they received from the gaoler are extended and refined. Girls like Molly, Yvonne, and Violet are conditioned to find sexual excitement under the whip because it is the only quasi-erotic experience permitted to them.

One might doubt if much pleasure was derived by the girls who were whipped between their open legs as well as across their buttocks. Carrington, as the publisher and perhaps the part-author of *Secret Talents,* is lighting a fuse under the English penal system.

As many Victorian and Edwardian readers knew full well, there were certain institutions were girls were whipped—the houses run by James Miles at Hoo, Miss Cotton at Leytonstone, Mrs. Walter at Clifton, Bristol, among them. The whippings and birchings were public knowledge and were much like Sir William Hardman's account of such punishments in 1865. Women were chastised "on their naked posteriors....publicly and indecently exposed in shameful nakedness."

Secret Talents reflects a moral irony which existed in truth. Whether dealing with a girl of fourteen like Sarah Barnes or Elaine Cox, or a young woman such as Ann Turner or Susan Webb, the authorities in a reformatory were scrupulous. There were no boy-friends, of course. Every effort was made to prevent the growth of lesbianism. Masters and matrons were vigilant to deny even the opportunity for masturbation.

And yet, as such Carrington non-fiction as *Studies in Flagellation* pointed out, there was another side to this judicial prudery. Mr. Miles would be seen, most afternoons, walking to a certain room accompanied by Elaine, or Sally, or Sarah, or Tracey, or one of a hundred other girls. Beauty at sixteen years old, the classic profile of fair-skinned English beauty, the yellow-blonde hair worn in a silken sweep across her head, like a fine veil falling on her shoulders.

It was, perhaps, noticeable, that the young nymph was dressed in blue working denim, a short jacket and tight working-jeans. Walking behind her, a punishment-strap dangling from his hand, the master was thus able to observe the long slim beauty of her legs and thighs, the taut feminine rounds of Tracey's bottom.

But, as Carrington knew, once in that soundproof room, the mask fell from the pretence of moral discipline. Tracey was made to mount astride a padded leather vaulting-horse and lie forwards tightly along it. Her wrists were strapped to the two wooden forelegs. With no witnesses present, the master was free to stroke her long sweep of yellow hair, kiss her lips and face, even to unbutton himself and make Tracey suck his erection.

Perhaps he did none of these things. What he would certainly do, however, was to undo the working-jeans and pull them down and off—with Tracey's panties inside them. Each of her ankles was now strapped to a rear leg of the vaulting-horse. In this pose, her thighs were braced open astride the horse, her taut young buttocks stretched wide as she lay forward, straddling. The master's hands would adjust her position lovingly, his fingers loitering over her hips and thighs, between her legs and buttocks.

The zealous chastiser had chosen the strap because it could be used long and repeatedly. Despite its ferocious sting, the red welts faded in a few hours. Yet, at sixteen years old, Tracey was being conditioned to associate her ordeals inextricably with sexual arousal. The master's fingers which felt and squeezed gently between her legs as he pulled her pants down might have been those of her boy-friend preparing her for some furtive sex.

For what could Tracey hope? Would the master change his mind, laying down the strap and mounting behind her as she lay astride the vaulting-horse? There were no witnesses, nothing to stop him straddling the padded leather behind her as she sprawled forward. He could thread his erection between her legs or impale Tracey's bottom on it, just as he chose.

If there was another person in that room during these sessions, it would be a second culprit straddling another vaulting horse. So the master might contemplate Tracey and Noreen side by side, or Tracey and Debbie, or any combination that he chose. Even if he unbuttoned himself and made use of Tracey and Noreen simultaneously, his word would always be believed against theirs.

This is the world which *Secret Talents* mocks in its account of the Countess Marie Rossenloff. "Those girls would put up with anything the Countess suggests rather than be returned to prison. As far as their appearing to like being whipped, they do not; it's simply that they know they must do it, and so they concentrate their thoughts on lascivious things and actually bring themselves to the spending point."

So we are left to imagine Tracey, her slim sixteen-year-old thighs tightening rhythmically on the leather flanks, the roundness of her young buttocks tensing and pressing, her yellow blonde hair sweeping aslant her face as she lay with blue eyes closed and lips gently parted. In a more healthy society, Tracey would have had a boy-friend to bring her to sexual fulfilment. Here things were otherwise. Mr. Miles could justifiably boast that he had used the whip to cure Tracey of wanting boy-friends. She had been conditioned to accept quiet a different order of pleasure.

Secret Talents is a novel and not a history-lesson. Yet any reader in the early twentieth century who thought it bore no relation to reality must have been going through life with his intelligence blindfolded. Chief Inspector Drew admitted as much to a select committee of the English House of Commons. It was Carrington's crime, in part, to excite readers to sexual enjoyment by the books he published. Yet his even graver crime was to mock the birch and the whip—the orb and sceptre of English moral order.

Carrington's own story continued until his death in 1923 and is too long to tell here. He remained a "wanted man" in England, living out his life in Parisian exile. Perhaps Inspector Drew thought that was punishment enough. The inspector's blood was still boiling at the French rebuff which told him that a girl's pubic hair was an innocent adornment and not—as English law maintained—a gross and lewd disfigurement. For another fifty years, until the 1960s, Mr. Drew's law prevailed. A nude photograph of a girl with her pubic hair shaved off was legal. If she still wore it, the photograph was an offence, punishable by imprisonment. There is, as they say, a moral in that somewhere.

Richard Manton

Chapter I

My dear friend:

It gives me great pleasure to inform you that I have received your most welcome letter, and am happy in the thought that you sometimes think of me. I am delighted, too, to know you are enjoying such splendid health.

Really, my dear, I thought you had quite forgotten me after all these years, but I see you haven't, and I am glad. Yes, I am very happy and contented and, like myself, I have retired from active life. I have lived my life —my professional life, I mean—and I intend to devote the remainder of my days in travel and—well, you know my great weakness.

It is strange that you should ask me to write my memoirs just when I was about to write them for myself, and now I believe I shall do so. And I hope you will enjoy as fully in reading these pages as I have enjoyed them in the flesh.

Well, where shall I start, my friend? Suppose we start at the very beginning—all careers have a beginning somewhere, you know.

Up to and including my fifteenth birthday there is precious little to tell, so I shall skip over that; it has nothing to do with this tale and will—I dare say—be rather tiresome.

Up to the age of fifteen I knew nothing of love, except, of course, the love one had from a parent, and the pets I had, so I can think of no one thing which might be called responsible for the strange and delightful life I have led. So, to sum up the whole thing, I guess I was born for love! How could it be otherwise when it has been the one ruling passion of my whole life? Love! Yes, that was it, and believe me, my friend, I have had my share.

There are few, few things concerning my early life, however, which I think would be of interest here. I was an only child. We lived in a pretty little home in the village of H——, and in my childish way I was happy. I never had to attend school like the other children, since father provided a private tutor, and an ugly old witch she was, too. She was very strict with me, and I can well remember how she used to scold me when I romped about the gardens with my pet poodle, telling me it was vulgar to show one's legs; nor could I visit with the other children who passed our home.

And it was this very strictness as much as anything else, perhaps, which led my active mind into other and stranger channels.

I guess she was what we call today a 'prude,' and I believe she disliked herself. So you see, my friend, I was kept in close confinement, as it were.

But, with all her faults she was a very learned person, and I have many, many times profited by her teachings.

Mother was very kind to me, and I always had the things I craved.

Father earned a wonderful living for us, he was a skilled mechanic, inventing many optical items used to this day, and for which he received a great deal of money.

When I received a scolding from my teacher, I would run to Mother, and always I would receive her kindest consideration, to say nothing of her kisses. But she had implicit faith in my tutor, telling me I must mind her as she knew best.

I must tell you of a little incident concerning this strange woman. At the far end of the gardens there was a tiny lake, or pond, and one day I asked permission to wade in it. But my tutor was horrified! It was scandalous! The very idea!

Do you recall my saying a moment ago how I believed it was this woman's meanness as much as anything else which led to the strange things I did? Yes? Very well, let me emphasize this here.

One day as she and I were walking through the gardens I was struck with the idea that I wished to remove my shoes and stockings and wade in the pretty pond, but what was my surprise to have this simple request refused me! What harm could possibly come of it!

I suppose I am no different than anyone else; had she allowed me this simple pleasure, I am sure nothing would have come of it, and what happened as a result of what I did, wouldn't have happened at all. Having been deprived of the pleasure, I promised myself that, unbeknown to her, I would do that very thing!

The next afternoon I watched my chance. On the pretense of taking my poodle for a walk, I slipped away and ran to the pond. It seems to be a human trait to lust for that which is denied us. Whether that is true or not I do not know; I do know, however, that I yearned for that pond as I had never yearned for anything else in my life.

The poodle, nearing the pond and thinking it quite

alright, ran into the water. Standing there watching him splash about made me all the more eager to partake of this pleasure, and the more I watched him the greater became the longing.

It's a strange thing that such a simple thing can lay the groundwork for one's whole career, isn't it? Yet, such was the case. Had I been allowed to wade at the time I asked my tutor, everything would have passed as before; now, standing there knowing I was contemplating something forbidden, made the desire all the more pronounced!

Now it happens that I had never been in the water, and as I stood there contemplating the pleasure my poodle was having, I was taken with the idea that I, too, would like to splash about in it.

To think is to act—and this thought has been my constant companion. Making sure no one was about, I stripped off slippers and stockings, and holding up my already short skirt, I waded in! The water felt delightful on my feet and ankles, and for minutes I stood there. I wanted to go in deeper, but, as I have said, I had never been in such a large body of water and the thought frightened me.

The next day, however, I tried it again, and this time I managed to get in to the bend of my knees. It was wonderful! I did this twice more, the fourth day being detected by my ugly tutor who ran to Mother with the startling news that I had wilfully disobeyed her!

Again I cried, and again Mother consoled me and made me promise to always obey my tutor, since she knew best.

A week passed, but my desire to wade was ever present. It was Sunday. Tutor had left for the day. Father, too, was away, and mother was busy about the house. Knowing I would never have such a favorable chance again, I raced for the pond! Naturally, I had gotten over being timid, and this time I became more daring!

Knee-deep no longer interested me. Besides, there was something delightfully naughty about the feel of the water on my legs! What it was I didn't know, of course; I knew only that it was the most wonderful sensation I had ever felt, and the deeper I went the greater the sensation!

I went deeper and deeper, and then, to my dismay, I found the lace at the bottom of my drawers was wet and that the legs were wet half-way up! I was frightened! I knew Mother would be furious if she discovered this, but the desire for the feel of the water was predominant! Quickly I hurried up the bank and removed the offensive garment, and after spreading them to dry I hurried back into the pond! Free, now, of the troublesome and peaky thing I waded out, and this time the water quite touched my cunt! Oh, what a thrill it was!

I mention all this to show you that in my innocence I knew nothing of myself. I knew nothing of the thrills one might enjoy through the medium of one's cunt, so, of course, I knew not that I was experiencing that first spark of young womanhood which comes to all girls. All that I was interested in was the fact that it felt so nice I thought I was in Heaven! Indeed, I was so overcome with the strange emotion that I quite overlooked the fact that my dress was trailing in the water, but, strangely enough, this bothered me not in the least.

The Heavenly feeling I refer to seemed to center deep between my thighs, and as I wondered what it could be, I put my fingers there only to find the strange sensations increased, for my fingers had come in contact with that tiny sentinel which guards the abode of bliss and which, until that moment, I never knew I had.

It was, as you may have guessed, my clitoris, that little jewel of an organ that was to play such an important part in my life in the years to follow!

Do you remember, my dear, how you used to delight to lie with your face between my legs? And how you delighted to kiss and tenderly suck that tiny red tongue, as you delighted in calling it?

Well, it was that same tiny morsel I found that day as I stood hip-deep in our little pond. So, do you realize now what an important part my ugly tutor played in my later life?

I was frightened as well as happy, and as I dried my dress before returning home, I promised myself many more wading parties in that little pond; I thought the water was responsible for those strange and Heavenly sensations I had experienced.

And that, dear friend, was the very beginning of a life of utmost pleasure.

Then came a change in my life. I found myself deprived of the pleasure of wading, and it's just as well—I might have become an addict to that dreadful practice known as self-abuse!

About this time it was discovered I had a most unusual voice.

I had been singing in Sunday school, and our music teacher often remarked of the wonderful future in store for me. This I accepted as most compliments, but I continued to attend to my music. Then one day our choir master visited our home and was closeted for some time with Mother, and I learned that he had spoken with her regarding the unusual quality of my voice. Mother spoke with Father about it, and it developed that something should be done about it.

Then followed four months of intensive study. I practiced faithfully and soon it was learned that my voice was far beyond anything they had even conceived and it was suggested that I be sent away where I might study under masters, and thus develop what they termed my good fortune.

But Mother and Father refused to listen to this. They did, however, consent to hire a music teacher, but as this change necessitated the removal of my other tutor, I was overjoyed.

I expected another old witch, of course, but anyone would have been preferable to her, and I praised the good Lord when she finally packed her belongings and left.

For a few weeks I was quite alone. I had no tutor, my only studies being that of music and I attended Sunday school daily. Also, I had plenty of time to run about the gardens, and you may rest assured the little pond came in for its share of attention. Ah, if that pond could see and hear! But ponds do not see and hear, and if it enjoyed my presence it did it in silence, for everyday I bathed there. Sometimes in complete nakedness, at others partly so, but always my little cunt came in for its share of fondling.

As the days slipped by. my feelings kept pace, and it was then, for the first time, I took notice of my breasts. They grew larger and firmer and rounder, and as my fingers caressed them a thrill swept over me—and I noticed, too, that my legs seemed rounder and more firm.

And there was something else too. I noticed that the hairs about my cunt grew darker and darker, and thicker and thicker; my cheeks grew redder and my lips took on a cherry-red hue, while my eyes seemed to grow large and there was a brighter look in them.

I noticed, also, that I experienced more and more thrills and that they became more and more pronounced just before and just after my "sickness." I knew not what caused this, but I wasn't to be left long in doubt, as you shall see.

One afternoon about this time Mother informed me that she was expecting guests. It seemed the "guests" were her niece and her husband-to-be, and since they had long promised to visit us, they took it upon themselves to visit us before their marriage.

The following day they arrived, bag and baggage. And now, as these two young people were to furnish a spectacle that prompted and hurried upon my career, it is no more than right that I describe them here. The girl was about twenty and very pretty. Shapely she was too, and her complexion was superb; all in all one might sum her up as beautiful.

Meeting such a girl in later years I would have promptly put her down as one literally dying to be fucked, and five years later when I became a lover of women's charms, I invariably chose just such a girl, and for the simple reason that she was animate and that she would comply, willingly, with every request.

Her lover was equally good-looking. Five feet eleven, very handsome, slightly dark with wonderful eyes, I fell quite in love with him. They seemed devoted to each other and were seldom out of each other's sight.

Now, it must be remembered that I was just approaching young womanhood, that period in a girl's life where so little is required to ignite the spark of passion. I remember that when near this man I would blush, and hot flashes came over me thrilling me to the core.

Both were very nice to me, and as I recall it now this man would cast longing glances, and had his future wife not been present there is no telling what might have happened as I am sure I would have welcomed him to my arms.

Life is a strange thing. A thief is forever finding something to steal; a drunkard is forever being offered wine; and so it was with me. Awhile back I said I believed I was made for love; I repeat it now; it was as though temptation was forever being thrown in my path.

Let me illustrate. A day or two after their arrival I had taken my poodle and had started off for a walk. At the far end of the gardens, and not far from the pond, there was a little summerhouse.

As I neared this I heard someone laugh and recognized the voice as that of the bride-to-be. My poodle had bounded off to his favorite swimming place, thinking, of course, that I would follow; but another idea occurred in my mind. Both liked to play pranks on me, so why not play one on them? I would creep up and frighten them!

As I neared the tiny building, however, I delayed my surprise attack; I heard something of what they were saying, and my curiosity being aroused, I listened. My heart was beating wildly; I knew it was an evil thing to eavesdrop, but my shameful curiosity was aroused.

My eagerness to hear was further aroused when I heard her say: "Oh, please, dear, wait until tonight; we can take a walk up the road and then you can have all you want!"

I wondered what it was he wanted? Thinking it might be something good to eat, perhaps, I crept closer and found I had a clear view of the interior of the place, and what a sight met my eye!

They were standing in the center of the bowerlike place. Their arms were about each other, their mouths were joined and they seemed lost in the affectionate embrace. Then their lips parted and they stood for a long moment staring into each other's eyes.

"But, darling," he was saying then, still clasping her in

his arms, "it's been almost a week since I've had anything! I'm bursting for it! Here feel for yourself!" Then, as I stood there breathless, my eyes fairly bursting from their sockets, he pulled open the front of his trousers! His great tool came out!

"Here," he said, placing her hand on it, "Feel how hard it is, dear! Please!"

Then clutching her in a tighter embrace, their lips met in another clinging kiss, her hand now working up and down the pokerlike thing she held in her hand! For one breathless moment I watched her as she toyed with that thrilling thing, and then something else occurred: His arms which had been clasping her now slid down; his hands clutching the firm cheeks of her bottom! My eyes staring, I watched as he slowly drew up the dress! Up and up! Now it was at her hips!

Suddenly my mind went back to my old tutor! How she was forever telling me how vulgar it was to expose one's legs. Yet, here was a man pulling up a girl's dress!

What was more, she seemed to enjoy this freedom! Was it possible, I thought, that this girl liked being denuded in this startling manner!

Truly she must have, for now her dress was up to well above her waist and the man was toying with and feeling all over her bottom and back which was entirely devoid of anything like drawers or other under-garments!

I felt the perspiration burst out on my face; my lips grew hot and dry, while a sensation yet unknown seemed to take possession of me. Still the picture lingered. Her hand continued to work up and down his big affair; he continued to play with the naked cheeks of her lilly-white bottom!

Again the picture changed! As one they moved to a broad couch-like seat and here he pushed her down, but not for a moment did they lose their advantage; he continuing to toy with her naked bottom; she to play with his iron-hard tool! Her legs fell apart, and at the same time his hand came from behind her and slid into her now fully exposed crotch! What a picture I was witnessing!

Naked from her breasts to the tops of her stockings, her thighs well parted, she seemed to relish the feel of his hand as it toyed with the thick black curls at the base of her belly or quite slid into the crimson gap buried in its folds! Again the picture changed.

Her hips were moving and her hand quickened its up and down motion on his toy, and then he suddenly dropped to his knees between hers, and while I stared, hardly daring to breathe, he plunged his face into the forest of black hair, kissing and tonguing her cunt in a frenzy of delight!

I didn't know it then, but how many times since have I experienced that delightful thrill of feeling a lover's tongue exploring the inner cavity of my own cunny! Ah, that young man was an artist; someone had taught him his lessons well.

For a minute, it seemed, he kissed it, and all the time she showed by the very expression on her face that she loved this strange sort of kiss! Her head rolled from side to side; little moans escaped her lips, and her hips began moving! Her hands came down to his head; I thought she was trying to force his mouth away, but I discovered she was holding him even tighter to her! He lifted her thighs to his shoulders, wrapped his arms about her hips!

She was moaning aloud now! She stiffened, gave a little startled cry and her hips jerked violently, while her eyes stared and she muttered: "Oh's" and "Ah's" at each new attack!

Then, with an "Oh, my God!" on her lips, she threw her head back; she held herself rigid for fully a minute, and then she collapsed in an inert heap before him, her hands falling to her sides and her thighs falling from his shoulders!

Wondering what ever had happened, startled to almost screaming point, I watched him bring the end of his cock to that lovely red gap he had been kissing! With his hands on her hips he forced himself against her, driving his cock deep into the glistening slit!

I thought he must be killing her, so violently did he plunge it into her! Now her legs came up and about his back, while her arms circled his neck, and now they were both swaying backward and forward! Then with a firm, forward thrust he drove it into her—just as I thrust my finger into my own cunt! Ah, God! No one can describe the sensation I experienced at that moment as I gave down my first maiden spend! My knees trembled beneath me; I gave a gasp, so intense was the thrill!

My finger, thrust to the last knuckle into my burning cunt, was bedewed with the thick starchlike fluid while streams of it, it seemed, gushed down my hand and forearm! But what's the use of trying to describe it to you, my friend? How many times have you complimented me when I would pour that elixir of love into your willing lips? How many times have you told me I was the best suck you ever had? Who, then, is a better judge than yourself as to the amount I threw off that first time I went-off?

How many times have I longed to live over those first thrilling moments of my young life? But I must get on with this first installment of my story.

They became more quiet; her legs slid down from his back, and then, free of her clasp, he withdrew his cock from her, and I noticed then that it was but half its former size. Now he took his seat beside her, but I noted how careful she was not to cover her charms.

Instead, she sat there, her skirt well above her waist, and for the first time I had an unhindered view of her pretty cunt. It was far larger than mine. Its color was deeper and it was surrounded with thick, black hair, while the cunt itself gaped open and a trickle of thick white stuff ran from the bottom and dripped on her skirt, but which troubled her not.

As he seated himself beside her, she lifted her left thigh and placed it across his lap. Then she carried one of his hands to her cunt, and as his fingers divided the red lips and bored into the dark interior she placed her nearest hand upon his half-limber cock and toyed with it, he slipping his arm about her and kissing her lips with soft, clinging kisses.

Now and then their lips would part and they would say something I couldn't hear, but at last, when it seemed she was about to eat him entirely with her passionate kisses, she said: "Now, Paul, darling, suck me off again!"

Then, instead of kneeling between her knees as he had previously done, he slid to the ground and lay full length on his back. For a long moment she stood staring down at him. Then, with a deft motion of her hands, she swept the dress up to her breasts and fell astride his upturned face which disappeared into the thick fleece!

Reaching over with one hand she grasped his cock which was again in a wonderful state of erection, and worked it up and down not unlike she had previously done and then, her face wreathed in smiles, she leaned down and took it into her mouth and began sucking it in and out, he all the while kissing and tonguing her cunt!

I remember wondering at the time what I would do if a man were to place his hand on my cunt, to say nothing of kissing it! I knew I would have died on the spot! And the game went on and on—how long I can not tell, and then, after both had acted as though they had received electric shocks, they lay still.

Rising, at last, she turned and kissed his lips, saying:

You darling lover, you! How you did come that time! It almost choked me, there was so much!

Again I wondered what could have happened, but it was no use; it was far too much of a mystery for me to solve. I might have remained and watched further had not I been overtaken with another violent spasm of pleasure, and again my hand and arm was drenched with the goodly amount of creamy jissim which gushed from me! My head was in a whirl! I was shocked beyond anything I had ever experienced!

I waited to see no more. Quietly I crept away and made my way to the pond and here, without even the formality of removing my shoes and stockings, I waded in, never stopping until I was tittie-deep!

Wasn't that the most ridiculous thing you ever heard of, dear?

Perhaps you have felt the same way after watching two passionate persons perform the rites of Venus, and if so, you can possibly understand my feelings.

However, after I had been in the water perhaps five minutes, I came to my senses somewhat, and then I realized what I had done.

Knowing I had to face Mother and that I was due for a dreadful scolding, I went my sorrowful way back to the house. But what was my surprise and delight to find that I could enter without being seen by her!

Quickly I ran to my room, that had been set aside for me, and here I changed into dry clothing, and returned to the lower floor without a single soul ever becoming the wiser.

As I opened the door to go out again, the two lovers were walking up the gravel path toward the house, a tranquility on their faces that defied one to even guess at the strenuous exercises they had so recently indulged in.

Even in my innocence I marvelled at this, for even the cool water of the pond had failed to quench the fire that raged within me.

Naturally, I was anxious to again witness those strange scenes between the two lovers, and shortly after dinner I was fortunate enough to see them again slipping off to the garden, where I was sure they would repeat the seminal banquet, but just as I was about to follow them, a girl friend entered the gate and came to me.

She, like myself, was taking singing lessons at the parsonage of the Sunday school, and being something of a pianist, she thought to play and we could rehearse at home. My chance of again witnessing the lovers' duet was, of course, out of the question for that time.

Do you understand now, dear friend, how I was being led into that path which has no turning back? Is it any wonder that I became the rage of all Europe? Do you wonder that I was the talk of every city I visited? Is there any reason to doubt why I shouldn't have become one of, if not the most talked-of women?

But wait. If you think I had had enough, then listen to what followed and judge for yourself if it was wholly my fault. But do not think for one moment that I am complaining of my past; I am not. I have been far too happy in my life to even think for a single moment that

I have done wrong. Nor has it given me the slightest moment of regret as to whose company I kept, and that goes for the future, too.

That I believe I was born to love I can prove in a few brief words. Consider for a moment the young man who chooses art as a profession. Some little thing has, perhaps, inspired him to paint. He takes up the study, and what happens? From the very first he is thrown in with painters—artists, we call them—and their instructors and fellow students. Everything is art in his life. He sees it, lives and breathes it. He sees it on every hand, and so, in a few years he becomes an artist; at least he's called one.

Take the case of the student who takes up medicine. In college he hears nothing else. He attends classes, sees surgeons operate on outcasts; his mind becomes imbued with surgery. And, so, he in turn becomes a surgeon. Do you see what I mean? Very well, then.

Instead of becoming a painter or a surgeon, I took up the study of love—and all because I was reared in the very arms of love and lust. Seeing it on every hand is it any wonder, then, that I lived for it?

To prove to you that I saw it on every hand, let me prove it; let me tell you of another delightful scene I witnessed, and this right in my own home. As I said before, I had been assigned to another room, mine having been put to the disposal of one of our guests. It happens that this room adjoined the one occupied by Mother. It connected with hers by a door, and over this door was a transom. There was another entrance to my temporary place of abode, but this led to the porch. I mention this door since it's to play a role in the scheme of things.

That evening at table I discovered that the following day was Mother's birthday. After supper the lovers suggested that we gather great bunches of flowers with which to trim the house, and as there seemed no end to them, I readily agreed. So, the following morning we three were out gathering the multicolored buds, and by noon the house had been gaily decorated.

Nor did this prove irksome, for the lovers—as I choose to refer to them—were forever making love to each other, and I was being treated to many thrilling sights. Indeed, they seemed to have gotten over the idea of hiding their love-making from me, and many times during their stay I had seen his hands slide up beneath her dress when they thought I wasn't looking.

And that day was no exception. They toyed with and petted each other at every opportunity, and by supper time I was sure I was to witness another episode of their thrilling love-making. But in this, however, I was wrong; if there was anything of a dreadful nature it was after I had retired to my room.

But I wasn't to be deprived altogether. All evening my parents seemed gay and happy (a rare thing, I might mention) and as I retired to my room something seemed to prompt me to look into their room.

On the porch was a short stepladder, which Father used in trimming the bushes and vines, and I carried this into my room through the porch door. Placing it against the door leading directly into their room, I climbed it and discovered I had a splendid view of the interior. The room, however, was vacant; they had not yet arrived.

Taking advantage of the interval, I quickly undressed and donned my nightgown. Then, just as I was ready to again climb the ladder, I heard someone moving about in the next room. With heart beating wildly—for I had never before spied on any one except the lovers—I climbed the ladder.

Father was sitting upon the side of the bed removing his shoes and stockings and he was gazing at Mother who stood before the mirror taking down her hair. She had already taken off her waist and stays and the upper part of her splendid body was covered with but a chemise of the finest lawn, and since it was cut quite low, I had a splendid view of both her full, firm titties almost to the nipples.

In order to unloosen her waist and stays she had unhooked the skirts, and these hung about her rounded hips threatening, it seemed, to fall from her with every movement.

All this I took in at a single glance. Then I turned my gaze to Father who had finished his disrobing, with the exception of his drawers, and was sitting on the bed as though waiting for Mother to finish her undressing. I had never before seen a man naked, and was surprised to see the profusion of black hair on his chest and which seemed to cover the whole front of his body and quite disappear in the front of his drawers.

In the meantime Mother had finished with her hair and had turned, facing Father. She asked if she shouldn't put out the light, but Father answered:

No, dear, it's seldom I have a chance to view your beautiful body, so as long as this is to be in honor of your birthday, let me have you completely nude.

Mother laughed a little. Then, with a toss of her head and a shrug of her shoulders, she pushed the little straps from her shoulders, allowing both the chemise and her skirts to fall to the floor, and the next moment I saw, for the first time in my life, a stark naked woman! And what a picture she was! In all my travels I have never seen a more beautiful woman naked!

Quickly she moved to the bed, as though ashamed of her nudity, and placed her arms about his neck. They kissed; not as the lovers had during their love making, but soft, clinging kisses, such as I had never seen before, and all the time one of his hands wandered all over her body and thighs, she lending herself willingly to his every touch. He tired of this, it seemed, for his hand slid down into the thick fleece, where it toyed for a moment, then down between her thighs. For a moment she held her legs together and then, as he reclined her on her back, she allowed them to fall loosely apart.

Sitting on the side of the bed facing me, I had a wonderful view of her full-fledged cunt! For a minute or two he played with it, and then he suddenly stood up and let drop his drawers, and as he turned to place them over the back of a chair, a sensation of the sheerest delight swept over me, for his stiff cock stood out from his belly like a bar of iron!

I had but a moment to view the wonderful thing, for a moment later he turned his back again and settled down upon the bed again, and here they lay kissing each other for several moments! Then, as though he could no longer stand it, he quickly mounted her beautiful body! It was the same as I had already witnessed between the lovers, only instead of rushing about the business at hand, everything seemed to be deliberate and with care.

First he applied the head of the wicked-looking monster to the lips of her cunt, and then he began forcing it into her, driving and pushing until it was in to the hilt! Like the girl in the summer-house, Mother raised her legs and clasped them about his middle, and then the battle began in earnest! Sighs and kisses were exchanged with the same freedom as those of the lovers, but their action seemed to lack that fire and fierceness I had previously witnessed.

But, like all fucks, this one ended like all good fucks

should end, and Mother twisted and squirmed as he
shot his boiling sperm into the innermost recess of her
trembling soul, and both lay for several minutes as
though dead. Father was the first to move and as he
relieved her of his weight I could see the same whitish
fluid running from the bottom of her crack as that I had
seen in the summer-house, though Mother's crack
seemed to be larger and gape further open. At that time
I was anything but a connoisseur of feminine charms,
and my first impression was that Mother's cunt seemed
greatly inflamed, but this was due, no doubt, to her age
and the fact that I had passed through those soft por-
tals.

For a few moments she lay there panting. Father,
too, seemed in great need of rest, for his cock had fallen
to but half its length and was hanging down between
his thighs. Then Mother arose and went to the dresser
from which she produced a towel. Returning to the bed
she dried first his affair and then her own. This done,
she seated herself again and leaning over him began
kissing his lips, and then she suddenly changed her position again.

Now she devoted her attention to his half-limber affair which she toyed with and caressed, and then, in
answer to something he said and which I couldn't hear,
she suddenly leaned down and took the end of it between her lips and sucked it!

Now, I haven't given you a hint as to my own feelings as a result of watching this strange and exciting
affair, and this is because I can find no words to convey
my meaning. What I was doing or did I have not the
slightest knowledge; I know only that I had drawn up
my nightgown, and as Mother took the end of Father's
cock between her lips, I bathed my hand with another
prolific dose of my girlish sperm which, because I

hadn't drawers on this time, gushed down my thighs unhindered, and that I so lost control of myself that I slid down the ladder lying on a heap on the floor in a near exhausted condition.

Remember, again, that I was rather young at the time, and found it rather trying to withstand the rigors of continually going-off on my fingers, and that accounts, perhaps, for my weakened condition at that time.

Later, however, I managed to crawl into bed where I fell into a troubled sleep. I say troubled. It was troubled only in that it was filled with the most wonderful cocks in the world, and though I fought frantically·to grasp one that I might use, the wicked things eluded me with the most surprising energy.

And, so, I witnessed another orgy of the sexes.

As long as I can remember I never saw my parents kiss each other, nor did I ever see them in bed again, though I watched several times.

I have often wondered if that little affair hadn't been something which took place only on special occasions —like a birthday!

And another strange thing about it was, that the next morning neither of them seemed to show the slightest hint of the wonderfully thrilling party they had had the previous nite. But, after all, hadn't it been the same way between the lovers that time I saw them after leaving the summer-house?

Chapter II

A few days after this the lovers returned to their respective homes and I was again left to my own reflections, and many hours I spent going over the wonderful things I had seen.

I hinted in no uncertain terms to my girl friend as to the wonderful things I had seen, but she would blush and turn away as though she didn't wish to discuss the subject.

And so for two whole weeks I was left alone. The pond no longer lured me, I lost interest in my poodle and there's no telling what might have happened had not Father returned at that time with my new teacher. This was my music teacher.

Why, I do not know, but I was suddenly taken with the idea that I didn't want another teacher. I had been alone so long, the thought of another ugly old woman to pester me was sickening and I realized my days of freedom were over.

Very well, I thought, If I'm to have another teacher, why not have one more romp at the pond? To think is to act. Since there was no one to watch me—I hadn't seen my new teacher as yet, since she had retired to her room—I hurried to the pond. Pond lillies were in bloom and the surface of the water seemed covered with them.

Then another idea occurred to me: I recalled the thrill I had had that day I had entered the water fully dressed! Why I had gotten a thrill out of this I have never been able to determine; I know only that the thought persisted! Making sure no one was about, I plunged in! I had long since become used to the water, and I no longer feared it! My skirts floated up about me as I waded deeper and deeper, and in less time than it takes to tell it, I was in to my neck, and here I had a wonderful time. I thought this about the most dreadful thing I had ever done in my life, and I knew Father would punish me if he discovered that I had gone near the pond, but I didn't care! The water felt delightful on my body and I sported about in it for nearly an hour.

I was a sorry looking sight, indeed, as I climbed out, but I had the lillies and I was happy. Quickly I stripped off my wet clothes, squeezed the water out of them and spread them to dry. Then I entered the pond again. I had often gazed at my nude charms in the glass since seeing my mother naked, and now as I stood there in the clear water I discovered that by standing quite still I had a clear reflection of myself.

I noted her same hips and legs and breasts; I noted, too, the same colored hair at the base of my belly and the same cunt, though I wasn't nearly as developed as she, though I had hopes.

Finally, after my clothes had dried, I wandered back to the house.

I expected, of course, another old hag, but what was my surprise to see sitting upon the porch beside my mother, one of the most beautiful women I had ever seen! Never shall I forget that shock!

Here, instead of an ugly woman, was a perfect beauty, not a minute over twenty years old, and when

I say she was beautiful, I mean just that. Not only was her face beautiful, but she was beautiful all over. As you will find a little later, I got to know that beautiful body in every detail, and the more I knew that girl the more I delighted in kissing and petting her, as you shall see!

At table that evening I couldn't keep my eyes from her, and I must have acted the dummy indeed. I could eat but little. Both Mother and Father chided me about it, but I passed it off saying I didn't feel just exactly right. Had Mother known my thoughts at that very moment, I would have been horse-whipped and Vera would have been driven from our home.

After dinner, however, I had a chance to further admire that beautiful creature. Mother suggested I show her about the place, and a moment later Vera and I were walking through the gardens.

Her hair was of that deep brown color; her cheeks were rosy-red and her full lips were like ripe cherries, while her teeth, white like the snow of early winter, were even and firm. I noted her swanlike neck and the narrow, slanting shoulders, and I took note of her dainty ankles and tiny feet. All this I saw that first evening as we wandered about the gardens, but I was to see more of her a little later.

I was to see her beautiful legs and thighs; her full, rounded hips and bottom-cheeks; the slender waist; the full, firm breasts with their tiny pink nipples; and above all I was to see the most beautiful cunt I have ever seen, even to this day!

Even that first evening, when I saw but her facial charms, I fell desperately in love with her! I was overjoyed at this sudden turn of events! I laughed and cried in turn; I danced all about her, picked flowers and forced them upon her and, I guess, made a fool of myself in general. But I just couldn't help it; I was that happy.

Though she noted my actions, she paid no attention to it; her only reaction being to take me in her arms and kiss me as tenderly as a mother would kiss her only child, and I felt that we were to become the most wonderful friends.

Later that evening she told me that we were to become lovers at heart, but it wasn't necessary for her to tell me that: I was already her lover at heart.

Ah, how little did I know then what she meant by that remark!

Oh, God! What pleasures I have had in your arms, Vera!

Years after, while basking in the arms of another woman, I always fancied it was you and your charms that were passing beneath my lips, and it was you who were trying to satisfy my endless craving by offering to my hungry lips that pearly nectar with which you were so plentifully endowed!

I remember only too well that first night in our garden. We had wandered to the summer-house, that same summer-house in which I had witnessed those strange scenes. There, seated upon that same couch, she took me in her arms and kissed me! Perhaps it was due to the great influence that summer-house had over me, or perhaps it was my love for her, but whatever the cause, I gloried in her kisses.

Not only my lips did she kiss, but my cheeks, eyes and even my throat did she kiss, and her kisses were far different than any I had ever received before. When kissing my mouth she would quite cover mine with her own, while the tip of her tongue would caress the inside of my lips. She did this a dozen times, I guess, each time a little more deliberate, and each time sending a delicious thrill through me until I thought I was literally dying of pleasure.

Looking back at that night I am convinced I would have been an easy conquest for her, for she had instilled a strange thought within me. Though I had never heard of such a thing, I was taken with the idea that I wanted to kiss her all over! I wanted to do something dreadful to her! Something naughty! But, to save my life I could not think of a single thing to do.

A few moments later we raised from the couch and retraced our steps. I led her by way of the pond. Somehow I felt free with this wonder woman. I felt so free, in fact, that I told her of my former delight in wading in the water, and how my former tutor had forbidden me going there. She laughed at this. Then she told me I might wade whenever I so chose, but that I must be careful since I was in her care then, and she made me promise I never would wade there unless she was with me. To this I gave a solemn promise.

Later we sat upon the porch, and here again I came in for a lot of kissing, but Vera was clever. She knew only too well how easily she might spoil it all by hurrying matters with me, and she would stop kissing my lips just when I was feeling the best.

She wished to know all about my studies; how far I had advanced; in fact she wanted to know all about me; and many of her questions I thought strange and far from the point. I wanted her to hear my voice, but she refused to let me sing in the night air, at least until my voice got stronger and settled. In later years I realized how true this was when I saw any number of girls ruin their voices by abusing them.

Later that evening she took me to her room, and here she allowed me to assist her in the unpacking of her trunk, and here I saw things I had never dreamed of. All sorts af the finest underwear, dozens of pairs of the finest hose, several beautiful nightgowns and several dressing gowns. One would never have guessed this girl had to teach music for a living, for her wardrobe was equal to that of a Princess.

Later she told me how she came by all the pretty things I saw.

And that night before I retired to my own room she gave me another of those clinging kisses, and how it did thrill me!

The days which followed proved to be a perfect paradise to me.

Never in the least did we seem to tire of each other. We were always together. Mother, too, had the utmost confidence in her, and Father never gave us a thought. And so, my love grew and grew.

One afternoon, about a week after her arrival, we discovered that both Mother and Father were going to the city on business, and as soon as they left I suggested we go to the pond and wade. Vera was willing and off we went. Happy in the thought that I could do as I chose in the matter, I stripped off my slippers and stockings and began paddling about, while she sat upon the grassy bank and watched.

Becoming used to this I ventured out further and Vera, seeing that the lace of my drawers were almost touching the water, said:

You had better pull them up, dear, or you will wet them.

I did this, but I found I still lacked something. I wanted to go in naked, but I knew Vera would never approve of that, and right there I lost an excellent chance with this beauty. She told me later how it thrilled her seeing my naked legs.

You see, my friend, how I dwell upon all this? It

isn't that I wish to tire you; it's simply that I delight in relating every little item of our conversation, and the strange things which led to a much clearer understanding between us. It was, I believe, the most wonderful period of my whole life; at least I thought so at the time.

I recall how I asked her to remove her slippers and stockings and come in with me, and how she declined saying she was 'unwell.'

This required considerable explaining on her part. She asked me how old I was and when I told her, she explained the whole business.

I had come out of the water and was sitting beside her, and I couldn't help but thrill when she explained to me all about the 'periods' a girl experienced once every month. She told me I was passing into womanhood, and I'll never forget the way in which she looked into my eyes when she told me I must be getting to be quite a full-fledged woman. And there was another splendid opportunity gone. Little did I know she was waiting for me to make the first suggestion to something more intimate.

The afternoon passed somehow and we returned to the house for dinner, only to find that both my parents had been detained in the city and would be unable to return until tomorrow. Left by ourselves as we were we found it much more convenient to converse on the porch, and you may rest assured we took the opportunity to cuddle in each other's arms, to say nothing of an endless number of kisses.

She suggested that we retire. I agreed, though I would have rather remained there on the darkened porch, that I might bask further in her clinging kisses.

Our rooms were separated by but a narrow hall; the doors being opposite. She said:

Since we are so alone, dear, perhaps we had best leave the doors ajar—then I can hear if you call me?

I thought this a splendid idea; we could talk to each other as we undressed. I couldn't be satisfied away from her, even in sleep!

I recall how quickly I undressed and donned my night gown, and how I crept to her door. Why, I do not know, but I wanted to see her when undressed! And I'll never forget the thrill I had when I peeped into her room! She was standing before her mirror, taking down her hair and arranging it for the night! Nor was that all!

She had partly undressed; that is, she had taken off everything but her little under-vest, an extremely short and transparent little garment, and this was furled up over her splendid behind, leaving her naked from well above her hips to her heels!

What a thrill that was! For long moments I stood staring at her! Her legs, hips and bottom-cheeks looked beautiful to me, but it was as nothing compared to what happened a moment later. Raising my eyes I discovered that she was looking directly at me, though she was still looking into the glass and had been watching me for some moments. Then she turned, resting her palms on the edge of the dresser. Like the back, she was naked in front; more so by far than her rear, for the tiny garment she wore was cut so low I could see both her breasts naked to the very bottoms!

Speechless, wonder showng in my eyes, I stood there gazing at her beauties, but my eyes were riveted upon the patch of hair that almost covered her beautiful cunt! And it was Vera who broke the spell.

Naughty! she whispered, beckoning me toward her. Why do you stare at me so?

Rushing into her outstretched arms, I said:

Oh, Vera dear! You are so beautiful and—and I love you so!

Silly little girl, she cooed, kissing me again and again. I'm not one bit more beautiful than you!

Though there was a few scant years difference in our ages, we were almost of an equal height, so we found it quite convenient to reach each other's lips as we stood clasped in one another's arms.

Evidently Vera knew the time was ripe to carry her caresses further, for she said:

You are beautiful, dear, but you are unfair!

Unfair? I asked, startled the least bit.

She nodded.

Of course you're unfair—You are so covered while I am so uncovered——

You mean——!

Again she nodded.

Why not stay here with me tonight, she cooed, kissing me lovingly and squeezing me in her arms. Then, too, she went on, It's so warm, and—and, well, we could sleep without anything over us!

Again our lips met and clung. Then pushing me away she let drop the tiny garment. Forcing it down over her full, rounded hips she let it drop to the floor, the tiny thing laying like a tiny bit of fluff about her feet! For a long moment I gazed at her, thrilling as I had never thrilled before! Then her hands drew the little shoulder straps from me, and while I stood as though petrified, she dropped my nightgown to my feet, leaving us both stark naked!

Isn't this so much nicer? she asked, leading me to the bed and seating herself on the edge, and at the same time drawing me down beside her.

Wouldn't you like to spend the whole night with me? she asked.

I remember the strange light in her eyes as she hugged me close to her breast, and the flushed cheeks which fairly burned mine, but I thought this was due to the pleasure she anticipated in having me with her the whole night.

Oh, darling, I cried, kissing her again and again, I'd love it!

Rising, she quickly doused the nightlight, while I scrambled into her bed. I was quickly followed by Vera, who took me in her arms and kissed my lips, cheeks, eyes and throat! Not satisfied with this, she buried her face in my hair, this little act quite forcing my face down to her swelling breasts! The moonlight shone directly across the bed giving me a perfect view of the lovely orbs as she pressed them against my face! I wanted to kiss them and I don't know why I didn't!

I could eat you with kisses! she cried, coming back to my lips again and fastening her open mouth over mine in the most maddening kisses she had ever given me.

Don't you just love it? she asked.

Oh, Vera, I answered, hardly knowing what I was saying, I love you so!

Taking it for granted that I was hers, she rolled me on my back and leaning over me she kissed my face and throat! Oh, darling, she cried, kissing my titties and mouthing the erect nipples, while little shivers of maddening delight dominated my very soul!

I love you so, she cooed, sliding her hand up and down my back and gently patting the firm flesh of my bottom, I could eat you alive with kisses!

Oh, darling, I cried, I am yours to do with as you like!

Then lie still, my darling, she cried, coming up over me and again kissing my lips, And I will give you the most delightful thrill you have ever had! I love you so!

And the next moment she started kissing me all over, while one of her hands played with the curls about my cunt! I was in a Heaven of delight! I couldn't lie still! My bottom moved on the linen sheet; my hips were set in motion, and all the while her lips swept up and down my body and legs! Not a spot escaped her hungry lips! From my breasts to my feet her lips rained kisses! For several seconds she contented herself with my feet, then up my legs ran her lips, to my cunt which she kissed and tongued in a frenzy of delight!

Circling my hips with her arms, as though to keep me from escaping her, she fastened her mouth to my slit, giving me those same open-mouth kisses, and then as my thighs fell loosely apart and I grasped her head between my hands, she drove her tongue into me!

I felt the same sensations I had felt when watching the lovers!

I realized I was going to come, and I tried to tear her face away, but she held me in a tight clasp, and then it happened! Now, instead of trying to force her face away, I held it pressed tightly to me; I no longer thought it dreadful to kiss one's cunt! I recalled how the lovers did it; I remembered how he feasted his lips on it; I pictured Father sucking Mother's cunt, and here was a girl doing that very thing to me! The thought was maddening! Arching my hips I held her pressed tightly to me and went-off, little moans coming from her as she felt the very essence of my soul flowing into her mouth—and then I fainted.

How long I lay thus I do not know, but when I opened my eyes it was to find her lying partly upon me and she was tenderly kissing my lips. One of my thighs was clasped tightly between hers, and there was a gentle movement of her loins.

Oh, God! she cried, kissing me. How I love you!

And I love you, too, Vera, I answered, more calm now.

Then she insisted that if I really loved her I should do something to relieve her suffering, and when I asked her what I could do, she answered: Kiss me, dear! Kiss me just as I have kissed you and make me flood your lips with my love-dew!

Oh, Vera, I cried, I would love to do that to you! I love you so! Come! Lie over on your back and I shall prove to you how I love you! And as she quickly turned over, I bent down and put my face between her thighs and attacked her lovely cunt with a passion which truly surprised myself! It was heavenly! I loved it!

I felt her grasp my head between her hands; heard her beg me to put my tongue in—all of which I did—and then she arched her hips, and the next moment my mouth was flooded with her warm dew!

She lay quite inert, and it was several moments before I realized what a dreadful thing I had done; that I had re-enacted the scene I had witnessed in the summer-house. But, strangely enough, I didn't think it improper. I thought, on the other hand, that it was quite fitting between lovers, and Vera was my lover! No matter what she might think, I was her lover!

She was lying quite in the same position as when I had kissed her cunt, and turning, I thought she too had fainted, for her eyes were closed and her head was thrown to one side. Then I again dropped my eyes to her lovely pussy! It was beautiful! The lips, instead of lying far apart, as I had noted with the lover and Mother's, was but a tiny crack and it was pinkish and it quivered the least bit!

I wanted to kiss it again, but before doing this I turned and looked into her eyes, only to find that she hadn't fainted but was smiling down into my eyes.

Isn't it wonderful, darling? she asked, moving her hips a little, and for answer I lowered my face and kissed it again and again!

Then a strange thing happened. I felt one of my legs being lifted over her breasts! Her hands came to my hips; drew me down, and the next instant I felt the tip of her tongue slip into me, and then, though I had never heard of it before, we performed a perfect "sixty-nine!"

I can remember every detail of our love-making as though it was but yesterday, and as God is my judge, my friend, we both went-off no less than three times before we fell apart! And then we—or rather I—fell asleep.

How well I remember waking (I thought I had just fallen asleep) to find it broad daylight. We lay for some time clasped in one another's arms, kissing and petting. Then she whispered:

You had best go to your own room, darling. What would your Mother say were she to find us together like this?

I rebelled against leaving her; I wanted to stay; I loved her a thousand times more than I had the previous day, but her better judgment finally won me over and I returned to my room and dressed, though I vowed I would never be out of her sight another minute!

You think, perhaps, that I had had a dreadful night of it, but such, my friend, is not the case. I never slept better in my life than I had that night. And when I awakened I was as refreshed as though I had never heard of Vera, and anyone seeing me as I dressed would never have guessed how we spent the greater part of the night.

Do you see now how I was being led into the by-ways of love?

The months which followed that night was Heaven to me. True, I had not tasted the pleasures of a man's kisses, nor the feel of his cock boring into my very vitals, but I learned all there was to know about it without the real experience of actually feeling it, as I shall here relate.

The days which followed were heaven. My singing lessons were a delight, and to wait upon Vera was my chief aim. I kept her room literally banked with flowers, and as the fruit season came around I heaped the various items upon her.

But it must be remembered that Vera did not allow me to plunge into my new-found pleasure with that utter disregard I might have experienced. Oh, no indeed! She was far too much of an artist to allow me to become disgusted with it all, and it was three days later before I was allowed any freedom with her. That day we walked through the gardens. Coming to the summer-house she told me she was obliged to go to the city that afternoon, but that she would return in time for dinner. This made me sad; I didn't want her to go away, even for an afternoon.

I know what's the matter with you, she said pushing me over on my back and kissing my lips. You think I don't love you—is that it?

I nodded my answer, for this was just what I thought.

Very well, she continued, slipping one hand underneath my dress and patting my thigh, Just for that, you lie still and I will show you, my dear!

Dropping to her knees she raised my dress and pressed her face into my crotch, kissing and tonguing my cunt until I went-off into her mouth! It was heavenly! I thought I was dying from sheer joy and happiness, so great was the amount of jissim I gave her!

The fact that I had had nothing since that first night, accounts, no doubt, for the unusual volume I gave her. It must have been voluminous, because she told me it was! Indeed, I must have been a very unusual person in my younger days, my friend. I have had any number of persons—both men and women—tell me the same thing.

I well remember a very handsome Hungarian gentleman who delighted in kissing a girl like that. Wealthy, he kept a dozen girls for that very purpose. It was their sole duty to hold themselves in readiness at all hours of the day and night, that they might be ready at his beck and call. He told me he had chosen these girls from scores he had tried, and had chosen them from the others because they were prolific "spenders." Then came the startling information: It was to the effect that I was even better than any of those he maintained in his castle, and to prove it he gave me a diamond necklace.

I then told him of my first music teacher, and he asked me to get in touch with her for him, that he would give her a thousand marks every time he had her that way. But I am digressing.

After I had had my pleasure I wanted to give her the same, but she put me off; she told me she had just come "sick." I insisted that she had told me that before, but she said she wasn't unwell that day; she simply told me that so she wouldn't have to go into the water, and that she preferred to lie on the bank of the pond and watch me wade.

However, she promised me no end of pleasure as soon as she returned from the city, even promising that she would make me "do it pretty" for her.

It was a surprisingly long day for me. My poodle and

I wandered all over the place. We went to the pond, romped the wood, but in spite of that time hung heavy on my hands. I had taken a seat in the summer-house, and here I allowed my thoughts to wander back over all the thrilling things I had seen and heard. But it was Vera who held my thoughts. Being separated from her for even a few hours was nothing short of torture, and I couldn't get my mind off her nor that dainty little cunt of hers, that beautiful object I had so come to love and adore!

Oh, how I loved it! There hadn't been an hour since I first had her that I didn't want to pop my head beneath her dress and suck her!

Having seen the lovers together, and having seen him suck her, I, naturally, thought it the most natural thing in the world. I recalled how she had taken his cock into her mouth and sucked him.

But hadn't Mother done the same with Father? I could feel my face burn with blushes at the mere thought of allowing a man to do that to me! Still and all it must be quite nice; both women seemed to have enjoyed it. I recall how the girl in the summer-house had thanked her lover for "coming" so profusely in her mouth!

Certainly Vera had "come" in mine. Then I wondered if men did it in a girl's mouth the same way? This mystery must be cleared up at the earliest possible moment; I would ask Vera all about it as soon as she returned! Surely she would know all about it!

And sure enough Vera returned about dinner time. I could hardly wait until I could get her alone, and shortly after dinner she told me to wait for her in the summer-house as she had to take care of herself before joining me there.

I knew, or thought I knew, what she was doing; she

was bathing herself; she wanted to be as neat as possible, since she was going to allow me to banquet on her spermatic sweets. She didn't know it but I would have much rather she wasn't quite so particular about herself, since I had come to love the deep, penetrating odor of her person. Years later I came to love this more and more; there is something thrillingly delightful about the odor one gets from a pretty girl's cunny.

And then, in the very midst of these strange thoughts, Vera came to me. I thought her even more beautiful than any time I had ever seen her, and I sprang into her willing arms and covered her face with kisses. But alas—I had forgotten all about her "illness."

She wouldn't allow me any liberties whatever; even when I hinted that I wanted her to kiss and caress me she put me off, telling me I must be patient and wait until she was entirely well, and then we would have another wonderful party.

Then, just when Vera was well again, which was the second following day, Mother informed us that she and Father were obliged to go to the city again and would be unable to return until the following evening, possibly the following day. I remember how sincere she was when telling me how nice I must be to Vera; that I was to obey her in everything, do as I was told and be a good girl generally.

How well I remember the expression that came over Vera's face at hearing Mother tell me all this! I saw her catch her underlip between her teeth—a habit she had when unduly excited—while the deep color came into her cheeks. Indeed, she showed me in a dozen ways that she was overjoyed at the prospect of being alone with me for a whole night and day, and you may rest assured that it was a dreadfully long time before my parents departed. I could hardly control myself, I was so filled with wicked desires!

How we got the dishes washed and put away I do not know; but at last they were finished and arm in arm we hurried to the the music room.

And now, my friend, I am afraid you are going to doubt what I am about to tell you now. I know you will call me a liar when I relate to you the various things that happened that night, but, as God is judge, every word is the gospel truth. Not only that; I am going to relate it word for word, as near as I can recall it.

To begin with, you must remember that we had promised this night to each other. You must remember that Vera had promised we would have another party as soon as she was "well," and you must not overlook the fact that I was just as much of a Tribade as herself.

As I said, we hurried to the music room, and though I was hardly aware of what was to happen, I was hardly able to start putting my thoughts into practical use. It was different, however, with Vera.

She knew all about what was going to happen; as she told me afterward, she, too, had been looking forward to that night. First Vera pulled all the shades down. Then she arranged two lamps so their light would shine all over the room; I can remember every detail as though it were but yesterday. Then, when everything seemed to her liking, she turned to me. Taking me in her arms she kissed me again and again, then:

You really love me, dear? she asked.

I nodded my answer; I couldn't find words to tell her how much!

And you wish to make me very happy? she asked.

Again I nodded my answer. Looking straight at me

she said: You are sure you know what I mean, little puss?

Oh, Vera, I cried, I'm ready to do any and everything you say!

Then go to your room and undress, she whispered, her eyes bright, her breasts heaving, then come here!

For a long moment I gazed into her eyes. And you! Will you be undressed too?

Hurry, and don't ask silly questions! Go!

My heart beating wildly, I rushed to my room. I knew we had nothing to fear; we were alone in our home; the curtains were drawn and we had the entire night before us!

Quickly I slipped out of my clothes. Without waiting to make such preparations as one would deem necessary under the circumstances, I hurried back to Vera, but as hasty as I had been, I found her already undressed and waiting. How she ever got out of her clothes so quickly I never knew, nor did I ask. I rushed into her arms like a crazed person! Our nude bodies met with a resounding smack, and for long moments we stood there, our breasts crushed together!

Then she led me to a broad couchlike affair and pushed me down.

I tried to get my face between her shapely thighs, but she would have none of this; she had other ideas about what was to follow.

You must be patient, my dear, she said, kissing me. We have the whole night before us, and we must go slow. You must conform to the program as I have thought it all out—won't you do that?

I could only nod my head in answer.

The program, as she termed it, consisted in placing me upon the couch, in a position not unlike that assumed by the girl-lover in the summer-house. And I, finally getting the idea of what she wanted, allowed myself to be placed in the position best suited to her needs. First she lay me full length, with my thighs well parted.

Then she leaned over me, kneeling on the floor herself, and began kissing me all over! Will I ever forget that night! Like the first time I had had her, she licked and kissed me from head to foot, ending the performance by sucking me most deliciously, and as you well know—from experience—I wasn't long in giving her a just reward!

And even after I went-off, she continued to kiss it gently, a little act she keenly enjoyed. Ah, Vera was a skilled artist, my friend. She knew how to best distill delight—and proved it a moment later when I wanted to suck her; she put me off, saying that she had other and better things in store for me.

Leaving me on the couch she hurried to her room, from which she returned, carrying a cardboard box. Opening this, she produced an article which she called a "dildo." You know all about these things, so I won't tire you with a description of it. Enough to say, that it was a beauty; indeed, it proved to be the most perfect one I have ever seen. It was slightly over eight inches long and about two in diameter. It looked just like the one I had seen in the summer-house, even to the hair and balls; the only difference being that the one she had possessed much larger balls; the idea being to give the receiver of it a far greater dose of its contents than is possible from a real one.

I have often thought of this very thing, my friend. Has it ever occurred to you, my dear, why so many women will take up with a man almost repulsive to her? Do you know just why this is? No? Then let me tell you this: It's the man who is capable of ejaculat-

ing the greatest quantity of sperm who is the ladies'
man, and this coupled with unlimited powers on his
part makes him the fortunate one, indeed! I know, my
darling; I have had many such!

Ah, it was a clever man who invented that particular "tool!"

Naturally I was filled with wonder about the thing,
and undoubtedly asked many foolish questions, but
Vera smiled and fastened the thing on me; she insisted that a demonstration of it would answer all my
questions. I must have looked rather funny as I stood
there with the strange instrument fastened on and strutting almost straight up in the air, but I wasn't left long
with my reflections before I was grasped and forced
down upon the couch, and Vera was impaled upon it,
and in less than five seconds its entire length was into
Vera's belly.

Having gotten the thing well planted into her cunt,
however, she rolled me over, making me mount her on
top and here, changed into a man as it were, I was
obliged to work the thing to her satisfaction. The result of all this was, as you can possibly imagine,
highly satisfactory to Vera, if it wasn't to me, for after
working away at her for some ten minutes she went-off
and, as I had been previously instructed, I pressed on
the big bag squirting her cunt full of the warm milk
with which she had been primed.

I wanted to try it, of course, but Vera would not listen to this; she said I was far too young to be penetrated
with that monster; besides, she had something else far
more appropriate for me.

The result of this, as you can readily guess, was a
delightfully naughty sixty-nine, during which I went-
off no less than three times while Vera, more seasoned
than I, went-off five or six. Then, the sharp edge hav-

ing been taken off our appetites, we retired to her room.
Here spread out on her bed I asked her many questions,
and she told me the story, in brief, of her life.

It seemed she was one of several sisters, and while
still quite young, her father had married a second time,
her own mother having died a year before. This step-
mother was very cruel to them. One day she and her
oldest sister ran away from home. Each had quite a
sum of money so they lived in fine style for several
weeks. Then, having decided that their money could
not last forever, they sought employment and were
fortunate in getting it. She (Vera) got a place in a
singing school, and it was here she discovered she could
sing, and before very long one of the instructors took
her in hand and taught her in spare time.

Now, it happens that there were some two hundred
other girls in this school, and, as is common in such
places, one is sure to find a chum, or pal, with whom
a girl would find happiness. Vera, being very pretty
and full of fun, had no trouble in finding several girls
she liked, and from these she chose one (A Miss Adams). This was an English girl, very pretty and talented, and seemed greatly devoted to Vera. Then,
about a week after forming friendship with this girl,
Miss Adams asked Vera to sleep with her.

Both knew this was forbidden, but liking each other
as they did both took the chance. It turned out, however, that Miss Adams had something far more interesting on her mind than sleeping, and as Vera was of an
affectionate nature, the other had little or no trouble in
convincing Vera that kissing was something of an art.

This acquaintance ripped into a real love affair between them and they were never happy when out of
sight of the other. Naturally, Vera developed into an
out and out Tribade. Nights were not enough; every

afternon they would meet on pretense of studying, and would always end the session by sucking-off each other at least once.

It being a recognized fact that Vera and the Adams girl were lovers, Vera accepted an invitation to spend the summer holiday with her new friend. At Miss Adams' home they renewed their love-making, sleeping together every night and wandering about the country-side every day. It seems this girl had a brother, and one day, when their stay was about up, this young man happened to run across Vera, who was sitting beside a small stream close to the house.

She rather liked this handsome fellow, and made little or no effort to fight off his advances. When he got over-zealous, however, Vera attempted to call a halt, but the handsome brother thought otherwise. Instead of resisting, he became rather nasty over Vera's refusal to accept his attentions, and then he told her, in no uncertain terms, that he had witnessed her (Vera) and his sister in bed together and that he had seen them sucking each other.

This of course frightened her, but still she wouldn't give in to his advances. Releasing her, he said:

Very well, young lady, since you are too nice to let me have my fun I'll just report you to the police. There is a law against such practices, and if I am not greatly mistaken you and my delightful cunt-lapping sister will find yourself locked up in jail! Vera was badly frightened. He really made her believe there was such a silly law.

This so frightened her that she consented to do anything he said, if only he would not tell of what he had seen. This was the very thing he had been fishing for, and his demands were that she allow him to fuck her. There was nothing to do under the circumstances but comply with his outlandish command, and that very afternoon he took her deep into the woods. She almost died when he lay her down and uncovered her charms, but she covered her face with her arms to better shut out the horror of the thing, but her closed eyes couldn't keep out the fact that he was soon upon her and between her thighs, and was trying to ram his cock into her. Frightened half to death, her heart going pit-pat, she hadn't a very clear conception of it all, and in answer to my questions as to whether he hurt her, she didn't know. She was far too frightened to know anything else beside the fact that he penetrated her to the limit, and after a most savage poking he went-off into her.

Strangely enough, she found herself liking him after this strange rape, and this, coupled with the fact that he held his threat over her head, compelled her to meet him again that evening. She expected to be half killed again, but what her surprise to find that instead of hurting her, it felt delightful, and the harder he did it, the better it felt. That night he took his fill of her, giving her three splendid fucks there on the grass.

Finding herself in love with him now, she consented to go to the city with him the following afternoon. Here he rented a room; she didn't like the idea of going into a room with him, but after a short session of petting she allowed him to strip her stark naked and lay her across the bed. Passionate by nature she literally made him fuck her the entire afternoon!

A few days later she and her girl friend returned to school, but not until she had tasted his splendid rammer no less than a dozen different times and was sorry when she was obliged to leave him.

Shortly after returning to school she allowed one of the professors to fuck her a few times, and it was during this blissful event that she had the misfortune to become pregnant. She consulted her friend, the professor, who took her to a medical man who caused her to get rid of it, as she termed it, and after that she swore she would never have anything to do with a man again.

But, like most women, she was weak. The doctor who had assisted her had been very kind; he was good looking, and soon she was listening to his pleadings; the result of this was that she allowed him to "have" her twice a week over a period of several months. She used to meet him at his office, and at his instructions she was able to avoid pregnancy in the future.

But after all this she still retained her love for the girl friend, though this friend was never to know that she (Vera) had let several men fuck her.

During all this I had become deeply interested, and it was then that I told her of the wonderful things I had witnessed between the lovers, and Mother and Father. My descriptions were complete if they weren't correct, and seeing that I already understood something of the business of sex, she told me about all there was to know.

Among other things she explained how her affairs with the various men she had met made it possible for her to take into her cunny such a wicked looking thing as the dildo; she told me the difference in men; how some men liked men and couldn't get satisfaction with the prettiest women; how there were clubs scattered all over Europe where men met and enjoyed sexual affairs with each other. She told me how much more a man could ejaculate than a woman; how her friend, the professor, had taught her to suck him, and how she became a devotee after the second or third time, even getting something of a thrill out of it the very first time. She told me of those who considered it "unnatural" to kiss and caress one's mistress in such a manner; she confessed that there was a certain amount of degeneracy in man when he mingled with other men, for sexual purposes, but that it was considered quite alright for girls —there being no known laws against it.

Naturally I had been an interested listener to all this, and when she asked for my reaction as to whether I thought it unnatural for one girl to caress another in that manner, I promptly pressed my face between her thighs in such a convincing kiss that she rewarded me with a most unusually wet kiss.

And so we spent the night. It was a perfect Eden to me. No one to watch for, having the entire house to ourselves to do in as we pleased, my excitement knew no bounds. How well I recall the result of that kiss! I remember how, after I had sucked her, I, with a sly wink, asked her what she thought of a girl who would surrender her lips and tongue to another. Taking me in her arms, she said:

I think it perfectly dreadful, little naughty, but as long as I am to be your instructor, and you insist upon learning all there is to know about it, I suppose I'll have to do the dreadful thing, and turning, she dropped her face between my legs in what I supposed was the most delightful series of sensations I had so far experienced. I hate to dwell upon this particular event, and above all, I do not wish to tire you with a description of it all, but there was something about it at that particular time that I shall never forget.

We had already indulged in several loving embraces and the fiery edge had long since disappeared, so it was rather a lengthy caress she was obliged to render before it had the desired results.

I recall how she arranged me. I was lying upon my back and partly on my right side. My right leg was out

almost straight, my left one drawn up, the heel of this
foot being hooked behind her neck.

Her left cheek rested on my right thigh, her left arm
was under me and clasped about my waist, her right
hand resting upon or toying with my belly and titties.
Propped against the pillows I was in a position to gaze
down into her eyes while her lips pressed the gentlest of
kisses on my pussy, now and then letting the tip end of
her tongue glide along between the lips. Would you believe it, my friend, when I tell you that that caress lasted
well over an hour? That every time I approached the
spending point she would stop, look up into my eyes
and wait until the desire to "come" had passed from
me? That is the reason why I so clearly recall everything
about it; that's the reason I shall always hold it as
the most thrilling "love affair" I had ever had, up to
that night!

And so we spent the night. With nothing but a light
coverlet over us we slept the sleep of the just. But,
strangely enough, we were not overtired; there was
something refreshing about it all, something which produced sleep without exhaustion, and we awakened in
the morning quite refreshed, though it was nine o'clock
before either of us opened our eyes. Sitting upon the
side of the bed, Vera confessed her love of being about
the house in complete nudity; she said she had often
done this when alone, and the idea seemed to delight
me. I was thrilled with it!

The most remarkable thing about it all is, that I so
quickly grasped the idea. It seemed delightful! Three
minutes later we were in the kitchen preparing breakfast, our only covering being slippers on our feet. I believed I had never been so happy in my life. Not satisfied with being about the house in complete nudity, I
opened the rear door and dashed into the garden, never

stopping until I was fully a hundred feet from the house.

Startled, Vera called to me to come back, but there was nothing to fear; our house set well apart from any other and there was little or no danger of being seen. When I explained this to her, she also came out, and here we stood allowing the warm sunshine to drench our bodies. And from that instant, dear friend, I have been a devotee of the nude, going about without the slightest covering whenever possible teaching the idea to others. I have appeared in plastic-posing—which means that I have appeared among many intimate friends in a perfectly naked condition, I have attended a naked ball where some five hundred persons appeared in equally naked condition, and I have spent days on end in a garden of a friend of mine in London without the slightest trace of covering. There were at least thirty women there who delighted in going about naked; but all this and much more I shall relate in good time.

Arm in arm we wandered to the pond where we enjoyed a pleasant hour splashing about in the water. Drying off in the sun was another favorite sport with us —but we had to return to the house; there was no way in knowing just when Mother would return, and above all, we didn't want her to catch us in that scandalous condition.

It was fortunate, perhaps, that we were tied down to a certain extent or there is no telling just what might have happened to us.

Vera became like one possessed. Returning to the house she hurried me to her room. Producing the dildo and filling it with warm milk she made me fuck her again and again—.

I begged her to try it on me; I wanted to be penetrated with the wicked thing, but she wouldn't do it, though she did put it on herself and touched me with the tip end, and here I learned she spoke the truth regarding the pain necessary to a penetration.

There is little more to tell, my dear, at least nothing you have not already heard; and to retell it would be but a repetition of what I have already related. And so I shall skip over the vast number of things that happened between Vera and I, and give you a recital of the more interesting and stranger things that awaited me. Enough to say, that I was still a virgin—in flesh, if not in mind—when Vera and I parted. And you may rest assured our parting was amid tears. We swore to remain true to each other, but I soon found plenty of temptation which caused me to quite forget my first real love.

Chapter III

After something like a year and a half my voice developed to a point where neither Vera or our Sunday School teacher could have been of any assistance to me. Indeed, I had quite passed beyond both, and if I were to do anything about it at all, it would be necessary to go somewhere where I might gain the necessary finishing touches.

It had been arranged that I was to go to Austria, where I might finish my musical education. Vienna being the popular place at that time, I was sent there. I was heart-broken when it came time to leave my parents and Vera, but I soon got over it, and I might add here, that it was the only time in my whole life when I really felt bad about anything. I thought, too, that it would be a dreadful thing to be cast among strangers in such a far country, but to my surprise I found it delightful.

I found many other girls and young men there, all studying voice-culture. They were unusually nice to me, as were as the aged instructors. One in particulai was unusually patient with me.

Never having been away from home before, he was sympathetic in his efforts to make me comfortable, and

I spent a week in his home where both he and his delightfully-pleasing wife did everything possible to make my stay a pleasure.

But, unfortunately, they were Puritans. Can you imagine me being with Puritans. Can you imagine me being Puritanical, my friend? Me, above any one?

But I wasn't to be under their jurisdiction all the time. I saw many things during the study hours that quite awakened me. At home I had heard of almost every kind of Love; In Vienna I was to see it.

I was to see it on every hand. You remember that at the time I went there, there was a Governor in charge who certainly must have believed in "Free Love." Besides being rather lax in the enforcement of civil laws, he was really a despoiler, a vulgarian. His Court reeked with scandal. It was common gossip that he abused his wife and kept a dozen whores in constant attendance.

This influence spread. His subjects, copying him, did likewise.

The theaters were nothing more than brothels where the most indecorous practices were indulged. Men and women alike wandered unhindered backstage, and here the most brazen flirtations were carried on. All of this, of course, I missed; I only mention it here to convey to you the deplorable condition Vienna found itself in.

An old castle had been converted to a school, and here every passionate thought was expressed, though, of course, in a more guarded manner. But there were any number of things that couldn't very well be hid, and through it all I found myself in a most unusual frame of mind. Chief among other things I found myself wanting a male companion. I saw dozens of girls who made no effort to hide the fact that they had lovers. Indeed, some three or four different ones even went so far as to suggest some friend they had, or knew. But I declined. But it wasn't because I didn't want a male friend. Indeed I was burning with desires for one; I wanted a man's embraces; Vera had poisoned my mind with thoughts of possessing a handsome man, one who was sympathetic and understood real love.

My real objection was the danger involved. I had never forgotten Vera's experience; how, after allowing her professor friend to fuck her a few times, she had to spend days in bed while a doctor relieved her of the "after-effects," and I didn't want any of that.

But that in no way diminished the desire for a lover. No, indeed. I longed for it yet I dared not make any desires known.

It had been arranged before hand that I was to maintain a small cottage during my stay in Vienna, and about a week after my arrival I was successful in getting such a one as suited my needs. Also, I was supplied with a very pretty and charming maid, and while she was unusually smart and quite happy in her new environment, she was not for me—at least not in the manner I preferred. After that my education was rapid, as you shall see.

I had attended school something like a month when my professor suggested to me that I have what he termed "a try out" with a local booking agent he seemed to be well acquainted with, and the very next day he took me there. This agent happened to be a Spaniard, and though I had never taken kindly to Spaniards, this one proved to be most unusual in many ways. To begin with he took kindly to me. He told me quite frankly that I had a very wonderful voice and encouraged me into acccepting a place with a small opera company operating under his supervision. It wouldn't, he said, amount to very much of anything, but it would

give me the "atmosphere" I needed, as well as get me
used to appearing before an audience.

Naturally I accepted this generous offer, and the following day I was interviewed by the manager of the
opera company. I had a most interesting talk with him,
and then, quite without warning, he said:

Now, my dear, let me see your legs.

And though he said this in a very matter-of-fact manner, I was somewhat taken back with the suddenness
of it. Seeing my cheeks turn to a flaming red, he
added:

Have no fear, my dear—to me legs are something to
hold up the body, nothing more.

He then gave me to understand that besides a voice,
I must possess very pretty and shapely legs, since the
costume I would have to wear would be rather revealing, and thus assured I got over my timidity and quite
brazenly lifted my dress. But I quite overdid it. Catching sight of my reflection in a large mirror, I discovered
my dress was high enough to not only display my legs,
but a considerable portion of my hips and belly, and
this, coupled with the fact that I was wearing but the
briefest possible thing in drawers, gave him a view of
everything else he might have cared to look at.

But it so happened, he cared nothing for me aside
from viewing my form, for he never so much as placed
his hand on me, nor did he make the slightest suggestive remark aside from telling me, quite frankly, that I
had the most beautiful legs, hips and buttocks he had
ever gazed upon, and the whole affair ended by my being engaged.

I was so happy I burst into tears. My rise so far had
been sudden, and my good fortune quite overcame me.
The old gentleman allowed me to have my cry, and
then I felt better, and I was told to report for rehearsal

the following morning, naming the place where the rehearsals were being held.

That night, I wrote mother, telling her of my good fortune, and I'm sure she found traces of my tears on the pages.

Somehow it never occurred to me to investigate the type of theatrical company with which I was joined, and it didn't reveal its true worth until the following day, the day on which I reported for my first rehearsal, and as you might have already guessed, I wasn't left long in doubt.

The company, as I recall it, consisted of some fifty persons, thirty of which were women and girls, the remainder young men.

My first surprise came when I viewed the type of dress one was supposed to wear at these rehearsals. I use the term "dress." If a pair of short, lacy drawers can be called a dress, then they were dressed. But this, in itself, was not so bad when one considers that they changed from street clothes in plain sight of the men members of the company, some even going so far as to literally strip stark naked before them. And, strangely enough—I thought—the men seemed to take little or no notice of them; and it was with much misgiving that I likewise stripped off my outer clothes and took my place with the others.

But don't think I wasn't aroused, my dear. Having been away from the caresses of Vera for so long a period, and having none other with whom I might indulge my passion, I became quite smitten with some of the girlish charms I saw so freely displayed. Indeed, I became quite overcome with them.

And the talk among them! Everyone, it seemed, had a sweetheart, and each one seemed to be vieing with the others in their descriptions of them. This one had a boy friend who possessed the most wonderful cock in the whole world. Another boasted of the wonderful party she and her friend had attended: There had been endless quantities of wine and champagne, and long before midnight the whole crowd had taken off their clothing and finished the night in the various beds supplied for the purpose, the heroine of this phase of the story boasting of the fact that she had had two men at one time.

Very startling to say the least. No one seemed to pay any attention to me; they simply took me for granted. But it being but a rehearsal I got through with it somehow. There was two full weeks of this, and by that time you may rest assured I became quite used to the whole thing, even to the point of going about almost completely naked, and before the opening of the show I had forgotten all about such a thing as modesty and found myself undressing—quite nonchalantly—in the presence of the male members.

And when this idea of modesty had forever been banished from my thoughts, I took to it like a duck takes to water. Indeed, I quite surprised myself. And do not think for a moment, my dear, that I hadn't chances to pick out a lover. Indeed, no! There was a never-ending line to choose from. It being a new show, and a good place to pick out new beauties, the stage and wings were constantly filled with men and women who, as I stated before, flirted in the most brazen manner, and while several of the girls listened to the giddy tales whispered into their ears, I remained aloof; I wanted none of them; the man who was to get my maidenhead was to get it through pure love, and not for the thrill of the thing.

A little later I shall tell you of an experience I had with one of these old rues, but first let me tell you of still another experience I had with a member of my own sex; it will enlighten you in two or more ways; it will show you the type of women I found myself thrown in with, and it will explain why I was more or less willing to take up with aforementioned old scapegoat.

As I have already mentioned, the opening of the show came about this time. I had become quite used to appearing in various stages of undress among the members of the troupe, but the opening night was quite something else again, and I'll never forget the thrill I experienced when the curtain went up! As I have said, my costume was brief. It consisted of but a tiny, fluffy skirt which flared out about my waist, while the waist—if you could call it such—was nothing more than a bit of gauze which left both breasts naked.

My part in that show was small. It consisted of saying but a few lines, and I sang in the assembly numbers, but it wasn't that that bothered me; it was the almost complete undress I was obliged to wear. Now, it also happens that I was caused to stand beside our leading lady—or primadonna, as she was known—and it was she who was always whispering encouraging words into my ear. And it is to her more than anyone else, to whom I attribute my success in later years.

This woman was about thirty years old. Besides being very beautiful, she had a splendid voice, and at that time was all the rage in Vienna. She was the whole show, of course. That opening night the stage was a sea of flowers. Baskets and boxes of them sat about everywhere.

There was nothing of the drama about the thing; it was a simple little Shakespearean thing chosen, primarily, for its erotic songs, a part quite suited to our primadonna. I well recall a little scene in the last act.

It represented a flower garden. In the center of this bower-like place was a flower-decked couch, and upon this reclined our leading lady. Just before the curtain descended on this last act, I was supposed to step close to her—while she lay upon the couch in almost total nakedness—and sprinkle flower petals down on her up-turned face. I was doing very nicely until she touched my thigh with one of her hands, a little act which quite startled me, and at the same time she was whispering something to me. What it was I never found out, but from what happened that night I can guess it was something very nice.

As is the custom on opening nights, the "elite" gave our prima-donna a party, backstage. I had heard considerable whisperings going on and from what I heard I gathered it was to be something most unusual, and so I gracefully made my exit. I was hardly ready for a wild party as yet. The following evening, however, I heard all about it, and then I was doubly glad I hadn't taken part, for the whole affair turned itself into a most awful orgy in that everybody, both members of the company, as well as the men and women guests, stripped stark naked and every method of sexual pleasure was openly indulged in.

The second night I didn't escape quite so easily, however.

During the last act, when I had to sprinkle her with the rose petals, she whispered to me telling me to come to her dressingroom as soon as I could after the closing scene. Wondering what she could want with me, I mentioned it to some of the others. I saw them shrug their shoulders, meaningly, but they said little. But I was determined to know something about it; the apparent mystery which seemed to surround my question prompted me to delve into it, and so I managed to cor-

ner a little blond. When I asked her what our primadonna could possibly want with me, she smiled faintly,
and said:

She's awfully nice—if you like her kind, and she gives
those she favors wonderful presents—and then she
turned and walked off leaving me quite as much in the
dark as ever. What she meant by that I hadn't the
slightest idea—but I was soon to know.

Upon entering her dressingroom, I found her still
dressing.

Sit down, she said, smiling very prettily, then: What
happened last night, my dear? You didn't stay for my
party? What happened?

I made some excuse or other, and she went on: Ah, I
know! You are a very naughty girl! You had a lover
waiting for you; but you should have invited him here,
to my party! He would have enjoyed it, I'm sure!

And she looked at me from beneath her long lashes
in a very naughty manner.

I then discovered that she wished me to go to her
apartment with her, and since I could not gracefully refuse, I accepted her invitation. The others had already
departed when we emerged, and a few moments later
we entered her carriage and were driven off to what
proved to be her "hotel." This was a very famous re-
treat among the sporting gentry at that time, and here
she maintained a suite. Nine in all there were, and until that time I had never seen anything nearly approaching it in splendor. Two large drawingrooms, an elegant
diningroom, a dressingroom, and last, but not least, a
beautiful sunken bath, and everything was literally covered with flowers. It was indeed a fairy-bower if I ever
saw one.

Left alone for the moment, I cast my eye about. I
saw many small pieces of statuary, and these were of

the most erotic kind, many depicting various women of
past fame and all nudes.

At the end of the drawingroom I first entered there
hung a life-size painting of herself. It was a nude. She
had posed for it at the foot of a flight of stairs, she said,
and I believed her, for the artist had brought out every
detail of her body and limbs, even to the patch of
golden hairs on her lower belly and her lovely pink-
lipped cunt. And while I stood admiring it, she joined
me.

Does it look like me? she asked, slipping one arm
about my waist and pressing me against her body.

I made some remark about it—it was complimentary
I remember—and her answer was to pat my bottom in a
caressing manner and kiss me. Perhaps it was what I
said about the picture, or it might have been that she
took me for granted, but whatever the reason, the lady
said:

Do you know why I have invited you here, darling?
and when I answered in the negative, she said: Seeing
you in that naughty little costume caused me to think I
would love to have you for a whole night—you would
like to stay and sleep with me, wouldn't you, dear?

I made some silly excuse about having to be home—
which wasn't true—and she promptly sent a messenger
with a note telling my maid that I was staying with her
that night. It was just like that.

It was obvious that this girl had been in the habit of
having her own way. However, I made another attempt
to get out of it; I had no idea of what was in store for
me, and though I hadn't the slightest objection to
spending the whole night with her in her bed, I didn't
want to get caught there and have her stage a party like
the one she had had the previous night. I hadn't the
slightest desire to be ravished by a man I didn't know.

I said: But aren't you afraid I'll disturb you by remaining here with you all night?

Nonsense, she cried kissing me again and again.

Besides, I'm going to enjoy holding you in my arms and kissing you all night.

No longer was I in doubt as to the part I was to play that night, and this time when our lips met I quite gave her the tip of my tongue, a little act she accepted as answer enough.

Stepping to a tassled cord, she summoned a maid.

Prepare my bath, she said to this domestic. We are bathing together. Then place wine and eatables on the table. Then you may go.

All very commonplace, I thought.

Come, she said when the maid withdrew. There is no need of us being uncomfortable; besides, I seldom wear anything when about my rooms. Come!

That this woman knew what she was doing was proven a moment later.

Leading me into a dressingroom she went about the business of undressing quite as though she were alone, and I, having long since gotten over the idea that it was prudish to go about naked, quickly followed suit, neither of us stopping until we were stark naked.

I couldn't help but wonder what Vera would have said had she seen me walking about those rooms in complete nakedness, and I couldn't help but wonder what she would have thought could she have seen us a few moments later reclining in that wonderful sunken bath!

The sight of this splendid woman electrified me. I thought, too, that she was even more beautiful than Vera, but I've often wondered if that thought wasn't prompted by having her naked and so close?

Lying there in the bath she became quite caressing,

and I, having been without a companion so long, returned her caresses in a manner quite convincing. They
must have been convincing, for she said:

Come, let us get out and dry! I am dying to kiss your
lovely body but I can't very well put my head under
water! And as though that wasn't enough, she slipped
one hand into my crotch and toyed with my cunt for a
moment, adding: It's beautiful, darling! I don't think
I'll be able to wait till we get on the bed!

But she did wait. In the outer room we found still another maid arranging the table with good things to eat,
and even the presence of this girl didn't deter her. Filling two glasses she handed me one. Then standing facing each other, she said: A toast to your darling little
cunt, dear; may it never be without a companion, be it
tongue or cock.

Somehow I managed to say something appropriate
about the golden hair that surrounded her cunt, and
then we seated ourselves, though we didn't sit with our
arms about each other as Vera and I had done that day
at home. The food was delicious and I did full justice
to it. I also indulged in considerable wine and champagne, and long before we left the table I was more than
willing to begin the oral festivities. During our supper
she gave me to understand that she loved to be about
without clothing, and that she loved to be with another in the same state; all of which I heartily agreed to.

Suddenly she sprang to the piano.

Sing for me, she suggested, seating herself and running her fingers over the keys. Perhaps it was the wine;
I don't know. Maybe it was due to the unusual condition I was in, but whatever the cause, I sang that night
as I had never sung before, and when I finished, she
raised from the stool and took me in her arms.

What a silly girl, she cried, kissing me. How utterly

foolish to expect you to remain with our little company when you should be making a name for yourself in the various capitals of Europe!

I couldn't believe that this girl should take such an interest in one like myself. But I was quite mistaken, as you shall see.

Come, she said, leading me toward one of the bedrooms. We are but wasting time. Besides, the night is short enough as it is!

On the bed she became quite spoony.

Where do you receive your lovers? she asked, leaning over me and gazing into my eyes, and when I told her that I had never had a lover she could hardly believe it.

Lie here on the edge of the bed so I can see for myself if you have ever had a lover!

Helpless in her hands, my head filled with the fumes of the wine and champagne, and eager to surrender myself to her in any manner she liked, I did her bidding. Taking my thighs upon her shoulders, she drew the lips of my cunt well apart and gazed into it. I could feel her hot breath upon it, she was that close.

As God is my judge, the child's a virgin! she cried, hardly believing it herself!

Knowing that in another moment I was going to receive the hottest kisses, I grasped her hair and drew her face close! It was a daring thing to do, of course, but I was so overcome with emotions strange to me, I couldn't help it. But it wasn't without its reward. Her mouth pressed tightly to it, she shot her tongue into me as far as she could reach, but a half dozen stabs with it quite brought on the dissolving period, and before I realized it I was shooting my nectar between her lips!

This so maddened her that she literally threw herself upon me and astride my upturned face, her cunt rubbing against and between my hungry lips and my tongue doing its part to produce a like spend from her! What a night! It was like she had said; there was going to be little sleep for either of us that night!

I became like one possessed! The feel of her unusually long tongue exploring the depths of my cunt drove me almost mad! Not satisfied with hers, I explored the lower regions, that dale between the snowy cheeks of her bottom, and here, strangely enough, I found a new delight!

Later I am going to tell you of my little Rose—that being the name of a very pretty and talented maid I had later—and how she delighted in forever finding new ways to thrill me. It was her greatest delight to bury her face between the cheeks of my bottom and tickle me there with the tip of her tongue.

And though it was the first time I had ever heard of such a thing, I found myself liking it, and we gave each other an endless amount of delight in this manner.

And so it went all through the night. But, since we were but human, we needed rest and at last fell into a peaceful sleep.

In the morning I felt little the worse for my night's pleasures and aside from a slight smarting in the region of my cunny, I felt quite myself. She, however, called me a little leech—

A bath and a delightful breakfast, and then, when I was about to depart, she gave me a beautiful ring. It was a small diamond, mounted into what resembled for all the world, a tiny cunt—and I have kept it to this day. She insisted it was a perfect picture of my own little pussy.

After such an experience I felt I really belonged, so to speak; I took more kindly to the strange conversations I heard all about me, and I began to rather like my surroundings. To give you some idea of the freedom

with which these girls discussed the most private subjects, let me tell you of a short conversation I had with
another girl of our troupe the following evening.

Evidently this girl had been watching for the very
thing I displayed. She said: "How did you make out
with our leading lady last night? Was she as nice as
you thought?

I tried to be a little uppish. I thought, too, it was
rather a delicate question, so I said: "What caused you
to think I went anywhere with her?"

She shrugged her shoulders, and without looking up,
said: "You are wearing one of her keepsakes in the form
of a ring. She never gives them except to those with
whom she's spent a night, so don't be offended, dear.
It's a sort of badge of servitude, and she gives them only
to those with whom she's had the pleasure of spending
a night. And," she went on, raising her head this time
and looking at me, "spending a night with her means
just one thing—I know, I spent a night with her myself."

So, I thought. The whole troupe knows about it, do
they? Well, what of it? I had had a wonderful experience, to say nothing of the real good it had done me,
so why worry about who knew it? I noted that three or
four of the others wore the same sort of ring; besides, I
might find it to my advantage to be nice to this primadonna.

A week passed. It having become known that I had
spent a night with this tribade, I was invited to parties,
but I refused them all.

But I didn't refuse my friend when I was again invited to her apartment. Indeed I was rather looking forward to it; having again tasted of the bliss to be found
in this woman's arms, and a whole week having elapsed,
I was quite willing to spend another night with her.

But what was my surprise to find, upon entering, a party of six other girls besides ourselves? My new sweetheart must have noted my confusion, for she said: "These are all friends of mine, dear, so please make yourself quite at home." I noted, too, that each and every one wore a ring similar to mine, and as this emblem constituted a sort of brotherhood, I began to feel more at home.

I also learned that these girls were members of splendid families and were in the habit of getting together from time to time for an out and out romp.

All were very pretty and shapely and not a single one of them was over twenty years old. Among them, however, was one, a very pretty little thing, that couldn't have been a day over fourteen, and I learned later that this was true. I also learned, and to my great surprise, that she was an out and out Tribade; that she was greatly sought after by women of the "elite," and that her greatest delight was to administer to women who delighted in oral satisfaction. She made not the slightest secret of it, openly solicited women to her arms, and that her greatest "hunting ground" was the theater where she made it a practice to enter the various dressing-rooms and here, beween scenes, she would pop her face between the thighs of anyone who took her fancy, or would have anything to do with her.

She was one of the most lascivious girls I had ever met, openly declaring her liking for me, and hoping I would let her prove her liking.

It was shortly after midnight when we entered the apartment, and before one o'clock we had all imbibed more or less freely and were feeling rather frisky, but it was the fourteen year old girl who started the real festivities.

She complained of the heat. Then, without waiting

for an invitation, she quickly disrobed, never stopping till she stood stark naked before us.

This seemed to be the signal. I have noticed that in a party of this sort it invariably rests upon the shoulders of one to start things going, and it was this child-woman who started things off that night.

Dresses, slippers and stockings were being cast aside by everyone now, and I found myself following suit, and in no time at all we were undressed. Then our primadonna and the child-woman slipped off somewhere—a little act which caused wild speculation among us—and then I found myself in the arms of a very pretty and shapely brunette who began showering me with kisses.

About that time the others were forming in pairs and were slipping off into darkened corners, or bedrooms, and finding ourselves alone—or as much alone as it was possible to be—my companion began spreading her kisses. Lips were hot enough. Titties, shoulders, arms and legs quickly passed beneath her skilled lips, and it wasn't long before I felt her greedy mouth sipping sweets from my cunt!

After that things happened with such rapidity it was difficult to memorize them. Enough to say that before we slept I had had the fun of gamauching every girl there, and by the time I got to have the child-woman I guess she got rather a dry kiss; I know she had little to offer my willing lips.

And that night I was to learn something else about what went on at these orgies. It is a known fact that flesh and blood can stand about just so much, and after that some stimulant is necessary.

In this case it was the birch-rod. Never having heard of anything like this I was rather surprised. Our hostess, however, seeing that I was the novice of the party, took it upon herself to explain the whole thing, hinting, in no uncertain terms, that I was to be the victim of their lust. I was somewhat startled at this bit of news.

However, I knew better than to decline; I was in their hands, and I felt I had best submit to this indignity even though it did hurt.

It's a very strange thing, my friend, how quickly one can bring his or herself to liking a thing like that. I wasn't the only one whipped that night. I learned, and to my surprise, that many of these girls really delighted in being stripped naked and whipped on various parts of their bodies, and I learned, too, that there was really something in it. Why a person could possibly have a desire to be whipped was, until that time, something of a shock.

But I learned, however, that the birch-rod in the hands of one skilled in the art can produce almost unheard of pleasure; at least I found it so in my case. At first it hurt dreadfully, of course, but in a few moments it ceased to hurt so much. I felt I was being cut to ribbons; I knew my back, bottom and legs must be laid open with cuts, but nothing of the sort happened at all. I did, however, have a few ridges the next day, but these passed off and I felt not the slightest effects of it.

Believe it or not, my dear friend, but I have come to like it.

Again I am not going to tire you with a recital of all the things we did that night; if I did it would be but to repeat myself over and over again, and that you do not wish. You are well informed as to what goes on at a party of this sort, so there is little to add.

Enough to say, that I was initiated into the gentle art of eating and drinking from a girl's cunny; bon-bons and wine being the morsels in question.

Isn't it strange, my dear, the odd things one will think

of when in the passionate embrace of a loved one? I recall such a incident. One of these girls seemed prettier to me than any other. She was the proud possessor of an unusually well-formed bottom. The cheeks were round and plump and as smooth as ivory, and somehow I couldn't resist the temptation to covering them with kisses. She had evidently been operated on in this manner by our primadonna, for as soon as I made known my desire, *she* promptly offered the choice morsel to my lips, even holding the cheeks apart that I might more easily reach that which lies buried within, and I might add here that I didn't disappoint her.

Does the story so far convey to you just what sort of a life I was leading? And do these lines portray something of my own lascivious nature? Write me and let me know your true reaction.

I have this to say about it all. Had it not been for these parties among ourselves, I am sure, with my unusual temperament, I would have fallen an easy victim to some man hardly worthy of me.

I do not wish to appear egotistical in making this statement.

What I wish to point out is, that had it not been for the possibilities thus laid open to me, I might have strayed into a world where it would have been doubtful if I could have made the grade, and I mean by that that I could never have stayed in the opera, and after all that was my aim. I wanted to become a great singer, and I have achieved that ambition.

And through it all I have acquired a wonderful viewpoint of life.

I have found, among other things, there is a little badness in us all, and that it takes but a spark to ignite it to a raging flame.

Many, and infinitely worse things have happened

among our best people, the only difference being that they won't confess it. That's a queer bit of psychology, isn't it, my friend? Well, it's true.

I learned among other things that many men kept as mistresses very young girls, and that Eve—that being the child-woman's name—was kept by a wealthy man, though she spent much of her time at the home of an aged uncle.

I learned, too, that there is no end to the strange things a man will request of his mistress, be she permanent or be but a casual "pick-up," and in a few moments I am going to tell you of an experience I had with one of these.

But before going into that let me tell you of my success—I like to dwell upon that. Shortly after the event recorded above, I had an opportunity to become understudy to a famous singer of that day.

She was getting along in years, and through the influence of our prima-donna I managed to get into another show. This particular woman had been in the habit of having fainting fits; also, as I have already stated, she was getting along in years. She treated me very kindly from the very first. There was considerable study ahead for me, but I pitched into it with a will, and I am proud to say that it was this chance that gave me my opportunity to go to the top.

As is customary for one in a like position I was offered all sorts of opportunities to indulge my passion, many of these offers coming from aged men. True, I had had love affairs with various men, but they had been of a platonic nature and nothing came of it. Also, I managed to find a girl here and there who liked to be sucked-off, so you see I had little or nothing to worry about.

I recall one man among the others to whom I took

rather a shine to. Like many of the others he was wealthy. He gave me wonderful presents, and though he coaxed me for favors I always refused, though I can't say that I did not think favorably of him. Almost every girl had a lover; they talked of them among themselves, even pointing out their good points, but I listened. Had this man been the least bit pressing in making his desires known I would have fallen an easy victim. Of this I am sure.

I recall one night in particular. I might mention here that he was a splendid looking man, not a day over fifty, tall and well formed. He had asked me to dine with him that night, and I had accepted.

The place he chose was one notorious for its ribald parties, but I didn't mind that; I was in rather a strange mood that night. As is customary on such occasions we occupied a private dining-room.

This room, besides having the necessary table and chairs, contained a very inviting couch. I happened to be wearing a very becoming dress. At that time, if you will recall, the women were going in for the extreme in decolette and were trying to outrival each other—or so it seemed—in indecent exposure and, because it was quite the proper thing, I was also wearing a decolette gown which quite revealed both my breasts naked to well below them.

We enjoyed a delightful repast. Also, we consumed considerable wine, and it wasn't long before I began feeling rather frisky, and shortly after finishing our meal we adjourned to the aforementioned couch. This couch, as everyone knows, was there for but one purpose, and I wasn't so sure that I didn't want to put it to its destined use.

Then, too, he seemed more caressing than I had ever seen him; my lips weren't enough for him and he was soon passing his lips over my naked titties, kissing and sucking the nipples like a true lover.

That, however, was as far as I had ever allowed a man to go before that night, but that particular evening I felt randy, and I made not the slightest effort to resist him as he lay me over against the pillows with which the couch seemed covered.

At this point he took hold of my ankle and toyed with it; I knew what was coming but I didn't stop him, and soon his hand was working its way up my leg and thigh, even slipping his fingers into the lacy drawers I was wearing and toying with the curls there. Why I didn't put a stop to all this I don't know; I do know, however, that his fingers felt lovely as they toyed with my burning cunt, and it wasn't till he attempted to press his face between my thigh that I called a halt, and only then because I had gone-off twice. I was weak after that and I am sure that had he pressed his advantage a little more I would have willingly accepted his cock which even then was sticking from his trousers, he having liberated it with the idea of slipping it into me.

And to his everlasting credit he did not press me; he simply took it for granted that I did not wish it at that time, and though the man never got another chance like that, his presents never stopped coming to me. It was, as he said; "He lived in hopes."

Now I shall tell you of that strange experience I had, and let you judge for yourself just what temptations lay in wait for a girl.

The night I have in mind I received a basket of flowers. Strangely enough I hadn't sung that night, so I couldn't account for its reception. In the basket, and well hidden, was a letter. It was addressed to me. There being no longer any doubt as to who it was intended

for, I opened it. It was a request that I have dinner with
the sender. In still another part of the basket I found a
long slender box. Upon opening it I found it contained
a necklace of very fine pearls. Wondering why anyone
would send me such a valuable present, I put the matter up to one of the girls.

"You're a lucky devil," she said after reading the letter.

"Lucky?" I asked.

"Lucky is right. Why couldn't I get an offer like that
from the old duffer!" She seemed peeved at what she believed her ill luck.

"Tell me about it," I prompted her. "What does one
have to do?"

"That's where the funny part comes in," she smiled.
"Think of getting a lot of money for simply peeing!"

"Peeing?" I asked mystified.

She nodded. "I know a dozen different girls he's had
out to his place, but I've never been lucky enough to
get asked; I guess he doesn't like my kind."

"But tell me," I insisted, "What does one have to
do?"

She patted me on the shoulder. "Listen, dearie, if you
turn down this offer you're a far bigger fool than I could
possibly think you! Go ahead, you lucky devil!" and
with that she turned and left me.

I might have asked someone else; I wanted to know
something more about this "peeing" business, but there
seemed no one else there who knew very much about
him.

In the letter it said that he (the writer) occupied
number two box, and to avoid mistakes he was wearing
a yellow flower in his buttonhole. It also instructed me
how to join him outside the theater. I was to enter a

certain carriage which I would find at the exit, and here I would find him waiting, and here he would explain his wishes.

I had little time in which to make up my mind. The play was almost over, and whatever I did I had to do quickly.

Going to the little peephole, through which the players were able to see out without being seen, I searched the box in question, and there he sat. Naturally, with the theater in semidarkness, I couldn't see very well, but what I could make out he didn't look very dangerous. Then, too, I was to talk with him, in his carriage, and if I didn't care for his proposal I wasn't obliged to go with him. Anyway I looked at it, it had promise of a thrilling experience. As was the habit with me I made up my mind quickly.

I would go; just for the novelty of the thing!

Following his instructions to the letter I left the theater and entered the carriage, which was waiting at the exit. Sure enough, the gentleman was within and waiting for me.

"You are prompt, my dear," were his first words, "and I am grateful to you. You will find me a gentleman, so you need have no fear of me. Rest assured I shall treat you with every consideration."

"I am sure of that," I answered, by way of starting conversation.

Little, however, was said by either of us as the carriage traversed through the city, and it wasn't until we had entered a very beautiful villa that he made any suggestion as to what I might expect. Indeed, we were seated at table and had partaken of the delicious foods and the splendid wine before he enlightened me.

Then, quite nonchalantly I thought, he told me that

he cared nothing whatever for women; that is, he cared nothing for them in a sexual sense, and only those who appealed strongly to him.

I must have appealed strongly to him for he went into the business at once. Rising from the table he stepped to a closet and brought out a white dress. With almost the same motion he produced a purse and laid it beside the dress.

"In the purse there are one thousand marks," he said, "and they shall be yours if you will but don this dress and do my bidding. You have nothing whatever to fear from me. I admit my request is a strange one, but since I have given my word that nothing will happen to you which might harm you in any possible way, I will be delighted if you will but assist me, doing your simple part that I might enjoy myself in the only way I can. Will you do this?"

Really, I was thrilled. I had become reconciled to being alone with him; I could see nothing in his manners which might lead me to believe him insane and, in truth, I was beginning to get a real thrill out of it already. Besides, I would have something real spicy to tell my friends!

"Very, well," I answered, "I promise to go through with it providing I might rest assured that you will not whip or hit me or molest me any other way."

He nodded his agreement, then: "You will find your task simple, indeed. You have but to go into this room" pointing to one "and remove all your clothing. Then you are to dress in this costume. You will find slippers and stockings to match the dress in the room, and you will don them. But remember, you are to wear nothing but the dress, slippers and stockings."

Without further ado I picked up the dress and entered the room in question, he holding the door open for me and closing it after telling me to return as soon as I had changed.

I heard the door click shut behind me. It being too late to back out now, I hurried out of my clothes. Then, before dropping my last garment, I looked all about but could find nothing amiss.

There was nothing but a beautiful bedroom, dresser and chairs and wardrobe, which contained many other garments, to say nothing of an endless assortment of slippers and stockings. Slippers and stockings seemed to be a weakness with the old boy, I thought.

Choosing a pair suitable to my feet, I sat down to pull on the stockings and slippers, when a strange feeling that I wanted to make water came over me. This I thought was unduly strange for I had attended to my wants before leaving the theater just a short hour before. But the feeling persisted. Indeed, it grew on me as I sat there thinking about it, and I began seeking something into which I might pee. There was nothing I might use, however, so I slipped on the dress.

I tried to dismiss the thought from my mind. Turning to the door through which I had entered I was about to turn the knob, when I was again taken with the necessity of wanting to pee, and the need of freeing my bladder was so pronounced I couldn't see how I was ever going to stand it until I could get out of the house.

Thinking to hurry the matter I opened the door and entered the room where I had left him. As he had suggested I acted the dutiful wife. My hands were clasped in front of me, and my eyes were downcast, and all in all I must have looked very funny.

Wishing to say something I asked him why he had chosen me as his wife. He explanied that only such a girl as I could appeal to him, and that since I was an actress I could carry out the part as he desired it. And while he was telling me this I squirmed and twisted about so great was my desire to pee.

Finally, when I thought I could no longer stand it, I told him that it would be impossible to continue until I had been allowed to visit the privy, and will I ever forget his answer to this!

His reaction to this was rather startling. "No!" he said, looking at me, a stern look on his face. "And do not mention it again! When the proper time comes you may attend to your want, but not before!"

To say that I was frightened would be putting it mild. Then he handed me a bridal-veil telling me to put it on. This done to his satisfaction, he said: "Now answer all my questions just as though you were my legal wife. Will you do everything, such as a dutiful wife should do?"

"Yes, sir," I answered, somewhat cowed now.

"You will obey me in everything?"

"Yes, sir," I answered, sure now he must be a mad man. My bladder almost bursting, and my knees pinched together for fear of spilling it all over the expensive Persian rug on which I stood, I awaited his next command. I didn't have long to wait, either.

"Come," he said, leading me into another room. Here, in spite of the outside warmth, a great fire burned on the hearth, and before this lay a great bear-skin rug. Then without further ado he lay down upon this rug, his head resting on the head of the thing.

Then he commanded me to come and stand close to his head.

"Closer!" he cried, "that is right. You are now in the right position. In the future you must dispense with drawers; they will be in the way while you are acting the good wife."

I knew then that he was looking under my dress, and if he wasn't getting a good look at everything it wasn't his fault, for I was without drawers; I wore nothing, as I said, except the dress, slippers and stockings.

Then, when I thought I could no longer stand it and would surely pee then and there, he said: "Now step astride me!"

With an effort I managed to do his bidding. It was an effort because now I felt as though I was about to burst, so filled was my bladder. Hurrying to do his bidding, that I might get it over with, I moved up so I stood astride his chest, my feet at his shoulders.

"Now squat down," he said. I did this. He kept me thus for fully a minute; it was the longest minute I had ever been called upon to endure. I began to suffer in still another way; I found my legs were hurting me dreadfully; they seemed filled with cramps, and my knees ached. He must have noted my suffering, for he said: "Do you still feel that you wish to make water?"

Snatching my dress away so I could see his face, I nodded.

"Then," he said, a strange light in his eyes, "since you are my dutiful wife I command you to do it right where you are!"

I could hardly believe my own ears! Was I hearing correctly, or had the man gone completely insane! Then it suddenly occurred to me that the girl back at the theater had said something about this; something about getting a lot of money for simply peeing!

"Could it be possible," I thought, "that this man wanted me to do this dreadful thing on him!" I recalled having read something about a certain Russian Count who, before he could bring himself to have sexual connection with his mistress, insisted upon her pissing on him! Could it be possible that this man wanted me to do the same thing, and that afterward he would ravish me!

The thought sickened me! It wasn't that I dreaded the thought of doing this supposed dreadful thing on him; it was the fear that gripped me that I might in another minute be ravished by him. But my fears and dread were not to be taken into consideration; I had already stood for more than I could stand, and even as I squatted there over him I so lost control of myself that the floodgate was forced open allowing a solid stream of amber fluid to gush and spatter over his shirt-front!

Suddenly I felt thrilled at it all! The fact that he seemed to enjoy this most intimate thing to be done upon him so aroused my lascivious mind that I deliberately arched my hips that I might dash the stream directly upon his face! Nor was I alone in these thoughts. At the first contact his arms went about my naked hips and he quite lifted me directly over his open mouth! His mouth glued tightly to my cunt he was drinking my fluid in great gulps—

And at last I had no more to give; my bladder was empty.

But, if my desire to make water had passed, my desire to be sucked had not. I had been greatly aroused; the dreadful act instead of sickening me had forced my unusually lascivious nature to the limit! One of my hands went to the back of his neck; his hair and the back of his collar was drenched, but I cared not for that!

My desire then was to go-off; that it might not have fitted into his scheme of things I cared not; I was burning hot! Moving and twisting about, rubbing my cunt all over his clinging mouth, I drew him tighter and tighter, and then I felt the time rising within me!

I went-off! I saw him smile with his eyes (that being the only part of his face I could see since the rest was buried in the thick curls) and I realized then that he was enjoying it all and that I hadn't carried my play too far. But the double shock had been far too great for me to stand. With a long-drawn sigh I collapsed upon him, only to roll to the floor helpless against defending myself had this been necessary which, thank the lord, wasn't.

Instead of mounting me as I thought he would, and which I was powerless to prevent, he satisfied himself with simply rolling off with me, and here, his face still between my naked thighs, he contented himself by simply kissing my aching gap. And it was at his own initiative that the play ceased.

Rising to his feet he stood looking down at me; then he did a strange thing. Bending down he drew my skirt down over my legs thus shutting out the sight of my nudity. "You had best rise and take care of yourself," he said in a low voice, "You are quite wet."

Almost reluctantly I raised to my feet. "I am wet," I answered, raising my single skirt to well above my waist with an utter disregard that I might be inviting him to further liberties.

But my guardian angel must have been spending her entire time watching over me that night, for the gentleman made not the slightest effort toward molesting me, and I re-entered the bedroom quite as intact as I had first left it.

Here I bathed myself and hastily dressed. It had been a rare novelty to me, but I would feel better about it all when I was safe back in my own rooms. He was waiting for me when I came out of the bedroom. I thought he appeared somewhat crestfallen, and I couldn't help but thrill inwardly at the thought of the strange story I would tell my friends.

When he saw that I was smiling, and that I wasn't

angry at anything that had happened, he said: "I sincerely hope you will not think too harshly of me, my dear—I am unfortunate in that I am unable to enjoy the embrace of a woman nature's way, and I wish to thank you for your kind consideration in assisting me."

Fully dressed, now, I felt more or less safe, and smiling, I said: "Please do not make any apologies; I, too, have keenly enjoyed it all, and whenever you wish it I shall be only too glad to come to you again."

Think of my surprise, then, to hear him say that he would never call upon me again. I thought that there might be something about me he disliked, but I was mistaken in this. He complimented me very highly for my conduct; he said I was the best subject he had ever had but, unfortunatley, he could never get the same thrill by having the same girl a second time. Then he handed me the purse; I had earned it, he said, adding, that I should wear the necklace in memory to a blessed event.

Perhaps I couldn't look at it as a *blessed* event, but I did remember it for many days as one of, if not the strangest event I had ever experienced. I accepted the purse, of course; it wasn't that I was in such great need of money; I had saved my earnings and my pay was good; I would use it in one grand party for my friends.

Though it was all very strange I must say that he was one of the most perfect gentlemen I have ever met. True, his desires were most unusual, but that was nothing I need worry about; I have met any number of men whose desires were far stranger than his, and they were far from being gentlemen.

It is needless to say that I arrived home alright, and no one was ever the wiser though later I told our primadonna about it; her only reaction being a shrug of her shapely shoulders and a faint smile. "You will get used to all that and many other things," she said. "Men seem to think a diva is something unusual, and as long as they are silly enough to believe that, we might as well reap the gold harvest of their thoughts."

She told me of dozens of men she had had that way, and I was surprised to find that there were women— many of them—who were equally guilty of the offense mentioned.

It had been a most wonderful experience for me. The money and necklace I cared little or nothing about; it had been an experience just suited for me in that it was of assistance to leading me by easy stages into a life of freedom and ease. It was, by far, the most weird experience I had had, but it had had its effect upon me.

I no longer feared being naked in the presence of men, since I had already been sucked-off by one. It was, however, the last affair of its kind I ever experienced in Vienna.

A few weeks after this event I was called upon to take our diva's part. She had been stricken down and was unable to carry on. This had its good points; one night I was interviewed by a celebrated gentleman. It seemed he had been in the audience. In fact he had been attending constantly for a week. It further developed that he was about to open another and far bigger opera in Frankfurt, and I was engaged for the part of Juliette.

At last I was made, as they say in the theatrical world!

I was given a wonderful part and I received many wonderful presents, and I have them to this day. I had taken an understudy, just as I had been understudy to our primadonna, so I was able to leave almost at once, and a few days later I departed the wonderful city that had been so instrumental in providing me with so many thrilling and delightful experiences.

I found to my great delight that a very beautiful villa

had been provided for me by my new manager. I thought, of course, that I would be called upon to pay —in a manner such things are supposed to be paid for —but he proved to be a harmless little fellow; he seemed to think it pay enough if allowed to kiss my hand, which he did at every opportunity.

Chapter IV

One might consider this the second part of my story, my friend, since it is the beginning of a far different life than I had been living, for it was here in Frankfurt that I was to meet the man who was to become my first real love!

You remember, my friend, how I told you I believed I was born to love? Well, I am more convinced of it than ever. Think back for a moment: Even before I left home I met a woman who opened my eyes to the joys of sex. True, it was an unnatural love to be sure, but what of that? I have never suffered from it; I acquired something of an education through it all, and though it was the wrong kind of an education—as some will try to make you believe—it had its advantages in that it was to provide me with the talents necessary in the years to follow. Such talents, I firmly believe, are necessary to a career such as mine.

I believe I have already mentioned that I was desirous in wishing to retain my virginity until I came to age; if I didn't I am mentioning it now. Even before I left Vienna I had been taken with the desire to have a lover, but I held off; even passing my eighteenth birthday, that age when it is quite proper and fitting for a maiden to be regally and royally fucked.

Even when making the journey into Frankfurt I was overtaken with these thoughts. I believe I had arrived at the age when it would be good for me to accept the love of a man, and as I reflected on my past life I was suddenly overcome with the desire for a man!

Yes, that was it. I was in love without a lover—a most amazing state of affairs. It, however, never occurred to me that I was to have one so soon.

The day following my arrival in Frankfurt my manager had provided me with a housekeeper. It happened, however, that I wasn't to keep her; she for years had held the position of wardrobe-mistress in the various productions and was quite well versed in things both upon and off stage.

She was a motherly old soul and I was quite taken back when, that very day, she said: "I do not wish to presume, my dear, but when do you expect to be joined by your lover?"

The question coming from her amazed me. At first I was inclined to resent this bold remark, but I thought better of it—and I have always thanked myself that I hadn't been harsh with her.

"My lover?" I asked, showing surprise at the audacity of her question.

For a long moment she stared at me, then: "You have a lover, have you not?"

"No," I answered, "I have no lover. Why do you ask?"

"I hope you will forgive me for mentioning it," she began, "but don't you think it quite necessary—to your voice, I mean?"

Then it suddenly occurred to me that I had heard something or other about this, and I wondered if I could be mistaken in this woman's true meaning? Here I was a total stranger in a strange city with few if any friends. In the late past I had never been without a girl upon whom I could lavish my caresses, and I suddenly felt rather alone. Also, I wondered if it were possible that this elderly woman had designs on me? Feeling somewhat frisky at the moment I decided to put her to the test; she wouldn't be so bad; and an old tongue was better than nothing.

Laughing, I said "I am sorry, my dear, but I have no male love; mine, in the past, has been lady lovers," and I stretched languishly, at the same time allowing one bare leg to jut out between the folds of my gown, the only article of clothing I was wearing at that moment.

She shook her head. "You are a very foolish girl," she said. "It is all very nice to have a sympathetic girl friend, but if you won't think me over bold I would say that you are abusing yourself in not taking a real lover—you understand, do you not?"

There was a merry twinkle in her eyes as she said this.

Becoming more daring, I said: "You mean I should take one who will caress me in the manner I like to be caressed?"

She nodded. "You will find it necessary in the developing of your throat muscles. Please do not think I am presuming too much," she went on. "Indeed, I am quite serious. You must do this, or sooner or later you will lose your voice," and turning, she left me alone with my thoughts. You may rest assured my thoughts were conflicting.

The rest of the day I spent between reclining on a beautiful little flower-decked porch and fussing about a well-appointed kitchen.

To give you some idea of how the thought gripped

me, let me tell you of how I ate my dinner that night. I had dismissed my housekeeper and had set the table for two places. I fancied I was entertaining my lover, and to make the picture complete I wore but a thin dressing-gown and mules, being careful that the gown was open down the front. It was foolish, of course, but I was having a grand time of it. Later, when "we" finished our dinner, I fancied he carried me to a broad divan, in the living-room, and here he kissed and kissed and kissed me. Oh, I don't know what I thought!

I found myself eager for a man! I pictured him as a strong man; one qualified to administer real, brutal love—

Then, the following day, a strange thing occurred. It was as though my prayers were being answered. A carriage stopped at my door. From it alighted my aged manager, and with him was one of the handsomest men I had ever seen! From behind the curtains I gazed at him; I had no eyes for my manager; and he was handsome; black, silky hair—Ah! he was an Apollo!

They entered. To my surprise—and joy—this man was to play the part of Romeo, in the play in which I was to star.

Never shall I forget the expression that came over his handsome face when he was introduced. For almost a full minute, perhaps, I stood staring into his eyes, and it was he who broke the spell.

"Really," he cried, his voice low, "I had no idea I was to play next to an angel!" We all three laughed at this, and after a brief visit my manager left us. He had many duties to attend to, he said, and bowed himself out, leaving me to speculate on the outcome of it all.

Even in those first few moments I couldn't help but wonder how wonderful it must be to be fucked by a

man such as this one! And even then I promised myself
the pleasure of having this man in my arms! Yes! He
would be my lover!

Even then I was speculating on how best to lure him
to my bed.

In the theater one sees nudity on every hand, and I
realized it would take more than mere nudity to bring
about a union between us.

I might add here that I *was* dressed somewhat scanty;
my only garment, besides a short silken under-vest, was
a kimono of pale silk, and low bedroom slippers on my
bare feet, and I took advantage of this scant apparel to
bring about a better understanding between us. "I must
beg your forgiveness for allowing myself to be caught
so," I began, motioning to my dress.

"Pray forget it," he said. "I quite understand. It *is*
rather warm and I am delighted in that you are considerate enough of your own comfort to dress accordingly."

"But," I insisted, a wave of almost uncontrollable lust
sweeping over me, "I am almost naked!" I laughed to
show I wasn't frightened.

"Pray! It is no matter," he said smiling his sweetest.
"Again let me say I think your dress is quite satisfactory.
However, since my visit here was but to meet you, may
I withdraw?" He kissed my finger tips and withdrew be-
fore I could say a word to stay him.

I was vexed with myself. Why had I said such a foolish thing!

I spent a dreadful night. My thoughts were filled with
nothing but that wonderful man. There was one consol-
ing thought, however. That was, that on the morrow he
would call again, and I promised myself that I would
never be so silly again. In reality I had meant to call attention to my scant dress hoping in that way to attract
him to my arms, but he was a gentleman, and took my

remark as a desire on my part that he withdraw. I cursed myself for a fool!

If he had but known the easy conquest I would have been I am sure he would have stayed with me, and instead of kissing my fingertips, he would have had something far more substantial than fingers to kiss. After he departed I slipped out of my gown and under-vest and donned my nightgown. Standing before my glass and viewing my image, I patted my hairy mount, saying aloud: "Very, very soon, my dear, you shall have something far more thrilling to caress than a mere tongue-tip."

The following day was a long one for me, though he came shortly after lunch. Taking advantage of his suggestion that I dress for comfort rather than for convention, I was wearing an outfit not unlike that of the previous day; the only difference being that my gown was of black georgette, and I wore black silk stockings.

My idea of the black gown was to accentuate the whiteness of my body and limbs. Somewhat daring, don't you think, my friend?

But I can tell you I was desperate; I had been pricked with Cupid's dart—it remained but to be pricked with my lover's!

This time he complimented me on my thoughtfulness in dress.

"Do you realize that you are very beautiful?" he asked, "And that I'm afraid I shall never be able to withstand your nearness?"

I thrilled as his eyes swept over me, for while my gown covered, it did not in the least hide the outline of my body and legs! "Nonsense," I laughed, "You have seen any number of handsome women, and you seemed to have survived."

We seated ourselves upon the divan. There we went

over the lines of the play. You are familiar with the play "Romeo and Juliette" so I won't tire you with the story. Enough to say that the balcony scene is unusually thrilling. Romeo, as you know, is supposed to climb the balcony, and here he is to meet his mistress, Juliette, and Juliette is supposed to have just gotten out of bed and is wearing but a nightgown.

If you will recall, I told you earlier in this story, that the whole of Europe had gone mad over exotic scenes both in and out of the theater, and I had been given to understand from the start that this particular scene in our coming production was to be enacted in a somewhat unusual setting. Instead of wearing a nightgown, I was supposed to wear a white georgette dressing-gown, and as we sat there scanning our lines, he came to this particular situation. "You are being called upon to assume a most unusual role," he said without raising his eyes from the page.

"Yes?" I said. I also kept my eyes riveted to the paper.

"Yes," he said. "I hope, however, that you will have no objection to wearing the scant attire this scene calls for."

"Why should I?" I asked, trying to answer nonchalantly. "After all it's all in the play, and the play's the thing, isn't it?"

"I'm afraid it won't be all play on my part," he said.

"Indeed? And why not?"

"Because," he answered, "Carrying such a beautiful lady, and having one so beautiful as yourself quite nude might prove too thrilling—I might drop you, you know."

I laughed at this. I knew we were treading on dangerous ground, but I didn't care; I was more than ever determined to win this handsome man to my arms! "Don't tell me," I said, laughing, "that I will be the first naked woman you have held in your arms!"

This time it was he who laughed, then: "I would rather not talk of that. However, if I have ever done anything like this, the lady was far less beautiful than yourself."

"That is very beautifully said. I hope, however, that you will not be so overcome that you *will* drop me— That, I'm afraid, would be too dreadful for words!"

"Rest assured I shall not," he said.

How we ever passed through this day without a demonstration from him I shall never be able to tell, for God knows, I did everything possible to impress him. On three distinct occasions I recrossed my legs, each time giving him a full view of my naked thighs to the very tops, and each time slowly drawing the folds of my scant gown over my knees.

Yet, nothing happened.

The following day it was the same thing, and the day after that.

By this time we had familiarized ourselves to the extent that we were ready to go over our lines together. That is, we were far enough advanced to practice our parts.

That day I had dressed very carefully. I was careful to the extent of ridding myself of everything except the lacy dressing-gown and slippers, and the gown being a buttonless affair, I was looking forward to practicing the balcony scene, though I was careful to hold my gown together until that thrilling scene was to be enacted.

But again nothing happened. True, we went over everything again and again—but for some unknown reason he didn't think it necessary to practice the balcony scene.

Finally I came to the conclusion that if I were to get anywhere with this man I must make the advances myself. Going about practically naked seemed to make no impression on him whatsoever.

True, he never failed to compliment me on my attire, but compliments did little to quell the burning within my aching cunt!

It might be mentioned here that I had managed to get a very good maid, and my housekeeper was relieved of the burden of caring for my home. This maid, however, was the worst kind of a greenhorn; I doubt very much if she knew there was more than one use for her pussy; I had given her hints enough, but she simply looked at me when I would flit about in complete nakedness.

And, so, without even the comfort of a likeable maid, I found myself getting desperate. Something had to be done. I said: "Why not arrange to have dinner with me tomorrow night! There is no reason why you shouldn't, is there?"

He hesitated a moment, then: "Why—I would be delighted! No, there is no reason why I shouldn't."

This was my first real step in paving the way to love! Real love! Already I pictured myself lying naked in his arms! Already I felt his lips kissing and caressing me from head to foot—

"You are unmarried?" I asked, hardly knowing what I was saying.

"Whatever gave you that impression?" he asked.

I shrugged my shoulders. "I don't know," I said, "I should hate to be the cause of trouble between you and your wife—I am glad, however, that you have none! I shall be expecting you—early!"

I'll never forget the strange light in his eyes as he kissed my fingertips at parting!

Believe it or not, my friend, I took an opiate that night before I could go to sleep. I didn't want to sleep;

I took it for the simple reason that I might hurry the hours until I was to see him again.

The next day everything was hustle and bustle. I am the world's worst cook, but I managed, with the help of my maid, in preparing a delightfully cooked dinner. This done, I dismissed my maid, telling her I would not need her again that night; that she was free to visit her relatives if she chose.

From the icebox I produced several bottles of champagne and the choicest wines, placing them in a convenient place at table.

Then I took a bath. It lacked little time before he would arrive and I wanted to be at my best that night! This night! That's right! It was this night! My wedding night! This was the night I was to surrender my maidenhead! The night I was to be ravished in every pore!

Dried, after a highly perfumed bath, I arranged my hair. Then I began speculating as to what I should wear. It must be something unusual; of this I was sure. Already I had appeared before him in next to nothing! What, then, could I wear?

Finally, I chose a black chion dressing-gown. It was a daring thing, but I didn't care, I was desperate! Beneath this I wore a short chiffon undervest. Standing before my glass I viewed the result of this and even I blushed. If this didn't turn the trick for me, then I would give up all idea of ever winning him to my arms.

The gown came to about midway between my hips and knees, and since it was cut away daringly at the top, it was necessary to wear the frail under-garment or my breasts would have strutted bodily out of the gown. And while I was gazing at my reflection in the mirror, the bell rang! My hour was approaching! Snatching up a pin, I stuck it into my gown, to hold the thing to-

gether. Slipping my bare feet into low mules, I hurried
to the door!

I noted he looked at me strangely. Entering and kissing my hand, he said: "Your maid—she isn't here?" He
couldn't seem to understand why I should have attended door for him.

"My maid," I said, "has been called away on account
of sickness, but fear not, my friend, I have a splendid
dinner for you!"

I wondered how I could be so calm in the face of
those thoughts.

I saw him gaze at me, and I knew he was thrilled at
what he saw, for this time the gown concealed nothing;
even the hair about my aching cunt was fairly well
revealed.

"I shall have to be your serving maid tonight," I said
as I flitted about him. The dinner, as you can guess,
was a huge success, and long before it was finished we
were both chatting away at a great rate. We consumed
much wine; we both seemed to possess unusual thirsts.

"Let the table go," I said as we went toward the living room. "My maid shall attend to it tomorrow; besides, we might feel like eating something later!"

I must have made a rather startling picture as I sat
there beside him upon the divan, my scant gown open
down the front revealing both my legs naked to almost
the tops. Ah, don't think I hadn't worked out a fitting
campaign. I was desperate, and I was daring. Of course
one could hardly expect a lover to make improper advances while seated at table, but at table I had added
to my already daring plan!

I had brought a bottle of champagne into the living
room, and by way of starting the daring plan I had in
mind, I said: "Now let us drink to the success of our
dinner, and our friendship!"

Even when saying it I could hardly control my voice. Knowing that in another minute or two I would have him in my arms was enough to thrill any one, wasn't it, my friend?

Very graciously he filled two glasses, and handing me one, we repeated the toast, and as I sat there holding the glass I realized that the moment had arrived! My well-thought-out plan was about to materialize! Leaning against him, I said: "We should seal our friendship with a kiss—isn't that the proper way?"

I saw his eyes glance quickly at the windows! Then he slipped one arm about my waist and kissed me, and as his lips met mine, I deliberately spilled the contents of my glass across my thighs, at the same time giving a startled "Oh!"

Quick to note this, he drew his handkerchief and attempted to dry me. "It's nothing," I said, "I shall go and change it!"

With heart beating wildly, for now I was going to do the most daring thing of all! Quickly I slipped both garments from my shoulders, kicked the mules from my feet! Then I gave a piercing scream and threw myself down across the bed, in what was supposed to be a beautiful faint!

In an instant he was at my side! Seeing the apparent faint, he grabbed up a bottle of salts and pressed it beneath my nose. My eyes fluttered open. He placed his arms about me and kissed my lips again and again, then: "Whatever happened? Why did you cry out?"

I smiled. "I saw a mouse," I answered, "and I—I guess I fainted."

Remember, my dear, I am an actress, but it took every bit of my skill to act timid then, for I was stark naked and I was in the arms of the man I loved! I made a feeble effort to arise, but he held me down. "Please, dear," he said, holding all the tighter.

"But, darling," I cried, laughing faintly and trying to blush, I'm stark naked! What must you think of me!"

"I think you are the most beautiful woman I have ever seen," he said, kissing me again and again, "and I want to hold you in my arms, just like this, forever and ever!"

What could I do? While saying this, one of his hands had crept down to the hairs on my lower belly! I made not the slightest move to stop him; and as his hand slid further down, my thighs fell loosely apart and his searching fingers quite took possession of my cunt!

"I love you! I love you!" he cried.

My arms slid about his neck. "And I love you, too," I answered, and kissing his lips, I added: "I have loved ever since I first saw you, and though I am still a virgin, I want you to make me a woman!"

Our lips met in a clinging, soul-stirring kiss!

Raising his lips from mine, he whispered: "Will you be mine! Now! Here! Right here on your bed! I shall never be safe to myself until I have had you—body and soul!"

"You already have my soul, my darling, you have but to take my body—It is yours to do with as you like!"

"Then lie still and let me seal our love with a kiss!"

With a bound he was down on his knees and pressing burning kisses squarely on my cunt! The wine, my mad desire for him, the thrill of it all drove me almost mad! Grasping his head between my hands, I held it there and went-off! No longer did I attempt to hold back! His arms were about me! His hands clutched my naked body and his greedy mouth sucked and tongued my cunt in a frenzy of delight!

Again I went-off, and this time I almost fainted dead

away, so intense was the shock! And while I lay there, my thighs still parted to his eager gaze, he quickly stripped off his clothes, a moment later springing, naked, into my waiting arms!

With a dexterous motion he placed the head of his monster of a cock to the flushed lips of my cunt and pressed it in where, thanks to the many tongues and my own fingers, he soon passed the barrier!

If I ever experienced a pain as a result of this, I know not; I know only that I was penetrated to his balls, and from the way he drove it into me, I thought he was trying to get them in too!

At last I was being fucked! Too late now to turn back, I bucked upward against him with all my might! Mad with lust for each other, we were like two animals! Holding it far into me, he went-off, and almost instantly he began again! Our lips joined, our tongues darting in and out of each other's mouths, we fucked like mad! All the pent-up passion of years standing was now let loose! How many times I went-off I can't remember! How many times he filled my cunt with his prolific spend, I do not know!

I know only that I was supremely happy. I had never been so happy in my life! For a long time neither of us moved; just lay there soaking in bliss. Then he gazed into my eyes. "Do you think this is acting on my part," he asked, "or do you believe now that I love you?"

"Of course you love me, Paul, darling. But let's reverse the question; don't you think I am the one to ask that question now that I have given you the one thing a girl has to give?"

I am not going into the details of all the things we said to each other that night. Many of them are too sacred to repeat, even to you, my friend. Enough to say that we swore eternal love for each other, and I believe he really meant it; I know I did.

But if I refuse to tell you of the things we said, I won't refuse to tell you of the things we did—You have a perfect right to that after the thrilling letter you wrote me, you naughty boy!

After relieving me of his weight he went to the bathroom, returning with a basin of warm water and towels. Bathing and drying me between my thighs, he bent and kissed my cunt in one long, clinging kiss.

Then he lay down beside me, took me in his strong arms and kissed me. Then it was that we talked. But talk did little to satisfy me: I had heard from both Vera and our primadonna of the joys of toying with and kissing the male organ. One of my hands stole down to it and my fingers clasped themselves about it; it was but half stiff, but I loved it. I squeezed and pressed it. It grew larger. I continued to caress it, and it grew and grew. Soon, however, it had swelled to full erection and I could no longer span it with my fingers. I thrilled with the thoughts that at last I had taken such a monster; I wasn't very well informed regarding the sizes of men's cocks, but I knew enough to know that this one was of an unusual size. Would you like to learn something about it, my dear? Yes? Then listen: It was, by actual measurement, just nine inches long from base to tip. Oh, it was a beauty, I can tell you. It was fully two inches thick (or fifty kilometers, if you prefer) and set in a bed of thick, crisp hairs. His balls filled both my hands, and they, too, were thick with hair. Wasn't it a beauty, darling? And is there any wonder that I fell so desperately in love with it?

During the short time I had been toying with it, one of his hands was busy with me. From hip to titties his soft hand caressed, and then, no longer able to stand it, he said: "Oh, darling, I love you so! Please let me fuck you again!" And he made as though to roll me on my back, but I would have none of it.

"Wait, dear," I cried. "Wait until I have proven my love for you, too! Let me kiss your lovely cock! Then you can have me whenever you choose!"

I scrambled out of his arms and slid down upon the bed. God! How handsome it looked then! Standing straight up in the air, its ruby head almost bursting with inward blood pressure!

Stooping, I kissed the purple and pink head! Staring at it and working my hand up and down its length, I became fascinated! I loved it! Dropping again, I kissed it once more! But I wasn't satisfied; I wanted more of it! Rising to his elbow he stared down at me, hardly believing what his own eyes saw being enacted before them! I kissed it again; this time with open lips, and I heard him give a little gasp as I quite swallowed the head! Still I wasn't satisfied! I felt something was lacking! With a downward lunge I plunged it far into my mouth, and then I sucked it with all my might! He was trembling; he tried to draw it from between my lips, but I wouldn't have it! I was out to show him that I too could love; that I was no half-baked mistress! I wrapped my arms about him, held him in a tight embrace, and seeing that I wasn't to be done out of it, he clutched my head in his hands and holding it far back into my throat he delivered the contents of his massive balls deep into my mouth! Nor did I give up my position till the last drop had been given me, all of which I eagerly swallowed!

Then, and only then, did I allow it to slip from my lips, and coming up over him, I kissed his lips again and again! "There," I cried, "I, too, have shown my love for you, darling! And now you can fuck me to your heart's content!" And as though to prove my word, I straddled him and placed the still hard head to my cunt and gave a downward lunge against it, taking it in to his balls!

You may rest assured, my friend, that I left nothing lacking in my love for him that night. When he tired of the sport, I sucked him back to erection, and three times I sucked and swallowed the sperm from his lovely crest.

What more is there to tell? How, further, may I convey to you the wonderful things we did that night? Why try when you know all too well what happens between persons who dearly love each other?

Enough to say, that after a most thrilling night, we slept only to renew our pleasing occupation the following morning. Then Paul left me, promising to return as soon as he had attended to his affairs.

My maid found me still in bed when she returned after her night off, and I guess I scandalized her puritan mind by the way I saw her staring at me, for I made not the slightest effort to hide my nudity from her gaze.

Of course, every girl suffers more or less after a night such as I had had, and I was no exception. I was happy in the fact that I had lost my useless maidenhead, however, and for the first time in my life I realized what it meant to be without one's love. I remembered, then, that I had allowed him to leave without his breakfast, and I promised myself that the breakfast should be served always after this.

Lying there against my pillow, thinking of all the delightful things that had happened to me the previous night and that morning, I became frightened. I recalled how Vera had told me of her few nights of love, and how she became pregnant as a result of it. And then I brightened. Why worry about it? Besides, it was worth it! What I had done I did for love, and if I was with child, it would be a baby of love.

I dismissed it from my mind; the damage—if any— was already done, and I had almost a full month to go before I would know anything about it!

Then I got to wondering about my maid. I wondered if she had discovered that I had entertained a man all night, and that he had slept with me? My thoughts were interrupted by her entering my room. In her hand she held the bloody towel, that same towel with which Paul had removed the traces of my maidenhead, a maidenhead gone forever. She seemed frightened, but I explained it away by telling her that I had had a slight accident.

After breakfast I played the piano. I wasn't very much of a musician; I played but for my own amusement. I sang. I tried out a piece I had been having some trouble with and found that I had not the slightest difficulty in reaching the unusually high notes.

This caused me to wonder if my ability to reach these notes wasn't due in some way to my recent experience with Paul? I recalled what my temporary housekeeper had told me about having a lover whose cock I could suck! Could this be a result of that? Could it have possibly been a reaction so soon! I promised myself that I would ask Paul about it as soon as he returned!

If this was true, then I would acquire one of the most famed voices on earth, because I loved it! I adored it! I had thought that kissing a girl's cunt until she spilled her love-dew into my mouth was the height of delight, but it was as nothing compared to sucking my lover's cock!

My thoughts lent wings to my feet! I flitted about the house with an abandon which quite startled my maid! In my eagerness to do something even more startling, I dropped off my gown and ran all over the place in complete nakedness.

I saw her eyes following me, and I knew she was shocked beyond words. "Very well," I thought, "If you are so easily shocked, then as soon as Paul returns I shall give you something to be shocked about!" I laughed inwardly as I pictured the expression on her face when she would see the costume I wore, then!

Wishing to be ready when he did arrive, and hardly wanting to be disappointed in the fun I was going to have, I brought out the tiny under-vest I had previously worn. As I have already said, it was the very briefest thing I had ever seen; cut low enough at the top to almost expose both my breasts, and so short that it came to but my hips in length, and so transparent as to amount to exactly nothing as far as concealment went, it was a naughty garment, indeed. Still, it lacked something. Can you imagine anyone wishing to appear in anything else than that, my dear, and still wear something?

That was my thought, strange as it seems. I wanted to be as near naked when he arrived as it was possible to be! And above all, I wanted to shock this silly girl as she had never been shocked before!

Any minute now he was due to arrive; he had promised to have noon-day meal with me, and it lacked but a few minutes to noon. A plan of daring entered my mind! Why not make it a real naked reception! Why go about it half-way! Why, indeed?

Picking up a pair of shears, I cut the tiny garment up the front, making a gown of it, the tiny ribbons over my shoulders alone holding it from falling from me.

Watching from my bedroom window, I saw him coming up the gravel walk! Calling to my maid to admit him, I took a final look in my glass! I heard him enter! Drawing the top of the thing well back from my titties, I quickly stepped into the room and went to Paul, my arms raised to greet him!

Even Paul gasped at the daringness I displayed, but I quickly whispered into his ear my intention in shocking my silly maid, and he, great actor that he was, quickly took the hint! "You darling," he cried, holding me off at arm's length and gazing at me. "You are a million times more beautiful than I thought! You're adorable!"

And drawing me close and slipping his arms about me beneath the garment, he hugged me close, kissing and tonguing my mouth with all the zest he could muster. And all the while my maid stood staring in awed wonder.

But Paul wasn't done yet. Falling in with my own lascivious acts, he carried it a bit further. Picking me up in his strong arms, he carried me into the living-room and to the divan. Pushing me over on my back he kissed my breasts, neck and face like a madman, and all the while from the corner of my eye I saw the maid staring at us. I became more daring. Taking one of his hands in mine, I carried it to my cunt, patting the back of his hand as he fingered the naked lips, I, throwing my legs well apart and whispering into his ear.

Looking toward the door again, I noted that she had disappeared; the loving display had undoubtedly been a little too much for her sensitive nature. But our love-making went on until I thought I would surely lose the delightful load I had been saving for Paul.

The delightful fellow while ardent in his attack, wasn't so foolish, but what he knew when to stop, and as we lay there cuddling each other, I told him why I had adapted such an outlandish attire, and how he laughed. "What you need is a more sympathetic maid," he said, "and I shall attend to it at once, today. I believe I know the very one for you."

Rising from the divan, he called the maid. "Here," he said, handing her some money. "This will carry you over until you find another place. You may pack your things at once."

Though I felt sorry for her, I believe she was glad to go; such carrying-on as she had witnessed that day proved too much for her puritanical nature.

He kissed me and promised to return in an hour, and after he had departed I bid my maid adieu. I stretched out upon the divan to await my lover's return, and I couldn't help but think how happy I was. A position in the world of art, a splendid income from which I could prepare for the future, a splendid cottage to live in, and above all, a lover! Strong, handsome, young and animate and armed with the most noble prick with which to fuck me!

Paul found me radiant, indeed, when he returned, bringing the information that he had engaged the services of a charming maid and that she would report to me the following day.

"Oh, Paul, you darling," I cried, pulling him down beside me, "I love you so, I never want you to leave me again!"

"And I love you, too, dear," he answered, kissing me again and again, "and I feel that I never want to leave you again—even to sleep!"

There was plenty more said that afternoon, and it all ended by him taking up residence there with me. Then I told him of my conversation with the woman who had acted as housekeeper for me, and how she hinted at the necessity of my having a lover; one whom I could gamahouche (I used that expression to him, then) and the great good I would derive from it. "Is that so?" I asked, looking him in the eye.

"I'm afraid it is," he answered, smiling. "At first I didn't want you to do that to me—"

"Why?" I interrupted.

"Well," he hesitated, looking off toward the window, "I realized, dear, that it was a dangerous thing for you to do, and—"

"Why is it dangerous?" I asked.

"Well, you see what happened—"

"And does that mean that every time I kiss you—like that—that you have the same thing happen?"

"I'm afraid so, darling," he answered. "It's a dreadful temptation to 'come' when one holds it in their mouth, as you did!"

"But I 'came' in your mouth when you did it to me, didn't I?"

"I'll say you did, darling, and that's the way I want you to do, every time I caress you like that."

"Is that a promise?" I asked, kissing him.

He nodded his answer—and five minutes later we were proving our promises to each other—and how!

During the night he told me it was necessary for him to be away for two or three days, and that he would spend his entire time with me. It seemed he owned some land in a distant part of the country, and as there were taxes and other things to take care of, he was forced to be away.

I wouldn't allow him to leave, however, until my new maid arrived, and I'll never forget the radiant smile that crossed her pretty face when she noted my scant attire. Not at all like the other country girl, who seemed frightened at my semi-nudity, but a pleased expression. She seemed to take it for granted, and I was sure she would be everything a maid could be.

After Paul left me, I arranged to visit the city. Paul was a great admirer of pretty dressing-gowns and chemise, and since he had insisted upon buying them for me (he felt he had a perfect right to do this, since he was my accepted lover) I couldn't very well refuse.

I found, upon my arrival back at the cottage, that my new maid, whose name was Geneveve, and who in the future I shall call "Gene," was not only a worthy maid, but a housekeeper as well. Everything was as spick and span as when I first entered the cottage, and to my further delight I found her in the act of preparing something for my dinner. She said she knew I was to be alone for a few nights and wanted to assist me in everything.

That she did assist me in everything was proven that very evening, as you shall see.

After our dinner (I had insisted upon her eating with me) I took a book and was reclining beneath a light. I had been reading but a few moments, when I was attracted by her standing close beside me.

Wondering what she wanted, I asked her, and was surprised to hear something like this: "Madame has such lovely long hair; perhaps she would like to have me comb it for her?"

There was something delightfully refreshing about the girl; she was wearing a little dress, of the type commonly worn by domestics at that period, and she was beautifully formed. Through the thin waist I could easily detect her firm breasts, the nipples of which seemed to be trying to press themselves through the thin material.

Also, I had detected the whiteness and plumpness of her thighs, as she moved about here and there, and this coupled with her strange request regarding my hair made me think kindly of her. I also wondered if it were possible that she knew more about things than I had as yet learned. The book I had been reading wasn't unusually interesting, so I made up my mind I would question her a little.

It also happened that I delighted in having someone play with my hair; I had an unusually long head of it, and sometimes I suffered headaches from it, though not since I had had Paul.

"Why, yes," I answered, smiling sweetly, "I would love to have you comb it for me."

I was wearing, as was usual, but a thin dressing-gown and low slippers, and I was lying in a more or less revealing position, but she seemed not to notice this.

Without further delay she arranged the pillows beneath my back and shoulders, and a moment later was letting down my hair.

After a few moments, I said: "What prompted you to think I liked having my hair done?"

"My last mistress liked having hers done. It was long, like yours."

"Did you like waiting on her?" I asked.

"Yes, madam. She was very kind to me."

"And why did you leave her?"

"She took a husband, and is travelling in India," Gene answered.

"I see. And if she hadn't married, would you have stayed with her?"

"Yes, madam, I liked her very much."

Womanlike, I became interested in this other woman. "Tell me about her," I said. "Tell me everything of interest about her. Was she very pretty?"

"Yes, madam, she was."

"And you have seen her in an undressed condition—like I am?"

"Oh, yes, madam. I have seen her undressed many times. In fact she was always undressed when I done her hair and massaged her."

"Oh, you massaged her too?"

"Yes, madam. You see, my former mistress liked wearing low-cut dresses, but unfortunately she had rather small breasts, so she used to have me massage them every night and morning."

"That is interesting indeed," I said. "And did your treatment help them, and did you like doing that?"

"I didn't at first, but after two or three times I got to like it."

"That's strange," I said. "What could there be about it that you didn't like? I can't imagine any one not liking pretty breasts."

"Oh, it wasn't that I disliked massaging them; it was something else."

"Something else?" I asked, interested and warming to the subject.

She nodded. "I hope you won't misunderstand, but —well, she liked to have me take the points between my lips and suck them."

"Indeed! And how often did you do this?"

"Every night and morning, madam," came the ready answer.

"I see. And you liked doing it?"

"At first I didn't, but after a while I liked it."

There is no telling just where this might have led to had not I, at that moment, received a caller. I was hardly dressed to receive visitors, and I had Gene receive them while I hurried to my room to don suitable covering. It proved to be my aged manager, however, and was bringing still another member of the company that I might meet her. She was a middle-aged woman, rather motherly I thought, and this proved to be so, although she was unusually broad-minded for one her age. We spent a pleasant hour, and then she left.

The spell had worn off, and since Gene had about finished my hair, I retired to bed where I read myself to sleep.

I was awakened by my maid, who smilingly told me breakfast was waiting, and as soon as I bathed she would have everything ready.

Think of my surprise to find her following me into the bathroom, where she assisted me at my toilet, insisting upon sponging my back and drying me. This was rather a new experience to me; I had had maids, but never one who waited upon me hand and foot.

After breakfast, however, I was in for another treat. The morning was bright and clear, and it was dreadfully warm, and as I reclined before an open window, Gene said: "You know, madam, lying there makes me think of my former mistress; she delighted in taking sunbaths each morning—while I arranged her hair—"

"And sucked the nipples of her titties?" I interrupted, smiling.

Gene laughed and nodded her head.

"Alright, dear," I said, "you can arrange my hair, and then, if you're very good, I'll let you suck the nipples of my titties. Mine, however, are rather nice, don't you think so?" and I threw the folds of my gown back to better reveal them.

Having been without my lover's splendid cock throughout the night, I was feeling unusually randy that morning, and I thrilled anew when Gene answered: "They are very beautiful, madam, and I should consider it something of an honor to be allowed to massage them."

"Very well," I answered, "since you think them so nice, suppose we let the hair go for the moment, and come here on your knees, so I can determine if you are so good as you are trying to make me believe?"

I noted the change in her at once as she knelt beside me. Her cheeks were flushed and her eyes were bright, and if I was any judge at all, this girl knew more than she appeared to know.

I noted, too, that she didn't attack the nipples at once; instead, she traced little lines about both my titties, starting at the base of each and circling them in little spirals, coming to the nipples as a last resort. I use the word "resort" because that is the word best suited to it, for I could see from the moment she started on the unusual job, that she was trying to arouse me. And she did arouse me, too.

Finally I said: "Really, dear, you are even better than my lover; but he's not so stingy with his kisses!"

I saw the strange light in her eyes as she raised them and stared into mine, and I went on: "Naughty girl! I'll bet you did something else for your former mistress, if the truth were known!"

I thought at first that I had carried my naughty suggestions too far, for there came a strange expression over her face; it seemed as though she was frightened, but a moment later I found she wasn't frightened. She said: "I didn't want you to know, but—well, I did have to do something else!"

She blushed a little, and I said: "I knew it, you little dear. But don't you think for a moment that that makes any difference to me. I happen to know that many women employ girls for all sorts of reasons; I myself have had girls, so you needn't hold any secrets from me. Now tell me, dear, what was it you used to do for her?"

Gene blushed deeply for a moment, then: "She used to make me play with her curls—there," pointing in the general direction of my pussy.

She still wore that strange expression about her eyes, and I said: "And I'll bet you liked that, too, you little pet, didn't you?"

She nodded, then: "Like I told you, I didn't at first, but I did after the first few times."

It was a strange thing, this unusual experience with my maid, a girl I knew little or nothing about, but as I said, I was in a strange mood that day and I found myself liking her more and more with each passing moment. Then, too, there was something charmingly feminine about Gene. And I was suddenly overcome with the desire to see her little pussy. Then it occurred to me that if I was quite careful and didn't hurry this strange flirtation I might develop a real friendship with her, and if I hadn't mistaken my guess Gene would prove a splendid alternative when Paul would be obliged to be away.

But there was one thing I fully intended doing, and that was, that whatever happened between us it would be of her own solicitation and not by any act of my own.

I said: "Very well, Gene, you little dear, if you are a really good girl I'll let you try it on me a little later, but in the meantime you might continue to kiss and caress my titties—it makes me feel dreadfully naughty," and gazing at her in a most suggestive manner, continued: "That's what my lover, Paul, does before he gives me his lovely big rammer."

Smilingly, Gene did my bidding. Her lips skipped all about my breasts, sucked the nipples in turn, and showed in a dozen ways that she was perfectly satisfied with her lot.

But I didn't want to spoil it all by hurrying matters, so after a few moments, I said: "There Gene, you delightfully naughty girl, I guess you best stop your naughty sucking for a little while; you've got me as randy as can be," and I playfully pushed her off. "After lunch perhaps I'll have you entertain me again—if you are good!"

I could see the disappointment in her eyes as I said this, but I was determined to make her wait for the "good things" I intended offering her red lips.

About the middle of the afternoon, however, I began putting my plan into action. I realized of course that it wasn't fair to Paul to develop a flirtation with even this little maid, but my lascivious mind conjured all sorts of strange and Oriental ideas; I wanted to be entertained; even Paul's wonderful cock hadn't robbed me of my thoughts of a pretty girl. Indeed, I had already given promise to myself that I was through with women and girls, and it was Paul being away as much as anything else, perhaps, which led my thoughts into these weird channels.

Besides the low divan there were several other pieces of furniture, and among these there was an old-fashioned piece which resembled a bed-chair of the type used by elderly women during their reclining years. It had, too, a sort of foot-rest that could be used when one wished to partly recline, and by using the foot-rest one could almost recline in the strange thing. I had thought it about the most uncomfortable thing in the house, but my eyes fell upon it as about the best possible medium with which to bring about the desired results.

"You naughty girl," I said, dropping off my gown completely and seating myself in the wicked-looking affair, "this morning you make me feel dreadfully nice with your lovely lips, and since I'm to be alone tonight, I feel I can't wait for my lover's kisses, so come here on your knees and please me." I tried to be calm, but I guess I overdid it a little, for her cheeks became flushed and her eyes again took on that strange light I had previously seen.

Remember, now, I was stark naked, and I thrilled as I watched Gene's eyes sweep over me. Noting this, I said: "And if you're real nice about it and make me feel good, perhaps I'll let you do my hair down here," touching my hairy mound.

That Gene was more than willing to get at the task was plainly shown by the manner in which she went about it. Watching her for a few moments, I said: "Tell me, dear, how did it come about that your former mistress insisted upon your doing such a delightful thing for her?"

Then, for the first time, a frightened look came into her eyes, then:

"I suppose I might as well confess—you will find it out sooner or later anyway." There was a faraway look in her eyes as she went on: "My former mistress—the one before my last one, I mean—mislaid some of her jewelry, and I was accused of taking it. The police made a great ado about it, and I was taken to the workhouse."

The sincerity of Gene's story was proven a moment later by the appearance of tears beneath her lashes, then she dropped her eyes, saying: "But why should I trouble you with all this—"

"Oh, but I wish to hear it," I said. "Your story interests me; go on; tell me all about it."

"Well," she went on, "my former mistress was a great friend of the lady who accused me of taking her gems. That night, shortly after I had been confined in the workhouse, my mistress found her jewelry where she herself had placed it, and the lady who had been a friend, the same one for whom I worked before coming to you, took advantage of the situation by coming

to me and telling me she would see to it that I was let
out at once providing I would work for her as her maid.
Naturally I was overjoyed and promised anything. It
was some time before I discovered the discrepancy in
her statement, but it wasn't long before I discovered the
true state of my late mistress's intentions toward me;
for though I had never given my former mistress any
reason to think that I liked her in any other than a
purely platonic nature, my late mistress took a deeper
interest in my well-being. I didn't, of course, want to do
the things she hinted at my doing, but she continually
held it over my head that she had taken me from the
workhouse, and if I didn't do her bidding, she would
see to it that I was returned there at the earliest possible moment."

"Well?" I encouraged her, seeing that she hesitated.
"What then?"

"It was then she insisted upon me playing with her
breasts."

"But," I hazarded, "you told me but a few moments
ago that you liked doing it. Don't tell me now that you
were fibbing me."

"No, madam, I wasn't telling a lie. It was true that I
didn't want to do it at first, but, as I said, she held it
over my head, and I was obliged to do it, and—well, I
got to like doing it, I guess."

"Then," I said, smiling prettily at her, "seeing that
she was getting you to go that far, she insisted that you
do her other hair; is that it?"

She nodded, blushing as she did so.

"And you got to the point where you liked that, too,
huh?"

Again she nodded, then: "Yes, mam."

"Very well," I said, smiling, "forget all about the
theft of her supposed jewels. Personally, I don't believe

a word of it, and I think it most unkind in her making you do something you disliked doing. But aren't you just the least bit glad, now?" And I reached out and encircled her waist with my right arm and drew her close.

She smiled then and nodded her head, the index finger of one hand tracing little imaginary figures on my belly.

I had been deeply touched by her story; it was not the first time I had heard of such practices having been put into effect when one wished to gain their ends; but that did not in any way lessen my desire to indulge this girl's arts to the full. I said:

"Now that you have told me so much, my dear, tell me this: Why did your mistress wish you to kiss and caress her titties—that part of the story interests me."

"Because she liked it," answered Gene.

"And how long were you called upon to do this before she wanted you to 'do her hair,' as you refer to it?"

"About a week."

"Did she ever tell you why, or give an excuse why she wanted you to do this?" I asked.

Gene nodded, then: "She said her lover complained of her breasts being so small."

"Oh. So her lover was in the habit of seeing her breasts? Yes?"

"Yes, madam."

"And did this woman's lover know that you were sucking her titties?"

"Yes, madam, he did. In fact he encouraged it," came the ready answer. "She gave me to understand that their wedding would be delayed until such time as her breasts were fully developed."

"And you believed this silly story?" I asked.

"At first I did."

"And afterward—weren't you glad she taught you such a delightful pastime?" I asked.

She nodded her head again.

"Now about the other hair," I said. "Isn't it true that you liked doing that, too?"

"I'm afraid I did—though I didn't at first."

"And what was the reason for wanting that hair done?" I asked, still holding her close to me.

"She said her lover liked it best when her—her thing was completely bare."

"Her thing?" I said, smiling.

"Her pussy," came the ready answer.

"And didn't you like her pussy—afterward?" I asked. Gene nodded, though she blushed this time.

"Was it as pretty as mine?" I asked, nodding toward my own.

"Oh, no!" came the startled answer. "It seemed far bigger, and the hair about it was of a dirty black—not at all like yours!"

"Thanks," I said, patting her bottom caressingly, "that is quite a compliment, indeed!" A daring plan came into my mind. There was no longer any doubt as to what Gene had been taught by this other woman, so why, I thought, shouldn't I profit by the other's trouble?

I said: "That's a strange coincidence, Gene. It happens that my lover also likes the hair on my pussy well out of the way when he kisses it. Does that shock you so very much?"

Shaking her head slowly, she said: "Why should it shock me? All men—at least I have been given to understand that all men—like to kiss their mistresses—that way."

"Don't you know?" I asked, increasing the movement of my fingers on the girl's bottom.

"I have never had a lover," came the ready answer.

"You mean," I said, somewhat startled, "that you have never allowed a man to diddle you?"

Gene shook her head. "Never," came the quiet answer.

"Do you mean to tell me," I said, becoming interested now, "that during all the time you were being called upon to assist your former mistress, her lover didn't try it upon you?"

"Oh, yes, indeed," came the quick answer. "He offered me fifty marks if I would allow him to do it to me just once, but in some way my mistress discovered it and they had a terrible scene, and she threatened to have nothing further to do with him."

"But," I insisted, "you were willing, were you not?"

She smiled and nodded, then: "My mistress seemed to get a lot of pleasure out of it, and"—

"How do you know that?" I interrupted.

"Well," she went on, "I hope you won't misunderstand, but—well, I heard her groaning one night and thinking he was hurting her, I went into a closet adjoining her room, only to find that he wasn't hurting her—"

"And what were they doing?" I asked, slipping one hand beneath her short dress and patting a smooth thigh.

"He was doing it to her. They were on her bed, and —and they were all undressed and he was on top of her."

"And?" I encouraged, warming to the subject.

"Well, after that I used to watch them every night. Oh, Madam!" she went on, seemingly startled at her own confession, "please do not hold it against me, but, well, I just couldn't help watching them!"

"I know you couldn't," I answered, patting the warm

flesh of her bottom, "and I know just how you felt, too. I once watched two lovers, and oh! the most dreadful sensations swept over me, so I know just what happened to you then, too!"

"What?" came the ready question.

"You wanted a taste of his lovely rammer, too, didn't you?"

She blushed and nodded.

"I'm glad you admit it, dear," I said. "Every girl wants a man to slip his cock into her pussy, and you and I are no different than the others; the only difference being that I allow mine to fuck me, and you have yet to have it. But don't worry, dear, you won't have to peep at Paul and I; there is no door on my room, and just to prove that there are no secrets here, I am going to have you serve us breakfast in bed, just as soon as Paul, my lover, returns. Will that shock you very much, dear?"

She shook her head. "I'd love it!" she said, eagerly.

Gene didn't know it, but her ready answer gave me another thought! It was weird, I'll admit, but my lascivious nature drove me on and on to greater heights! If Gene was so eager to see a man and woman in each other's arms, and in a compromising position on her bed, then I would not only make it possible for her to witness a real love-battle, but I will solicit her assistance as well! I would have her in our bed with us!

Wild with desire now as a result of my wild thoughts, and wishing to bring her under my own powers, I said: "Now that we understand each other, dear, tell me the truth: Didn't your toying with your mistress's pussy give her considerable pleasure? And didn't she cause you to continue until she 'came'?"

Gene blushed deeply, but she nodded her head.

"And isn't it true that you liked to make her go-off—that way?"

Again she nodded.

"And if I were to tell you that I felt dreadfully naughty and wanted to go-off, wouldn't you consent to assist me, too?"

Once more she nodded, this time quite eagerly, I thought.

"And if I allow you to do it for me, will you promise never to tell?"

She nodded again, and I went on: "Then hurry to your room, dear, and take off all your clothes—then hurry here!"

I thought this suggestion startled her the least bit, but she did my bidding, returning a few moments later as naked as the moon! I too was naked, and I'll never forget the expression which passed over her face as her eyes swept my nude form! And you may rest assured, my friend, that I too feasted my eyes on her unusual nudity! She was positively beautiful, but what drew my attention most was the tiny patch of golden-blond hair above her cute little cunt! Throwing myself down upon the divan so that my bottom was at the edge, my left foot touching the floor, I waited, my right arm drawn up close to my bottom!

She seemed to know what was needed then, for she quickly knelt between my thighs where, in awed wonder, she stared at my wide-open slit! "Isn't it pretty, Gene?" I asked, giving a slight upward thrust of my loins, a motion she could hardly mistake.

She settled down, that she might better gaze at it. "Isn't it beautiful!" she whispered, and then, as though unable longer to resist it, she leaned close, pressing her lips to it in a long, clinging kiss!

And that, my friend, was the beginning of a most delightful courtship between little Gene and myself. Is it necessary to tell you that I, too, tasted the delights of her blond thatch? Is it? Well, you are quite right in assuming it.

That night I had Gene into my bed, and here we abandoned ourselves like only two tribades can. She was marvelous! That day and that night we indulged our passions to the full, and I'll never forget how she thrilled at the thought of her waiting upon Paul and I, and how she blushed when I threatened to tell him of the delightful things we had done together. There was nothing the child wouldn't do, I believe.

When Paul returned and I told him what a wonderful maid he had brought me, he too was glad. "Perhaps," he said, hugging me close to his chest, "you will find her even a better maid than you first thought."

"Is that why you suggested this particular one?" I asked, returning his kisses and showing in every way that I liked the idea.

"Well," he said, "it's quite the fad to have a 'talented' maid these days. Besides, there might be times when I can't be with you."

The morning following his arrival home I suggested that Gene serve us our breakfast in bed. Paul favored the idea, and I was somewhat surprised to note the girl's willingness to assist us, even slipping out of her clothes and feeding us. Nor did we make any effort to hide our nakedness. Indeed, I thought Paul took an unholy delight in showing her his erect cock, its erectness due, undoubtedly, to the lovely child's blond nudity.

All that day Paul and I wore but dressing-gowns, insisting upon Gene remaining in complete nakedness; a little task, by the way, to which she took to kindly if not readily.

"You old darling," I said that night as we lay upon the bed and I toyed with his erect cock. "I believe you even have designs on my little Gene!"

"I'll admit it, dear. And why shouldn't I, too, have her?" he asked. "You've had her a score of times," he continued.

Somehow a strange idea that I wanted Paul to have her came over me.

"Would you really like to have her?" I asked kissing him.

"If I thought I wouldn't lose you," he said, kissing me.

"Of course I wouldn't be angry. Nor would you lose me," I said. "Only yesterday the little imp told me she was wild to be fucked, so you might as well do it here in bed as anywhere; it will be but a matter of days before the little imp will entice you to her arms!"

In answer to my call, the little beauty came into my room; she looked charming in her little nightgown, but at my suggestion she let it drop, springing into my arms, perfectly nude!

What a night that proved to be, my friend! She squealed and cried when Paul thrust his big cock into her, but we were both unmerciful, and long before he went-off into her belly she had become reconciled to it and returned his caresses with a will!

Nothing was hidden; everything was done just as though there had been no third person. Nor did that end it; Paul proved to be worthy of two women, and Gene came in for her share of pleasure.

During the week that followed, Paul and I went into our work with a will, and long before the opening date of our performance we were able to put on a complete dress rehearsal, very much to the satisfaction of our manager.

Then came a change in my life. At last I was a recognized primadonna! A diva! My ambitions had been realized!

That night, after the initial performance, or opening as it were, I was tendered a party backstage. We knew, of course, that this was the custom at that time, but Paul and I had arranged a little party all our own; we wanted to be alone; we wanted to celebrate the success of my first venture. And I might add here, my friend, that my success had been assured. That night I was showered with the most costly presents I had ever received. Everyone seemed to be trying to outdo everybody else. A great table had been laid there on the stage, and this dinner was attended by the most famous persons in Frankfurt. And just to give you an idea of the type of party it was, let me say here that they insisted upon my appearing in the costume of our closing scene.

But there is considerable difference between wearing scanty dress in some certain scene in a play and wearing the same clothes at a social gathering, but evidently I hadn't known my Frankfurt. That I did not, was brought very much to my attention that night. Among our guests was a couple I must mention here. The genleman was easily thirty-five, and his mistress—I was to learn that she was his mistress—about twenty. The gentleman was wealthy and a collector of rare books. It so happened that these two were responsible for the delightfully elaborate dinner tendered me, to say nothing of many of the more costly presents, among which was a book, at that time most rare.

I knew nothing whatever of these two delightful people; it must be remembered that I had been in Frankfurt but for a short time, and most of if not all of that time had been taken up by rehearsals and the almost constant attention shown me by Paul. However, I found them most congenial, and at parting that evening, Paul and I were invited to spend the week-end with them.

I wasn't so sure I wanted this; I would have most preferred to be alone with my lover, but Paul, who was far better acquainted than I, thought it best that we pay them a visit. This we did.

Upon arrival at our host's home, however, we discovered they had other guests, but they were a jolly crowd, and long before the last couple left we discovered that most, if not all, of them were members of a Love-cult of some sort or other that had been making history in those parts.

Later, as I was preparing to retire, I was visited in our suite by our hostess. She was wearing a long velvet dressing-gown, and I noted her utter disregard in showing her naked legs. She said:

"My dear, did you read the book Herman gave you?"

"Yes, I did, and a most unusual document it was, too."

The book, by the way, was "Opus Sadicum," which, as you undoubtedly know, is a treatise on cruelty; the author, one DeSade, being an advocate of whipping, and various other degrees of punishment. I recalled at the time I had scanned the book that I wondered how anyone could possibly get any pleasure inflicting punishment on another. One chapter in the book, however, held my attention more than any other. This was the chapter describing a character named Roland who, not satisfied with stripping and whipping girls in the most brutal manner, must satisfy himself by having connection with them in the "rear passage" or bottomhole.

Thinking this a good chance to clear up the matter, I said:

"There is one chapter in your book which is not at all clear."

"Yes?" she answered, settling herself in a more comfortable position.

"Yes. It concerns one Roland who preferred to have his women in a manner not prescribed by nature—"

"There are many such modes," she interrupted, a strange look in her eye. "Just which one do you refer to?"

"I refer to the one where this Roland prefers his women by the rear route, if I may refer to it that way. What I don't understand is, how can a man get satisfaction by penetrating a girl in that strange manner?"

"That is quite simple," she said. "It is an art practiced since the days of the Caesars, and is practiced to this day. Indeed, I might add that it is much more in vogue these days than during the Christian period. Don't tell me you have never tried it."

I laughed. I knew very little about this splendid-looking woman and was hardly ready to confess everything to her. "I'm sorry, my dear, but I must confess that I have not."

"Then by all means do so at once. You will find it a most thrilling experience." Rising, she came and stood close by my side, then: "You gave your lover your maidenhead—why not give him the rear one?"

We stood looking into each other's eyes for a long moment; she, undoubtedly, trying to fathom me; certainly I was trying to ascertain hers. She broke the silence.

"My real reason for stopping in to see you, dear, is to see if you wouldn't care for a little diversion—something to raise your pulse; a little whipping, for instance?"

"You mean—?" I asked.

She shrugged her shoulders, then: "I have a very unruly maid; it serves to arouse my lover's passion to no
great extent," and noting the look in my eye, continued: "Come along, my dear; I'm sure you'll enjoy it."

I might add that at the moment I was wearing but
the briefest of undervests, and seeing delay, she said:
"Don't bother dressing, dear; you couldn't possibly have
on less than I," and by the way of proving her statement, she opened her gown proving to me that it was
her only garment.

Imagine, then, me walking into the well-lighted living-room all dressed up in a tiny undergarment of the
thinnest possible gauze.

All of this may have little or no interest to you, my
friend, it is written for the sole purpose of showing the
real character of my lover; how he fostered this visit;
how he was a friend of long standing with these people
and had been in the habit of visiting them and taking
part in the weird entertainments there. The whole
thing, briefly, was to initiate me in their Free Love
cult, and I, ever seeking thrills, calmly walked into a
nest of the worst sadists in all of Europe. Nor was that
all. After a buxom lass had been led naked into the
room and frightfully lashed, all four of us stripped stark
naked and I found myself paired off with this other
woman's lover. Not satisfied with this, he insisted upon
spending the remainder of the night with me and here,
for the first time, I tasted what was supposed to be the
joy of being diddled "the back way."

Needless to say, my friend, that I became a frequent
visitor at our new friends' home, and here, thanks to
theirs and to their friends, I found my education ad-
vancing with leaps and bounds.

But I won't linger longer over my stay in Frankfurt.
Enough to say our stay covered two years, and as we

were to close in a few weeks, I had the good fortune
to receive a visit from a producer of operas who was
about to open in Pest, and was eager to get my signa-
ture to a contract. Then, as though fate had laid in
wait for me, Paul also received a splendid offer, which
was to take him on a long tour.

There wasn't the slightest doubt but what I would
have taken this offer, but there were a number of reasons which hurried my signing.

First, I was about to lose Paul. Second, I had already
been touched by another beside Paul (nor were these
two the only ones). And third, was for the reason that a
splendid-looking young fellow accompanied my new
producer and with whom I found myself falling desperately in love. His name was "Arpid" and that night
as Paul and I lay clasped in each other's arms, I fancied it was Arpid who held me.

Indeed, I even called out the name Arpid when at
the height of my passion, so great was my desire for this
young man. But Paul was nice about it. He told me to
go and enjoy myself; that I was free, and though he
would never forget me, I was free to take another lover.

I mention here that I never saw Paul again.

Chapter V

I have often wondered at the strangeness of my own nature. For two years I live with a stranger, the same man who had the pleasure of taking my maidenhead and initiating me into the mysteries of sex, and yet at the expiration of those two years I hadn't the slightest regrets at leaving Paul.

Some people will say that a woman cannot have two loves and have the second as passionate as the first. That, my friend, is not true. And my case, too, was different than most women. There wasn't a spot on my body, from the tips of toes to the end of the longest hair on my head, that hadn't at some time during our two years been inundated by his prolific spend, nor was there a single method known to man that Paul hadn't tried upon my body.

You may dispute that, but I can safely say that that is true.

And what is stranger still, perhaps, is the fact that I wanted it that way. Paul's moods were strange, as were mine. I have known him to literally tear the most costly garments from me and ravish me in the most unheard-of manner; I have had him in my dressing-room, just before I was about to enter upon the stage. I believe this lent strength to my voice, for standing there, feeling his prolific sperm trickle down my thighs from the overdose he had so recently given me, made me thrill in my work.

I have had him in a railway carriage; in a carriage; I recall how once we were riding through the park, and how I made him fuck me almost under the very eyes of the driver who sat on a seat directly above us—Oh, I could tell you of a hundred crazy things we have done, and yet, the day I left Paul I had not the slightest regrets.

With Gene it was the same thing; a kiss and a well-filled purse was all that passed between us as I left her, though tears showed on her lashes. I was told later that Paul took her with him, but of this I know nothing, nor did I care; my mind was on but one thing, and that was my darling Arpid!

The trip from Frankfurt to Pest I thought would never end. Fifty hours on a train alone and burning with desire for a man I knew little or nothing about!

I arrived in Pest about the middle of the afternoon, as I recall it, and never shall I forget the welcome that awaited me. It seemed the entire populace had turned out to greet me. Many of these people were strangers to me, and many I already knew. Among others, of course, was my manager and Arpid.

As soon as it was possible, I shook off the others, and entering their carriage, was driven off. My manager had arranged for me to occupy an entire suite in the city's best hotel, and we were driven directly there. A hurried tour of the place convinced me that my ideas had been carried out to the letter. My suite consisted of twelve rooms and bath. This bath was the nearest approach to the Roman idea it were possible to produce. The plunge itself was entirely surrounded by mirrors;

even the floor was one vast mirror, as was the bottom of the plunge. In one of the larger rooms I had had erected a miniature stage, even to the curtain and drapes.

The rest of the apartment consisted of three or four bedrooms, lounging and dressing rooms. My inspection over, I suggested dinner, and here again fate seemed to guide my future.

My manager, delightful old soul that he was, found it impossible to remain, even for the time necessary to dine with me; I made out as though I was dreadfully disappointed, but I wasn't; in my heart I was overjoyed at the prospect of being alone with Arpid!

If I had thought him handsome when I first laid eyes upon him, he was a thousand times more so now, and when I found that I was to have him all to myself, my joy knew no bounds—for weeks and weeks I had thought of nothing else but Arpid, and now that I had him I was more determined than ever to possess his handsome body.

I might add here that Arpid was far better looking than Paul—at least I thought so—was far younger and of a better family. Indeed, his every action showed "culture."

In spite of the fact that he was Hungarian, he spoke German fluently.

He had spent all his life in schools and colleges. Indeed, he had but finished his final educational period, and at the time of my meeting him he was touring Europe, and had stopped off to visit his uncle, my manager.

Dinner was an event long to be remembered. Besides the wonderful food, we consumed large quantities of wine, and though I flirted outrageously with this handsome boy, it was plain that I had a novice to contend with. During the entire dinner my bell was kept ringing by friends and acquaintances who demanded to be received, but to all I turned a deaf ear, pleading a severe headache and making appointments for the future.

Mad with a lust that was rapidly consuming me, I began my attack on Arpid. Begging to be excused for a moment, I dashed to my room.

Here I stripped off my clothing and donned a tiny, transparent under-vest and a pair of the briefest possible drawers, both garments of the finest dawn. Over this I wore a transparent dressing-gown, its only fastening being a tiny ribbon about my middle. Thrusting my bare feet into low bedroom slippers, I hurried back to Arpid! I saw him give a start as I swept back into the room, my gown flowing behind me, showing both my thighs naked to the very tops, my breasts strutting bare about the top of the under-vest!

During the half-hour that followed I was anything but selfish with the exposure of my charms! I was getting desperate! Taking advantage of the moment when I happened to be out of line of vision, I deliberately drew out the tie-cord of my gown, allowing it to flow open about me! Catching sight of myself in a mirror, I thrilled at the sight, for I may as well have been stark naked, so revealing were the tiny under-garments! My gown, almost falling from my shoulders, had at least the effect I desired; his cock, almost as large as that of a young stallion, lay along his thigh beneath his trouser-leg, and the thought of possessing it, having it driven into my burning cunt, was fast driving me wild! But still he made no effort to take me.

For more than an hour I had been seeking a means to make him stay all night with me, and then, as though in answer to my prayers, a most violent thunderstorm broke through the heavens.

Here was a chance I couldn't possibly let slip by! Since Arpid was too timid to declare his love for me, then I must declare mine to him!

"Oh, Arpid," I cried, springing into his arms and hugging against him, "I am so afraid! The storm frightens me! Please promise me you won't leave me alone tonight!"

"But, but—!" he went on, evidently frightened half out of his wits at the thought of having to stay a night in a lady's apartment.

"Please, Arpid, my darling," I went on, cuddling against him like an affectionate kitten, "I know what you're going to say! You're wondering what my friends will say when they find I have had a man in my rooms for a whole night! But I don't care! I'm frightened! I can't let you go! See!" I said, pointing to an open door. "That shall be your room, dear! It's right next to mine, so that if I get too frightened, I might call you! Please, dear!"

How I did it I do not know, but I got his promise to stay the night in my apartment! Mad with a desire to bring this to a conclusion, I pushed him into the room set aside for him!

Hurrying into my own room, I quickly slipped off the frail garments I had been wearing, and waiting for him to climb into bed! Knowing that it was quite the custom for Hungarians to sleep without night clothing, and feeling certain that he, even here in my apartment, would do so, I put out my light and waited!

I heard the bed springs creak beneath his weight! There came a more violent crash of thunder! I darted into his room! With a single sweep of my hand I threw the cover from him and naked I threw myself into his arms, being careful that I landed astride his hips!

"Oh, Arpid!" I cried, "Hold me tight! I'm so afraid!" and slipping my arms about his neck I nestled close, thrilling anew as I felt his darling cock pressing against my naked bottom!

The man who couldn't be tempted after this, wasn't human!

And Arpid was no exception. In an instant his arms were about me! Our mouths met and clung! Aroused himself, he rolled me over upon my back and getting between my thighs! One of his hands came down, that he might steer his mighty cock to my slit!

"Oh, Arpid," I cried, "What are you doing to me?" at the same time putting down my own hands, not to force it away, but to assist in steering it to my hungry, burning cunt which, a moment later, literally sucked it in to his great balls!

Arpid might have feared me in the outer rooms, but here in bed he proved himself my master. In my short career as a fuckstress I had never met a man like that. Three times in all he shot his scalding sperm into me without even withdrawing between times, and even then I didn't let him rest! Wild with an unsatiated desire, I bent over him, toyed with and played with his half-limber cock! Then, with a little cry of happiness on my lips, I stuck it into my mouth and sucked it back to erection! It was the longest cock I had ever seen until that time, but its length chased me not! Rising from my charming position, I got astride his hips where— with a single downward motion—I impaled myself! With long strokes, I slid my cunt up and down its towering length—.

And so, my very first night in Pest was spent in the arms of a man I had come to love at first sight. Nothing was spared. Like myself, Arpid was made to love, and I had not the slightest trouble in teaching him the various modes of pleasure, and at the very first touch of his lips and tongue to my cunny, he all but ate me alive!

He became my slave, eager to satisfy my slightest whim or desire.

A little later I shall tell you of how, in the presence of my guests, he abandoned himself to me.

It was noon before we attempted to rise from bed, and only then when Arpid promised to come and spend the night with me again.

After he had departed, I gave my attention to the many cards and letters I had received; these had been left by my earlier callers who promised to return when it was more convenient for me to receive them. All day long I received these guests. My rooms were banked with the choicest of cut flowers, and that night Arpid and I sprinkled our bed with the petals of the choicest of them, and upon these the delightful boy ravished me throughout the hours of the night.

The following day I threw open my door to my friends, both new and old. These proved to be the "elite" of Pest. Men and their wives rubbed shoulders with kept-women and their lovers. Young and old they trouped through my rooms, leaving tokens of endearment; some in the form of trinkets, others of great worth.

Three hundred women, in all, passed through my rooms that day, and when I say they were the "elite" of Pest, I mean just exactly that, for not only were they wonderful by birth, they were beautiful as well.

Among them were two sisters. Their names were Anna and Nina W—.

Scarcely twenty years old and as beautiful as the most costly Dresden dolls. I remember how they seemed to hang back until the last of my guests had departed, and how, upon being presented to them, one of them handed me a letter. Upon reading it I found it had been written by a very dear friend of mine in Frankfurt, and that it was a letter of introduction to the sisters.

I recall the many things my former friend had told me regarding the thrilling exploits she had had during her stay in Pest, and since the letter stated, in no uncertain terms, that Anna and Nina might prove worthy of a better acquaintance, I asked them to stay and have dinner with me. This they readily agreed to, and as most of my guests had already departed, and my door had been closed to any late stragglers, I soon found myself closeted with my two new friends.

Strangely enough I felt like I was meeting old friends in these two girls; I also knew by the letter of introduction that I need have no fears that these weren't quite my equal.

While dinner was being laid, I said: "This letter of introduction makes me feel as though I am but renewing old acquaintances; your friend has often told me of the delightful times she had had during her stay in Pest, but I didn't at that time, of course, know that the girls she spoke of were you two."

"I hope," said Nina, smiling and gazing at me from beneath partly lowered lips, "she did not tell you all the things we did."

"I'm afraid she did," I answered. "There were no secrets between your friend and myself. She told me, also, that you girls disliked the idea of wearing clothing—is that correct?"

Anna said: "That's quite true. And since Grace has written us about the same thing regarding your delightful self, why not drop pretending?"

Nina nodded her approval of this, and I said: "Then

why not make ourselves comfortable? You are staying to dinner with me, and I would delight in having you both for the entire evening. Besides, I have any number of chick dressing-gowns we might don."

Smilingly, we three entered one of my dressing-rooms, emerging a few moments later clad in but hip-length gowns, the handsome sisters making not the slightest pretense of fastening them about their naked bodies. I saw their eyes sweep over me from head to foot, for like them, I allowed mine to fall away from my shoulders.

Dinner was announced. Our maid, well trained, paid little or no attention to our outlandish dress—or undress—and during the repast we consumed considerable wine. Later, having finished dinner, and while we were lying about in another room, I said: "My friend hardly did you girls justice, when she referred to your unusual beauty."

"Indeed," answered Anna, rising and coming to my couch and seating herself beside me, "You are not so bad to look upon yourself."

I'm not going into the details of all the things we did before the return of my lover Arpid. Enough to say, that we became very well acquainted before another hour passed, and I found them everything I had heard of them.

Becoming more calm, after the first outburst of passion, I said: "Your friend, in Frankfort, told me something of the good times you used to indulge in here. Tell me more about it—tell me something about yourselves."

Between them I learned that they were of wealthy parents; that they lived in a mammoth house, and that they were allowed to go about as they pleased. Parties in this home of theirs seemed to have been something of an event, so I said: "What about those wonderful parties you had there? Tell me about them?"

The girls exchanged glances, then, Nina, shrugging her shapely shoulders, said: "Why shouldn't we tell her —she'll be wanting to attend one, so she will know what to expect."

"Bad as all that?" I asked, settling myself in a more comfortable position.

"Worse," answered Anna. "Want to hear about it, and what to expect?"

Nodding my approval, she went on: "Well, to begin with, what goes on is common knowledge to everyone else. In the first place, we meet at our home twice a week. Here new members are discussed and voted upon."

"Voted upon?" I repeated.

"Exactly," Nina went on, telling the story. "Every now and then some member of our club as we call it, has a new member she or he wishes to introduce. At the Monday night meeting we discuss this person, and a committee is appointed to look into the past history of that individual. This checked, we vote to either take in, or reject that person's name. If accepted, and it's convenient for everyone concerned, we hold the initiation that Saturday night."

"Something about that word 'initiation' does not sound so good," I said, laughing, though undaunted. "What's the idea of the initiation?"

"To assure strict secrecy," she went on. "If one is called upon to do a so-called 'dreadful' thing, and has to do it in the presence of a mixed group, that one isn't going to tell on someone else about something he or she has seen or knows."

"Sounds interesting," I said. "Tell me more about it."

"First, the candidate is stripped stark naked. If it's a girl, she is led, blindfolded, into a room where the men are assembled. These men, naked of course, are assembled about the room, while she, still blindfolded, must point her finger to one of the men. She must go on her knees before this man and suck him off, and she's never to know who the man is, except that he's one of our crowd. If it's a man, he is subjected to the same performance, the only difference being that he is taken before the girls who, like the men, are nude, and here he must suck-off some designated girl. If everything goes as expected, then we unmask the girl, or man as the case may be, and then we abandon ourselves to the pleasures of an out-and out orgy. How does it sound, my dear?"

"It's alright," I said, "but there is one thing that isn't quite clear: Why must the girl, or man, be blindfolded? Why not allow the candidate to choose his, or her, partner?"

"That," said Nina, "is where the spice of the thing comes in. The candidate never knows who he or she had that first time. If it was not for that the candidate would be sure to pick someone whom they particularly liked above someone else."

Does this seem strange to you, my friend? If it does, let me tell you that in every part of Europe people of the so-called 'better class' were forever forming some sort of lovecult or other, so there was nothing remarkably strange about the entire affair, as far as I can see. After all, who are we—you and I—to judge others?

This, however, was the state of affairs in Pest at that time. I could go on for hours telling you of the strange affairs that I know were taking place every night in the week. But that is not my idea; I am not writing a history of other persons' affairs; this, as I told you in the beginning, was a history of the more exciting things in my own life, so I shall stick to that, digressing only when it is necessary to bring out some particular point in my story.

Anna and Nina were more than willing to spend the night with me, but I begged off. There were many other nights, I said, and I had to reserve a place for my latest lover, Arpid.

"So," Nina said, "you already have a lover? You work fast, my dear. I was hoping to assist you in the choice of one."

Knowing Arpid was due any moment, I did not bother to dress, but lay on a broad couch just as we had finished our party. Lying there I began going over in my mind the description of Nina's and Anna's party, and the more I thought of it the more interested I became.

Arpid came in, and seeing me lying there in complete nakedness, must have excited him considerably, and you may rest assured that I came in for considerable loving; and you may rest assured that Arpid had hardly gotten used to his new playmate as yet, and was slightly put out when I asked him to lie with me there on the couch; the darling boy was for getting his face between my legs, a little trick I would have gladly welcomed had the two girls not taken about all I had to offer for the moment.

We spent a delightful night, however, and though the girls had done considerable toward abating the hunger I usually had for it, I managed to give Arpid a few wonderfully long-drawn-out fucks and sent him to sleep by taking his wonderful cock into my mouth and sucking a splendid spend from it.

Never having heard of anything like that, Arpid was wild with delight at the thought of putting the end of his cock between my lips and going-off there; but he was dreadfully bashful; he confessed that I had been the first woman he had ever had. I then conceived the idea of teaching him something of the life.

The following afternoon Nina and Anna called on me, and I went into the subject at once. There being no secrets between us, I told them my plans. I told them of all the delightful tricks I had taught him, how I had taken his "cherry" and how I wished to initiate him into being more brazen in his methods. I had a reason for this; I really loved Arpid, and I wanted him to share the pleasures I had arranged for myself. The girls were delighted with the prospect of teaching Arpid, and at my suggestion both stripped stark naked, hid themselves, and then we three waited for his return.

Soon we heard him coming. He found me, as before, lying completely naked, and once again he wanted to start in. "Please, dear," I said, kissing him, "hurry and undress!" Never will I forget the sight when he re-entered the room, his great cock sticking almost straight up along his belly. Again he wanted to mount me, but I held him off.

"Get astride my chest, dear," I said, "I want to have your lovely plaything where I can kiss it!" His eyes shooting fire, he did as I directed. I had propped myself up against the pillows in such a manner that I was in a splendid position to take his noble charger, and after toying with it for a few moments, I signified my desire to take it. Smiling, his bone-hard tool leaping in my hands, he leaned forward. I knew the girls were watching, and I was determined to put on a good show. First I licked it all over! Then, fearing it might explode, I quickly took it between my lips, and Arpid, having learned his lesson, pressed nearer, sending it far into my mouth!

But the battle was short-lived; my warm mouth was too much for the novice, and just as the first gush of his cream came from it, I gave the signal and the two nude beauties rushed upon us!

Arpid was wild, but between us we got him quieted and he became quite reconciled to his fate. Indeed, he flirted so outrageously with the two girls that we finally agreed to let him have both of them. It isn't very often that I have shared a lover with another woman, but we couldn't very well do otherwise, since it was my ambition to awaken him to the point where he would agree to joining the secret "club" the girls maintained in their home, and long before the evening passed, Arpid was willing to agree to almost anything.

And I might add that Arpid got all the sucking he needed that day, for with the three passionate women operating on him, he was of little use to me that night.

Three weeks later our new show opened, and I might add that the show was a huge success from the very start. Invitations were pressed upon me from so many different sources, I found it impossible to begin to take care of them. They came from the first families in Pest.

Ministers, businessmen, bankers—and all these I turned over to the two girls, Nina and Anna, for it was upon them I depended to choose the most worthy of my attention.

That's a strange way of putting it, isn't it? I use the word "worthy" and I mean just that. My two friends, knowing everyone in Pest, chose only those they thought I cared to see. If this one seemed a prude, her or his name was discarded. If this or that couple had children, their names were discarded.

"Here," Nina said, holding up a letter, "is a person you should cultivate."

"Yes?" I answered, taking the letter. "Who is she?"

For a long moment Nina looked at me, then, "Have you ever been whipped, my dear? For love, I mean?"

"I have," I answered, "Why?"

"Then by all means go and see her; but if you have a tender skin then stay away."

"Sounds interesting," I offered, "Tell me more about her."

Then followed the strangest story I had yet heard. This woman, it seemed, was a Russian. In her early twenties, very beautiful and greatly sought after not only by the wealthy men but members of the nobility as well, she was an enigma; a paradox if there was one.

She had caused more men's hearts to flutter than any one person in all Pest, by her daring dress, or undress; she invited the handsomest men to her villa, only to have them thrown out bodily; she had a positive fetish for appearing in public in the most bizarre dress; she had had herself driven through the streets, reclining in her carriage wearing but the thinnest possible night-dress; she received her guests in plastic; never wore a thread of dress within her home, and had once entered a celebrated hotel and walked the full length of the dining-room stark naked. I listened to all this from the lips of the two girls, and wondered.

"Her lover?" I asked, thinking that at last I had found a woman who could be true to one man.

"She has none," came the startling answer.

"A girl-lover, perhaps?" I offered.

"If she has one it has never been found out," answered Anna.

"What, then, does she do for her entertainment?" I asked, interested.

"Now we're right back where we started from," offered Nina. "The delightful creature depends on her whip to furnish her pleasure."

I was becoming more and more interested in this

wonder-woman, and made no secret of my desire in meeting her. "You know her?" I asked.

"I've had the pleasure," answered Anna, "and I do not care for her very much. Nor does Nina."

"Why?" I asked. "I can't imagine you disliking a pretty girl," looking at her in a decidedly naughty manner.

"Who's a better judge of that than you?"

"Naughty! But tell me more about this woman," I said. "Perhaps I shall call upon her; I have her invitation, you know."

"There's very little to tell," offered Nina. "That is, there's precious little anyone knows about her except that she maintains a dozen maids, and that she goes in for active flaggelation. Aside from that there's little known about her."

"You intrigue me," I said. "Please let me see her letter."

Scanning the letter, I noted the date she would expect me; it was for the following day, and I was expected to dine with her, and that I would have ample time before the performance that night.

"This is very unusual," I said. "Here I am being invited to this woman's home to take dinner with her, and I have never had the pleasure of meeting her. I supposed one paid a visit to me before I was expected to return the call,—"

"But that's where you're wrong," suggested Anna. "It is done differently here. Besides, she has already been here; she was among your guests at 'at home' day."

"Indeed. It's strange I do not recall her. However, since that is the case, I believe I shall call, as she suggests."

In truth, I was all excited to meet this strange woman,

but I was hardly prepared for what I was to witness the following afternoon.

The following day, at precisely two o'clock—the time set—I was driven to her door, and was ushered in by one of the most beautiful girls I had ever seen. This was shock number one. Shock number two came at the same moment; this latter was caused by the most unusual dress I had ever seen a supposed domestic wear. It consisted of a little purple jacket, tight fitting about her waist, and a skirt, if the thing could be called a skirt, for it was but a stiff ruffle about her waist and flared out straight from her, leaving her stark naked from her waist to the tops of her purple stockings. On her feet she wore heavy shoes, commonly worn by Russian peasants.

I noted, as I followed this girl through the hall, that her bottom and thighs were marked with long, red weals, and I wondered if it were possible that this beautiful girl had recently been the unhappy victim of her mistress's wrath?

A moment later I was shown into a luxuriously furnished room where I was immediately joined by this Russian woman, whose name proved to be Rosenloff. Her full appellation was "Countess Marie Rossenloff."

Something of a name, don't you think, my dear?

But it wasn't the name, however, that bothered me; it was the most fantastic dress that went to make up her costume. I use the words "dress" and "costume." The "costume" consisted of a crown into which she wore a dozen ostrich feathers, and that was her costume; she was otherwise stark naked!

If ever in my young life I wanted to laugh outright at anyone, it was this strange woman. But after looking her over, however, I became more or less used to it, for she was very beautiful; her body was well formed and unusually fair, and it was evident that she had taken good care of herself.

"You do not object to my dress?" she asked, seating herself in the direct rays of the sun. When I assured her I did not in the least object, she said: "I thought you wouldn't; I have been given to understand that you, too, like to be about in the altogether."

"That is quite true," I said, "but I'm afraid I do not limit myself to the indoors." I wondered if the Countess got the significance of this. Evidently she did, for she said: "We are the pioneers, my dear. Sooner or later everyone will discover the be. efits derived, and will be going about stark naked."

My visit to this woman's home had been brought about by curiosity alone. A woman who has no male lover, yet will walk into a hotel in a state of complete nakedness, must have some direct reason for doing so. I put her down as a conservative; and I mean by that, one who chooses her lovers, and these lovers were a select few among the girls and young men. In brief, I put her down as an out-and-out tribade; a lover of her own sex. Wishing to draw her out, so to speak, and perhaps learn for certain just what she might be, I took the bull by the horns. And I might add here, my friend, that I found it something of a delight and joy in gazing upon her nude charms.

Here I was, practically a total stranger to her, yet she greets me in complete nudity! Knowing, as you do, that I have a weakness for well-formed girls in the nude, I might be forgiven for gazing with a certain amount of longing upon this splendid young woman.

Her hair was corn-yellow, there was the unmistakable slant to her eyes, her nose was rather small, and her mouth, though well formed, was unmistakably Russian. Like women of her race, she was big boned, though not too much so; her breasts were full and well formed, and, I thought, unusually erect, while the nipples were pointed and stiff and quite cherry in color. Her waist was small, her hips full and well formed, her bottom-cheeks were beautifully rounded and plump, and her thighs were things of beauty! Round as apples and as smooth as ivory, they tapered down to graceful, dimpled knees. Her calves were tapering, her ankles were small and her feet were unusualy well-formed. But that wasn't all I found myself fascinated with; what took my interest most was the fact that there wasn't a trace of hair about or above her full-lipped cunt which she seemed bent on my seeing in all its glory.

Thinking to get at the bottom of all this mystery, I said: "I can quite understand your desire for being about in complete nakedness.

"You are very beautiful." I smiled as I said this.

"You, too, are very beautiful," she said.

"My face is—at least so I have been told."

"Ah, but your body, too, my dear."

"Indeed. I didn't know that you had seen me in the altogether."

"Yes," she said, touching a button a stand. "I happened to have been in Frankfurt, and there I had the pleasure of seeing you in your opera, and you were marvelous as Juliette—particularly in the balcony scene."

"Indeed. I seemed to have been a precedent in the art of appearing in almost complete nakedness, in the opera."

"Enough," she said, "to convince me that you are beautiful. There is one thing, however, that I don't understand: Why have you never removed your pubic hair?"

"That's strange," I said, smiling. "I was just wondering the same of yours. I have so much, and you have none; I'll admit, however, that it makes your cunt more beautiful." I thought this would surely open up the conversation a little, but she merely said: "That is very complimentary, but I did not remove them for beauty's sake; it was purely for sanitary reasons. Not only am I without the useless hair, but my maids are compelled to remove theirs also."

Wishing to be a little more daring, I said: "I once suggested having mine removed, but my lover, at that time, said it would be a shame to remove it; he said the hair just shaded it enough to make my puss beautiful." Allowing this to sink in for a moment, I added: "And what does your lover say about yours? He likes 'bare facts' I presume?"

Before the Countess had a chance to answer this, however, a maid, in answer to my host's summons, entered, and here again I was the least bit shocked, for the maid, another very beautiful and shapely girl of eighteen, entered, her only covering being unusually high-heeled slippers and the tiniest apron I had ever seen, and while I was busily engaged in summing up the girl's fine points, the Countess said: "Why did you keep me waiting, Molly?" and without waiting for an answer, continued: "Hold yourself in readiness for my call; then come and bring the whip; I shall lash you between your legs. In the meantime, bring a bottle of my choicest wine and two glasses."

I had been watching the maid during this, and I couldn't help but note the expression on her face as she listened to her mistress' scolding: The color mounted to her cheeks, she bit her lower lip, a brightness came into her large eyes, and I was sure the faintest trace of a smile crossed her pretty face. Then she bent her knee, and turned and walked from the room, my eyes followed her, and I could easily understand what Nina meant when she said the Countess's maids were the prettiest in Europe; her bottom-cheeks were beautiful, and I should know for the girl, in the rear, was stark naked.

I was on the point of asking questions regarding this girl, when the Countess interrupted. "You were asking about a lover, were you not?" and when I nodded, she went on: "I have none; in fact I have never had one, if you were referring to a man lover."

"How, then, do you get your pleasure—if that's a fair question?"

I watched her now; I wanted to note the reaction to this.

She shrugged her shapely shoulders. "Sounds funny to you, no doubt, but I have no desire for a man; I am quite content with my maids; besides, they understand me."

I saw I would have to change my tactics; I hadn't, so far, gained the slightest bit of information; I would have to do something unusual to gain the facts I wanted. I said: "I surely cherish your wine; it is dreadfully warm," and I fanned myself with my handkerchief.

"Oh, my dear," she said, "I'm sorry. I quite forgot myself; I was so comfortable I quite forgot my guests. You will stay for dinner, won't you?"

"I haven't made any other arrangements," I said, "and will be delighted to stay; I rather like your arrangements here." This had the desired results, for she promptly said: "Then why not make yourself comfortable by slipping off your clothes? You are not bashful?"

"Hardly," I answered, smiling. "Too many persons have seen me naked, to be anything like modest."

Then: "You forget, my dear, I have a lover."

The Countess remained in her position on the lounging-chair as I started to undress. "I shall have one of my maids to assist you," she said, touching the convenient button again.

I laughed. "I'm almost afraid to trust myself with such a pretty girl," I said, giving a slight little wiggle with my hips, and before she could find an answer to this, the maid appeared. This one, however, was one I hadn't seen as yet.

"Assist Madam——with her slippers and stockings," said the Countess. Up to that point I had removed but my upper garments, and I was surprised to see how quickly this pretty girl went at the task assigned her. Quickly kneeling, she slipped both hands beneath my dress and up along my leg to my knee. Remembering, then, that she had failed to remove the slipper, she quickly removed this, and once again her hands slid up along my leg. Watching the Countess, I made it appear as though I was having difficulty with my skirts, and was delighted to note that instead of watching her maid, she was watching the uncovering of my upper charms.

Glancing down, I happened to catch the maid's eye, and I noted the deep color in her cheeks; she was deliberately taking her time about removing the garters, and catching the hint, I said: "Be careful not to stretch the elastic, my dear," then again turning my attention to the Countess, I said: "Are you in the habit of whipping your maids simply because they happen to be delayed in answering your summons?" and then I felt the unmistakable sensation of soft fingers stealing up my thigh, far, far too high to get at the garter!

"That's why I asked you to call today," the Countess said, moving with that languor common to one under the influence of another's presence under certain circumstances. "This is punishment day."

"Indeed," I said, making believe I was surprised at

this choice bit of information. "Then I am in luck. I have never witnessed anything like that."

Hidden beneath my skirts, as they were, the maid's hands were taking advantage of the golden opportunity, for while one hand toyed with the elastic of the second garter, the other slid along and quite came to rest among the curls that lay hidden there. Holding my waist momentarily between the Countess and me, I looked down only to find the naughty maid staring up into my eyes, and if ever a signal passed between two persons, one passed between us; and I am sure the pretty girl read my thoughts.

Naturally, I wondered at this. Why, I wondered, would this girl deliberately flirt this way with me? Was I to learn something further about the inner-doings of this mysterious house?

The stockings having been removed by this time, I pushed the skirts and drawers down over my hips, letting them fall about my bare feet. There was an unmistakable flush on the Countess's cheeks; one I hadn't noted before, and she seemed to be centering her attention on my hairy crack. Very well, I thought. If you enjoy looking at it, my dear, I shall have the pleasure of feeding it to your clever mouth before I leave here today!

But I was never more mistaken in my life, my friend, as you shall see. That the Countess was eager to get at the punishment business was manifest a moment later when she said: "If you are really interested in what is about to happen, my dear, come along to my punishment-room," and she raised languidly and motioned toward a curtained doorway. Grabbing up the bottle and glasses, I said: "I will enjoy it far more if I am fortified with this," waving the bottle on high, and following her to the doorway.

Turning to the maid again, she said: "Have Yvonne come to me in ten minutes—I shall punish her first."

Here was a most unusual event in my young life. I had already done many strange things; I was no stranger to the ways of the flesh with both men and women, but this was the first time I had ever stripped stark naked and followed an equally naked one into a darkened room for the purpose of watching her give vent to her pet maid in the form of a severe whipping to another, but because I had promised to discover all the mysteries possible within this house I would go through with it regardless of what happened.

What was my surprise, then, to find myself in a cute little bower-like place, the only article of furniture—besides a large bearskin rug on the floor—being a broad, low couch and upon which she threw herself in a position which quite conveyed to me her intention.

"Why do you whip these pretty girls?" I said, dropping down beside her and slipping one arm about her nude waist, and carelessly dropping the other hand upon her smooth, warm thigh.

She had removed the silly headdress and was partly lying and partly sitting, her thighs quite well apart. Looking into my eyes, she said: "A few moments ago you asked me a question—regarding a lover, and I told you I had none." While saying this she deliberately raised her leg and placed it across both mine, and once again I could hardly mistake her meaning. However, I did not take advantage of this apparent offer to go further, but contented myself with patting and toying with the warm flesh of her well-turned thigh. Nodding my answer, she went on: "That was quite true; I have no use for men. Nor is it possible for me to enjoy the embraces of a woman until I have first been aroused by watching another suffer under the lash."

Again I nodded. "I can partly understand that," I said.

"There are, however, exceptions to that rule. Seeing your beautiful body, and knowing something of your past, it would require but precious little attention to arouse me fully. You know what I mean, do you not?" giving a dreadfully naughty look and moving her belly in little rotating motions.

I understood fully enough, but I did not propose to be caught in any of her traps. I said: "Doesn't it arouse you to have so many pretty, nude girls about the place?"

"At times. They are very skillful, and delight in pleasing me, but one tires of one after awhile. Your presence, however, has aroused me to no little extent," and gazing at me from beneath her long lashes, she added: "You do not misunderstand me, do you darling?" at the same time moving her belly again.

I laughed. "How could one be mistaken—in you?" I said, sliding my hand up along her thigh and bringing my fingers to rest upon the soft lips of her cunny.

"I thought you would understand. Now if you will but go down upon your knees and dissolve me, I shall be able to furnish you with a very pretty little show."

There was not the slightest doubting her meaning now, and though I found her very desirable I had not the slightest intention of allowing myself to become a victim of her wiles. It also occurred to me that she was the least bit brazen about it; you know, one does not go about it in such a manner, and her actions conveyed the impression that I was being led into some sort of a trap from which I might find difficulty in extracting myself. So, sparring for time, as it were, I said: "I'm sorry, dear, but you seemed to have forgotten about me. You see I, too have to be aroused; so why not wait until after you have punished one of the girls—I will feel more like it, too."

"But you don't understand," she said. "You see, it's this way: If I were to go about it without first being relieved—you know what I mean, dear—I would be sure to soften and fail in my duty. The whipping, I mean, would be a failure; it wouldn't bring about the desired results."

I was thinking fast now. Here I was in this strange woman's home, naked, in the most compromising position and being literally invited to "go down" on her without the slightest indication of her reciprocating. How, I wondered, was I going to get out of this fix?

True, I wasn't the slightest bit afraid of her; I was too well known in the ctiy of Pest to think for a moment that anyone would dare lay a hand on me. It was that I did not want to be caught in any traps; blackmail was far too prevalent at that time for me not to know the pitfalls one can so easily walk into. No, indeed! If I were to do this woman's bidding, then she must return the favors bestowed upon her.

I have always tried to live a Christian life (that may seem strange coming from me, but it's true) though I had long since given up the idea that prayers could be of any possible assistance to me, but that afternoon an unspoken prayer was answered. I had been taxing my brain for a way out of the present difficulty, when the curtains parted, admitting a girl. It was the same beautiful creature who had removed my stockings, and like myself, she was in complete nakedness.

"Yvonne is ready, Madam," she said in a low voice.

"You have prepared the whip?" asked the Countess, relieving me of her leg and coming to a sitting position.

The girl nodded. "Everything is ready, Madam," came the lowered voice.

"Very well," came the dismissal. Turning to me, the Countess said: "You would like to be in the room where I inflict the punishment, or would you rather remain here and watch through the curtains? I am sure the latter would be the best; Yvonne would be sure to respond with far greater freedom if she thought she didn't have an audience."

I was thinking fast. "I believe I would much rather remain here—if the punishment-room is in close proximity to this."

"The next room," indicating the heavy curtains at the far side, at the same time rising and walking toward them in what I thought an abrupt manner. Turning just before passing between the drapes, she said: "I shall have the couch drawn close to the curtains, that you might recline while watching."

Then, as though they had been waiting for that very signal, two girls entered the room and without a word moved the couch, with me still upon it, close to the curtains. One of these girls was the one who had announced Yvonne's readiness, and you may rest assured signals again passed between us, signals that I was to find had been readily understood!

Leaning forward and carefully parting the curtains, I gazed into the next room. It was a strange place, if ever I saw one. All about the place were strange pieces of furniture, if one may call all sorts of devices such as these, furniture. There were pulleys, strange looking benches and chairs, and all equipped with straps.

There was an affair not unlike one sees in workshops; what is known as a "horse" on which mechanics saw boards, though instead of the flat top, it was almost knife-sharp. I was to learn afterward that this unusual piece of furniture was known as the "Berkley Horse," a very wicked and cruel affair, to say the least. However, the thing had little or nothing to do with what I was about to witness, so I shall refrain from describing it further.

The Countess, when I gazed through the curtains, was pulling on a glove. This, I was to learn later, was for the purpose of protecting her palm against the ravages of the whip-handle, a wooden affair commonly used in northern Russia.

This, adjusted to her satisfaction, she picked up the long-lashed "knout" and flicked it wickedly through the air. A shudder passed through me! "Could it be possible," I thought, "that she will use this wicked instrument on a girl!"

My speculations were cut short, however, by the appearance of the girl Yvonne, the girl who had served us with wine.

And here I was to witness what I believe was the strangest affair I had ever heard of. And then, as though the devil himself was to pilot me through the strange affair I was to witness, the girl, the one who had announced Yvonne's readiness, and had removed my slippers and stockings, glided noiselessly into the room.

When first I saw her she was wearing the apology for an apron, but now she was stark naked.

"You shouldn't have come here," I said in a low tone, pulling her down beside me. "Your mistress might not understand; she might take it upon herself to punish you, too."

The girl smiled and cuddled her smooth warm body close and whispered into my ear; "There is no danger of that, since it isn't my day to be punished." I thought her rather composed.

"Not your day?" I asked, surprised at this strange remark.

She shook her head, then: "We have certain days to be whipped; mine comes again next week."

"Then you have already been whipped for some offense?"

She smiled faintly. "There was no offense," she whispered.

"When, then, does she whip you girls?" I asked, pressing amorously against her. "Your body should be reserved for kisses."

She pointed toward the curtain, then: "If you will but watch you shall see why."

Again I applied my eye to the crack between the curtains.

The Countess was sitting on a divan, her right leg across the left one. The girl, whose name I learned was Violet, was standing in the center of the room. Suddenly the Countess rose and came directly in front of the girl; she was swishing the lash through the air.

"You were dreadful today! Why did you keep my guest and myself waiting! Were you trying to intimidate me!"

"No, madam," came the faint answer.

"Is that all you can say, 'No, madam'!" and without waiting for the other's answer, went on: "Then there is another matter. Why did you enter Pauline's room last night, when you know I have forbidden you girls entertaining each other!"

The girl dropped her face. "I'm very sorry, Madam. It shall not happen again."

"That is no excuse, and for your forgetfulness I shall give you an unusually severe whipping! Now kiss my feet!"

Without a word the girl dropped to her knees and clasping both the other's feet in her hands rained kisses all over them, raising them one at a time and quite caressing both the instep and pinkish sole.

This done, the Countess said: "Now kiss the whip."

Obediently, the girl did this, clasping it in both hands and kissing the lashes and wood-handle.

Obviously, the Countess seemed to have forgotten all about me, her guest, for after making the girl stand and submit to having her hands fastened to two straps and these drawn up far above her head, she said: "You are very pretty, Yvonne, and it's a shame to stripe your lovely body, but it shall be! I am dreadfully hot today, so I am afraid I shall strike hard! But don't worry, my dear, you shall have your reward—afterward!"

The lash fell across the tender flesh, making the girl lunge forward!

Drawing the nude girl closer, I whispered: "Why does she whip that girl? She has done nothing to warrant such a beating!"

The girl, snuggling close in my embrace, nibbled with her pearly teeth at the lobe of my ear, then she whispered: "I wish it were me she was whipping! I love it so!"

"You love to be whipped!" I asked, hardly believing my own ears.

"Yes! It's the only way in which we are allowed to enjoy!"

"Tell me," I whispered, "Doesn't your mistress ever allow you girls to relieve each other's suffering—in bed, I mean?"

"We are allowed only the pleasure from the whip—she whips us until we have enjoyed!"

"Then?" I asked, caressing the flesh of her belly and thighs.

"Then we have to caress her—with our lips and

tongue, until she enjoys!" The girl seemed greatly moved now; there was little doubting the sincerity of her statements.

I took another look between the curtains before putting my next question. The girl was still struggling beneath the lash; her back and thighs showed red marks, and I knew that there must be an end to this strange affair before many moments else she would kill the girl. I said: "Do you enjoy doing that to her?"

"I love it!" came the ready answer.

"Would you like to do it to me—now!" I asked.

Instead of answering the girl slid quietly to the floor and between my knees! I couldn't be mistaken now! I raised my foot, put it upon the divan and instantly her hands came to my crotch! Carefully she smoothed the hairs back, and holding the slit quite open, applied her half-open mouth to it! Wild with desire for it, I strained her face close! Her tongue came across the clitoris! Toyed with it for a moment, then, like a javelin, it darted into the depths like only one trained in the art can do!

Now I turned my attention to the occupants of the next room.

Strangely enough, I no longer thought the Countess cruel. Indeed, my friend, I thought it quite fitting that she should whip the girl!

It's strange, isn't it, how quick one can change from a tender, mild person to a cruel, wanton one. That was me. For the first time in my life I gloried in the suffering of another! I thought the Countess quite beautiful in her radiant nakedness! I thought, too, the other beautiful!

I never gave it a thought at the time, but it was a bit of sexual psychology worthy of a deeper consideration than was mine. Perhaps it was due to an inborn cruelty;

it might have been caused by my unnatural and over-wrought lascivious nature, and again it might have been brought about by the feel of that trained, sensitive mouth gnawing at my sex, and the fluttering tongue that explored the very depths of my aching cunt, but whatever it was that caused it I found myself wholely taken with the picture before me.

What I had first thought cruel was now beautiful! That the whole affair was nothing short of a ritual never entered my mind until a moment or two later! The girl, her fists clinched, every muscle of her splendid body drawn taught, was staring at the ceiling! Her legs were well apart! Her loins were moving in spasmodic little jerks! Now they rotated! The cheeks of her well-formed bottom opened and closed!

Then, when it occurred to both that the proper mo-ment had arrived, the girl cried "Now! Now! Oh! My God—I'm coming!" and at the same instant the Count-ess directed the blows upward between the well-parted legs, bringing the tips of the lashes well into the ex-posed cunny of the other in a series of well-timed blows!

Nor was that the end of the performance. At the same instant that the girl went-off, Madam, the Count-ess, stiffened, grasped her breasts and squeezed them, and uttering a low moan, she too went-off! It was too much for my torn nerves! I felt the crisis arriving! Clutching the other's head between my hands and pressing it tight, I allowed the floodgate to open, be-dewing the javelin-like tongue with what I supposed was the most abundant spend I had ever let down, the shock of which almost caused me to faint!

Indeed, it was some moments before I was able to again direct my attention to those in the other room, and here I found the picture changed. The girl had been released and was kneeling before the Countess who sat—or partly lay—on the divan, her thighs well parted, one of which hung over the other's neck while Yvonne toyed with and kissed the wide open, glistening box of her mistress!

More calm now, I drew the girl up beside me. "Tell me," I said, "Does the Countess do the same as she is having done?"

"No," she said, shaking her head, "She never does! And she would kill me if she were to know that I had done it to you! She even refuses us the pleasure among ourselves!"

"Have no fear that she will ever find out," I said, kissing her gently. "But I want to know more about this woman," I continued, "I want to know why she never is active in her pleasures. Can't you arrange to visit me very soon? She allows you to go out, does she not?"

"Yes," answered the other, "but she watches us every step we take! I'm afraid!"

Again I looked through the curtains. The picture was the same, except that the Countess was now reclining, quite as though she had forgotten she had an audience. Motioning the other ahead of me, for I had seen quite enough, I followed to where I had left my clothes.

"Tell me," I said, for we could talk more freely here, "Why don't you leave this dreadful place? What is there to keep you here?"

There was a wild look in her eyes. "I don't know," she answered, glancing with her ever-widening eyes toward the second set of curtains, "I don't know!"

"Has this woman something which she holds over your head? Something she might use against you, that would hold you here against your will?"

"Oh, yes! No! Oh—I don't know! I don't know! I'm frightened!"

Hers was the strangest actions I had ever seen in my life. That the girl was either insane or lived in dreadful fear there was no doubt. But how, I thought, was I to get to the bottom of the secret? How was I to find out the mystery of this den? What was the hidden secret here?

I gave it up. "Bring me the bottle from the other room," I said.

A moment later, with this in my hand, I drank deeply. I wondered why I didn't dress and flee this strange house. But I didn't. Why I didn't I do not know, though no great damage resulted by staying.

"Well," said a voice off to one side, "how did you enjoy the little performance I staged for you? You are an actress, so you should be able to judge."

I found it was the Countess, still naked, and just— I thought—as pretty as ever. "It was splendid," I said, trying my best to smile, and making, I guess, a rotten job of it. "I enjoyed it as I have never enjoyed anything in my life." Trying to be flippant, I added: "Won't you have a drink? Personally, I always insist upon wine—after an attack like the one you just enjoyed."

The Countess threw herself down upon another divan. "I am disappointed," she said, "I didn't in the least enjoy it."

"Indeed!" I said, lifting my brows, "You seemed to, if I am any judge. What was the cause of your disappointment?"

"It was your fault," came the startling answer.

"My fault?"

"Yes," she said. "I had planned on having you as my victim. A pretty woman always excites me."

"I am sorry," I said, "but I could never stand it to be punished like that. However, I am dreadfully sorry."

"Oh, I didn't mean about the whipping," she offered, quite brazenly I thought.

"No?" I said, toying with the half-emptied glass.

"No. I was looking forward to having you suck me."

The brazenness of the woman startled me. I said: "What prompted you, my dear, to think that I would do anything like that?"

She partly raised from the divan, looked at me with wide eyes, then: "Can it be possible that I have been misinformed?"

I smiled. "I have no idea of what you have been informed of, but of this I am sure: I am no garbage bucket for anyone—even a Countess, so-called!"

She stared at me for long moments, then: "I'm sorry, my dear; I did not understand. I hope you will forgive me."

An instant after I had rebuked her, I had been sorry, but the words slipped from me. I softened, however, and said: "It is quite alright, my dear. I didn't mean to slander you, and I am sorry."

I began drawing on my stockings. "You are going?" she said. "I had hoped you would stay for dinner. I shall be dreadfully disappointed if you do not stay."

I gazed at her; I knew I had her bested. "Are you in the habit of allowing your guests to suffer while you enjoy yourself? I, too, am but human, you know." I continued dressing.

She raised and came to my side. "What did you mean by that?"

"I mean," I said, "that watching two pretty women, as I have had the pleasure of watching you and your Yvonne, if that is her name, has greatly aroused me, so I shall have to return to my own apartment for a like relief. You offer what appears to be delightfully tasty, but I, too, have something to offer, though you have seen fit to ignore it. Tell me," I went on, giving her a splendid opportunity to get her fill at my secret charm, "Is mine so repulsive as to cause you to decline it? Especially after having expected me to take yours? Am I correct in that?"

For a long moment she stared at me, then: "Am I given to understand that you would partake providing I would return the compliment?"

"You will have to draw your own conclusions about that part of it," I said. "What your presumptions are matters little to me. The fact remains, however, that I, as I have already said, am human. I am dreadfully sorry, but I must have relief; watching your delightful game has aroused me dreadfully; nothing short of a cock measuring two hundred and fifty meters would come anywhere near satisfying me."

The Countess seemed greatly put-out that I would not stay. But I was persistent. Turning at the door, I said: "You must come to see me. And inasmuch as you delight in having a pretty girl, I shall take great pleasure in furnishing one or two for you."

So you see, my friend, I did not gain much by this visit. True, I had had the pleasure of having a very talented girl perform for me, but I had set the Countess as my game, and like her, I was disappointed.

Anna and Nina, who were almost daily visitors at my apartment, I found waiting for me; they had been waiting to hear the results of my visit.

"The huntress goes forth to conquer and returns empty-handed!" cried Nina, springing up to embrace me, smiling the while.

"Not entirely," I said, passing into my room that I might get out of my clothes. "I'll admit my trip wasn't entirely a success, but it wasn't without a certain amount of success; the Countess has some very pretty maids," looking at her from the corner of my eye.

"But I'll bet a pretty penny you didn't capture the Countess," she insisted. "If you did, you are the first that ever did."

"Nina, dear," I said as I settled myself about to enjoy a rest before going to the theater, "there is something about that house that is next to terrifying, and I would give much to penetrate its secret." Both girls listened in rapt attention as I related everything that had transpired in the Countess's home. I described with minute detail everything as I remembered it. I told how she had almost openly solicited me; how I had had the pleasure of beating her in her scheme (if she had schemed) by allowing the maid to cool my raging passion, and I told them of the brief conversation between the girl and myself.

When I ended my recital, Anna said: "Alright, my dear. You wanted to take the matter into your own hands, and you have failed. "Now we'll tell you the truth of the matter. No, don't look so startled; you would never have been satisfied until you made that call, and now that you have satisfied yourself—and got nowhere—we'll tell you what we know about her."

"Tell me this first," I said. "Why do those girls remain there for the sole purpose of being whipped? What power does she hold over them, and why are they deprived of the pleasure afforded most young women who crave the flesh?"

"One question at a time, dearie," suggested Nina. "Let us take them in the order asked. To begin with, this woman, as you undoubtedly know, is a Russian. She is, or thinks she is, of a class who delight in lording it all over those beneath her. She was reared, undoubtedly, in an atmosphere of mock splendor; lived and breathed wealth—though she might have been deprived of it herself—and power. Inborn, imbued, as she undoubtedly was, with the thoughts of wealth and power, she could think of nothing else. Then came the moment when she could grasp wealth; how no one knows; it's enough to know that she has it and that's all that matters.

"So far so good. The second phase is this: The girls do not remain with her through their own initiative; they are held there quite against their will. Why? Listen carefully and I shall tell you. Our friend, the Countess, has a brother. Like her, he is a low beast—I have met him and know, as has my pretty sister. At the moment he is chief jailer at a prison in Budapest. He rules like a Czar; the people of Budapest look upon him as something akin to the unnatural, and that is exactly what he is; an unnatural beast.

"Now, then: The beautiful girls our friend the Countess maintains in her spacious home are provided by this wealthy brother. He knows all about his sister and keeps her provided with pretty and talented young women. These girls have been arrested at some time or other on trumped-up charges and held there against their will. With his unholy power this is easily done. Believe it or not, that prison is the worst den of iniquity in all Europe. Men of great wealth—and women, too—frequent the place for this sole purpose of holding orgies of the most awful sort. During these orgies, and that's all they are, the most fiendish and brutal practices are inflicted upon the inmates. Men and women—mostly women, though—are stripped stark naked, fastened to, or on, strange instruments of torture and here they are brutalized to the point where it is not at all uncommon for the victims to die. The more beautiful of these are shipped to the delightful sister (the Countess) and are held there under pain of death. Now: As far as the girls liking the idea of administering to the sensual desires of the Countess—to say nothing of liking the lash—is because they are instructed by the noble brother. They are deprived of the pleasure derived from men; it is true that they are not allowed to frequent each other's rooms, realizing that if they disobey a single laid down rule for them they will be returned to Budapest to finish their days in prison.

"We know for a fact that that has already happened. Now for the final reason of this strange incarnation in that strange house: Those girls would put up with anything the Countess suggests rather than be returned to prison. As far as their appearing to like being whipped, they do not; it's simply that they know they must do it, and so they concentrate their thoughts of lascivious things and actually bring themselves to the spending point for the sole purpose of entertaining their mistress. Does that explain it, my dear?"

"Partly," I answered. It was, without doubt, the strangest story I had ever heard. "Tell me this," I continued. "Why does she have the girls wear such strange undress? Why is her home decorated with the most obscene pictures all devoted to whipping, and why, above everything else, does she wear such an asinine headdress and go about otherwise naked?"

Nina laughed. "For one young woman you have a happy faculty of asking questions. Answering the first question the answer is this: "If the girls were allowed clothing they might try to escape; naked they wouldn't get far. Her home is decorated with whipping pictures for the simple reason that there is little else on her mind; the strange headdress you refer to is a direct symbol of her insanity."

"You mean," I ventured, "that the woman is insane?" I began to realize how silly I had been in laying myself open to an attack from her.

"Crazy, yes," answered Nina, "but crazy on one thing; otherwise she is quite sane."

"Why didn't you tell me this?" I asked.

"Why try telling you anything—you would have gone anyway."

I saw the truth of this and did not press her further.

"There is one thing, however, that isn't at all plain," I said. "How can one get pleasure—sexual pleasure—in watching another suffer?"

Both girls looked at me for a moment before Anna said: "Think back for a moment, my dear. Weren't you highly excited at witnessing the show?"

I wondered at that. I wasn't at all sure whether it was the sight of their nakedness or the whipping. "I don't know," I said in answer to the direct question. "I am somewhat in doubt about it."

"Enough to want to put it to the test?" asked Nina, gazing at me from beneath her lowered lids.

"What do you mean by that?" I asked, mystified as to her meaning.

"I mean," she said, "do you care enough about it to want to put it to the test? If you do, it can be arranged."

"How?"

"By making up a little party and visiting the prison in question; I know the very person who would be delighted at the chance of going with us; say a party of four?"

Something snapped within my brain! The thought intrigued me!

"Why not?" I thought. If there is a chance to visit this den and discover if I, too, have an inborn desire (unknown to myself) to witness another's suffering, then why not take advantage of it!

"How can it be arranged?" I asked, trying to be tranquil.

"Easily," answered Anna. "We can arrange it for one week from this Saturday. If you will recall the Monday following next Sunday, your theater is closed; it is a Saint's day. We could leave right after Saturday night's performance and have plenty of time to enter into the spirit of the thing; then you could return either late Sunday night or early Monday. In any event, it would give you plenty of opportunity to rest for your Tuesday night show."

The thing seemed cut out for me. I gave it considerable thought in those few moments, then: "Are you sure there will be no danger in this wild scheme?"

"None whatever. We have both been there and suffered little or no damage to our delicate persons."

"And this other person; a woman, I presume? Who is she?"

"Her name is Bernice——; she is in her early twenties; she is one of the most beautiful and prominent women in Pest, and maintains one of, if not the best-known, whorehouses in all of Europe."

"Great God!" I cried, "Is there anyone you don't know! But never mind—go ahead with your plans; I'm crazy to see the place!"

Well, my friend, I suppose by this time you have quite given me up as about the worst person in the world, and I don't see how I can blame you either.

But if I have pictured myself to you as a wanton, it was but to prepare you for my further adventures; adventures which quite outshone any I have yet related.

With me it has been to seek something new and startling; something to stir the blood; that would rise the temperature; something to thrill one from head to toe—and I got it in Budapest.

As you undoubtedly know, it isn't such a long run between the two cities, and we made it that night, arriving at the prison in the early hours of dawn. Nina and Anna having made all the arrangements, we were royally received. An excellent breakfast, a few hours rest, and we were ready for the busiest day and night I have ever spent.

The prison itself wasn't much; just one of the many of its type found in the older cities throughout Europe, and this one was no exception to the rule. Low, grimy, filth everywhere, it was a sight for Satan himself, and I guess he presides over it with consummate, if not extravagant infinity.

It was enough to cause one to turn away, but the gaiety of my friends with their expectations of something unusual in the manner of orgy, led me on. And I'm not sorry, in a way, that I remained. True, the things which I saw, nay, even took part in, the experience I gained as to the inner workings of the human mind, to say nothing of the delightful creature I found there and who was to become my maid, all compensated me, I believe.

The fourth member of our party, the one chosen by Anna and Nina to make the quartet, was a very beautiful and talented young woman by the name of Bernice——, a young lady of Spanish extraction, and known, like most famous women at that time, as "Madam Bernice."

During the journey I had had a chance to study this woman, and the longer I was in her company the more I liked her. Raven-black hair, a dark, olive complexion, beautiful features, well-formed and firm breasts, a small waist, full-rounded hips, thighs as round as the most perfect spheres, tapering calves and ankles, small, well-turned feet with unusually high arches—a mark of distinction in itself. Added to that she was unusually intelligent and liberal to a fault. I found myself delighting in her drollery and wit.

Daring, too, she was. Like my friend, the Russian Countess, she had an almost unholy delight in appearing in public in the scantiest of dress. Strange still, she was welcomed into the most wealthy and famed homes in both Pest and Budapest; wealthy dames thought it something of an honor to be seen in her company, and many of them—thousands, if you please—frequented her spacious home and indulged in their passion to the limit.

I shall tell you much more of this a little later on.

I found that she had, on several occasions, visited the famous prison and was on excellent terms with the Russian warden. Indeed, I found that some of her prettiest girls were brought from this dreadful place, as were several young and handsome men, and of this I shall have more to say a little later.

Our reception into the warden's office was an event I shall long remember; he (the warden) was the nearest approach to a pig in human form I have ever seen outside a circus; most Russians look more or less like hogs, but this was the great grand-daddy of them all! The man weighed close to three hundred—I was to feel his great weight before I left the den-like place. Like his famous sister, he sported the high cheekbones, the slanting, Mongolian eyes so common among the lower classes of Russians, while his nose was flat and broad and appeared, as I first sighted it, as though a great slice had been taken from its base, leaving the great holes of his nostrils looking like miniature caves.

Not a very pretty picture, one might say.

Moving one's vision further down the broad, flat face, one came to what was supposed to be a mouth, but which resembled a cave, in which one saw a few long, yellow teeth. The chin, or what there was of it, wasn't much and this was covered with a two-or-three day growth of light-yellow beard. His great head of corn-yellow hair was unkempt, and his eyes—unusual in the Russian I thought—were set close together, a feature which has always caused me to fear to trust.

His shoulders were unusually broad, his body was massive, as was his belly and hips. His legs were like pillars, while his feet, encased in monstrous shoes, were things of dread.

Add to this a profound hatred for water and soap, and you have what might prove to be a rather unique picture of the gentleman.

Believe it or not, my friend, the mere sight of this monster in human form sickened me—yet, I was to know him much more intimately within a short time! Startling, isn't it?

Madam Bernice, however, didn't seem to dread him. Rushing upon him in the most unorthodox manner, she sprang into his waiting arms, kissed his frog-like mouth with what appeared to be a frenzy of delight. Hanging about his great shoulders and smiling into his eyes, his great hands moulding and pressing her bottom-cheeks through her thin dress, she cried: "Think of it darling! I leave a thousand of the most handsome and powerful men in Pest, ride most of the night on a stuffy old train just to be with you again! Just for the pleasure of having your wonderfully big cock again! Tell me you love me, Mike!"

"Sure I love you!" he cried, holding her out at arm's length as though she were but a doll. "And you'll get it, too! Get it as you've never got it before! And you,

Anna, my angel!" he cried, dropping Bernice and taking Anna in his great hands and tossing her up in the air amid a flutter of flying skirts. "So little Anna has come back to be properly fucked! Ho! Ho! Well, like Bernice, the little half-black Spanish-nigger, you'll get it too!

"And you, Nina!" grasping the laughing girl in his soiled hands. "The most wonderful little bedfellow in the world! The little one who knows how to cuddle one between her pretty little thighs! Ho! Ho! The hottest little cunt in all creation! Ho! Ho!"

Then, as though I had been invisible until then, his pig-like eyes fell on me. "So!" he cried, pushing the others aside and rushing upon me like a crazed bull. "So this is the new beauty you were telling me about! Ho! Ho! Well, my darling, I'm going to make your trip worthwhile! I'm going to give you a dose of sperm that will still the very action of your heart! I'll drown it! So I will!"

You think that dreadful, my friend? You think this quite the most unusual incident you have ever heard of? Yes? Then listen to this and judge for yourself just what sort of a man I found myself confronted with. Having finished with his description as to what I might expect, he tossed me up and astride his massive shoulders and hurried toward a stone-paved room where a great plank-constructed table was being prepared by a half-dozen girls brought from the women's section of the prison.

Guards, less gigantic than my warden, though no less cruel in both looks and demeanor, followed us, each carrying a kicking, squealing bundle of laughing, shouting femininity, said femininity being Anna, Nina and Bernice! Nina, seemingly gone mad with the spirit of the thing, literally tore the upper part of her bodice away, bared her breasts! "Look!" she screamed, leaning close and rubbing the erect nipples across his eager lips. "Aren't they beauties! Don't you love them! Suck them, you dog!"

Anna, held in the embrace of another guard, a fat little pig of a man, was suffering his kisses, one of his hands, the while, caressing her bottom-cheeks, the other probing into the cloth of her dress! "Fool!" she cried, snatching up her skirt that he might have unhindered use of his probing, searching hand, "That's no way to feel one's lover! Feel how slippery it is! All ready for your lovely cock!"

Bernice, more daring, perhaps, than the rest of us, broke away from her escort's embrace. Jumping upon the table, kicking bottles and glasses out of her way, she was tearing her clothes from her body! Waist, under-vest, skirts and lacy drawers, all went by the board! Na-ked, now, save her slippers and stockings, she broke into a most obscene dance! Danse du ventre!

But I had but a fleeting peek at all this. The warden, whirling like a dancing fool that he was, kept me busy holding onto his shaggy mane that I might not be dashed to pieces on the paved floor!

"Look!" he cried, stopping and holding me aloft with his powerful, ham-like hands. "Look, a blond! A beau-tiful blond! Fair enough to be of my own fair Russia, yet selfish enough to hide her crowning beauty from my gaze! Zounds! Is the woman dead?" tossing me upon the table and clawing at my skirts.

"Strip! Get out of your clothes quickly! It is the only way!"

It was Bernice whispering into my ear! Somehow, though I'll never be able to explain how, I seemed to catch the spirit of the thing!

With clawing fingers I tore at the fastenings of my

dress and underthings! My waist quickly followed the other things! Not satisfied with this, the warden was clawing at my slippers and stockings, pulling them off! I tripped, fell sprawling upon the table, and here the denuding was completed! As naked as a new-born baby I was lifted again in his powerful hands! With one hand beneath the crook of my right knee, the other under the small of my back, I was held aloft while his carnivorous mouth sought out the treasures of my nude body!

Nina and Anna were upon the table now, and a moment later they too were naked and were submitting to the indignities of their partners! Laughing, shouting, kicking their legs this way and that, offering their hairy cracks to probing fingers and tongues, the mad scramble went on! I knew it was useless to resist; I gave myself up to the maddening caresses of the frog-like mouth—.

What an orgy! Bernice, under the very eyes of the awed girls who had fallen back from the table, was being fucked by a guard!

Anna, who had succeeded in freeing her partner's cock from his trousers, was astride his lap and was riding up and down upon his hard cock!

Nina, the more eager to show her eagerness for her partner, was kneeling before the other guard and was sucking his tool, sliding it in and out of her mouth as though it was the last she was ever to get!

Myself? You are wondering about me? What I was doing all this time? Well, I was being sucked-off! The warden, seeing that I had at last given way to his seeking mouth, had laid me upon the table, while he, on his knees before me, was holding my thighs in his great hands and was feasting his great mouth on my most secret charms!

Why not resist? Why not fight them off? One might well ask all these and more questions. But why? Hadn't we gone there for an orgy? And if we refused to enter into the vile performance, would we not be forced against our will? The answer was yes. We would have been forced; so why not submit peacefully?

That is exactly what we did do; we submitted peacefully.

I expected, of course, that the brute would ravish me after the delightful service he had just rendered me, and I wasn't at all sure I didn't want him to, but he didn't; at least not just then.

Instead, he raised to his feet; gazed about him, not unlike one who had just committed a great theft and was afraid he had been caught.

Bernice, in the meantime, had been freed of the weight of her partner, and coming to the warden, clasped her arms about his neck, kissed his still wet mouth, and cried: "You old darling, I've got to have at least a dozen new girls, and you've got to furnish them for me!"

"Of course, of course! Why not! Ho! Ho! Of course I shall! And the price will be a hundred rubles and a fuck each! What say you to that, you half-nigger wench! Ho! Ho! What say you to that?"

I wondered at the strange names he called her, but I was to learn that Bernice was wise to the ways of the Russian warden.

"Of course I'll pay the price, great pig! Why not? Lead me to them, oh, keeper of my cunt, and you shall have your gold! Lead on!"

"What is it now?" I whispered in Bernice's ear while the great warden was mustering his guards.

"We are going for an inspection of the prison, and mind you, say nothing to those who hurl insults at you.

Here, put on your slippers, for we shall climb many stairs and the way is hard!"

"Like this?" I asked, startled the least bit.

"Why not?" she asked, smiling and patting my belly. "Your blond beauty will be a treat to their tired eyes; especially that one between your ravishing legs."

"Fie!" I cried, rubbing amorously against her. "It's not half as pretty as yours."

"You think mine pretty?" she asked, cocking her head to one side.

"Sweet enough to eat!" I quickly answered.

"Be careful, darling," she cooed, rubbing in turn against me, "or I'll take you literally and offer it to you!"

"Is that a promise?" I said, "And can I depend on it?"

"You may—providing I might have yours at the same time!"

The great warden had gone on ahead, and the other two girls were grouping about us, thus cutting off further promises.

"Isn't it grand!?" cried Anna.

"Isn't it just too lovely for words?" cried Nina.

"Wait until you've had a taste of the warden's giant cock!" cried Anna. "He'll be sure to take you in on his bed! You're new to him, and he always falls hard for a new girl! Like it?"

"Wait until I've tried it, and then I'll report," I answered. "Anyway, if it's as nice as I've heard, I think I'll like it!"

"You think you will? I know you will! I've had it half a dozen times and know! That's why he didn't diddle you here on the table; he's waiting until he gets you on his bed; and once he has you there, baby, you'll know the meaning of a good fucking!"

A few moments later we heard the blowing of a whistle, and as this seemed to be the signal for us to come on, we trooped across the flagged floor and into the men's section of the great prison.

Will I ever forget that experience! Think of being a prisoner in that dreadful place and having four stark naked women stop before your cage and flirt outrageously with you! It was the most cruel thing I had ever seen. Men, their eyes sticking almost out of their heads, staring at us as we wandered along the various corridors in front of them. Would you believe it, dear, that there were men who had been incarcerated there for months, many of them for years, without even so much as a peek at a woman? Would you believe it when I tell you that more than one of them openly masturbated themselves right before our eyes? Would you believe it when I say that those three girls stood as close to them as it was safe, and allowed their scalding fluid to splash upon themselves as they ejaculated?

That is as true as the gospel, my friend.

Nor were the girls alone in their taunts. The guards, taking to this mode of torture, lent their lascivious aid by calling attention to our various charms, mine with the others, but being careful not to let any of the caged brutes get their hands upon us.

Finally, having spent at least an hour touring the men's section of the prison, we entered a large room. This proved to be part of the women's section, though they were never allowed to enter this room unless called. The place really sported a rug upon the floor, and there were several easy chairs and two or three couches scattered about the place.

"Line up the women," the warden said to one of the guards, "and march them in here in two's!"

And so, I was to learn, we waited for the parade of

the younger girls. And since this would take several minutes, the guards and the warden made good use of their wait. Anna and Nina wasted little time in getting the two guards on two of the couches, while the great and handsome warden took both Bernice and myself upon his lap.

"Naughty old cunt-lapper!" she chidded him, patting and caressing his cheeks. "I suppose you'll have butcher —with that giant cock of yours! But don't forget our bargain, you old pig! I'm to have a dozen girls—if your old musty jail can furnish that many—and for every one I choose you have got to give me a fuck! Do you understand that, old Frog-face!"

"You think I can't!" cried the warden. "Ho! Ho! You think I can't! No! Very well, half nigger, I'll take you both! I'll ram your guts out! Ho! Ho! I'm as fresh as a new-born baby! I haven't had a woman today! Ho! Ho! You will see! Ho! Ho!"

The girls were led in, and were as quickly led out again.

More were led in; like the others, they were stark naked, and they were led away. "What is it?" cried Bernice, pulling his shaggy hair. "What is this?" Some kind of a new game? Where's the good-looking cunts? Bring on something with a little style! Something my clients will rave over! For a hundred rubles I should have queens, you old pig!"

And through it all the warden laughed in uproarious gaiety. It was all very funny to him. Perhaps he was happy in the thought that he was to ravish me, a new woman to him, a blond like his dear Russians. More girls were led in. These were better, and Bernice beckoned to one; she was to remain; the others were dismissed.

Holding back, her eyes downcast, her hands trying to

hide her charms, she was jerked in front of Bernice, and here she underwent a series of questions. Interested, I listened. Many of the questions were of a decidedly personal nature, but to them all the girl nodded her head; she was willing to do anything, go anywhere, if only she could escape from that den of iniquity. She was chosen as the first inmate of Bernice's house of ill fame.

"You see!" cried the warden, pinching Bernice's nipples. "Ho! Ho! You see! One woman! One woman you choose! Gold! One hundred rubles and a fuck! Ho! Ho!"

Others were led in. They were all shapes and shades. And only the young ones were brought before the prospective buyer. It was a modern slavemarket, where women and girls were chosen for the nude beauty and ability to please men—and women, for Bernice maintained a resort which was patronized by as many women as men.

Finally, after almost a hundred were led in, Bernice managed to get a full dozen; Japanese, Hungarian, Swedes and Italian made up the quota, and only the most beautiful were chosen.

Then I made an announcement. Taking advantage of the warden's anxiety to have me, I said: "My dear, do you suppose it would be possible for me to find a maid? I have none, you know."

"Why not! Ho! Ho! Why not? A hundred rubles apiece! Ho! Ho!"

"But," I said, kissing his cheek and carrying his hand between my legs, "you wouldn't charge me a hundred rubles, would you? Remember, you are to have me a little later."

"Ho! Ho!" he cried, squeezing my breasts. "Ho! Ho!

I have you already! You can't escape me! How can you? Ho! Ho! A hundred rubles and a fuck; that's the price! Take it or leave it!"

I was frightened. I saw the uselessness of trying to bargain with the brute. He must have his gold, and I was getting damn good and tired of his constant "Ho! Ho!"

"Let one of the guards take me through the women's wards," I said. "We can save time that way, and you shall have me all the sooner."

This, strangely enough, seemed to tickle his fancy, and I was allowed to wend my way through the prison. And here, stranger still, I found a girl who instantly took my eye. Calling her to one side I questioned her. She was just fifteen. Very beautiful and shapely, and I wondered why Bernice hadn't seen her. Then, upon further questioning, I discovered that she was being reserved for a future date when she was to be whipped before a company of select women guests who were expected the latter part of the following week.

This I gained from the obliging guard.

When I asked him if I might take the girl to one of the tiny cells to question her further, he said: "And what do I get out of it, if I do?" There was a mean leer in his evil eye. I said: "What do you want?"

He answered: "The warden has you picked for a little party, and he'd kill me if he knew I asked, but the price is a fuck, young lady!"

"Done," I said. "Shall it be now or later?"

"Now," he said, "and a promise from you that you won't tell!"

It is needless to go into the details of it. Be it enough to say that in the very cell in which I was to hold a private interview with the girl, I submitted to the guard's embrace. Nor was I so dreadfully putout over it, either, for the guard proved to be something of a man, performing his duty in rather a pleasing manner.

A few moments later I had the girl in the cell. Her name proved to be Rose, and she stared at my nudity in ever increasing wonder.

"Tell me, Rose," I said, taking her in my arms and kissing her, "how would you like to be taken away from here and become my maid?"

Her eyes filled with tears, and it was some moments before she could answer, then: "Oh, Madam, if you will take me away from this awful place I'll be your slave for life! I'll die for you!"

"You won't have to die for me, little dear. On the other hand, I want you to live for me; I might ask you to do strange things for me, but I'll never whip or abuse you. Do you think you could obey me in everything, Rose?"

"Oh, yes," she cried, her eyes wide. "I'll do anything!"

"Anything?" I repeated, slipping my hand beneath her ragged skirt and patting her smooth flesh.

"Oh, I wouldn't care what you asked me to do. I would do anything! "You are wealthy, and I'm sure that if you ask they will let me go with you!"

She said this with so much meaning I believed I couldn't be mistaken. "Will you do something for me, Rose?" I asked.

Nodding her eager approval, I said: "Will you take off your dress, little dear? I want to see you naked; just as I am!"

Quickly, her eyes wide in wonder, she slipped off her dress, the only garment she wore, and stood naked before me. My eyes swept over her girlish form, and what I saw pleased me. "And if I take you away with me will you give me your solemn promise that you will never refuse me a single request, no matter how naughty it might seem to you?"

There was a strange light in her eyes. "I'll do anything," she answered, her voice low, pregnant with meaning. We sealed the bargain with a kiss, and I returned to the sitting-room, leading Rose, now dressed, by the hand.

"I've made my choice," I said, indicating the girl by my side.

"Ho! Ho!" cried Frog-Face. "Ho! Ho! You can't have Rose! You can't have Rose! Ho! Ho! Rose is being saved for other guests!"

Bernice, quick to note my plight, came to my rescue. "Then the deal is off!" she cried. "The girls I chose you can keep! There are others I can get, you pig! And you'll not get the thousand and more rubles! 'Ho, Ho' over that, you old pig!"

I expected a scene, but there was no scene; old Frog-Face was far too eager for the gold to allow Bernice to get away with her threat.

"Alright! Alright!" he cried. "Ho! Ho! But she'll cost you plenty! A thousand rubles! A thousand rubles is the price! Ho! Ho! A thousand rubles for the pretty Rose!"

"You're a fool!" cried Bernice. "A hundred it is, and that's far more than she's worth, you thieving pig!"

Crestfallen, beaten at his own game, the warden led us back to the prison proper and into the room with the table. Here we found a great spread laid out. We dined and wined. Bernice whispered to me: "Now you'll see the real show, and after that he'll take us both to his bed, so prepare yourself for a buggering you'll never forget!"

"I fooled the old pig," I whispered. "I had to fuck the guard before he would admit me to Rose's cell."

"For God's sake, don't let the old bastard find it out or he'll kill the guard! I know him! He's the worst brute in all Europe!"

Bernice, with all her experience, seemed frightened, while I, strange as it may seem, was looking forward to an engagement with the monster! I wanted his monster cock! I hadn't seen it as yet, but all three girls had boasted of its great size! Then, too, he had promised to take both Bernice and myself to bed with him, and that in itself was enough for me! Just then I would have done anything to be with this black-haired beauty!

Even then, perched as she was on the monster's knees, I couldn't keep my eyes from her thatch! It was thick and entirely surrounded her cunt, and it grew far up on her belly, ending in a little point just below her navel!

But my thoughts were cut short. Two girls were led in; they were naked. They were larger than any Bernice chose, but they were well-formed and sturdy. Briefly, they were quickly tied down and brutally whipped until the blood ran in streams down their bodies and thighs, and they lay in a dead faint.

It was brutal—and through its brutality I found myself liking it! Something within me stirred at sight of the blood! I believed I had never felt so hot in my life! One hand stole down to the front of the warden's pants! Sensing my meaning, he separated his great legs, allowing my fingers full play! A moment later I had his great cock out! I gave a gasp! It was truly a monster! By far the largest I had ever seen! My fingers could not span it, it was so big!

Still, I was overcome with a desire to have it! Forgetting the strange scene being enacted before us, I dropped to my knees before him, kissed the purple head, tried to take it between my lips, but it was far too large! Blind, now to everything else about me, I kissed and tickled with my tongue the orifice; squeezed and stroked the great column; bit the head; ran my mouth up and down its entire length! Screams, cries and shouts were mingled in the bedlam of noises! Soiled hands clutched my head, pressed it with ever increasing pressure against the throbbing head of that wonder-dart, trying, it seemed, to drive it into my mouth! Somewhere—it seemed to be far in the offing—I heard Bernice cry aloud like a banshee!

Pandemonium had broken loose! Other guards rushed upon the scene!

I was forcefully dragged off! Clutching hands tossed me, as though I were a feather, to the stone-paved floor! Naked feet; feet shod with hob-nailed shoes trampled me, ground me to a pulp—or so it seemed!

Through all this maze I saw other women rushing upon us. These were the women from the wards; women too far gone to mingle with those whose cells we had visited! It was as though the very beasts of hell itself had been turned loose upon us! Somewhere in the distance a great gong clanged. It was enough to raise the dead from hell, so great was the crashing beat of its gigantic hammer; but it was dimmed by the inferno of babbling, screaming voices!

I tried to creep away, but I didn't get far. Great, hairy hands clutched me! I was tossed high in the air! A great beast of a man, far more heinous than the warden—if that were possible—was dragging me away! I screamed! More screams! Other hands clutched me; were trying to drag me away from the foul beast that seemed bent on carrying me off to his den—.

I had fainted. When I opened my eyes I was upon a bed, a very dirty bed. Startled, I tried to sit up, but I was forced gently back against the pillows. "Lie still." It was Bernice. With her were Anna and Nina. No longer were they the beauties of yesterday.

"What ever has happened?" I asked, trying again to sit up.

"We seemed to have arrived at the most opportune time," answered Bernice. I thought her unusually calm in the face of what I thought must be the end of the world, if one were to judge by the din somewhere outside the door.

"What is it?" I repeated.

"There has been a mutiny; but it's alright now; the guards are putting it down."

"A mutiny," I cried, fearing the worst. I had heard of such things happening. Nina was gazing through a crack in the door.

"It will be all over in a moment," she said. "They are driving the prisoners back."

"Here. Drink this." It was Anna pressing a bottle to my mouth. The wine tasted good to my parched lips. In a few moments the warden came in, and we learned what had caused the trouble.

It seemed the sight of us walking through the prison before all those men had been too much for them. They had overpowered a guard; took his keys and liberated the others, and then, like the beasts they were, they liberated the women, and the combined gang had rushed upon us. Not a few had been killed; many had been injured, and not a few had managed to make their escape.

"It's alright!" cried the warden, brandishing his great, hairy fists above his head. "They couldn't stand up under these! Ho! Ho! I taught them what it means to cross me! Me! The new Czar of all the Russians! This will be the beginning of the overthrow of a tyrant! A despot! A new Czar shall rule—!"

He ranted on and on. Now it was all clear to me. He, like his egotistical sister, the Countess, was mad! Mad with a lust for power! I didn't know it at the time, but he, the warden, was the forebearer of the teaching of Socialism! A revolutionist! Here, in the very heart of Austria, he dared ot practice his unintelligent, bovine-like doctrine!

But this, my friend, was never supposed to be a treatise on political uprisings; it was to be brief, a history of the strange—the more strange—events of my life. I pictured, in the fewest possible words, the scenes which were later to turn all Europe upside down; I have tried to portray a picture of this beast, this monster who, strangerly enough, I found myself admiring.

Strange, isn't it? Like Bernice, the beautiful and talented girl who rested beside me, who had her choice of the most handsome and talented men of all Europe, I found myself admiring the beast.

To me—as to Bernice—he was handsome; such is the weakness of us, the weaker sex. Always wanting something we shouldn't have; forever clutching into the unknown; grasping for the impossible!

But the warden wasn't impossible—as I was soon to discover.

Bernice, taking advantage of his weakness, managed to get him down beside us upon the filthy bed; and like the child he was, he quickly forgot the terrible battle which even then was going on in a far section of the prison.

Toying fingers worked stealthily at the buttons and fastenings of his torn clothing; nimble fingers freed his great feet and legs of their nether coverings, and soon the great, hairy beast lay naked among us.

"Now, you old pig," cried Bernice, throwing herself

into his arms, "I shall pay part of my debt! You are going to fuck me!"

But the warden would have none of her. He wanted me! I was the new woman; and the dainty warden was forever seeking new women!

He mounted me! I thought I was being split up, so huge was his rammer, but thanks to his sucking-kiss, the wine and my unsatiated passion, I was soon penetrated as I had never been penetrated before!

Would you believe it, my friend, when I say that that man went-off three times into me before he relieved me of his great weight?

Would you think me silly when I saw that as soon as ever he could do so he mounted Anna and rode her to a most satisfying conclusion?

Again: Would you believe it when I say that after that he mounted Nina? Then Bernice, and then me again? Would you believe it when I say we spent the entire day in that room, and that he was the only one to share our persons? Did you, I ask, ever hear of such a man?

No, you never did, nor did anyone else. I lost track of the number of times the man mounted me; I know only that I paid a great price for Rose's freedom. Food was brought before us. Naked, we ate it. Wine was splashed about that den as so much water; we were drenched with it; this and the great amount of sperm that beast was continually pouring into us.

Taking advantage of my temporary freedom, I went to the door and looked out, and I was just in time to prevent a tragedy. One of the guards had dragged Rose into the outer room, and even as I looked on, he was trying to mount her! I screamed. The warden, at that very moment pentetrating the lovely Bernice, stopped his delightful task and rushed toward me. Seeing what was about to take place, he rushed past me and into the outer room where, with one well-directed smash of his great fist, he sent the other reeling arcoss the stone-paved room, to crash, a beaten, bloody mass, against the further wall!

If there was anything on God's green earth I didn't witness that day, then I do not know what in heaven's name it could be—and I was the happiest person on earth when at last we were allowed to depart. My education was—I believed—complete. Arson, rape, sadism, lesbianism, sodomy, nay, I had even witnessed murder! Before my very eyes I had seen men and women killed! Beaten to death!

But I had had an experience; I had learned that I was susceptible to the sound of the lash on naked flesh —but I had Rose! That little darling who was to mean so much to me in the near future.

I insisted that I take Rose with us; the others were to follow with a guard. Bernice, having previously imported women to her house, knew they would arrive; the warden would never pass up a chance to get his filthy hands on considerable more than a thousand rubles.

If you will remember, my friend, I had no servants of my own, so Rose was a very welcome member of my household.

I have always been glad Rose did not witness the frightful orgy which took place in that filthy bedroom; had she, I doubt very much whether she would have become attached to me.

Bernice returned to her home, but Anna and Nina went to my apartment. Here they took a prolonged bath (inside and out) and tumbled into bed for a much-needed rest.

Rose, having already seen me naked in the prison,

acted as my maid, and it wasn't until the two girls had
retired that I decided to bathe, and here I was given an
example of her true worth.

She insisted upon bathing me. From head to toe I
was shampooed and scrubbed. I found her apt in arranging one's hair, and I allowed her to do mine, and at
last I reclined on my bed.

I had assigned a room to her, but what was my surprise to find, upon awakening the following morning, that Rose, instead of going to her bed, had spent
the entire night sitting beside mine. Nor had she
closed her eyes even to nap. Never had I seen such
devotion.

When I questioned her about it, she said: "Have you
forgotten that I promised to be your slave?"

I smiled at this. When I first laid eye on her, there in
the prison, I had conceived a great liking for her; now
I loved her!

I said: "Very well, Rose; if you are to be my slave,
then brew me a cup of strong coffee." Then, think of
my surpirse, to find she had already done this, and that
it was even then warming over the table stove?

Then an unexpected event occurred. I was taken
down with a slight fever; my experience in Budapest
had been the least bit too much for me. Rose doctored
me, as did the two faithful sisters, but I grew steadily
worse. I called in my manager. He was wild, but there
was nothing to be done about it; I was ill, and I must
have a rest.

My doctor, fearing something more complicated than
a mere fever, prescribed a sojourn to Kaiserbad; he said
I needed the health-giving baths for which the place
was famous. Anna and Nina wanted to go with me, but
I declined their offer; I had other ideas; I wanted to get
away by myself; I was tired of the continual round of

pleasure, and I wanted to be alone with Rose; I wanted to complete her education.

The trip, as you know, was short, and we soon found ourselves in a wonderfully equipped hotel, and here I engaged a whole suite of seven rooms, two of which were equipped with baths; one a shallow affair for those who disliked water; the other a deep pool, or plunge, where one might sport about as one pleased.

I had furnished Rose with a complete outfit of clothing; not the type commonly worn by maids, but of a type not entirely unlike that worn by the Countess's maids, though far less scant, and she was busy arranging my things in various parts of the apartment.

I decided upon a bath. I went to the plunge. Slipping out of my dressing-gown, I slid down into the water. As you undoubtedly know, the water in these baths are kept at a constant temperature, and wading about in varying depths I found myself thrilled. Perhaps it was due to the warm water; perhaps it was on account of my ever increasing longing for the unknown, but whatever it was, I found something lacking. It wasn't complete. I called Rose. I was standing at the deepest part of the pool when she entered with nothing more than my head and the tips of my fingers above water.

Gazing up, for she stood just above me, I feasted my eyes on her perfect limbs that showed all too plainly beneath her widely flaring skirt, a little affair which came to but midway between her hips and knees and which flared from her at a rakish angle. The little dear must have realized I was gazing up beneath her dress, for the color came to her cheeks in ever increasing volume, and I could see she was not averse to having me see her charms.

So, instead of finding her presence something to console me, I found myself even worse off; her presence simply added to that something which seemed to be lacking.

Coming out of the water, I placed myself in her hands for drying.

So far I had done nothing more than hug and kiss her a little, but now, as she gently dried me, I was taken with another sort of longing for her. You see, my friend, being ravished with the warden's monster of a cock had not quite cured me; there was still a slight spark lying dormant within me; a spark which even then was burning into a flame which was to almost consume me a little later.

Going into my lounging-room I settled down on a broad, low divan, making her kneel beside me on the floor. Here, while she stared into my eyes with ever increasing wonder, I plied her with questions; and here I got the whole life story.

She answered all my questions and asked not one.

"I believe," I said, by way of opening the subject most dear to my mind, "you love me, Rose—Tell me why."

She smiled. "I do love you," she said in a low tone. "I've loved you ever since I saw you that first time—."

"In the prison, you mean?" I finished for her.

She nodded. I saw the word "prison" hurt her, and I never referred to it again.

"Tell me," I continued. "Was it because I really liked you, or was it because I happened to be naked? Perhaps you fell in love with my nudity, yes?"

"I don't know," she said. "I only know that I love you more than ever now. What I told you about wanting to be your slave is true.

"All my life I have wanted to be a slave to a beautiful woman, and you are beautiful."

"What did you think when you saw me that day; my nakedness, I mean?"

"I have often seen naked women; almost daily one sees naked women wandering about that place."

"Why?"

She shrugged her shoulers.

"Do you know why I was naked?" I asked.

Again she shook her head. "It was because I wanted a maid," I said, "and the warden wouldn't allow me to enter the place until I first undressed. Do you know why he made me undress?"

"Only too well," she answered. "He makes all the women undress who call there."

"And you don't hate me for it? Even when you know that he had me? That he ravished me?"

She shook her head. "Many women come there to pick out girls, and he does it to all of them; that's part of the price one must pay."

"Do you realize, Rose, that I did it for you, and not because I liked him?"

"Yes," came the ready answer. "And that's why I love you, and want to be your slave! I want to be abused! I want you to undress me and whip me! I want to lie naked on the floor and have you walk on me! I want to suffer for you!" Sincerity was written all over her face.

Very well, I thought, if you want to be my slave I shall make you one, but in a far different manner than you think!

I said: "Have you ever acted as lady's maid?

She shook her head, and a fear came into her eyes.

"Don't be alarmed," I laughed, "I'm not going to send you away; I but wanted to know, so I would know where to start with your education. But I could never bring myself to walk on you, Rose; you are far too beautiful to be abused in that terrible manner. There is, however, something you can do for me that would please me far more than anything you could possibly think of." I saw the light return to her eyes as I went on: "I used to have a maid just like you, and she did something for me which I dearly loved, and I wonder if you would do it for me?" And at the same time I slipped my hand beneath the short skirt and gently patted the naked bottom.

Her eyes were brighter now. "Oh, I will do anything you ask!" she cried.

"Anything?" I asked, sliding my fingers up and down between her firm bottom-cheeks. She couldn't seem to find words to answer this; just nodded her head, and I continued: "Very well, Rose, but before I ask you to do this something for me I want you to take off all your clothes, then come back to me. Now hurry!"

She darted away to her room. Taking advantage of her absence, I arranged myself in the most perfect position I could conceive.

Moving my bottom to the very edge of the divan was my first effort to complete the picture. I dropped one foot to the floor; the other I drew up close to my bottom, and here, my thighs well parted, I awaited her return. She shed her scant covering quickly, bounding back into the room almost before I was ready for her. She stopped stock-still, stood and gazed into my fully exposed crotch, for like herself, I was stark naked. And as I allowed my gaze to sweep over her girlish charms I realized she was even prettier than Gene, my former maid! I beckoned her to me. Making her kneel beside me again, my arm slipped about her, drew her close and kissed her lips again and again!

"Do you love me now?" I asked, holding her close.

"Oh, yes!" she answered scarcely above a whisper.

"Still want to be my slave?"

it was my efforts alone which saved her from a life a thousand times more wicked than that I prescribed for her.

All in all, I believed I was fortunate in getting such a talented girl for a maid, and beginning that very day she proved in a hundred ways that she was willing to do anything for me.

That night I took her into my bed. I talked to her for hours about my lovers; I told her I might call upon her to entertain me even when visited by my friends; I told her I was going to make some "great monster of a man" fuck her—and to all of this she willingly agreed.

Together we spent three weeks there, and then I returned to Pest.

The show reopened in a blaze of glory; I met all my old friends and many new ones. Among them I received a call from Bernice and, naturally, I welcomed her with open arms. I thought her more beautiful than ever, and it was due to the efforts of this same Bernice who made it possible for me to learn more about the innerlife of our talented and wealthy Europeans.

During the course of her visit, I happened to mention that I had never seen the interior of a house such as hers. "Then why not pay me the honor of a visit to mine?" she said.

Anna, who was present, said: "Before going to Bernice's home, why not visit some of the other places first? Then ——— would appreciate the splendor and beauty of yours."

"A capital idea," seconded her pretty sister. "I haven't had a real outing since you went away."

And so it was arranged. But there was more to it than just getting up and going; all the places, as I was to learn, were not like the famed house Bernice maintained, and a visit to most of them required something more than just a mere opening a door and entering.

And so, it became necessary to make a certain amount of preparation for this night's fun, and the witty sisters provided the necessary answer to it. First we must provide ourselves with men's attire. Also, we must wear little masks, and long black capes.

The following night after the show, we started out. All preparations having been made by the thoughtful girls, we entered a carriage that was waiting at the exit of the theater. I noted, too, that one proceeded us while another followed. I said nothing of my suspicions for some time, but seeing that all three coaches maintained the same positions I finally called the girls' attention to it.

Nina said: "Have no fears, my dear; just a little protection against the more unruly."

It must be remembered, my friend, that at that time there were a great many houses operating in the various cities throughout Europe, and since the police were lax in their vigilance (it seemed to be general knowledge that the police owned many of them) it was only fair to assume that some of these dens housed the more criminal element who were forever on the alert to trap the less wily.

Hence the two carriage loads of masculine protection.

We visited five of these dens that night, and while there is little to relate regarding our own experiences, a brief description of two of them wouldn't be out of place here.

The first one, a den which was entered by descending a flight of stone steps, was of the more common type found throughout Pest.

It was a cheap drinking place frequented by the lower class of girls who resided in the neighborhood, and where their favors could be purchased for drinks. There were no private rooms, no darkened corners where the couples might converse in private. Everything was done more or less openly and, as is common in such places, fights occurred with startling regularity. Enough of that place.

We had started, as one might guess, with visiting the more degraded places. The second one, while no less dangerous, was a little better. This was the meeting place for the working, or middle class, girls and young men, and was less conspicuous. I mean by that, that little rooms were provided, each room having a curtain, and it was a steady parade of couples entering and leaving them.

You must keep in mind that we were wearing men's attire, masks and long opera capes, and since members of the "upper class" were continually visiting these places, it wasn't at all uncommon to find visitors dressed somewhat like ourselves.

This second place, even though it was a little better than the first, furnished us with a little bit of excitement. It also proved to us that our "guards" were ever on the alert. We were approached by one of the other visitors of the place who asked for a drink. This girl was of the medium type, and after perching herself on the edge of the table, and going through the formality of adjusting a garter—a little trick common among them when they wanted to flaunt their wares upon an unsuspecting wayfarer—asked one of us if we wouldn't buy her a drink. That in itself wasn't at all out of the way, and we would have gladly done so, had not something else happened at that moment.

Before we could summon a waiter, however, we were approached by a villainous looking man who promptly insisted that we were trying to steal his darling girl, but the altercation was cut short by the timely appearance of a stranger who promptly delivered the would-be trouble-maker into the waiting arms of his mistress, said trouble-maker being of no further use to anyone that night, because he had a badly fractured jaw; and was still in the arms of Morpheus when we retired.

When I discovered our deliverer was one of our guards, I said:

"What a splendid man, my dears! I should like to know him better!"

Anna, being better acquainted with the brute, answered: "Leave well enough alone, darling! That brute, while he appears gorgeous, is little better than the man he ruined, and would as soon knife you as protect you; the only reason he doesn't is because he is being paid more for his work than he could possibly get from our purses."

As you can readily guess, I left our protectors politely alone.

The third place we visited that night was of the better class resort, and I really got something of a thrill there. Instead of being in a smelly basement, the place was off the sidewalk and we had to pass between two burly doorkeepers before we could enter.

I wondered if our eight "guards" would be denied admittance, and was glad to see they followed us; a whispered word from one of my companions seemed to have done the trick. Inside, however, they seemed to have melted away, but Nina said: "Don't be alarmed, my dear; they aren't far away—they haven't been paid yet, and until they get it, you couldn't lose them if you wanted to."

The place, besides sporting a dance floor of a sort, was lighted by gas-lamps, and all about the dancing section were tables where one could sit and enjoy the activities of the others, while sipping your drink. I noted, too, that there were several other groups, dressed somewhat like ourselves, sitting at the tables. They differed from us, however, in that in almost every case they were women, only an occasional man being present, though they all wore masks.

I remarked at this; the only answer being a shrug of the shoulder, and a lifting of eyebrows. I wondered at this.

Another strange thing about the place was that several of the guests received notes, or cards, or a whispered word from the waiter, and in almost every case the one receiving the summons left their group and entered through a door at the far end of the room and disappeared from sight. My curiosity being aroused, I called attention to this, remarking on the scarcity of men present.

"How do you know they're *not* men?" asked Anna.

"So," I thought, "It's *that* kind of a place, is it?"

Knowing more or less about the type of man who ran about dressed as a woman, I didn't think I cared for it. They were, as Anna so aptly put it, a sexless crowd unable to produce a "hard" even with the most beautiful girl.

The place was provided with a stringband, which furnished music for the dancers—which were chiefly women —and after a short stay we departed. Riding along, Nina said: "Having a good time, dearie?"

I laughed. "If seeing is having a good time, then I'm surely enjoying myself, but it's like coffee without cream —there's something lacking."

"Something to quell the raging fever?" asked Anna, reaching across and patting my belly.

"Something like that," I answered.

"Just what's on your mind, dearie? A man? Maybe a talented woman would do the trick?" This from Nina.

"Are you trying to flirt with me?" I asked. "If you are I'll take down my trousers." This caused a lot of lewd answers, then Nina said: "Alright, dearie. The next place we stop, you can turn yourself loose a little —only you've got to take your chance with what you get."

"Meaning?" I asked.

"Are you game?"

"The way I'm feeling," I answered, "I'm game for anything!"

A few moments later we were driven into a darkened street, and, closely followed by our "shadows" as we had gotten to call them, we entered a dimly lighted house not unlike the former place.

Here, however, the occupants were fewer and consisted chiefly of men, though, like the others we had seen, they, too, wore masks.

"Another one of *those* places, huh?" I said.

"Satisfied with anything you get?" Nina asked. "Just as long as you can get your gun off?"

This was a droll way of putting it, and I couldn't help laughing at the daring girl. "You seem well versed," I answered, "so suppose you pick out a nice 'gentleman' for me?"

"Done," she said, adding: "But knowing your weakness, dearie don't try returning the compliment; some night in the near future we'll take you to a place where you can go the limit, and where they don't wear masks."

"You interest me, my dear," I said, "so let us hope it will be soon."

A waiter was approaching. "Let me order," Anna whispered when the waiter neared the table at which we sat.

"Merry Wives," said Anna to the waiter, "Something to warm the red lane." He bowed. It was obvious he understood this strange request, for he said: "Perhaps the gentlemen would prefer being served in a private dining room?"

"Later," answered Anna. "For the moment we shall watch the dancers; perhaps we will find someone to dance with."

"Merry Wives? Something to warm the red lane? What in the world were you saying, Anna?"

"Just an expression to convey our needs, dearie. Our friend the waiter knows what we're here for now, so go ahead and pick out a partner; the best way is to pick out one you want then dance awhile."

"Good heavens," I cried. "Why all the secrecy? What's it all about?"

"There's no mystery about it, darling. Just a little surprise; surprises are always more thrilling, you know. Now take over there for instance; see the tall gentleman with the Vandyke?"

Nodding my answer, she went on: "The gentleman of the Vandyke happens to be the daughter of one of our wealthiest bankers, and whose desire runs to pretty women. She's looking over here now, and a nod will bring her running. Then suggest a dance, and see what happens."

"You intrigue me," I said. "Well, here goes!" and I gave the expected nod, which was immediately answered with another from the gentleman of the Vandyke. "Too late now to back out," whispered Nina, "for here she comes."

I approached her as she neared our table. "Dance?" I said.

This was the expected source of introduction, and as we moved about the dimly-lighted dance-floor I could see the other's eyes staring at me through the small holes in her mask.

"You dance divinely," I said, pressing against her, and receiving another in return. Something about this woman (for it was a woman) attracted me. Her mouth was pretty, as were her teeth, and what I could see of her complexion was unusually fair, and I found myself wanting to kiss her. I remembered, however, what I had been told about not returning the compliment, so I satisfied myself by awaiting the other's proposal. Glancing back at the table I had just left I noted that both Anna and Nina were walking out upon the dance-floor. My partner noticed it, too, for she said: "Your friends will be occupied for some little while, so why not join me in a drink?"

"At your table?" I asked, watching her eyes.

"I have a private little place, where we could be quite alone—besides," she continued, "I am quite thirsty."

Well, my friend, to make a long story short, I allowed myself to be led to a small room and here she pulled a cord. "A bottle of Benedictine," she promptly ordered. The waiter withdrew. "Won't you remove your cape?" she asked, tossing hers to one side.

"I would rather wait until the waiter has come and gone," I said.

Evidently the waiter hadn't far to go, for he rapped almost at once. "Shall I pay for it?" I asked, seeing that my companion made no effort to do so.

"It isn't necessary," she answered. "I shall take care of it before I leave." The waiter having pulled the cork, left us to ourselves. "Now the cape?" It was more of a command than a question. The cape thrown to one side, as was the high hat, I settled down upon a broad divan, my hair tumbling about my shoulders.

Hardly knowing how to begin the business, never having had a similar experience, I toyed with my glass, and waited.

"You have beautiful hair," she said, settling down beside me.

"You knew, then, that I was a woman?"

"Why else should I have asked you here? Besides, none but women are allowed upon the dance-floor."

"Then you, too, are a woman; one would never guess it," I lied, "by looking at your beard."

Her answer to this was to remove the beard, the hat she had already dispensed with. "Now that we understand each other we can feel more free, can we not?"

"I would feel more at ease were you to remove the mask," I said.

"You fear me?"

"Not in the least," I answered. "It's simply that I would feel more at home."

"And your own?"

"I would rather not: Perhaps we shall become better acquainted, then I would feel more like having you penetrate my identity."

I was wearing freshly pressed trousers, and the crease was unusually prominent, and with the index finger of one hand she began tracing it, up and down, up and down.

"You tickle dreadfully," I said, moving uneasily, but making no effort to hinder her. It was evident this girl wasn't at all sure of herself with me, for it was some moments before she became more progressive. Thinking to entice her, and having no idea of whether or not I was keeping the others, I leaned back amid the pillows.

This seemed to have the desired effect. Leaning partly over me, she said: "Would it interest you to know that I am rather wealthy?"

"Indeed. And how could that possibly interest me?" I asked.

She shrugged her shoulders. "I would like to know you better; you are very beautiful—what I can see of you, and perhaps I might be of service to you."

"That depends entirely upon yourself," I said with meaning.

"You mean that you would like me to remove my mask?"

"Would I be asking too much? I am here with two friends who are acquainted with the place; in fact it was one of them who suggested I dance with you."

"It appears that I am well known," she laughed, throwing off the mask and seating herself again by my side. "It doesn't matter; you must know why we are here?"

This being the first direct insinuation, I said: "Hadn't we best lock the door?" A thrill passed through me as this pretty girl took my hint as direct surrender, and I settled myself more comfortably amid the cushions. I knew that whatever happened was due to happen within the next minute.

Without further ado she again placed one hand on my thigh, but instead of tracing the crease in my trousers, her hand slid along to the fly and her nimble fingers were soon toying with the buttons, her eyes constantly upon mine. Then: "I would much prefer to have you completely nude," she said, quite slipping her hand into the opening she had made and bringing her fingers directly upon my cunt!

There being no longer a mystery about the thing now, I said: "That will be quite impossible here; another time, perhaps?"

"I would love to have you with me a whole night," she said, leaning down over me. "You are very beautiful—We could go to my home, some time? I have a lovely home."

I made no answer to this; by lying perfectly still, allowing free scope of her hand I believed answer enough. Her hand, in the meantime, had completed its exploration about my middle. Withdrawing it, she completed the undressing; that is, she unfastened the top of my trousers and drew off my legs. This done, she again knelt between my widely parted thighs and carefully rolled up my shirt! Naked, now, from the tops of my stockings to well above my waist, I awaited her attack! Then, a moment later, I said "Isn't it pretty?" at the same time raising my bottom and rotating my hips.

"It's beautiful!" she whispered, and then she pressed her half-open mouth to it! With eyes closed, my head turned to one side, I thrilled beneath her skilled lips and tongue! That she loved doing it there was no doubt, and all doubt was swept away a moment later when I bedewed her lips with a liberal dose of my come, all of which she carefully licked up and eagerly swallowed!

"You naughty girl," I said a few moments later as I raised from the divan and adjusted my clothes, "I never had anything half as nice."

"And you will see me again?" she asked eagerly.

Slipping my cape about my shoulders, I said: "The next time, my dear, it will be in that wonderful bed you told me about, and if you are half as nice undressed as you are dressed, I'm sure you'll find me willing in more ways than one!"

I really meant it, my friend. I liked her. She wasn't the type one finds so commonly about such places; she didn't have that masculine look, nor the tiny mustache one sees on a tribade's upper lip, and I fully intended making my way back there again—I was quite sincere about the "bedroom" part of it.

I found my two friends awaiting me when I came to our table.

"Had enough?" asked Nina, "Or is there someone else you'd like to try?"

But I had had enough. Besides, the hour was late; it was, in fact almost daylight when we started back to my residence.

Naturally, we discussed the events of the evening, and then we drifted back to the last place we had visited. Then, since neither girl held back anything, but freely told everything that had happened to them, I said: "I am rather smitten with your friend, the banker's daughter—I would like to see her again some time."

"If you're wise you won't," offered Nina. "Once she finds out who you are she'll pester you to death."

"As bad as that?" I asked.

"Worse. Why else would a girl make such a joint her rendezvous if she wasn't an out-and-out rotter?"

This made me open my eyes. I was glad then that I hadn't been so free to divulge my identity. Nor did I ever go there again.

"If you have had enough for one night, then let me get to bed; I'm near dead," cried Anna.

We had coffee before retiring, and Nina said: "Be a good girl, ————, and some night soon we'll take you to a place called 'Cupid's Nest.' "

"Sounds good," I answered, "but in the meantime, I'm going in my own little nest, so goodnight to you, my children."

You like my story so far, my friend? Is it the type you desired, and is it naughty enough to tickle your fancy? Write me and let me know; I am yours to command, my dear.

As you have noted, no doubt, I am mentioning only such events in my life which might prove of interest to you. I could go on and on relating the more trivial ones, but I'm sure they would prove of no interest whatever. Enough to say, that for a whole week I devoted my time to my rooms when I wasn't at the theater. There was much to be done. I had to devote much of my time to Italian; it was the one tongue which intrigued me, and my manager had hinted, in no uncertain terms, that a contract awaited me in Milan, where he expected to open another play.

I might mention here, my friend, that I had lost my lover, Arpid.

It was as much my fault, perhaps, as his own, but I couldn't take him to Kaiserbad with me, and when I returned I found that his father had traced him, and since he was but touring Europe before entering military college, his father had taken him back home with him.

I hated to lose him, of course, but as there was nothing I could do about it, and as there were numberless handsome men to be had at one's beck and call, I quickly forgot him. Besides, I had my little Rose, and between times, when I met an occasional man, her pretty lips and tongue were ever at my disposal, and many's the time I awakened in the morning only to find her still with her face between my thighs, and she always gave me a splendid sucking before I went to my bath.

At the expiration of a week, however, I found myself desiring something more substantial than one's tongue-tip. Rose was wonderful, and she loved me, but even her skilled efforts failed to appease the hunger which grew and grew within me.

I mentioned this to Anna and Nina; they were, as I have already said, almost constantly with me; they seemed to have forgotten their home completely, and the witty Anna said: "How about a trip out to Bernice's establishment? You promised her a visit, you know; she'll be wondering what's happened to you."

I had, of course, been looking forward to a visit there, but there was something else I had in mind which interested me still more.

I said: "I would fully enjoy calling on her, but there is still another place I would like to see first."

"Yes?" Anna said. "What is it? Perhaps we can help you."

"You can, since it was your delightful self who suggested it," I said. "I'm anxious to see this place you call 'Cupid's Nest.'"

"So," cooed Nina. "Our little diva's getting a hard-on! Well, I guess it can be arranged. When do you want to go?"

"Any time it's convenient for your delightful self," I offered. "The sooner the better."

"It can be arranged, of course, but it will take a few days. You understand, of course, what sort of a place it is, do you not?"

"I know nothing whatever about it," I said. "I guess I've fallen in love with the name of the place. Cupid's Nest," I repeated over and over again. "Sounds pretty good to me."

"You've got one of those, darling," laughed Nina. "Isn't it something to put into the nest that you hanker for?"

"You've guessed it, and I'll die if I don't get it damn soon!"

"Then Cupid's Nest it shall be, darling, but keep your pretty legs together a few days, and then you can open them as you please. In the meantime I'll see about it."

Seeing Rose lingering about as though wishing to hear more about it, and feeling dreadfully naughty at the moment, I said: "Can't I even open them for Rose—"

"Good heavens!" cried Nina, making believe she was shocked at the idea, "Has the woman debauched the child to the extent of making a cunt-lapper of her!" This caused considerable mirth, and not a little embarrassment to Rose, but she had long since proven herself a good little sport and enjoyed it as much as any of us. Both girls knew that Rose delighted in gamahuching me, and Rose knew that I was on unusually friendly terms with Anna and Nina, so what harm could there be?

A little later I shall tell you of her loyalty to me, and how at my own suggestion she allowed herself to be deflowered by a lover I was to meet, and with whom I lived openly.

But I am digressing, my dear; that part of the story will come in its proper place.

To return to the story. In due time, Anna and Nina completed the details necessary before we could enter the *sanctum sanctorum* of the Cupid's Nest. What a name! By rights it should have been called "Cupid's Dart" for that was what it really was; a place to receive that very thing.

The place was located on a street occupied, for the most part, by factories, but that did not in the least take from it the glaring splendor one found within its walls.

A brief description of the interior of this place is necessary at this point before one can begin to understand how the place was worked and maintained. To begin with, it was a most exclusive place, being frequented by only the "elite" of the social world, and no woman was ever allowed to enter, save those who became inmates, either temporary or permanent.

Sounds like something one reads about in the Arabian Nights, does it not? Such, however, is true. The front of the place was used as a beer-drinking garden; the ceiling was high and beautifully decorated with the works of several celebrated artists, said decorations being in the form of the most erotic paintings. The walls were like wise decorated. This room, which was large, contained nothing in the form of furniture except tables and chairs upon which the patrons sat, the patrons, as I have said, being men.

The place was brightly lighted, the whole was screened from the street by heavy velvet curtains. The waiters were men.

At the extreme rear of this room was an elevated platform. The front, or room-side, was covered with a latticework interwoven with vines growing sweet-smelling flowers. From this latticed hallway, for that's what it was, was a set of steps, six in number. At the head of these stairs was a door, and behind this door, which was heavily barred, stood a gigantic negro, and woe be unto he who tried passing that negro! It had been tried once or twice—to the great sorrow to those who tried it.

Behind this hallway-like space was the main room, or rooms, and it was these occupied by the "clients" who frequented them, these last being women, or girls, as the case might be.

These rooms, of which there were twelve, were beautifully furnished, each room containing a full-sized bed, a dresser, chairs, a clothes-closet and a washroom. There was but one lamp on this entire floor, and this, for obvious reasons, was seldom if ever lighted; the reasons for which I shall explain in due time.

The rooms mentioned were rented for periods ranging from a week to a month by women, both married
and single, for clandestine purposes, and here women
and girls with an over-animativeness could carry on
their love affairs without hindrance. The possibilities
were limitless; and though the owners of this brothel
were censured, they should have been rewarded.

They were censured, of course, by the good Christians, those Christians, those who believed not in the
pleasure of the flesh and dwelt only in a spiritual world
—when no one was looking.

There was every possible convenience within those
rooms, and here is the way the plan was carried out.
First, the woman or girl who was to occupy a room was
of necessity well-known. If she was a stranger she must
be vouched for by someone acquainted with the mistress; if accepted she paid the fee necessary for a given
length of time, and was given a key to a door of a house
on a street in the rear. Entering, heavily veiled, she
made her way through this house to the one in which
she maintained her one-room apartment.

Once there, she quickly made her way into the room
assigned her, and here she arrayed herself in the costume in which she wished to receive her partner; she
used her own discretion in this. When she was ready
for her lover she would don a domino and mask and
make her way through the hall to the latticed partition
which overlooked the drinking-room below, and here
she would have a commanding view of everyone in the
room, and here unseen, she would choose the man she
wanted. Having made her choice, she would indicate
to the big negro the man she wanted and he in turn
would see to it that the message was conveyed to the
right person.

Having made her selection, she would retire to her

room—all this having taken place in absolute darkness —and here, by the simple expedient of dropping the domino and mask, be in the costume necessary for a lover's embrace.

Isn't that a pretty arrangement, my dear? I think it was.

Nina and Anna having made the necessary arrangements for me, I repaired to the place. The mistress must of necessity know every woman who entered her establishment, but she was the only person who was let into the secret: You can readily understand why this was necessary. Being well known, however, I hadn't the slightest difficulty in getting a place, or room, and I lost no time in getting into it, and I was less time in getting out of my clothes.

Then I went to the latticework partition and gazed out upon a sea of faces. It was remarkable the great number of handsome men who frequented the place. There was at least fifty there at the moment and I had no trouble in choosing the man I wanted. Indeed, it would have been difficult in choosing between them; they were all handsome—the homely ones never came twice.

Waiting until I saw the message delivered to the right man, I went back to my room, threw off the domino and mask and settled down upon the bed to await my pleasure, and as you might have guessed I didn't have long to wait; no gentleman will keep his mistress waiting, and these were all gentlemen. True, they weren't all wealthy, nor were they all of the "elite," but they were handsome to a fault, and were known for the "staying-powers" when in the arms of a passionate woman.

I won't tire you with a detailed account of all the things I did that first night: Enough to say, that he was a wonderful man in every way—and I'm sure I sent him to his home that night satisfied that it would have been impossible to extract another drop of his precious fluid. Briefly, I maintained that room for a month, going there direct from the theater whenever the call of the flesh demanded—which was often. If a certain man was unusually nice, if he had a large cock and objected not in offering it in any manner I chose, he would be sure to get a second invitation to visit me.

Then there was another advantage to all this. If one felt in a mood for variety, all you had to do was to tell the man to leave after he had given one or two demonstrations of his manly powers, and then you simply chose another, and no one was the wiser.

Would it interest you to know, my dear, that several of these men had handsome incomes from these women, and yet never knew who the women were? Such is the case; I have ample proof of that statement.

The first incentive, naturally, is that this sort of an arrangement called for a lot of unnecessary preparation. Why, one asks, should a woman go to all this bother for the sake of meeting some man? Why not go to any one of dozen hotels or houses set aside for that very purpose? There are a thousand reasons why all this is necessary—if a woman wants to keep her secrets.

There are scores of women in every city who are not properly mated to their husbands; convention being the prime fault of that. She might be of the ultra-passionate type, while her husband is quite the reverse: She might be the type who craves certain caresses—both active and passive—but is denied them by said husband; he might be the type who wouldn't hesitate to kiss the cunt of his mistress, but wouldn't for the world do the same for his wife, nor would he dream of inserting his cock into her mouth—he could never lower her to do *that!*

What better way, then, than for her to engage a room at this delightful place and take her fill of the good things in life?

Shall I tell you of other possibilities within those walls? Yes?

Then listen: I had often talked at great length with the woman who runs that house, and she told me many strange things, and though there were no names mentioned, she held back nothing which might lend fact to the telling. She told me of a certain married woman who greatly loved her husband and wanted a baby by him. But he, unfortunately for her, didn't want her to have a baby; in spite of the fact that he was an amorous man and fucked her every night and sometimes in the morning before arising. But at the expiration of each put-in he compelled her to take a careful douche thus preventing her from becoming with child.

She didn't like. She coaxed him to make her withchild, but it was no use; he insisted it would ruin her figure, and that ended that. But it didn't end it with her, however. Determined to get herself "caught" she set about putting a most witty plan into action.

Now there was not the slightest reason why she shouldn't have gotten in the family way, for there were thousands of men who would have given an arm each for the mere privilege of spending an hour between her adorable thighs, but she loved her husband and would have gladly died rather than to have allowed another man fuck her.

She knew he went with other women once in while, and she knew she could do little about it since most men had their mistresses, so she hit upon a very witty ruse. First of all she wrote her husband a very pretty letter. Two or three days later she wrote another. This was followed by a third, a fourth and a fifth, each letter a little more daring, each a little more naughty. She said she dare not divulge her name, but made no secret of the fact that she was smitten with him, and would never rest happily until she had possessed him.

Like most men he fell for the ruse at once; a beautiful lady of refinement and culture wanting him to diddle her was a little too much for his sensitive nature. A day or two later he received another letter. This one informed him that the lady would be at the Cupid's Nest on a certain evening, and if he would promise to meet her there, abide by the rules of the place and never seek to find out her identity, and was willing to satisfy her constant longing, he should be at a certain place—she named it—and he should be wearing a yellow rose on the lapel of his coat.

If he did this, she would know he was willing to meet her, and she would be there on the date set, and he would be conducted to her room, and here he might have his fill of her person, and at the same time give her a greatly longed-for pleasure.

Everything worked out as she desired it. He appeared wearing the rose; she went about engaging the room, and at the time set he had the good fortune of being conducted into the good lady's room where he made short shift of pleasing and gladdening her heart.

Thinking, of course, that he was with some social butterfly whose only thought was to be royally and properly fucked, the good man did a wonderful job, such a thing as douches being the least of his thoughts. The result of that single meeting was a beautiful baby boy, and he was glad.

Shall I tell you of still another and far more thrilling case? Yes? Then listen to this, for it's but another ex-

ample of the possibilities in this wonder-house, though
you'll admit it the strangest case you have ever heard of.
Indeed, I couldn't think of a better illustration than
this one.

Shortly before my advent in Pest, there lived a young
and very beautiful girl. She was scarcely seventeen, and
was one of two children, the other being a brother. This
brother was some six or seven years her senior, and like
his sister, he was unusually handsome. Tall, straight,
wavy black hair, broad of shoulders, he was a handsome
man. And, as in such cases, he was greatly sought after
by the ladies. Indeed, he sought the ladies, too.

Then, by some strange twist of the mind, the girl fell
in love with her handsome brother. Her interest in him
grew, as did her love for him, but of course she dared not
tell him of this.

Finally, the thing became an obsession; she could
think of nothing else save her handsome brother. Now
it happens that this girl had never tasted the joys of a
male member; no man had ever touched her, nor had
she ever been pricked with the desire for a man, and
now, for the first time in her young life, she felt the call
of the flesh. She couldn't, of course, divulge her secret
to even her most trusted friend; she had to suffer alone.

A month passed. During that time she read all the
books she could find on the subject of love, and since
the book shops sold lewd items almost openly, she had
little trouble in getting several of the better-known
works. And since these books pictured the various ways
in which men and women enjoyed the carnal acts, her
education grew. And with her education grew her passion.

Desperate now, she began throwing herself in her
brother's way.

Wealthy, as they were, he had plenty of time to indulge his passion for books and women, and spent hours at a time in the gardens reading. The sister, who we shall call Eve, because that wasn't her name, made it a point to appear before him in this garden. Becoming more brazen, she began wearing less and less clothing, though she never let on that she knew her brother saw her. But nothing happened. If he became smitten with her freely exposed charms, it only increased his desire for other women.

Eve tried every conceivable thing and trick she could conjure, but she couldn't entice her handsome brother to her arms.

She knew he went out with girls, and this annoyed her. She got to following him, but this did little good. She persisted, however, and finally she happened to follow him one night when he went to the Cupid's Nest. Eve was no fool. She knew something about the place—as did most sporting women—and after a little inquiry here and there, she got the whole story.

Her happiness knew no end! With plenty of money to do with as she chose, she rented a room at the above mentioned place.

But, as will sometimes be the case, she spent several nights there before she saw her handsome brother, and then her thoughts quite carried her away. Without delay, she sent him the word he had expected to receive from some handsome dame, and hastened to the room designated, and having been there several times, he knew exactly what to do—and he did it.

With wildly beating heart, she lay there listening to him undress, thrilling anew with the fall of each garment. And you may be sure the happy fellow lost no time in gliding into bed with the wildly passionate girl where, after exchanging kisses of every kind, he gave her proof of his manhood again and again.

He must have found her tender little cunt most pleasing to him, for it was hours before he had enough of it —and just before he left, she pressed a prepared note into his hand; it was to the effect that she would expect him the following night and that he must not fail her, since she had fallen desperately in love with him.

A kiss was his answer that he understood her whispered command.

No longer a maiden, a smile on her beautiful face, she settled down to rest and dream of another night with her handsome brother!

The next night she watched him dress and noted the great care he took that he might be at his best with his new love—little dreaming that his new love was his own sister.

What mattered it if she commit incest with her own brother? Did she not love him? And hadn't he whispered in her shell-like ear that he loved her, even though he didn't know who she was?

Her carriage was waiting when she slipped from her home, and she was quickly driven to the street upon which the secret entrance of the Cupid's Nest was located. Without delay she slipped into her room. Ten minutes later, clad in but the kimono, she tripped to the lattice and gazed down into the room.

Her handsome brother had not yet arrived, but she hadn't long to wait. Pressing the prepared note into the negro's hand, she watched him deliver it, thrilled to her pretty toes when she saw his face light with inward pleasure at reading it!

She slipped into her room. Naked from top to toe, her well-developed breasts heaving with inward delight, her cunt throbbing with longing for the feel of his lovely rammer, she threw herself upon the bed and waited!

Last night she had been a novice; it being the first time she had ever been with a man, she was the least bit timid. But tonight! Tonight she would be different! Tonight she would return some of those thrilling kisses he had bestowed upon her! Tonight she, like he, would banquet on the spermatic sweets she had so often read about! She would abandon herself like those girls she had read of in the naughty books; she would drink pleasure to the full!

This is something of a glowing picture I am painting, my friend, but it is just as it was told to me by the lady who maintained that wonder-house, and she got it from the girl herself. Why was this?

It was this way: Seeing that the same girl chose the same man every night, the woman became curious. She had the man followed; learned where he lived. She had the girl followed, and learned that both lived in the same mansion. When I asked her why she did this, she gave me this explanation: She said she had from the very first noted the strange similarity in their looks, the color of their hair, and so on, and after making the discovery that they lived in the same house, she questioned the girl and got the truth from her.

So you see, my friend, I know the whole story, though I hadn't the slightest idea who they were, nor did I care. I only know that for a full month this girl and her brother occupied the same room, and that she became pregnant by him.

But she was clever. One night she saw him with another handsome young man, and knowing the man was of splendid family, she passed up her brother and invited this other man to her arms. Then, by what I thought was a very clever ruse, she managed to acquaint this man with her identity, and the fellow, thinking he had been the only one, he married her—and they lived happily ever after.

I am going to end this letter here, my dear, but I shall write you again tomorrow. It's short I know, but I'll have plenty more to tell you very, very soon, and I'll tell you of my visit with my friend Bernice and what I saw there.

Chapter VI

There is little to tell of the month that followed my entrance into the famous Cupid's Nest. For almost the entire month I fully enjoyed myself there. Nights when I did not care to go, I gave my key to one of the girls; they were in no suffering need of men; they knew everybody in Pest and men were the easiest things they could get.

However, if I remember correctly, I promised to tell you of our trip to Bernice's house. It was nothing more, as I have already said, than an out-and-out whorehouse, but it differed from the others in that she catered to none but the most select patrons; men and women of the nobility.

Bernice, having been made acquainted with my desire to visit her, had come to see me. "If you want to see something more or less unusual," she said, "make it a point to come out Sunday night."

We asked no questions as to what she hoped to show us; we simply went that Sunday evening. We went as soon as it was dark enough to enter her place with safety, and I'll never forget it. It was, without doubt, the most elaborate place I had ever seen.

A mansion, set well back from the street, and this

street in the very center of the most fashionable homes in the city. When I questioned her about this, she said: "Why not? None but the 'elite' come here, so why not have it handy?"

"But I would think the ladies would complain," I suggested.

She shrugged her shoulders. "Why should they? They find it convenient here."

"You mean?" I said, "that some of your patrons are women of the fashionable set? That they live close by?"

She smiled. "That's why I asked you to come tonight. About a dozen of them will be along in about three hours; tonight they're holding one of their parties." Seeing that I couldn't grasp the significance of all this, she went on to explain.

"Their parties are conducted somewhat along the lines of those who run the Cupid's Nest. The only difference being that they are less secretive about it. Being that kind, and moving about among the elite only, they don't have to be so careful; every one of the nobility is their friend, they all know each other's secrets, so they don't have to be careful about what they do or say.

"When they decide to hold one of these events, which in most cases is on Sunday night, I send out invitations to the men I think desirable to them. Then, after they've eaten and drunk themselves full, the real party gets under way, and if I'm not very much mistaken, you are due to see an orgy that will put the one you witnessed at the prison in Budapest in the background."

I began experiencing thrills even then. "Supposing the witnessing of all this," I said, "overheats us? Then what?"

"Well," she answered, smiling, "I have plenty of girls

and ten men to choose from, to say nothing of twelve or fifteen men of the Nobility, so I see no reason for any of us to suffer very long."

"Cut it out, dearie," cried Anna, stretching herself out on a broad couch, "or I'll lose mine right here in my panties."

Please don't, cried Bernice apparently shocked at the idea.

It's nothing short of criminal to waste the precious stuff!

Huh! grunted Nina. Just as though you'd let her waste it!

Are you insinuating, darling, asked Bernice, that I would stoop to conquer?

I don't know about that, Bernice, answered Nina, but I do know you'd stoop.

Cat, Bernice answered her, then turning to me, continued:

Would you like to see my home, my dear? While we're waiting for the fun to begin?

Seeing me rise to follow her, then hesitate, she said:

Never mind the two cats; they've seen everything I've got in the house.

By-the-way, Bernice, I said, as we passed from the room, I haven't seen any of the girls I'm told you keep here. And that puts me in mind of something else, I continued. Where are the girls you purchased in Budapest? You've got them here, of course?

Not as yet, my dear. They're not allowed to mingle until they've been examined; we call it 'exile.' I have plenty of others, however; would you like to see them?

—and the men, I added, smiling.

Naturally, she said. Who wouldn't. You wouldn't like them, though; they prefer men.

Indeed, I cried. That kind, eh?

You'll see, a little later.

Would you like to hear a brief description of the place, my dear?

Yes? Very, well, then. As I told you, the place was very spacious. Four stories high it stood, great stairways carved from rare wood and carpeted with runners imported from Persia, candalabrums of the choicest glass, Louis thirteenth chairs on every landing, suits of armor here and there, satin and velvet-covered walls, ceilings adorned with pilasters formed and carved into seductive Cupids each armed with little arrows directed to a dying Venus, doorways topped with miniature marquees and each door lettered with the occupant's name framed in gold. And the rooms! Things of beauty, I termed them, each equipped with a large, springy bed, the walls covered with mirrors, a great one over each bed, a couch, several easy chairs, and the usual washroom, but these, instead of the coarse marble, were of onyx of every color and hue.

The three upper floors were given over chiefly to the "plaisir" chambers, the ground, or lower floor being reception rooms, lounging rooms, and one large amphitheaterlike room, though this was without the usual seats used by an audience; it was as Bernice said, they didn't want an audience to what went on there.

This room, since it's the only one of great interest of this part of the story, was furnished in the most elaborate style. The largest rug in all Europe, I believe, covered the floor, and it was worth a king's ransom. Six inches deep, it was, and into it was woven a man and woman in a most compromising position.

The walls and ceiling were frescoed with the most erotic paintings, while all about this great room were several broad, low couches while between them were heaps of pillows.

Standing in the center of this, I said:

It is the most beautiful I have ever seen. I stared in awed wonder; this room alone must have cost a vast fortune; I could easily understand why Bernice catered to the wealthy.

If you think it beautiful now, you should see it when filled with guests; tonight, for instance.

I hope to, I answered. I have been looking forward to it.

Passive or active? she asked, a merry twinkle in her eyes.

I'll look them over first, I answered. Then if they look good I might take you up on it.

Like the feel of the whip? she asked, smiling. If you do here's a good chance to get your fill.

Thanks, I said, but the only kind of a whip I like is the kind surrounded with hair, and about ten inches long.

She looked deeply into my eyes for a moment, then:

As long as you insist upon the hair, my dear, wouldn't a pinkish slit do—assuming, of course, that the hair was black?

There was something dreadfully suggestive about this; I said:

That puts me in mind, darling; if I remember correctly, you promised me a little party with a black-haired pussy, and I raised my hand to her curly locks.

That's a promise, my dear, she whispered, moving close and pressing her belly to mine. If you're still in that frame of mind after seeing the 'show' you'll find one somewhere about me—I get rather hot, too, after seeing a real show.

May I depend on it? I asked, rubbing her belly and gently pinching her pussy through her thin dress. Our lips met in a clinging kiss, and I'm sure I would have been a willing partner to anything she might have suggested had she but hinted it.

Wandering back to the others, she said:

Did you suffer any ill effects as a results of the warden's big tool?

Instead of directly answering this, I said:

Isn't it too bad he isn't more sanitary about his person? Isn't he a man, though?

Don't misjudge me, dear, but once a month I make the trip there, just to get it a few times, dirt or no dirt. Would you believe it, when I say that in a single night he topped me fifteen times, and that doesn't figure in the three or four times I sucked him off, either.

Such was Bernice. Such was the manner in which she freely discussed subjects few women care to discuss.

Back in the room where we left Anna and Nina, Bernice said:

Step behind this screen here and I'll let the parade in; our guests will be arriving any moment now, and at the same time you'll get a look.

The screen referred to was a transparent curtain which hung across a doorway. In the room it was dark, and being light in the larger room we could see everything. The "parade" consisted of the girls of her establishment who trooped up from the lower floor, or basement, where they maintained sleeping quarters, and here, looking through the curtain, I was given an agreeable surprise.

The "girls" trooped in. Bernice spoke to each in turn, patted this one's cheek, spoke kindly to that one, made some little adjustment to this one's hair, straightened another's dress, and then they passed on into the larger room where they were to entertain.

More girls trooped in. These last, of which there was a dozen, were treated to about the same thing, the only difference being that Bernice seemed more careful. You're properly bathed? she would ask one. Sure you haven't wasted your energy today? she would ask another. Remember, my dears, we are having several guests tonight, and I want you at your best.

Finally all of them had passed from sight, and we joined Bernice in the outer room. I said:

Your girls are beautiful, dearie, but where are the men I've heard referred to? I'm just a little anxious.

All three laughed. Bernice said:

I have twenty-two girls and they are all here, yet thirty-four persons passed through here; how would one account for that?

Good heavens, I cried. You mean to say that some of them were women? Am I that blind?

You are not blind, my dear, answered Bernice, laughing the while. It's simply that you didn't recognize them; not being on the watch for them you naturally missed them, and that was due to their dress.

The laugh, of course, was on me, but I didn't care.

As I was to find out a little later, many of them were men, but they were all wearing beautiful garments, all wore wigs, and all were painted and powdered to the point where they all looked more or less alike. So you see I could be forgiven for not knowing the difference.

A few moments later Bernice led us through a dimly lighted hall and into a small room which was located directly behind the large room in which the "entertainment" was to be held. Leading me to a position close to the wall, she said:

I am allowing you to witness something that you will remember for many a day, and all I ask in return is that you will remain in absolute tranquility. If our guests were ever to discover they had an audience, I would be ruined, socially and otherwise.

Depend upon me, I answered. She was directing
her instructions directly to me; Anna and Nina having already witnessed the "show" needed no instructions.

Then look, she whispered, touching a tiny protruber-
ance in the wall. I looked. I was suddenly startled to
note that I could look into the large room. Indeed I
had as clear a view as though I were really in the room;
not a single item escaped my roving eyes!

The secret panel—for that's what it really was—slid
shut. I had heard of such things; many old castles
throughout Europe were equipped with them, but this
was the first time I had ever had the pleasure of gazing
upon one. The thing, as Bernice explained it, was so arranged that one could see directly into the room without the slightest danger of being seen, a section of one
of the many wall-decorations being transparent allowed
this.

I'm leaving you three to yourselves for a little while,
she said. Make yourselves at home; I shall send up re-
freshments in a moment. She swept out of the room,
closing the door after her.

That secret panel held my interest above everything
else.

Opening it I gazed out into the room. Nina moved
over to my side.

Pick out the men from the women,—dear, she said.

I tried this, but it was impossible. Thirty or more
persons were moving about or sitting in that room, and
the more I gazed the less sure I became. "I give it up,
I whispered. If there are any men in that room I defy
anyone to pick them out. Anna assisted me.

See that one with a yellow flower in her hair? pointing.

She looks like a Jap, I answered.

And that one over there—the one with the ribbon about her neck?

I turned my gaze to where she pointed.

Another Jap? I asked.

She nodded. Brother and sister, my dear, and two of the most skilled in the whole establishment. Bernice picked them up in Tokyo; both were inmates in a Yoshiwara which, as you know, means whorehouse in Japanese.

Gazing about the room I could recognize Russians, Spaniards, one or two French girls, three or four Germans. One who sat quite alone by herself proved to be Arabian. Her duties, besides entertaining in every possible mode, was to dance. You have seen dancers, but wait till you've seen this baby; she's a tonic for those suffering a rundown condition.

Those others, I said, pointing toward a group in a far corner.

What are they? I can't seem to locate their nationality.

Octoroons, my dear, and the most talented and lascivious of the group. There isn't a thing they won't do, as you shall see. They can think up more deviltry than all the others put together.

A maid entered bearing a tray, bottles and glasses.

Ah! cried Anna. Champagne for the thirsty!

The maid, a cute little Parisian, almost nude, served us, then:

There is something else I might do? she asked in almost perfect German.

Not just yet, Jenny, answered Nina, pinching one of the girl's nipples. Wait until the party gets under way; then I'll call you and you can give me a good sucking; I'll feel more like it then.

Bernice seemed to have forgotten nothing to make

our evening complete. I called the others attention to this. Anna said:

You can have anything you like, dearie; Bernice is a great little provider.

I'm afraid I'll have to turn them all down, Anna dear. If I'm any judge of actions, Bernice is looking forward to having me spend the rest of the night with her.

So she informed us. You'll find her everything you can expect.

We conversed for some time, and then, quite suddenly I thought, the doors were thrown open and several women and girls entered.

Our guests are arriving, whispered Nina. The 'elite' of the male sex will be coming along soon now. Pointing them out one by one I found myself gazing upon a dozen or more members of the highest society.

I was still holding my mask in my hand, the two sisters were still wearing theirs. Couples, arm in arm, were constantly passing us. They would stop, those who recognized me, and I couldn't help but smile at some of the remarks they made, and all were not flattering, either. Before leading us into the ballroom, Resi led us through a short hall and to the stairs which led to the upper floor. Couples were ascending and descending the stairs, and all were stark naked.

Those descending seemed more at ease; those ascending seemed in a hurry, and the reason was obvious: The sight of so much nakedness was proving too much for the gentlemen, young and old, and the amatory maidens were hurrying them to the various bedrooms, that they might reduce the hard-ons and at the same time cool their own raging passions.

In the little room above, Resi laughingly said:

Our party is getting under way with a bang.

I can quite understand how those girls must feel, I said. The sight of all those thrilling stiff pricks has aroused me too.

Resi produced a bottle and glasses, and after we had drunk a toast to my success, Anna and Nina slipped away. We both laughed, for it was plainly written on their faces what was troubling them.

This, she said, leading me through the tiny room and opening a door of another, this is the room I have reserved for you and Ferry.

You seem to take it for granted that I have already won him.

If you haven't you will. Just as soon as he lays his eyes upon that delightful pretty little thing between your thighs, and here she placed her arms about me: he'll be sure to fall in love with you.

For a long moment we stood gazing into each other's eyes, then:

Has he seen you yet? I asked.

Resi nodded, and I went on: Then if it's sight of a pretty puss that's necessary to arouse him, what chance have I got?

Naughty! she cried, pressing her bare belly against mine, I believe you are falling in love with me! Or is it my pussy that attracts you!

Here was a direct challenge; one could not mistake her meaning.

I said: "It's both, darling, and if it wasn't for the fact that I wish to retain everything for Ferry, I would prove my liking for you right here and now!"

Do you really mean that? she asked.

And when I told her I did, and that she was beautiful, she said:

Then why not come and spend an evening with me— we can be quite alone, and—well, you wouldn't be the first! Our lips met in a clinging kiss, tongues playing their part in it.

Don't tempt me, darling, I said, or I'll be unable to delay a demonstration right here. You're very beautiful, you know!

Is it a promise, then? she asked.

Will this convince you? I said, dropping before her and pressing face into the thick fleece and touching the upper end of her slit with the tip of my tongue!

Or this? she answered, pushing me down upon the bed and pressing her face into my crotch and gliding her tongue far up into my box!

There, she said, rising her cheeks flaming, Now your pretty little cunt is well lubricated and ready for Ferry's unusually big prong! My room is directly behind this, and after I've tasted the bliss of one of my favorite's big prick we'll drop in on you!

But come; if I remain here another moment I'll be sure to take what you want Ferry to have!

We hurried to and down the stairs; making our way through the laughing, happy couples; Resi playfully touching a pussy here or grasping and squeezing an erect prick there.

Such an assemblage is bound to become the least bit unruly, but to their everlasting credit, not a man so much as touched me, though some of the girls were less careful.

Into the great room at last, Resi led me through the maze of people. They were standing everywhere, and I wondered how ever they would find room to dance. Some four hundred persons were there, and every one as naked as a new-born baby. Pricks, stiff, thinking, perhaps, that no one saw their actions, were boldly stroking the men.

Few gave us any attention at all; they were too busy

with their own partners, and two more naked girls meant little to them.

Gaining a far corner, Resi said: I've never seen them so free as they are tonight—I wonder what could have gotten into them?

Is a little playful fun barred? I asked.

Not in the least. The sky's the limit; it's simply that they have never acted with such freedom before! I could see she was excited at all this. I said:

It's just possible that some hot-blooded maiden will so forget herself as to take possession of one of those noble-looking pricks right here among the other guests.

I had a real reason for suggesting this, as you shall see.

Her eyes brightened. That, she said, is something I have forever longed to see happen, though I have never met one who would dare!

And if someone were to start the fad? I asked with meaning.

She stared at me; I believe I guessed her thought—

Come, she said, leading me along. Here is your future lover!

A moment later I found myself face to face with Ferry: He was talking to two girls, and like them, he was stark naked; sandals on the soles of his well-formed feet being his only covering.

A smile lightened up his handsome face at sight of me, and he came forward, gently pushing the others out of his way. Grasping both my hands in his, he said:

Without a mask, too! I had no idea you would come —to say nothing of allowing everyone to recognize you!

But you, I returned, smiling, are also without a mask.

He laughed. I'm afraid a little thing like a mask would be poor covering for me, and he dropped his eyes in a significant manner.

My gaze followed his, and what I saw thrilled me to

the core! I heard Resi give a little startled gasp! Turning quickly, I saw the wild light in her eyes, and she nodded.

Returning my gaze to his, I said:

How could I stay away when so many handsome men are present! We stood staring into each other's eyes! For a long moment we stood thus, then: I'm dreadfully angry at you, my dear!

Angry? What ever have I done to arouse your anger?

I moved closer; close enough to feel the smooth head of his stiff prick touching my belly! Those standing close enough to hear now turned their gaze toward us, stood listening! A wave of uncontrollable lust swept over me! I remembered what Resi had said—!

I am angry at you for neglecting me that night I invited you to my apartment!

But what did I do? he asked, slipping his arm about Resi's nude waist and drawing her close. Tell me, my dear, what did I do? He said this in a much lower tone.

It wasn't what you did, you dreadful man, I said. It's what you did not do that annoyed me! Do realize you didn't even kiss me, either upon entering or leaving, when you must have known I wanted you to!

My dear, I'm sorry. Really I am. And I'll see that it never happens again. Never!

And that isn't all, I said, becoming more and more daring.

Couldn't you see by my action that I wanted—this! at the same time placing one hand upon his glowing prick and working it up and down! I heard another gasp; this time from my left, and it wasn't Resi, either. Turning and taking a quick glance I noted several eyes upon us; I became more daring!!

Oh, but I'm dreadfully sorry, my dear. Had I but

known, I would have stayed with you. I thought him rather nonchalant about it.

Nonsense! I answered, quickening the motion of my hand. Why else do you suppose I donned that little gown, if it wasn't that I wanted you to fuck me! But never mind, I continued, you shall not escape me again, for right here you are going to fuck me!

And then, with a quick motion, I pressed down that noble prick to my aching slit! My other hand spread the lips apart, and standing on tip-toe, I directed the glowing head to it, pressed against it, and felt it glide in! Too late to resist me now, had he cared to, overcome undoubtedly, by the feel of my warm cunny clasped about his raging hard, he grasped me in his arms! His hands slid down to my bare bottom! He raised me, and at the same time he drew me close, sending it into me to his balls! My arms slid about his neck; my thighs instinctively rose and clasped themselves about his waist, and I found myself sitting, as it were, upon his hard dart, the head of which I felt lodged far up within me!

Still in this position, he carried me through the mass of packed humanity! Gasps, I heard on every hand! Isn't she beautiful!

Oh darling! Oh, lover! Give me your darling cock Fuck me! were some of the expressions I recall!

Do you want to know what happened there that night, my dear? Yes?

Then listen: On every side men were clasping women in their arms. I had started a new vogue. Bedrooms were no longer necessary for that act. Couples were copying our action—but all this I knew nothing about for hours. Remember, I had nothing like this for several days, and this, coupled with a most unholy desire for it, made me blind to anything else that might have been going on about me. Sitting, as I have already said, upon that hard prong, the head of which seemed lodged up between my hipbones, the up and down movements upon it at his every step, and the cries on every hand, arousing my passion to the maddening point.

My only thought was that at last I possessed my lover! The man I loved with all my heart was carrying me off; where to I knew not and cared less! Resting on his palms as easily as though I were a child, he carried me into a room, lay me upon the bed, and there I was fucked as I had never been fucked before!

Ferry must have been wild for it because he went-off twice before he withdrew and lay down by my side—

How long we lay thus I do not know. I kept no track of time; it was an almost continuous performance. Kisses, embraces, naughty words whispered into each other's ears, dainty touches, kisses showered upon each other's love-pets, all came in turn—

There was a dim light in our room, and now, for the first time, I realized where I was. I was in the very room Resi had set aside for me! How did you manage to bring me to this room, you naughty man? I asked, cuddling closer in his arms and kissing him.

It's the one Resi set aside for us—

Us? I said, mystified.

He nodded. Us, he answered. Are you sorry?

She should be sorry, silly, when she, like yourself, had it all planned.

The voice frightened me. Turning my head I saw Resi standing in the doorway of the room she said was where she intended taking her lover. I held out my hand. Quickly she glided to the side of the bed, seated herself; she was still stark naked. Leaning over me she kissed my lips. Happy, darling? she asked.

Oh, Resi, you dear! You can't know how much! and

again our lips joined. During this brief space, Ferry remained quiet, then:

This is a good chance for you to pay your compliments to her, dearest, and at the same time keep your promise.

What do you mean? I asked, hardly believing that this man could possibly know anything of what had happened between Resi and I.

Before you came into the ballroom you made Resi a certain promise, didn't you? he asked, smiling the while.

It's true, darling, whispered Resi. Ferry and I planned the whole thing before you arrived, and he was here in this very room watching us—You're not angry?

How could I be angry? Hadn't Resi planned it all for me and Ferry? Wasn't it she who made it possible for me to meet this man in the privacy of this beauitful room?

Of course I'm not sorry, or angry either, you dear, I cooed. Ferry would find it out some time, wouldn't he?

"Well," he said, "How about paying the debt?"

Here was a direct challenge. Could it be possible that Ferry sanctioned an affair between two women? Was it true that he was an epicurean? That he was willing to share me with another?

Resi seemed waiting; lying over me with her arms about me, she seemed waiting. "Does he mean it?" I asked. "Right here?"

She nodded, smiling into my eyes. "Think I wouldn't?" I asked him, turning my head and looking into his eyes.

"I'm waiting," he said. "Action is craved in this case."

There wasn't anything either of them could have suggested I wouldn't have done then. Forcing her gently off me, I turned and pressed my face into her crotch, but a moment later, she said: I'll take your word, honey, but please stop; if I go-off again, like that, I'll die. I'm sure of it!"

I pulled away. "Satisfied now?" I asked, turning to him again.

"You're a peach," he said, kissing me again and again, "and I love you, you darling!"

"What happened, dear?" I asked.

She laughed. "What didn't happen? You two no more than left the lower floor when all hell broke loose, and you should see my home now. It's a wreck."

"Oh, dear, I'm sorry," I said, "But you brought it all upon yourself, if you remember."

"Oh, I'm not complaining; it was worth it: You started a new vogue, and after this masks will be decidedly out." Then followed a description of what happened. Someone had seen his wife in the arms of another man and had beaten him terribly. This started a general fight. Several were hurt, not a few more or less seriously, and the place was a shambles.

"And where were you all this time?" I asked.

"When I wasn't watching you two lovers," she laughed, "I was in the other room" motioning toward the room she just left "in my lover's arms."

"And where is he now?" I asked. "I thought you were going to bring him in here."

She shrugged her shapely shoulders. "I haven't a derrick, so I guess I'll have to leave him there."

"Drunk?" I asked.

Ferry answered the question: "Fucked almost to death, I would say."

Resi laughed. "You're not so far wrong, my dear," she said, reaching across me and grasping his prick and shaking it. "The one I had is a single-shot affair—"

"Be careful the one you're holding doesn't fire in the air," laughed Ferry.

The spell was broken. "By their deeds ye shall know them," said a pretty golden-haired beauty, rising and stretching languidly, adding: "Hell! We all do it, and we all like it and we like having it done, too, so why make such a mystery over it?"

This girl was right in her statement. There wasn't a person in the room, girl and man alike, who wasn't a devotee to it, and I might mention here, that from that moment until the day Ferry and I left the city of Pest, the utmost freedom was indulged in.

I have seen more than one couple in a perfect "sixty-nine" without the slightest thought as to who happened to be present.

As for the Lesbian Kiss, it was just as freely bestowed. Everyone knew the relations between Rose and I: Ferry knew it and encouraged it. Does that seem strange to you, my friend? Yes?

Then let me tell you this: All over Europe groups were forming among the so-called "upper-class." Women of the smart-set, dissatisfied with the puny efforts of their husbands and lovers, were forming clubs. At first these meetings were held in secret. Later, when news began leaking out as to the type of affairs held behind doors, others wished to join, and soon one was considered strictly "out" if she wasn't a member of at least one of them.

Men, too, were forming themselves into groups. History was repeating itself. No, Rome and Greece wasn't being. outdone, if one cares to put it that way; it was simply that the wealthy and idle, living as they did in constant inactivity, found time hanging heavy on their hands. Like the women who came from Lesbos and other islands in Asia Minor, the women of Germany and Austria—and other nations as well—were practicing and introducing to others their intimate and lubricous secrets. Maids were being taught the Lesbian Kiss, and only those most expert in the art found favor with the wealthy women.

From this, nudism grew. Women were vieing with each other in indecent dress; and soon nudity became general at certain social functions—and that was the condition all about us.

Is it any wonder, then, that we took to it like ducks to a pond? Is it any wonder that we took to openly practicing our own arts? Ferry had openly declared himself by stating that his greatest pleasure was in kissing a pretty woman between her thighs: One girl, one of our own group, seconds this by stating in no uncertain terms that she loved it, both active and passive; and another, to prove her contention, takes her lover's prick between her lips and sucks him; and all this under the very eyes of a dozen persons.

Remember, my friend, much of this happened in my own apartment.

Resi spent considerable time with us; everyone knew she cared little or nothing for men, and many times during my stay in Pest, I have seen her solicit another girl and almost under our very eyes perform her most cherished rites.

I recall one afternoon in particular. Instead of being looked down upon by persons in the profession as a result of the scandalous affair at Resi's home, I was being besieged with offers to go to other cities. Managers from all over Europe (the news of Resi's ball was by this time common gossip) offered me contracts, but Ferry had prevailed upon me to hold off. His time was nearly up, he said, and when he left Paris he wanted to take me with him. That was his declaration of love, and loving him, I delayed signing a contract.

We had been living together for several weeks, and

since he had been such a constant lover in every possible way, closing his eyes against the affairs I was constantly carrying on with the girls, I thought I would give him a "banquet."

Anna, Nina and myself talked it over. The girls were delighted with the idea; it would be a fitting tribute to his faithfulness to allow him to share the love between Rose and myself.

We called Rose and asked her what she thought about it, and we couldn't help but rejoice at her eagerness to give herself to that handsome man. She had already been deflowered by the giant dildo, she was no longer a maiden—as far as a maidenhead was concerned —and we thought it fitting that she give herself to Ferry.

The afternoon in question arrived. I had told my many friends that I wished to be alone with my lover that last day and night, and they, realizing the truth of this and thinking that I was to depart from him forever, readily agreed that that was a fitting tribute.

But I wasn't alone with Ferry, as you shall see. We said nothing to Ferry regarding our plans; Resi, Anna, Nina, Rose, Ferry and myself being the only ones in on the secret. I couldn't very well omit Resi as it was she who made it possible for me to engage him.

Anna and Nina were, of course, my constant companions. They took charge of everything. A table had been laid for the occasion. Meats of the choicest cuts, foods of a highly spiced type, wines, champagne and liquors were piled about the place, and the entire apartment was littered with flowers. My bed, that bed upon which Ferry was to enjoy the nude charms of Rose, was covered with fresh cut violets.

Ferry watched these preparations but said little. Wise to the ways of women he realized that this was for him.

You have read history, my friends; you know what went on at the banquets of the ancients during Babylonian times; how Alexander the Great died of the excesses heaped upon him; how even the Armenians and Africans celebrated by giving great banquets where, after the guests had become heated with wine, they surrendered themselves to each other in every possible manner?

You have read how the women would lay aside one garment after the other until they were stark naked, and how the men, equally naked, would engage the women and girls in the most shocking manner and before the very eyes of anyone who cared to look?

Well, we went them one better. Instead of waiting till the wine had heated us, we stripped stark naked, our only article of dress being tiny rose-buds in our hair. Nudity of course was nothing new to Ferry; our guests had adapted themselves to being nude, and our apartment was seldom without at least one stark naked couple.

"Ferry, darling," I said, standing on tiptoe and embracing him, "this is to be in your honor. In a day or two we leave for parts unknown leaving our friends behind. We may never see them again, and it is for this reason I have decided to give you this party. Not only shall you feast on the good things we are to eat, but you shall banquet on the orgasmic sweets as well. Five of us have elected to provide you with every possible comfort and thrill, and all this because you have remained faithful to me when you realized I carried on a tender alliance with women and girls."

I saw his eyes sweep over us as we stood about him. "Five?" he asked, mystified. "Where is the fifth? I see but four of you."

"For days," I answered, "I have seen you watching

my maid, Rose, and I, as everyone else, have guessed your desire for her, and this day, and far into the night, you are free to enjoy her sweet and tender charms in any manner you see fit."

Our lips met in a long kiss, then: "No man could possibly be happier, my darling," he said, "than I have been with you. Your beautiful body has furnished me with pleasures I never hoped to have in the arms of a woman. You know my weaknesses, my desires, and you have offered yourself willingly and freely that I might enjoy you, so I can see no reason why I should seek other women."

"Ah, but that's no reason why you should deprive yourself of the joys we are about to so freely offer. Anna and Nina have long suffered for the feel of your splendid dart; Resi, while she has already done so, is eager for it again—she confessed it today. Then there is Rose. It isn't one in your station in life who looks with favor upon a ladies-maid, but Rose is different. Besides, the little imp will never rest until she's felt it stirring her womb and tickled her palate!"

No man was ever given a broader hint, was he, darling?

It took more than mere nudity to arouse Ferry, but at the mention of his having my pretty maid, his prick stiffened and rose against my belly. "I must, I suppose, go through with this?" he asked.

"As soon as ever we have dined," I answered leading him to table, "and after that our bodies are at your disposal to do with as you see fit! You have but to command, and the commanded one shall do as you direct!"

We drank a toast. Holding my glass on high, I said "Here's to your wonderful prick! May it this day hold its head high, that it might caress cunt and lip, and

never throughout the hours of day and night be without
our constant caresses!"

I shall not dwell upon the dinner; it has nothing to
do with what followed; it was simply a medium from
which we might keep ourselves supplied with good
things to eat and drink. The table had been laden with
the choicest fruits and candies—and we left it just as it
was, that we might return to it from time to time as
the spirit moved us.

The highly spiced wines and food had done their
work well, and this coupled with our unusually erotic
temperaments, left all of us in a very unusual mood.
Rising from the table, Ferry said: "Your party is well
received, my dears, and as long as this day has been set
aside for me, that I might enjoy myself at will, then let
us enter into the spirit of the thing with zest. Let us
give ourselves body and soul, let nothing we think of
be undone!"

To this we applauded. "Come," he said, leading us
into the front room where the others had placed two
broad couches close together.

Throwing himself down upon it and arranging us all
about him, he said: "It is understood that I am to be
master of ceremonies? That everything I propose is to
be carried out to the letter?"

We voiced our approval to this, and he went on: "In
all my travels about this great and splendid earth, of all
the peoples I have met and mingled with, and of all the
banquets and parties I have attended, I have yet to enjoy an affair like this. True, I have had women by the
score and in every conceivable position, but I have
never been the lone man among a bevy of beauties such
as your delightful selves. And so, I want to indulge my
passions to the full; I want to do things I have always

wanted to do but have never been given the opportunity of doing. May I look forward to all this?"

"Darling," I said, lying over him and kissing his lips, "you have but to command and your slightest wish shall be complied with, no matter what it is or how naughty it might be. We have tried to bring together everything to make this day of happiness and joy for you. Our own desires we have ignored, that you might have just such a day as you suggested." Turning to the others, I said: "Is that not the idea of this gathering?"

"Resi said "———— is right, Ferry dear, we have promised to do everything; this is your day. We have even provided whips, that you might indulge your sadistic fancies if you wish, and any one of us will willingly surrender our bodies."

The others voiced their approval, then he said: "Very well. Have Rose bring me that heaping dish of bonbons."

Rose, who had been standing at one side listening to all this, bounded to the table, returning a moment later with the desired dish, and this she handed to Ferry. "You," he said, looking at Resi, "shall be first, since it was you who suggested it, so come and sit here on the head of this couch."

Drunk with desire herself, her eyes flashing with inward fire, her breasts heaving with pent-up emotion, a smile on her handsome face, she did his bidding. "So," she said, seemingly satisfied as to what was to follow, "Having eaten all I can hold, I am to be stuffed otherwise—Is that it, Ferry, dear?"

"You're a good guesser, darling. Now spread your pretty legs!"

One by one he stuffed the bonbons into her lovely

crack until five had been squeezed in. Then making her hold the lips of her slit together with her fingers, that the candies might not slip out, she moved down to the foot of the couches.

The meaning of this was obvious to us all now. Making Anna take the vacated place, he performed the same rite with the smiling and happy girl. Nina was next. Having seen the other two and knowing what was to follow, she held the lips of her pretty little slit well apart and smilingly watched him slip the chocolate-covered dainties into her willing pussy. "You're next, darling," he said. But I didn't take my place as the others had done. Instead, I lay over him and smilingly watched down between my thighs as he poked and squeezed the semisoft substance into my cunt until, like the others, I had five.

Reaching over and taking one from the dish, I said: "The banquet won't be complete, dearest, without covering the adjacent parts," and I deliberately rubbed the sticky stuff up and down between the cheeks of my bottom, and what was left I rubbed through the hairs about my pussy.

You think this a strange thing to do, my friend? Yes? Well, when one considers this an ideal spot to kiss one's mistress, why not add to it by supplying something?

Arranged on the couches, our bottoms resting on the very edge and our thighs hanging down in front, and pillows heaped behind our backs that each might see the whole performance, he took his place between Resi's thighs and sucked the candies from her, while she, by simply working the inner muscles of her vagina, forced them one at a time between his waiting lips. Then, without moving from his favored position, he sucked her off.

Quickly he moved to Anna, and here he repeated the performance.

Next he took Nina—leaving her trembling as a result of his sucking kiss!

"It's time, you naughty boy," I said, lifting my thighs to his shoulders and clasping my feet together upon his back, "I can feel the sticky stuff melting within me!"

"Why shouldn't it melt," he said, "when it's the sweetest and hottest cunt in all the world!" And down went his mouth—not to leave his feast until every speck of the candy and the last drop of my jissim had been licked up!

"Now bring me Rose!" he said, throwing himself down upon the two couches, his legs well apart.

Rose, who had been watching this lascivious picture, sprang forward and settled down between his legs. We crowded about, watching, wondering what she would do now that she was face to face with the real test. But the little dear remembered her lessons. Grasping it between her hands she worked it up and down for a moment, and then she leaned down and kissed it. I saw Ferry give a start as her warm lips came to it. Leaning over I whispered in his ear: "Don't disappoint her, darling, but give it all to her."

Bending down over his belly and grasping the base of his prick in my hand, I said to Rose: "I'll hold it, dear. Put your arms about his hips and give it a good sucking and make the sap run out!"

And little Rose did just that. There wasn't the slightest doubt in the world but what she really wanted it, for she quickly took it into her mouth and sucked it. Rose, though she had never sucked a man, was no stranger to it; she had seen men and girls gamahouche each other, and she had seen Ferry and I in a similar pose, so the little dear wasn't entirely surprised when he shot his prolific spend into her mouth, not a trace of it remaining when she raised her face.

Then came the best part of the whole program. Eager and willing hands arranged her on her back. Smiling, she watched as Anna and Nina held her legs apart. Resi bent down and applied her mouth to the pinkish slit, lubricating it with her tongue. Resi didn't know that the two girls had already ravished her with the giant dildo, and was somewhat surprised when I guided the hard head to Rose's slit and watched Ferry sheath it to his balls!

If the child had ever spent a happy moment in her life, it was then when Ferry gave her the entire length of it and fucked her with long, powerful strokes. It was, as Ferry had often said, like all cunnies, in that it stretched beautifully and squeezed his prick in a firm and powerful clasp.

And so we spent the afternoon. That evening we adjourned to my bed, and here, amid the flowers, we abandoned ourselves in every possible way, and always Rose played a prominent part.

Too tired to continue, we listened to stories. When its erotic nature failed to do the trick, one of us would lean over and suck his cock to a state of erection. It was nine o'clock, perhaps, when Ferry made a strange announcement: "With everything in the world to make a man happy, there's still one thing missing," he said.

Wondering what in the would it could be, I said: "You have but to name it, darling, and I shall produce it for you."

"If I thought you could I would demand it."

"What is it?" Resi asked.

"It's a man. A handsome young man!"

"A man?" I asked, hardly believing my ears.

He nodded. "I suppose it's terrible, but I can't help

it. For years I've thought about it. I have talked with men who delight in it, and always they tell me the same thing; that I'll never know what a real thrill is until I have had a young man."

The quick-witted Nina came to the rescue, as it were. "Why not?" she asked. "Women and girls like to suck each other, so why should not Ferry satisfy his desire and have what he wants?"

"Why not? Why not, indeed?"

"But, Ferry, my darling," I cried, "where ever shall we get such a man?"

"Bah!" he scoffed. "The place is full of them. I'll bet I could get a dozen in a few minutes!"

With a bound I was out of bed. I summoned a maid. In brief I told her my needs and she, having received many presents from me, hurried off to bring a man to us. I'll never forget the expression on his face when I greeted him. I saw his eyes sweep over me, for I was naked.

"You would earn a hundred marks?" I asked in a low tone for I didn't want the others to hear. "And you will forget all about it afterward? Never mention to anyone what you will see or do?" He agreed to everything.

"Then strip off your clothes; I want you to be stark naked!"

I believe I never saw a man undress so quickly. Grasping me in his arms, he said "I wouldn't need a hundred marks to fuck you, young lady!"

"Very well," I said, "Then do as you are told; forget everything afterward, and you'll have not only the hundred marks, but I'll promise to let you fuck me before you leave!"

I thought this the best way in winning him over to our needs, and the good-looking fellow would have gone through fire and water for a promise like that.

But another surprise awaited him when I led him into the bedroom and he caught sight of the other four girls lying about one nude man. "I shouldn't wonder you'd want another man," he said, a wild gleam in his eye.

Then I explained his duties. He seemed surprised, but went willingly enough to the bed, and straddling over Ferry's chest quickly surrendered his prick to Ferry's lips. No foolishness here. Ferry had been sincere. It was, to his everlasting credit, the very first time he had ever had a man like that, and like most men who try it, he liked it; he made no bones about it whatever.

Indeed, he sucked-off the man three times that night—

The following morning, long after the others had departed leaving Rose and I alone with him, Ferry said: "I suppose you'll think me a brute, dear, but I'm looking forward to another affair with a man some time. It was the most thrilling thing I've ever had."

I sympathized with him, of course, but I was in hopes he would forget all about it; I felt quite capable of taking care of all his needs.

And so we bid farewell to our friends in Pest. Resi took Rose and made a lady of her. I learned some time later that she married a handsome man and was well-to-do.

I wonder if she ever thinks of me?

Ferry had many friends, and during our journey south, which was to take us into the Balkans where we were to visit several countries, we talked of them. In Vienna I expected to head a company in a new opera, but Ferry had asked me to hold off, and because of him I did so. In Belgrade we were hailed like incoming heroes; everybody had heard of my affairs in Pest, and everyone, or so it seemed was, anxious to greet me.

Installed in the leading hotel in the great city, I began receiving guests, and one of the first to call was a lady of the Austrian Court. She bore a letter from an official high in Governmental affairs, and the letter was to the effect that my presence was wanted at Court at the earliest possible moment.

"What does this mean?" I asked Ferry, handing him the letter.

"You'd better go," he answered, "or the old boy'll be sore."

I could gain nothing by questioning the Court girl, so I wrote an answer making an appointment for the following day.

Frightened half out of my wits I entered the Palace only to find that my presence was needed not by the man who had wrote the letter, but by the Emperor himself.

Now it must be remembered that at the time I write of the Court of Austria, the whole country had gone mad over some sort or other of cults, free-love cults being more in vogue than any known other.

Presiding over the Court was one "Duc de ———" (it is best to hide his name) who was considered by everyone as a leader in this cult-craze. It was also whispered that he was, besides being a despoiler of maidenheads, a man-lover and kept several handsome young men about the Court for his especial entertainment when so moved.

I had learned, too, that the Court ladies were made up of the prettiest women in Belgrade, that their love affairs were carried on under the very eyes of the Emperor who sanctioned it, and that they were maintained within the summer palace chiefly because they were unusually beautiful and their willingness to adapt the unusual undress worn by the ladies of the Court.

At last, after a ten minute wait, I was delivered into the hands of the famous Duc de ————. I found him charming enough, and had it not been for the fact that I already had a lover, I could have fallen in love with him. Finally, after leading up to the subject by degrees, he said "Our Emperor is planning a great ball at the summer palace here and desired your esteemed presence. Having heard your remarkable voice and witnessed your performance of Juliette, some time ago, he is desirous of having you as part of his entertainment." After a short pause, as though he were waiting for this to sink in, he continued: "You have no objection of appearing in such a scene wearing, of course, your stage costume?"

I smiled at this. "Why—I—I don't know," I answered. "The costume you refer to is—well, rather, what shall we say—brief, and I'm afraid such a costume would hardly do for a private theatrical. You see—"

"That," he said, "is the very reason our Emperor desires your presence. The costume, as you refer to it, should, if you wish to please our monarch, be even more brief."

I laughed outright this time. "Then I'm afraid it will be a near thing," I answered. "If I were to wear any less, I'm afraid the Emperor would have me thrown out—"

"The Emperor would enjoy it, on the other hand, if you would consent to appear in the nude."

"And where is this entertainment to be held?" I asked.

He seemed to take this question as an acceptance on my part, for he said: "The performance is to be held here in the Palace. Your partner—Romeo, if you prefer —is a handsome young actor, and a great favorite of the Emperor. You will like him I'm sure."

"And *his* costume?" I asked, smiling.

Instead of answering this direct, he reached over and patted my hand in an affectionate manner, then: "You do not seem to understand our Emperor, my dear. We have at the moment the Russian Ballet consisting of sixty members; an aerial act consisting of fifteen persons; a comedy act consisting of six more, and they all perform in the nude. Does that shock you, my dear?"

I laughed. "Pardon me," I said. "I wasn't laughing at that; I was just thinking how strange I would look wearing a costume, when the others perform stark naked. I *would* be out of place."

"Then it's agreed?" he asked, leaning across the table.

I shrugged my shoulders. "Is one in the habit of denying your Emperor?"

He seemed to take this question as acceptance.

The Duc, I mention here, was a Frenchman, his close connection with the nobility having been brought about by his willingness and eagerness to seek out and provide the most startling entertainment for the Court. Knowing the vast hordes of beautiful women about the palace were nothing more or less than whores who, like the Emperor and his right-hand man Duc de ————, were more than willing to do their part toward assisting in the scandal forever creeping out to a suffering public, I became more bold. I said: "I would prefer not to attend alone—You have no objection to my lover escorting me to and from the palace?" This was part suggestion and part question.

He pouted, inclined his head. "Is it necessary?" he asked. "You are expected to assist in the private entertainment for our Emperor, after your formal appearance, and—well, wouldn't the presence of—your lover, as you prefer to refer to him, be somewhat unusual?"

Such, my friend, was the state of affairs one found within the "circle" during those days. Without going

further into the details of the whole affair let me close
this part of the history by saying that I attended the
"party" in honor of the Emperor, and that two days
afterward, Ferry and I made a timely exit from the fashionable city, to the great displeasure of the Court.

We had intended spending a few more days there,
but, as I have said, we thought it best to leave. It wasn't
that I objected to the attention paid me; it was because
I knew it hurt Ferry.

And because there are other things to relate, events of
far greater importance to tell you, let us skip all this
and take up the thread of the story as to what happened a few days later.

We crossed the border into Serbia, and while the
Court here was no less impure than that of Austria,
there was far less scandal and gossip.

Wishing to be alone for a change, we took a delightful villa in a quiet section of the city Widin. Close to
the river Danube, we found it a delightful spot, and
here we spent several weeks, and they were, I believe,
the most pleasant I had ever experienced.

We journeyed into Bulgaria, stopping here and there,
enjoying the country and its restful climate. But now
Ferry became restless; something was on his mind. "I'm
worried," he said in answer to my questions. "Today I
saw an agent connected with the secret police of the
Austrian government."

"But what shall we do?" I asked, now a little worried.
We had done nothing to arouse the dislike of those
people. I expressed my thoughts to Ferry. "You don't
understand," he said. "It is not what we have done, it's
what you *haven't* done."

"Me?" I asked, surprised.

"Yes," he answered. "You don't know it, my dear,
but our friend, the Emperor, was disappointed with

your sudden departure from the summer palace, and he's not one to be brooked in his desires. Tomorrow we leave for Roumania. I have friends there."

That night, lying in each other's arms, we talked of all this.

He told me of a wonderful people he had met in a mountain just outside the city of Silistria; how I would love them. They were gypsies, he said, and though they were known outlaws and were almost constantly sought by the police, they were a friendly, kind and generous people. He had met them while busily engaged in writing a book, and though he had been held in a sort of bondage, he one day rescued the young son of one of the chiefs of the tribe, and as a result he had been accepted as a "blood-brother" to the tribe and was always welcome. "Besides," he said, holding me close and kissing passionately my lips and eyes, "you will find them the greatest lovers in the world."

I laughed. "And what would I do with lovers?" I asked. "Haven't I you? And did I not run away from wealth and Royalty so that you alone would possess me?"

"And didn't you give me Rose?" he countered. "Did you not allow me to satisfy my desires between her snowy thighs, just to make me happy? Oh, no, dear, it is my turn now. Once we get into the mountain fastness of these people and are conducted to their camp, I want you to indulge yourself to your heart's content."

Then followed a detailed description of their mode of living; their habits and loves; how they lived and practiced—openly—free-love, and how I would be expected to adapt their methods of living. He told me they were the most beautiful people on earth; that they practiced sanitation in all its phases, and how upon entering their fastess one must sacrifice himself, or herself, to some member of the opposite sex, as this was the only manner in which they could be positive of one's loyalty to them.

Strangely enough, I began looking forward to visiting these strange people. There was a certain amount of hardship one must endure before entering the abode, he said, but after that it was the nearest approach to heaven he had ever known.

And so I found myself eager to get under way; something about the whole affair interested me. I cared nothing of the so-called hardship. He had failed to explain this, and I had cared little about it.

Three days' travel by cart and stage brought us to the city of Silistria. This, as you know, is also located close to the river Danube and is famous for its delightful climate, and here we rested two days. Safe in Roumania at last, we felt more secure. We had shaken off the police, I hoped, forever.

Two days' travel by the most primitive methods brought us far into the mountains, and here our deliverers refused to go further. They shook their heads and gazed off toward the distant hills; nothing we could offer would entice them further.

"We will leave our baggage here," Ferry said, "and take with us but the clothing we are wearing. Come."

On foot we wandered on our way. I put explicit faith in Ferry; I knew he would never sanction this trip were there any possible danger connected with it, and since I had agreed to do and say everything he suggested, I followed him up the steep paths through the dense wood. We had started early that morning, and it was mid-afternoon when we were suddenly confronted by what I believed to be the most blood-thirsty creature I had ever had the misfortune to meet.

He came forward, and I had an opportunity to study the man.

Large, slightly darker than I had expected, great gold rings in his ears, black, curly hair fell beneath a wide leather hat. His worst feature, perhaps, was a wicked cast to one eye; he was the most murderous-looking person I had ever seen.

"Be not afraid," suggested Ferry. "He is but one of the guards, and as soon as he learns our business here, we will be conducted further into the wood where we shall meet an escort who will take us directly into their camp."

The "brute"—for that's what he looked like to me—asked many questions, and finally, having been convinced that we were not police, he conducted us along the path to an opening, or clearing, in the dense forest, and directed us along, pointing out the path we must follow. Quite without warning we came to a bend in the wooded path, and here, directly before us, was a stream.

Ferry saw the look of mystery in my eyes. Laughingly, he said: "This is the first hardship I referred to," and nodding toward the water, continued: "We have got to cross it."

I had hardly expected this. I said: "But it's deep, darling! How shall we ever cross without wetting our clothing?"

He laughed; kissed me. "One doesn't cross without wetting their clothes, my dear," he said. "If we were to enter the stronghold of these hospitable people wearing dry clothing, we would be laughed to scorn, and I wish to impress them with your willingness to comply with their scheme of things."

I looked down into the water at my feet. It looked black, and I could swim but little. Then another thought gripped me. Ferry, I knew, was a good swimmer, so there would be no danger of anything happening to me. I recalled the delight I had had back home, and how I had often gone into the pond fully dressed. I recalled how one Sunday, returning from Sunday school, I was overcome with the desire to go into the pond, and how without waiting to remove my little jacket, I splashed my way into the thing! The thought thrilled me! Why not? It's dreadfully warm, and the water would feel good on my body!

All these thoughts passed through my mind in a moment. Raising my eyes to his, I said "Very, well, my dear. I am ready when *you* are."

"You can swim?" he asked, and when I told him that I swam but little but was not afraid of the water, he said: "That will make it ever so much easier. I'll go first, and then I'll assist you down, and by resting your finger-tips on my shoulders, I will be able to get you across. Ready?"

Nodding my answer, Ferry turned and dove in. It was all very unusual, I'll admit, but we were like two wild children bent upon doing something devilish, and I for one was as eager as any child could have been. Coming up and shaking the water from his hair, he came back to the steep bank directly beneath my feet.

"Alright, honey," he said, smiling up into my eyes. "Lower your pretty little feet and I'll help you down."

"You won't!" I cried, a daring thought coming into my mind. "I'm going to jump! Catch me!" and without another thought I leaped down! I thought I would never come up, but at last I did, and then I found Ferry's strong arms about me. Happy, my eyes bright with the novelty of the thing, I laughed and shook the water from my hair, and a moment or two later we were across and standing upon the sandy bottom. Turning to look at the opposite side, I saw the villainous-looking creature we had first encountered staring at us. Raising my arm and waving to him, I was surprised to see him smile. I had thought him incapable of smiling, and after gazing at us for another moment, he turned and walked off and out of sight.

Standing tittie-deep, I unloosened my hair letting it fall about my shoulders. "Like it?" asked Ferry, smiling and coming close by me.

"I love it!" I cried, kissing him rapturously, "I could stay right here forever and ever! Oh, Ferry!" I cried, "I'm going into every creek and pool I ever see! No matter what the occasion or what manner of dress I'm wearing, I promise I'll plunge into the very first body of water I see!"

You have heard of a person having a fetish? One possessed with a thought or object above all else? Yes? Well, going into the water fully dressed had become a fetish with me. Then and there, standing in that unknown stream, I had become a slave to my fetish!

I told Ferry of it. He said: "You'll have plenty of chance, my dear. Remember, we've got to return through this same stream."

I had thought when I first discovered that we had to cross the stream that we would undress, and now, that I found something to entertain me, I was glad we hadn't undressed.

Climbing out and standing upon the sandy shore, my thin clothing clinging to me, I looked a sight, every line and curve of my body standing out in bold relief. "You might as well be naked, my dear," Ferry said. "That's the way I wish to be," I answered. "I want your friends to see me just as I am."

"I want them to see you just as you are, my dear. I want them to see your beautiful body, and I want you to display it willingly. "And above all, I want you to surrender to them; I want you to do as the others do. In a few moments we shall come upon their camp. Here the chief will embrace you. I want you to return his embraces, lend yourself to him in every possible way, accept any suggestion he might make; in short, you are to enter there with open mind; give yourself to them body and soul."

"And supposing this man, whoever he is, wants to fuck me?" I asked smiling.

"You are to do that, also," he answered.

"Then," I said with a toss of my head, "I hope he's better looking than the brute back there," pointing in the rear. Then moving along toward the sought-for camp, I said: "And you? I suppose you will flirt madly with some black-eyed damsel and fall an easy victim to her charms?"

"You don't understand, my dear," he said. "A man and woman entering here never violates a written rule —that of fucking his own mistress."

"Indeed," I smilingly answered, "It sounds interesting. But even though I surrender to another man, my dear, I will try to think it you I'm clasping between my thighs!"

Happy, contented, we hurried along the path, chatting every step of the way, and soon we came into a clearing, and instantly we were surrounded by a score of chattering children. One, more handsome than the others, made his way through them. Like the others he was naked save a cord about his neck, a gold-piece dangling from it.

His eyes brightened at sight of us. This, I was to learn a moment later, was the boy Ferry had rescued from a great bear, and after a most affectionate greeting, during which Ferry and the boy exchanged the most affectionate kisses, he ran off shouting to the top of his voice. The other children, seeing the welcome, began dancing and shouting about us, and amid this happy, carefree mob, we were led into the camp proper.

A giant of a man stepped out. He was a handsome man; his black hair hanging in clusters of curls about his handsome head. About his hips he wore a great bearskin; he wore it in such a manner that it covered but one leg; he was otherwise naked.

He greeted Ferry with the greatest of respect, kissing his lips very much as the boy had done. This giant had come from a low-roofed building without sides, the roof being held by a dozen or more posts. From it others were emerging. A quick glance showed them dressed very much like the large man, though not a few of them were without the slightest thread of covering, men and women alike.

Then Ferry and the giant having completed their greeting, turned to me. The giant's face lighted with smiles. "My mistress," Ferry said, by way of introduction, and instantly the other placed his great palms under my arms and lifted me off my feet. Holding at arm's length as though I were a baby, he said: "She's dressed! You know what that means, my friend?"

Ferry smilingly nodded. "That's why I insisted upon swimming the stream full dressed," he said.

Still holding me aloft, the giant said: "She's beautiful! And is she a good fuck?" This frightened me a little, but Ferry quickly answered: "She *is* beautiful. And lying deep between her lilly-white thighs you'll find a heaven of delight."

"Then," cried the giant, setting me down on my feet, "I proclaim her my bride for the night." And slipping the rope from about his hips he let drop the skin, a simple operation which left him quite naked. Others, now, came forward. "Take her away," said the giant, nodding in the general direction of another and smaller building close to the large one.

Ferry followed me, and just as we were entering the building, a beautifully formed girl stepped before him. She was stark naked.

Raising her arms about his neck and pressing amorously against him, she said: "My dear frieind—you forget Nattie?"

Ferry held her close, kissed her lips. "Of course I haven't, Nattie, and since you are without your badge of servitude I know you are engaged for tonight, but tomorrow," he continued, "you shall be my bride."

I heard no more. The girls into whose hands I found myself escorted me into what proved to be a sleeping-room. Many beds were arranged about the outer side, but the center was void of furnishings, and her dexterous fingers soon freed me from my wet garments. Naked from top to toe, I stood there among them. Towels dried me. My hair was combed and dried; hands patted and caressed me. "You are tired after your journey?" asked one of them in almost perfect German. Nodding my answer, one of them arranged a bed for me, and a moment later I lay full length upon it, the others kneeling all about me, smiling and patting my white body and thighs.

One went to the lower end of the bed and massaged my feet.

"You are a very fortunate girl," said another.

"Fortunate?" I asked, smiling. "I do not understand."

"For having been chosen by our king," she went on. "It is a great honor to be chosen by our king. He is a wonderful man, and tonight he will make you very, very happy—here," touching my pussy-hairs.

I was dreadfully tired, but as they continued to hover

about, and not wishing to offend them, I said: "You speak as though you were well acquainted with his charms. Tell me; has he ever cuddled you in his arms a whole night?"

"Once," came the quick answer. "He spends a night with every girl once. If he takes a fancy to some particular one he chooses her a second time. Otherwise he has her but once."

I noted among other things that one or two of them wore the usual skin affair about their hips; the others were stark naked. In answer to my question regarding this, one of them said: "Those of us who are without covering have been chosen for the night. Those of us you see wearing clothing have yet to be chosen."

"Which means," I said, smiling "that you are going to spend tonight in some man's arms?"

She smilingly nodded. "We spend every night in some man's bed."

"And what do you do throughout the long hours of the day?" I asked.

"They are not long hours," she answered. "They are all too short. From sunrise to dark we play and sing and dance. Sometimes we swim in the lake, or romp through the woods with our lovers. At night the men light great fires, then we sit about these and sing or dance and make love."

"And do you not ever make love in the daytime?" I asked, interested in this strange though straight-forward girl.

"Oh, yes. That is one of the many ways we spend so many happy hours together. We are taught to please the men when we are very young."

"And supposing," I said, looking very naughty, "you are unfortunate enough not to entice a man to your arms; then what?"

She smiled at this, then: "Then we flirt with them and make them go with us into the wood."

"And what do you do when you are with your lovers?"

"Anything he wishes us to do," came the ready and innocent answer.

"And am I supposed to do anything with the man who has chosen me for tonight?" I asked.

They all laughed at this. Then my new friend said: "You will find out tonight. A great banquet will be served, and afterward you will entertain us by lying with our king."

I wondered at this. Could it be possible, I thought, that I was to be offered to that handsome giant under the very eyes of all of them? I said: "But I supposed I was to spend the night in his bed with him. I would greatly dislike to have him fuck me before everyone."

They seemed greatly surprised at this. They exchanged startled looks, then one of them said: "Has not your friend told you of what we do? How we live?" And when I told her I knew very little regarding their ways, she said: "Be not afraid; we consider it a great honor when our king—what do you call it?—fucks us so everyone can see. After that every man wants to fuck us, and that makes us very happy."

The simplicity of the girl's statement was nothing short of refreshing. Here was a tribe of people who lived for the very joy of living; giving themselves to any man who desired their favors.

Nothing hidden. A passionate, high-strung people living a life of utmost freedom and ease with no other aim in life other than to make men love them; a people, as near as I could understand it, who gave themselves under the very eyes of brother and sister—Surely there must be something more to this than mere contact with men.

It was, as I was to find out a few hours later, a sort of ritual among these people. Instead of going at the business in secret and making a mockery of the thing, it was looked upon as a high honor.

"Very well," I thought, "I don't understand it very clearly, but I'll show these people that I, too, can enter into the spirit of the thing with the same freedom as themselves. If I'm supposed to accept the embraces of this or any other man, and I'm supposed to accept it in public, then I'll show them that I am not afraid! I shall join in the feasts, I shall sing and dance, I shall flirt with these men and, if I mistake not, I shall teach these handsome girls a thing or two they do not know!"

"You had best sleep," one of them said, handing me a glass of aromatic liquor. Then I seemed to drift off into peaceful rest.

When I awakened I found many changes. In the first place it was dark beneath the roof, but outside the whole place was lighted by many bonfires.

"You are rested?" asked a low voice close beside me. Turning I saw against the bright light the same well-spoken girl I had conversed with earlier in the afternoon.

"Much, thank you," I answered, patting her hand which rested on the side of the bed.

I stretched languidly. "I have slept long?" I asked.

"A few hours," she said. "It is nothing."

I took this for granted that she had remained by my side, and when I asked her this, she said: "I would have stayed anyway, but it was because our king demanded it."

"Why?" I asked, smiling up into her eyes.

She shrugged her shoulders, then: "So no other man would make love to you."

"Speak plain," I said. "I do not like riddles. What

you mean is, that you watched over me so no other man than your king would fuck me. Isn't that it?"

She smiled, nodding her head.

"Do you like to fuck?" I asked. Perhaps it was due to my unusual position among these people; maybe it was on account of my strangely erotic temperament and the thoughts that I was to enter into the orgy which to follow, but whatever caused it I felt dreadfully naughty; I believed I had never felt quite so much so, and I awaited her answer. "Sit here," I said before she could answer my previous question, and as she perched herself on the bed beside me I placed one hand on the smooth skin of her well-turned thigh and gently patted it. "You are very beautiful," I continued as a surge of lust swept over me, "and if I were a man I would consider myself lucky indeed if I were allowed to fuck you."

She smiled her prettiest, then: "It isn't the men who are the lucky ones, it is us, we women, who are lucky, for sometimes we have to tease them before they will fuck us. But come; the feast is about ready, and we must not keep our king waiting."

She led the way outside, and here I saw men with great arm's full of wood hurrying toward the various fires where other men piled it on, each heavy stick throwing great quantities of sparks high in the air. Everywhere I saw girls and young men in groups, talking or singing; children were gaily chasing each other about the place, and everyone was naked. The fire cast flickering shadows over their bronzed bodies, red lips and flashing eyes in evidence everywhere.

I stopped. "Where is my partner of the night?" I asked, smiling.

"I am taking you to him now," she answered. "He is waiting in yonder temple," pointing to a building directly ahead.

The soft pine needles felt as soft as the softest carpet beneath my feet, for it must be remembered that like my friend I was stark naked. Entering the low-roofed structure I saw the "king" at the far end reclining on a broad couch-like affair. He was lying on a mattress of skins, and beside him sat Ferry. A beautiful girl sat on the latter's knees, and a half dozen other girls were perched about the king. All were naked and were listening to the strains of a guitar,

Suddenly the king saw me. "Come!" he cried, brushing the others off like so much chaff. I hurried to the bed, threw myself down beside him and into his waiting arms. "She's beautiful, Ferry, my good friend!" cried the king, kissing and petting me in the most brazen manner. His great hands slid all over me, patting and gently pinching the flesh of my bottom, thighs, belly and breasts.

Everybody was happy and gay. "She's just as I told you, my king," cried Ferry, "but wait until you get between her powerful thighs and your great prick deep into her belly and then you'll think her beautiful!" It was plain to be seen that Ferry had partaken deeply of the powerful wines they brewed, for in the flickering light I could see the flush on his handsome face.

"And that, my good friend, won't be long!" cried the king. "See! They are already erecting the great bed upon which your mistress will pay her debt to the king where she will taste this!" carrying my hand down to his great prick and about which I wasn't long in clasping my fingers, though I couldn't span it.

My presence evidently had had its effect on the king, for his prick was as stiff as a board, and a thrill passed through me as I worked the loose skin up and down, and though it wasn't quite as long as the Russian warden's, I wondered how I was ever to take it all! I saw

Ferry making frantic motions; wondering what he could mean it was some little time before I comprehended. I noted, too, that the others were staring at me, as though they awaited something. I looked at Ferry again; this time I could hardly miss his signal! I felt the color come into my cheeks as I said: "And you, *my* king, are handsome, too, and I shall consider it a great honor, indeed, to share your bed this night, that I might possess—this!" and bending down I kissed the great, heart-shaped head!

I wasn't at all sure that I hadn't done a dreadful thing, but I was reassured when the others applauded convincing me that this had quite won me a place in their hearts.

A great bell boomed out its signal that the feast was ready, and we scampered like a lot of unruly children toward the banquet board.

These people may have had a certain amount of savagery in their souls, but they knew how to entertain their guests. Great tables had been brought forth and erected in the clearing, the entire place being illuminated by the soaring flame of the great fires.

At the end of the first table a place had been reserved for the king and I, as his "bride of the night," held the seat of honor at his right, the seat being elevated to a point where everyone could see us. The seat we sat upon was covered with the choicest skins of silver foxes, and the white-tipped, unplucked hairs tickled and caressed my naked bottom and back. Great platters of roast venison, boar and lamb were set before us. Tankards of highly spiced wines and liquors sat within easy reach of everyone. Bread, biscuits and rolls, nuts, figs and grapes were piled everywhere. A string band furnished music, voices, as clear as silver bells, echoed and re-echoed through the forest lending a bacchantic atmosphere to the scene. Old crones replaced the men who had attended the fire, and these, now joined with girls, were seated at table.

Children, boys and girls alike, were scattered through the groups or were lifted to the table tops where they assisted the others in the selection of foods: Indeed, one would have to witness the scene before they could get the full significance of it all.

Everyone was laughing, playing. Kisses were exchanged, hands groped everywhere. Ferry and his "bride of the night" sat on our left and they, as though to inspire the others to greater freedom, were indulging between mouthfuls of food and drink in the wildest revelry. I was beginning to fear the result of all this, but the king reassured me; the revelry, he said, was at its height, there was nothing else to do but copy their acts.

The singing voices broke into a sort of chant, weird, eerie and lewd. The voices continued, each stanza more and more indelicate.

Now the entire assemblage took it up; bodies swayed; feminine heads rested on masculine shoulders; men's hands toyed with and fondled naked breasts, their own hands stroking the now erect pricks of their partners. I saw Ferry's partner raise her cherry-red lips to his, saw their tongues mingle and twine about each other's, saw one of her hands capping and uncapping the ruby head of his prick!

"It's the mating song," whispered the king, lifting my left thigh across his right and slipping his hand into my fully exposed crotch and toying with my aching pussy! No longer afraid, I rested my head on his shoulder, gave him my lips, my left hand falling to his great, stiff prick!

Mad with an unknown lust, I drew my mouth away.

"I love you!" I cried, redoubling the motion of my hand.

"You are ready?" he asked, his voice low and kindly. "Ready to make the sacrifice to Venus? See?" he continued, pointing toward a group who were placing a great skin-decked bed-like affair in the very center of the clearing, "They are preparing the altar upon which you are expected to receive me. You are ready?"

It was a strange situation, I tell you. I had attended many strange and weird affairs; I had seen scores of men and women in every conceivable position and pose, and I have taken part in many strange and erotic affairs, but I had never been called upon to play a part in an affair like this. The significance of it all was plain: These people, bandits though they were, lived for the real joy of living, lived in an atmosphere of love and idleness, giving themselves to pleasure in the utmost freedom. Why, then, should I be afraid? Why shouldn't I, unknown to them as I was, give msyelf in a like manner? I would never see them again; they knew not that I was a primadonna sought after by Royalty, indulged and petted by the "elite" of Europe, looked upon as a shining light in society—all they knew was that I was their guest, that I was to sacrifice myself on the altar placed in the firelight that they might become more and more inspired to deeds to greater lust!

"Afraid?" I asked, gazing into his large, dark eyes. "Why should I be afraid? I love you. I love this" giving his prick another shake "and I want it as I have never wanted anything in my life!"

It was the last expiring acknowledgment of a surrendered modesty, if there was a spark of it left within my soul, and I thrilled anew as this handsome giant lifted me and carried me to the waiting groups assembled now about the great bed.

Though I was overcome with a lust I had never felt, I looked about me and saw many strange things. The elder women—hags, they called them—had disappeared as though by magic, and everywhere the younger ones were forming into pairs and were selecting advantageous points from which to watch the sacrifice of my body to the cult of Venus.

Placing me upon the great bed, the king lay down beside me, and now the music struck up another and stranger strain. It was, perhaps, to inspire me, and if so then it was a huge success—for there before their very eyes and in the leaping of the great fires I gave myself to him! Never shall I forget the thrill as he lay over me and drove that bone-hard tool into my vitals!

My mouth pressed to his, my arms clasped about his back, I raised my thighs and clasped them about his middle—and the battle began.

Voices seemed to float away in the great, dim distance, and in their place there came a tinkling of silvery bells. This was my imagination, of course. The voices had never ceased the naughty chant, I only thought they had; the ringing bells had been brought about by the feel of that lovely dart sliding in and out of my warm slit, each inward thrust making the great head caress my heart—at least it seemed so—each vigorous poke rousing a new sensation within my aching womb! A shiver passed through me as I went-off!

Again and again the warm balm flowed down keeping the warm pathway lubricated for the piston-like rammer which glided in and out, in and out with a steady cadence—Twice the handsome fellow went-off into the very depths of my soul before he relieved me of his weight—.

Our example had been copied by the others, and everywhere couples were swaying in each other's arms, heads were pressed between the thighs of the girls, here and there cherry-red lips paid homage to a partner's erect tool—

Ah, my friend, these people may have been savage, they might have lacked the refinements of life, but they knew how to partake of the pleeasures of sex.

As I was raised from the bed and carried to the king's abode I saw acts of the tenderest dalliance.

In his temple, as he called it, another bed awaited us. Alone now, I gave myself up to maddening pleasure with greater freedom. Mad with lust for that wonderful weapon I covered it with kisses, took the head between my lips and sucked it! I felt myself lifted up and astride his up-turned face, felt his face, as smooth as that of a girl, glide between my widely parted thighs and his lips come against my slit! In a perfect position to carry out the delightful act of love we abandoned ourself to the task at hand! Again I went-off, his greedy lips taking all I offered! I felt him tremble beneath me, I felt the base of his lovely rammer grow stout and leap within my mouth—and a moment later I received such a dose of his scalding fluid as to quite smother me—

But such deeds are but the prelude to greater and better acts.

That night I was fucked in a dozen different positions, and it was long after the hour of midnight before we settled down to rest.

Such, my friend, was my initiation into the mysteries of an outlaw camp. A beautiful breakfast awaited us as we emerged from his hut, and we settled down to a much-needed repast.

Here I noted another strange thing. Most of the girls and young men wore the customary skin about their hips; not over a dozen were without them. A question brought an answer to this.

"Those wearing them are free to choose partners for the coming night; those without have already been chosen."

It was a very pretty arrangement, I thought. I said: "But I have none. Does that signify that I have already been chosen by some man?"

"You were chosen last night," he answered. "Such a beauty as yourself was meant only for a king."

And so I spent my first full day in camp. But that didn't mean that I wasn't free to go and come as I chose. Indeed not. Shortly after our breakfast a group of radiant girls rushed me off into the thick forest and to a beautiful, sandy-bottomed lake. It was the morning bath, they said. Those without the skin rushed into the water; those with them simply dropped them about their feet and followed.

Soon a happy, mad crowd was splashing about in the refreshing water. We were joined by several men, and the hilarious gathering indulged in amorous play of every sort. Men whispered naughty words in my ears, suggestive little questions, but I refused them all.

I have been chosen by the king, I said, and after that I was left quite alone with the girls. The beautiful girl who had sat by my bed the previous afternoon seemed to be my constant companion; she drew me off to one side and out of hearing.

"You are happy?" she smilingly asked, leading me into deeper water.

"I love it," I answered. "I wish I could stay here for ever and ever. It is beautiful!"

"You like our king?" she asked, and when I told her I thought him wonderful, she said: "He must love you to want you for two consecutive nights—it is seldom he chooses one for more than a single night."

"Perhaps it's due to my white skin?" I suggested, to

which she shook her head. "I do not believe so," she answered. "Many white girls come here that they might share his great love but seldom does he have them a second night."

"Then I give it up," I laughed. "I am no different than any other; there are many of you far more beautiful than I. There must be another reason."

"There is," came the ready answer. Her eyes bored into mine, as though something was on her mind. "You like the caresses he bestowed between your legs?"

"Naughty girl," I cooed, slipping my arms about her and drawing her into deeper water. "Of course I like it; every girl likes to be kissed like that. But how did you know he did *that* to me?"

She smilingly shrugged her shoulders. "That he has chosen you for another night proves it; he chooses only those he likes, that way."

"Has he ever chosen you—that way?" I asked, pressing my belly against hers and holding her tightly in my arms.

She nodded her answer though the color deepened in her cheeks.

"You like it?" I asked.

"I love it! I adore it! The feel of a lover's tool is so much more acute after one has been kissed like that!" The girl was radiant now. Her full, well-formed breasts rested just above the surface of the clear water, their pink points arousing within me a desire to kiss and caress them! I said: "You're right, dear, with your king I had no other than to accept him in any manner he chose to have me, but were I to have my choice of the most handsome men on earth I would choose only those who would kiss and caress my cunt before allowing him to put it into me!"

This girl must have noted the strange light in my

eyes; she must have fathomed my desire, for she said: "Let us walk through the forest; we'll see many pretty sights, and afterward I shall show you my secret love-bower!" There was a tenseness in her voice that led me to believe I was to be let into a secret.

I would have kissed her had she not told me kisses between like-sexes were forbidden.

Through the forest we saw many couples, but we passed them by, but I saw enough to know that nights alone were not reserved for the pleasures of the bed; sights which in no way dimmed the desire I felt rising within me.

Slipping between the trees, she looking back as though desirous to hide our action from the sight of others, we went deeper and deeper, and soon we were alone. Suddenly she stopped, clasped me in her arms. "You will promise you shall never reveal my secret?" she asked, her eyes bright and shining, her breasts heaving.

I promised everything she asked, wondering the while what next I was to see. I hadn't long to wait. With a final look around, she drew me beneath a vine-like density, and here I received shock number one, for cuddled on a pile of skins was Ferry and his partner of the previous night, and they were naked!

"Is this the surprise you planned for me?" I asked, staring at her, wonder showing in my eyes. The other girl, a beautiful blackhaired beauty, jumped up, embraced me. "Don't be angry, dear," she whispered, "but Ferry has told me everything!"

"Everything?" I asked, hardly knowing what he had told her.

"Everything!" she answered. "Secret kisses are forbidden, but here, in this little bower, we may indulge our desires in any manner we please!"

Still puzzled as to why all this secrecy among a peo-

ple who took their pleasure where and when they liked,
I looked down at Ferry. He was smiling. "Don't be angry, my dear," he cooed, sliding one hand up my thigh
and patting my bottom. "Knowing your desire for a
pretty girl now and then, and having exchanged secrets
last night, we arranged this little meeting for you, and
here we might give ourselves without stint."

For a long moment I gazed down at him. Then I
turned my gaze on my friend. I said: "Naughty. Why
didn't you tell me why you were bringing me here,
when all the time you must have known I wanted this,"
slipping my hand into the black fleece on her lower
belly.

It is needless to go into the details of what happened
that day.

Instead of returning for the noonday meal, we remained in that tiny vine-covered, moss-decked bower. It
was exactly as my friend called it. A love-bower, it was,
if ever I saw one. And there, hidden from the sight of
anyone who might pass, we abandoned ourselves.

My friend had spoken the truth. She loved those secret kisses, and a hundred times, I guess, I buried my
face in her tender crotch where, with lips and tongue,
I sipped the sweets as they trickled from between the
vermilion lips—

That night there was another banquet, and after-
wards the king took me to his bed. Three nights in all
I received his maddening embrace upon his skin-decked
bed, and then, the fourth day, he left us.

I thought him the most handsome man I had ever
seen as he walked off through the forest. A broad
leather hat, a leather coat above green velvet trousers,
his legs encased in red hose and his feet shod with low,
silver-buckle shoes the soles of which were heavily
spiked against the ravages of the mountain rocks.

That day was another and stranger banquet, though it was a spermatic one. Our friends had prepared a lunch and had hidden it in the thick wood. Leading me to the lake where we enjoyed a refreshing bath, my friend and I slipped away into the forest. This, she said, was to be a more elaborate affair, and it was. In the little love-bower we found four other couples, four of the handsomest men I had ever seen, and six women, and I class Ferry and myself among them.

You recall the party we had given Ferry just before we departed from Pest? And how I got the good-looking young man for him? Yes? Well, this was another party just like it, only instead of two men, there were four.

"We are leaving in a few days," he said, drawing me down by his side and kissing me, "and this is in our honor. Today we abandon ourselves as we like. See!" and even as he explained, a handsome fellow leaned down and took the head of Ferry's cock between his lips and sucked it! The others crowded about us. One handsome fellow knelt directly behind us, his erect cock sticking up a rakish angle between our shoulders. Ferry raised his hand and clasped it, worked it up and down. "I suppose you'll hate me," he said, his voice a tremble, but I can't help it! For years I've wanted it, and today I'll have my fill if I die for it!" and without another word he turned his head and took the head of the other's erect cock into his mouth, allowing the man to push it in!

Fascinated, I watched the strange sight. Ferry, his eyes half-closed, abandoned himself to his new-found pleasure. I heard him moan, saw him move his lips—He was going-off, pouring his hot fluid into the mouth of the sucker before him! I saw the other move his hips back and forth, saw him place his hand upon Ferry's head and thrilled as I realized he in turn was filling my lover's mouth with a prolific dose of his spicy jissim—

What more is there to tell, my friend? You have been a member of many such affairs, you told me so with your own lips, so you must know what goes on at such functions. Enough to say, that we gave ourselves up to every possible sort of pleasure; we girls sucked each other, and we sucked the men. The men sucked each other's cocks, and we were fucked in every conceivable position.

We were out of sight of our friends; no one knew where we were, so Ferry and I enjoyed ourselves to repletion. A few days later we departed. Dressed in the clothes we had worn to that bandit camp, we started the return journey. Standing, at last, on the edge of the little river I gazed down into the cool black depths. Then I smilingly steppd in. Coming to where it was too deep to walk further, I gave myself into Ferry's hands and he swam the short distance with me. Standing on the opposite bank we waved farewell to our friends, and then we went our way. I never saw any of them again, though I have often wished that I might enjoy another week in their midst.

Ferry and I talked of the delightful times we had enjoyed with his friends and we fully intended returning to them some time for another and far more lengthy visit, but events that followed made it impossible for us to do so.

I must turn my thoughts to my work. My time being up I joined a company of singers touring the country. I bid farewell to Ferry; it wasn't to be a farewell forever; it was simply that he had been unexpectedly called to America where he had many interests, and I might mention here that I never saw him again.

Shortly after his arrival in the distant country, I received word of his demise, and with it came the news that I had inherited his vast wealth. I'm the least bit afraid I failed in my work after that; his loss was, I thought, greater than I could bear.

I promised myself that I would be true to his memory, that I would never allow another man to have me, but how weak we women are.

Then came even sadder news. It was to the effect that both my mother and father had been killed, and this so upset me I decided to travel. I booked passage to Italy. I had always wanted to visit Florence, and there I went. By traveling across Bulgaria, Servia and Albania.

I had been there but a few days, however, when I was overtaken with an urge to again taste bliss in the arms of another woman, and, since Italy's noted for its tribades, I had little trouble in finding a pretty and shapely girl. This but added to the urge for a man. I left Florence and journeyed south through Italy.

In Rome, during one of my many visits to the coliseum, I was approached by a man. Like myself he was a stranger, touring about the country. In spite of the fact that the man was nearly fifty years old I found him handsome and learned. Indeed, he didn't look a day over thirty-five, and I found myself delighting in his company.

Perhaps it was due to my thoughts of the coliseum and the wonderful amphitheatre, now gone, in which the Flavian games took place.

History having been my favorite reading for years I used to dwell for hours at a time on the wonderful things that happened there, and I many times pictured myself walking naked among them.

This man, whose name was Sir Ethelred Merwyn, told me many strange tales about the feasts and other events which took place within the walls of the crumbling edifice, and I was suddenly taken with the idea that I would like to know the man better: Having been so long without a lover my mind was easily influenced, and I soon realized that I desired something far more substantial than mere looks.

And so I set about luring this man to my arms. In invited him to my hotel to dinner, and we enjoyed ourselves to repletion.

Everyday we went somewhere. Then, when it seemed I could no longer stand it, I invited him to my apartment. I told him I felt dreadfully indisposed and would appreciate it if he would dine with me there. He did this, and I thrilled as I caught him viewing my thinly-clad body, for I wore but precious little beneath a lacy dressing-gown.

I continued to feel badly, and invited him to have dinner with me the following night, and again I flirted with him, growing less and less careful about hiding my charms. But a peep at my knee, a dexterous swish of my skirt which revealed a patch of white thigh or a scant view of one nude breast failed to thaw out the man.

This was Saturday night. As he left me that night I made him promise to call early the following afternoon. He must have dinner and lunch with me, I said. About noon he arrived. He suggested a ride, but I declined; I wanted a different sort of ride than the one he proposed.

We spent hours talking on his favorite theme, and it was late in the afternoon, before I succeeded in getting his mind off on something else. I finally turned to the subject of women, and this we discussed at great length. He spoke of the different nationalities, pointing out the good and bad points.

"You are very beautiful," he said, "and though you come from Germany I favor the French women."

"Why?" I asked. It was a direct question.

"Because," he said, "the French, as a whole, are the most beautiful in the world. Their habits are more correct, and they are best fitted to wear the conventional dress of the country."

He said many more things about the French women, all complimentary.

"You are mistaken about their dress," I said by way of getting to the point. "I have seen other women wearing dress the French women would never dare to wear; their bodies are hardly suited for the extreme in decolleté dresses."

"You speak as though you were well versed on the subject."

"I am," I said. "I myself have worn dresses no French woman would dare wear. Not alone their breasts, but their legs are hardly suited to the 'ultra' in dress."

I saw him give a start at this broad statement. We argued back and forth, and finally I said:

"I have many gowns here with me, and I will wager you that a Germna woman—myself, if you please—can wear the ultra in undress and still look acceptable."

This seemed to have the desired result, for he said: "You are making a rash wager, my dear young lady."

"I am ready to prove my statement," I said, smiling into his eyes.

For several moments he remained quiet; it was as though he was trying to gain courage to put the next question, then: "I am willing to lose considerable money to back up my statement, that a French woman is more daring in dress than any other on earth."

"Tell me how you know this, and perhaps I shall take you up on it."

"Very well," he said. "I was calling on a French girl one time, and, strangely enough, the same conversation came up. Just in a joking way I wagered her that she dare not don a costume consisting of less covering than one I had seen but a few days previous, and the daring girl took me up—and won my wager."

"And what did her costume consist of?" I asked, feeling sure I had him on the right track.

"That," he said, "would be unfair. I didn't tell her what the other had worn, and it would not be fair were I to tell you. Remember, it was you who started this, and it's me who is willing to back my contention with money." He was leaning forward now, expectantly.

"You sound sincere," I said laughing.

"I was never more so in my life," he parried.

"I am inclined to take you up," I said, laughing, "just to take the conceit out of you." Inwardly I was thrilled. I had given this man considerable opportunity to enjoy my caresses, but he had failed to rise to the lure, and now I wondered just what would move him. Instead of answering my pun, he drew from his pocket a large billfold, and from it he drew what appeared to be a considerable amount of money. This he lay upon a small stand. Rising, I went to the stand and picked up the money.

"I am inclined to take your wager," I said, "but unfortunately I haven't near that amount of money with me. However—"

"Your word is good enough for me," he interrupted. "You understand the conditions surrounding this wager?"

I smiled. "Your wager, as I understand it, is that I dare not appear here before you in as daring an undress as your French friend; is that correct?" and when he nodded, I went on: "As you say, this is most unusual, but I have brought it upon myself, so the only manner in which I might prove my contention is by appearing here before you in what I choose to term 'ultra-undress.' Is that correct?"

Again he nodded. "There is one condition under which I shall go through with it," I said, "That is, that you will never mention this affair to anyone. May I have your promise to that?"

Again he nodded. "I am a gentleman in every respect," he said.

Smilingly I turned and walked from the room. With wildly beating heart I slipped out of my already scant covering. Naked, I sprayed myself with a dainty perfume, turned and walked back to the curtain which separated the two rooms. I peeped between them. Sir Ethelred stood gazing at a picture above the mantle. With a quick movement I swished the curtains apart and stepped into the room.

I saw him gasp. Then, without further ado, he stepped to the tiny table and picked up the money. With a smile on his face he turned and handed me the cash. "There isn't the slightest question as to who has won this wager," he said, "and I take back what I said about women other than French. You are the most beautiful one I have ever seen!"

I saw his eyes sweep over me. I turned, allowing him to view me from every angle, scattering the money as I did so. Stopping before him, I said: "Your French friend—was she generous enough to invite you to remain with her, after she had won *her* wager?"

He came to me, took me in his arms. "What do you mean?" he asked.

For answer I raised my lips to his in a clinging kiss.

Leading me to a broad couch he kissed my face, neck, and shoulders and titties—and after he fucked me, he dropped to his knees between mine and "frenched" me. He, my dear, was the first man who ever did that to me;

men usually tongue-fuck their women *before* they fuck
them. But Sir Ethelred was different. He was an epicurean in his great heart. Leading him to my bedroom
I asked him to strip off his clothes. The sight of his naked body lent further lust to my already overwrought
body; I sprang upon him, kissed him all over and ended
by taking his cock into my mouth and sucking him off.

There were no secrets between us after that. He
asked me to tell him my story, and I omitted nothing.
He, in turn, confessed that he had on several occasions
taken good-looking young men to his bed, and that he
loved it. He remained with me all night, and proved in
many ways that he was something of a ladies' man.

The following morning he insisted upon my taking
my winnings, but I refused. "If I accepted your money,"
I told him, "you would always remember me as a whore,
and I'm not that; I take my pleasure for the pure love
of it."

This so delighted him that he proposed a series of
parties, and for one solid week we indulged in one orgy
after the other.

He told me of the shocking orgies which were for
ever taking place throughout Rome and promised to arrange that I might witness them.

One talks of Paris and the gay and exciting things
that happen there, but they are nothing as compared
to those of Rome. Through peep-holes one might witness scenes never dreamed of in Paris, but I won't tire
you with a description of them here; they are for too
shocking for even me to relate.

After a week with Sir Ethelred I left Italy and crossed
back into Hungary, and here I spent a happy month.
Here, as I have already told, the "elite" were vieing with
each other in every sort of vile and erotic entertainment.
A description of one will give you an idea of the sort of

entertainment they fostered. My previous visit to Budapest had made me acquainted with many members of the "upper-set," and I hadn't been in the city a day before I was being sought by members of this self-same set. The night of the day I arrived in Budapest I was invited to a great banquet given in the home of one "Madam Silvia Tugwell." Silvia, though in her early thirties, was the mother of a very beautiful daughter, and was noted for the spectacular parties she was for ever giving.

Living, as she did, in a spacious home, and being married to a man of great wealth, Silvia had had installed in the basement of their home a swimming pool, and the place had held more than one bizarre party. The banquet was to begin at nine o'clock, and I arrived at seven, and was just in time to partly over-hear a quarrel between Silvia and her vicious daughter.

This girl, though scarcely seventeen, had already been mixed up in one or two scandalous affairs, and was known to have carried on a flirtation with a captain of police, he having caught her in a raid, and demanded her favors as the price of silence.

"I don't know what the child will want to do next," cried Silvia, wringing her hands and carrying on at a great rate. "Now she wants to bring in a dancer to entertain my guests, and I know it will cause nothing more than another scandal. What shall I do! What shall I do!"

"Forget it, Silvia," I said, patting her cheek. "The child must have her fling, even as you and I."

Whether she got my meaning I do not know. I know, however, that nothing more was said about it until near the end of the dinner, and then plenty was said, and not alone by Silvia.

These functions, as one might guess, was the gather-

ing place for rues and their mistresses and, as in other
fashionable centers, the women were forever striving to
out-do each other in indecent dress, and Silvia's banquet was no exception. Myself? I wore a gown with a
little or nothing above my waist. My breasts, like those
of every woman and girl present, strutted bodily over
their corsage. The couples, eighty in number, were
from the first families of the city, and the women
and their escorts alike boasted of their lovers and mistresses.

Madam Silvia herself spent but one night each week
in her husband's apartment, the other six she spent in
the arms of her lovers.

Is it any wonder, then, that her vicious daughter,
moving, as she did, among the others of the "younger
set" shouldn't go in for the unusual?

I have, as you know, a pair of full, well-rounded
breasts, and long before the dinner was over more than
one gentleman present was viewing them, desire showing in every look. Much wine had been consumed, and
the dinner was rapidly drawing to a close when there
came a scuffle at one of the draped exits, and a moment
later a girl was seen to dash through the portiers and
run to the table. With a bound she sprang upon it, ran
the entire length amid the plaudits of the guests, and
finished the performance by doing a most lewd dance
in the very center. Does that sound unusual, my friend?
No? Well, then, let me tell you something more about
it. The beautiful black-haired daughter of Silvia was
stark naked.

Her mother, of course, was horrified, or pretended she
was, but the guests, and especially the gentlemen, were
delighted and insisted that the pretty child-woman continue her dance. After that she was handed from one to
the other until she had made the round of the table,

and the whole affair ended by her mother kissing her and thanking her for making the party a success.

But Silvia, however, had another treat in store for her guests who were to remain over night. A dozen couples, having come from distant cities, were supposed to remain all night, and being among these latter I too remained.

"You'll enjoy it darling," she cooed, handing me "Frenchy" nightgown. "It's so risque. Oh, darling, you'll love it!"

The "party" Silvia had in mind was to take place in the famous pool in the cellar the following morning. There was a story leading up to this affair which runs something like this: "Once, a few years previous, some woman of her acquaintance had given a cruising-party to several of her guests. A large yacht carried them into the Adriatic, and everything went well until the afternoon of the third day, and then the yacht sprung a leak.

There was little or no danger, but the captain ran the yacht upon a sandy shore for safety sake. The dining-room, however, they found to contain several feet of water, and someone in the party suggested what she called a "swim-breakfast" and this was seconded by the entire party. Then, just to give the thing "spice," they went into the dining-room wearing their night clothes, the ladies wearing their naughtiest night-gowns, the gentlemen wearing theirs.

Silvia, who had been one of the women, immediately copied the stunt, and once a year she gave what she called a "swim-breakfast" in her pool, only those being invited to attend being the "elite."

The pool having been arranged in the early hours of dawn, we proceeded into the cellar where we found everything ready and waiting.

It was, I do believe, the most bizarre affair I had ever attended.

The water had been lowered 'till it came to but the top of the table, and the chairs had been weighted down. We found steaming coffee awaiting us, and it was a gay crowd, indeed, who tripped down into the crystal-clear water, little 'Oh's" and "Ah's" escaping their lips at the contact of the cool water.

Sounds like a very "spicy" party, doesn't it? Well, to me it was the most asinine affair I had ever heard of. It was asinine because these fool women were wearing the Frenchiest sort of nightgowns of the sheerest possible texture (two or three, more daring than the others, wearing gossamer affairs without the slightest trimming) when they should, by every possible right, be naked.

After all, my friend, what is the difference between a woman wearing a nightgown of the sheerest possible texture, and another in complete nakedness? Think it over a little, my friend. Then add to this—if you can— how they look when wet.

Two or three of them hurried down into the water and waded to their places seemingly unmindful that their thin garments floated about the hips, while others, trying to appear shy, flitted about the edge, their gowns drawn up their thighs and begging the men not to wet them; the men, in the meantime, getting a splendid eye-full since they stood directly beneath the squealing women.

At last, however, they all waded in and were directed to their proper place by maids who waded hip-deep, and here again there was considerable squealing when they settled down upon the chairs.

It was Silvia's daughter again who turned a drab affair into a real honest-to-God naughty party, and thus

saved the affair from becoming a flat failure. The little
imp seemed to have been waiting until everyone was
seated before she burst in upon the crowd, and, as the
previous night, she was stark naked. Laughing and
splashing her way through the water, she rushed directly to her mother's side, kissed her and splashed water into her face.

Silvia was furious, of course. She remonstrated,
coaxed and pleaded, but it did not the slightest good;
Tillie (that was the daughter's name) was bent on
making it an out and out nude party and finally succeeded in tearing the gown off her mother, very much
to the other's—Silvia's—disgust.

This, of course, was wildly applauded by the others
who were only too glad that someone had courage
enough to do something to enliven a drab affair. The
gentlemen, seeing Silvia floundering about in absolute
nakedness, now took it upon themselves to denude their
partners, and though the latter made as though to prevent it, it was all too plain that they were doing everything possible to assist the men in the disrobing act,
and the result was that every woman, myself included,
was reduced to complete nakedness, and after the men
kindly removed their scant attire, we sat down to enjoy
a much delayed breakfast.

"Isn't it fun!" cried one.

"Isn't it just too naughty for words!" cried another.

"Don't you just love it!"

"Let's do it every Sunday morning!"

Everyone had something to say in favor of it, and
while those silly women was trying to get used to something they had wanted to do in the beginning, Tillie
had scrambled upon the table and was pouring coffee
and making herself useful in a dozen different ways, and
more than one male hand reached up and patted or

toyed with some charm the child-woman so freely exposed.

Silvia tried to make one desperate effort to get rid of her daughter, but Tillie wasn't to be put off. "You should talk about me! What were you sneaking into your lover's bedroom for last night if it wasn't to get a thrill! Oh, don't look so frightened! I saw you and him in bed together, and you weren't making such a fuss about being naked then!"

And while Silvia fumed and fussed, the others laughed at her misery, and the whole affair boiled down to what it should have been in the first place, namely, an out and out bare-ass romp.

That was rather a long description of a rather tame affair, my friend, but I couldn't help but describe the sort of affair that was forever taking place in that and other cities at that time.

Being alone (Sir Ethelred having continued his journey into the Orient) I spent several days in the offices of my attorneys, and after what seemed endless time, my affairs were in such state that I was able to travel again.

With more wealth than I could ever hope to spend I toured to France and hence to Paris. I had three distinct reasons for this. In the first place it was necessary to go there as I had affairs of Ferry's to settle; I had never been to Paris, and I wanted to replenish my wardrobe.

I had heard considerable about Paris and its gaiety, and as soon as I got settled in a hotel, I went on a tour of shopping. Being a stranger in the city I had asked one of the hotel clerks to suggest the best known places in which to buy dresses, and he had given me a card, upon which was an address, and telling me of the high quality of the garments sold there.

I visited this place late the following afternoon, and

it was in this "shoppe" that I had my first thrilling eye-full of what went on in this type of store. Having made known my needs to what seemed to be the mistress of the establishment, I was shown into the rear of the store, or "shoppe," as the place was known.

Like many other places of a like-kind, it was fitted out with a small stagelike affair upon which the models displayed the various gowns, suits, under-things and the like, but this shoppe differed from the others somewhat by showing live models instead of plaster ones. And while I stood waiting for the "show" to begin, another young woman entered and seated herself close beside me. I noticed that she smiled at me, and I returned the smile. Here, I thought, was a good chance to crack up an acquaintance; I knew no one in the great city and was desirous of company.

I noted among other things that she was unusually pretty, that her carriage was perfect, and that she sported a wonderful shape.

This interested me, as you might have already imagined.

There was another thing about her, however, and this was, that she was unusually pale. I wondered at that.

The mistress of the establishment had the kindness to introduce me to this handsome woman (I had previously told her I was a stranger in the city) and I found her charming, indeed.

I told her something about myself, she told me a little about herself, and all in all we found each other splendid company. She said that she purchased all her gowns in that particular shoppe, thus leading me to believe she must be well-to-do, and that being the type I sought, I encouraged her. When she discovered that I had traveled more or less extensively, she said: "You have been in Russia?"

When I told her I had never been in that country, but that I had had the pleasure of meeting several Russians and that I admired them a great deal, she smiled and said: "I am Russian, as you have undoubtedly noted."

"And I am German," I laughed. "We should make a good foil for these delightful Parisians." And so I gained another delightful friend.

I had never cared very much for French people; those I had met seemed to be narrow-minded and distant, but there is one thing to be said in their favor: When a Parisian does something, he or she does it well. And this held good in this shoppe.

The models, instead of being the plaster kind, were real live ones, and shortly after we had entered the place they began coming upon the little stage I have already mentioned. One by one they made their appearance, and it was these very models who gave me my first look into Parisian ideas and the way they did things.

The first model, a beautiful black-haired creature, came on wearing a long black cape and low slippers. Gaining the front of the stage the girl smiled down at us and dropped off the gown, and there before us she stood stark naked.

Nudity was no new thing to me, but this, I thought, was about the strangest thing I had ever seen. I called my new friend's attention to this, but she simply shrugged her shapely shoulders, saying:

"It is nothing, my friend. One becomes used to so much nudity, and we think nothing of it here."

"You have lived here long?" I asked.

"A year," she answered. "I like Paris very much."

Wondering what she meant about "so much nudity," I said: "You speak as though you were a frequent visitor here—Is that what you meant about the nudity?"

She smiled, then: "No. You see I have been a professional woman; I was a member of the Ballet, but I injured an ankle and" she shrugged her shoulders again "well, I never took it up again."

I found myself liking the woman more and more. I said: "I can quite understand, since you were an actress. It happens that I, too, have been an actress and am used to nudity, but one sees here and there one she like better than another perhaps." Pointing toward one of the models who was just coming upon the stage, I continued "That one, for instance. I am anxious to see her undraped; she must be beautiful."

My friend smiled. My lure had been taken, for she said: "We all have our tastes. For my part I would prefer the one over there; the little one who came on first. I could just *eat* her with kisses I think her the most beautiful of them all."

A thrill passed over me. This business of *eating* a girl sounded interesting. I said: "Strange, isn't it, but I was thinking the same of the golden-haired one."

My Russian friend thawed; my last remark had had its effect.

Reaching across and patting my hand, she said: "I do not wish to be misunderstood, but—well, the one you refer to *is* rather acceptable and can be had."

Taking the bull by the horns, I said: "Passive or active?"

"Both," came the ready answer. "You will find Madam ———— more than willing to accommodate."

We talked for a few minutes more, made a few selections, and as I was about to leave, my Russian friend said: "If I am understanding correctly that you are quite alone in the city, why not come and have dinner with me. I am quite alone this evening."

I made the necessary excuses, and finally accepted.

I discovered she had her own carriage, and into this we were driven to her apartment. I found it furnished with taste. Costly furnishings were scattered about everywhere. Rugs, many of them unusually costly, covered the floors, while in the center of the front, or parlor room, stood a low, broad couch. Upon this was the largest bear-skin I had ever seen, and it was white.

A maid took our wraps, and when she disappeared, I said: "That couch—it looks interesting," and I looked roguishly at her.

She dropped her eyes, and I wondered if I had overstepped.

"You will undoubtedly think me a dreadful person," she said, her eyes still cast down, "but, well—the gentleman with whom I share this apartment is not my husband."

I laughed. "Naughty," I said, "I knew it all the time, but do not allow it to worry you. I have had a lover at different times and I wish I had one even now."

"That makes it ever so much easier," she said. "I was afraid you wouldn't understand."

Her name, I learned, was Camilla. She was in her early twenties; what she had said about being a ballet dancer was true, and that she was the mistress of a gentleman connected with the Spanish government, and held a responsible position in the French capitol.

Summoning her maid, Camilla ordered wine. "Just an appetizer before dinner," she said, smiling. After two or three glasses of the wine Camilla began taking on life, and soon we were discussing—quite freely I thought—our affairs, previous and present.

Looking longingly at the skin-decked couch, I said: "It must be something of a thrill to entertain a lover while lying in his arms on such a couch."

She laughed. "I'm sorry I cannot furnish you with a desirable man at the moment, but —"

"Then I should have brought that golden-haired beauty with me," I said, giving a slight rotating motion with my loins. "I could do with her very nicely, at the moment."

"Tomorrow," she said, "if you have nothing important to do, I shall show you about our famed city, and who knows—perhaps we might find someone for you."

"Indeed! Sounds interesting!"

We enjoyed a delightful dinner, and long before it was time to depart, Camilla was telling me many things about her lover.

"That couch," she said, nodding toward the other room, "You would hardly believe me when I tell you of the strange part it plays in our affectionate encounters."

"Indeed," I said, "Tell me about it. I am interested."

'Would you believe that my lover, Henri, never receives me in any other than fully dressed? And that it is only after I have aroused him by performing strange rites, that he undresses me?"

Not wishing to ask a direct question, I said: "Lovers are strange persons, so nothing you can tell would surprise me!"

"Just the same," she continued, bent, it seemed, upon telling me about her Henri, "you have never heard of anything like what I am going to tell you. Would you believe," she went on, "that before he is able to have me, I must first straddle across his chest—while we are fully dressed—and pee-pee on his shirt-front?"

I laughed. "There are many men like that, so your story is in no way unusual." Then I told her of the strange experience I had had with the old man, and how he made me "pee-pee" all over him.

She laughed at this, then: "And that is the reason why I am so pale. Henri insists upon me taking something to increase the desire to pee-pee; it's something he heard of from a friend, though he says it's perfectly harmless."

I had my doubts about that, however. I said: "After that I suppose he is quite capable of satisfying you? Most men are, afterward."

"He's wonderful," she said. "I don't know why, but I rather like his strange ideas, too."

"And what does your lover say to that?" I

She shrugged her shoulers, a habit with her I noticed, then: "Then I send for my pet, at Mada's establishment; the black-haired one, I mean."

"And what does your lover say to that?" I asked.

"He's a dear, and doesn't mind a bit. He knows I like a girl, that way, and as long as I remain true to him I can have anything I like."

"And where is your lover now?"

"At the moment he is off somewhere" and looking naughtily at me, continued: "That's why I suggested seeing the city tomorrow, if the idea appeals to you, of course."

"Must we wait until tomorrow?" I asked. I thought this was sufficient to bring her to time, but again she failed to raise to the lure. Camilla was undoubtedly waiting for me to make the first move, but I was but acting; I fully intended it would be she who made the first move.

But I was doomed to disappointment; though I didn't find out the truth of it until the following day.

True to her word she took me on a sight-seeing tour of the city, and among other places we visited was a "massageparlor" in a secluded section of the city, and here I found the "massaging" was done not on one's back and legs, but chiefly between one's thighs.

And it was then I discovered that while Camilla delighted in having a pretty girl "entertain" her that way, she never did it herself. Upon questioning her as to why she didn't, she said: "I do not know myself. It's simply that I never desired it that way, I guess."

That ended that. Camilla was not for me; as long as she care nothing for it actively there was no further reason why I should look forward to a party with her. I did, however, find her rather helpful in my search for a man. She arranged a dinner party for me, and promised to invite a friend. Such affairs were common, she said, and I promised to come.

Camilla had suggested my wearing my naughtiest dress, and this I did. Wearing naughty attire was my greatest delight, and since it had been some time that I had had a man, I rather looked forward to meeting this promised Adonis.

I found Henri's friend rather good-looking, resembling, somewhat my former Ferry, and like him a connoisseur.

Camilla, it seemed, had written Henri making the arrangements for this meeting, and Henri, good soul that he was, had brought the gentleman with him, both arriving late Saturday afternoon. Dinner had been announced for eight, and I had plenty of opportunity to study my new acquaintance. My dress, as Camilla had suggested, was rather in keeping with such a gathering, and though it was delightfully naughty, Camilla went me one better.

Hers was a white satin affair cut in such a manner as to show both her well-formed breasts and showed off the outlines of her splendid figure by its tightness.

The dinner was a success, and I believed I had never enjoyed anything like it, and long before we left the table the wine had gotten in its fine work for all four of us were feeling quite kittenish.

It was Camilla, however, who started things off. I could see from the very start that she intended making it a real party, for all through the repast she flirted outrageously with him, and just as her maid placed coffee and cigarettes before us, she said:

"Perhaps you gentlemen might help ————— and I to settle a dispute."

Her eyes were dilated, her full lips were even more full and red, and the nipples of her breasts were firm and erect and looked for all the world like tiny strawberries.

"Indeed," answered Henri, "I hope you two beauties haven't quarreled on so short acquaintance."

Camilla laughed. "Nothing as bad as that, my dear; it's simply that we disagreed about women."

"Sounds interesting," Phillip (that being my friend's name) offering by way of assisting in what he must have known was to follow.

"Go ahead, Camilla, and tell us; perhaps Henri and I can help you settle your dispute'.'

"Yes, by all means tell us about it," chirped Henri.

"Well," began Camilla, selecting and lighting a cigarette, "it was nothing more than a dispute about women. I insisted that Russia produced the most beautiful women in the world, and —————, being German, insisted that Germany produced the most perfect women."

"What in the world would cause you girls to argue over a thing like that?" asked Henri. "I supposed I had settled that long ago."

"You might have settled it as far as you're concerned," chimed in Phillip, "but I, too, have my ideas regarding beauty."

"Indeed. And what *is* your idea on the matter? Tell us."

"Well," Philip said, eyeing me naughtily, "I quite agree with my little friend, here. If she is an example of Germany's women, then I agree with her, although your Camilla, Henri, is beautiful."

"Thank you," I said, patting his hand and smiling sweetly, "I at least have one friend among us."

"Not at all, not at all," he said. "I am quite sincere about it."

"One man will always stick up for his mistress, and having seen my darling Camilla naked many times—"

"Henri!" cried Camilla, making believe she was dreadfully shocked, "What will our friends think of us, talking like that!"

"But it's true, isn't it?" asked Henri, trying to tease Camilla.

"Just the same you need not advertise it. Besides, I'm but one woman, you know."

"Don't quarrel, don't quarrel," cried Phillip, "but tell us what started the argument."

"Well," began Camilla, "———— and I visited Madam ————'s place a few days ago, and we got to discussing the models—"

"So," cried Henri, "You've been cheating again, have you?"

"Not the way you mean, naughty,"· answered Camilla. "Remember, my dear, there are none but girls there."

"That may be true, but I happen to know what you passionate women go there for."

"Then you shouldn't go away and leave us alone for so long," cried Camilla. "Besides, a little kiss never hurt anyone, and if you'll recall, dear, you said I could go there if I'd promise never to flirt with some man."

The party was getting under way with a bang. The dinner over, we moved from the table and into the front room. The maid brought in champagne and glasses, and Camilla said: "After you have removed the dinner things you may go; we won't need you further tonight."

Camilla looked at me and winked. When she first proposed this affair she had asked me if I was game for a *real* party, and when I told her I would do anything she suggested and that the sky was the limit, she had said something about going a little higher than the sky, and I had readily agreed. And now that she had dismissed her maid I could look for anything.

Phillip and I had taken seats, and Camilla had thrown herself down in rather a sprawled position and was waiting for the drink Henri was preparing for us. This drunk and our glasses filled again, Henri settled down beside Camilla. "Now tell us something more about this argument," he said.

"Well, as I said, ———— and I happened to meet there to select new gowns, and as they began displaying the models we got to discussing them. They are of all nationalities, as you know, and I happened to say that I thought the Russian women were the most beautiful, and ———— insisted that the Germans were."

"Well," Henri said, as though to hurry Camilla.

"Well," Camilla continued, "we didn't get anywhere in our argument, so we decided to let you boys decide it for us. My contention was, that since the ballet was made up chiefly of Russian women, the world accepted them as the best formed."

"In what way?" asked Philip.

"Their legs, of course," said Camilla.

"Nonsense," I offered in my own defence. "The German women have as well-formed legs as any others."

"I quite agree with my friend," Phillip said.

"And I agree with Camilla," insisted Henri. "When I chose Camilla as my mistress I chose her from a hundred women of various nationalities. I know women, and Camilla has the most beautiful legs and thighs of any women I have ever seen."

Phillip, not to be outdone, said: "Again I dispute with you. I have never had the pleasure of seeing ————'s legs, but if what I can see is anything like the rest of her, then I am of the opinion that she is far more beautiful than your Camilla."

"Indeed, she is not," cried Camilla, "and I stand ready to prove it, too."

"Ah, but legs aren't everything," cried Henri. "A woman may have beautiful legs and be out of proportion otherwise. When an artist paints a nude he has, perhaps, a dozen or more models: He paints one's feet, another's legs, and still another's buttocks, while still others pose their head or breasts. No," he continued, sighing, "I'm afraid Camilla's right. You forget that I chose her from hundreds, and having seen her completely nude scores of times—"

"Oh, Henri, you're wicked! But thanks just taking my side of the argument," and she leaned over in his arms offering her half-open mouth to his.

"I'm afraid that lets me out of the argument," Phillip said with a great sigh. "I have tried to be loyal to you, ————, but I'll have to withdraw now."

Not to be out-done when it was plain that the party was just getting hot, I said: "You're just like all men, Phillip, letting me down like that."

"But, my dear," he cried, slipping one arm about my waist, "how can I uphold my contention that you're more beautiful when I have never had the pleasure of seeing you nude?"

"Then let us settle it this way," cried Henri. "Let the girls strip stark naked and—"

"Henri!" cried Camilla, trying to blush. "What a dreadful thing to suggest! I should die of shame!"

"I agree with Henri," Phillip said, looking into my eyes and seeing my answer there. "Let both girls strip stark naked. Then we will produce tapes and measure them. All over, from head to toe."

"How about it, ————? Are you willing to back your contention by going through with it?" asked Henri.

I shrugged my shoulders. "It's a dreadful thing to do," I answered, "but, well—I'll do it if Camilla will. I'm that sure of myself!"

"There," said Henri, hugging his mistress in a tight embrace and kissing her again and again. "Now let's see if you're game, Miss Camilla—!"

"You think I won't?" she cried. "You think I'd back out now?"

Raising from the couch beside Henri, she said: "Come on, ————! We'll show these two softies we're not the simple-minded kids they think us!"

Laughing, her breasts heaving, Camilla pulled me into one of the bedrooms and closed the door. "Thanks," I said, kissing her, "I need it dreadfully bad, and tomorrow I'll pay you back in kind!"

She said not a word to this, and we quickly undressed, even slipping off slippers and stockings. I had seen Camilla naked a few days previous, when we visited the massage parlors, but that night she looked like a marble statue. Her skin, lily-white, seemed even more white to me, and she was, I thought, the most beautiful woman I had ever seen in the altogether. Our wager and brags had been, of course, but a means to an end, and just as we were about to re-enter the larger room, she slipped her arms about me, saying: "You still game to make it an out and out party, darling? I'm dreadfully hot tonight, and I might shock our pretty eyes with what I do!"

"Lead the way, Camilla, my dear. I said I'd go through with anything you could suggest, and I mean it. I'm game for anything!"

"Anything?" she asked, a naughty twinkle in her eye.

"I'll do anything you do!" I answered. "And not only that, but tomorrow, or whenever we get the opportunity, I'll pay you back, just as I promised!"

She gazed into my eyes for a long minute, then: "May I depend on it, darling? I might take you up, you know."

"Fix it so I can have Phillip for the entire night and I'll promise anything—and I never break a promise!"

Snatching a single kiss, Camilla turned and ran into the other room. Naked as the day I was born, I followed. I saw Phillip's eyes sweep over me as Camilla and I posed in the center of the room!

"Naughty!" cried Camilla, trying to cover her cunny and breasts with her two hands. "Don't stare at me like that! It's dreadful."

For answer Henri pulled her down upon his knees, and here Camilla forgot all about covering her charms, and from that moment on the party was a huge success. The promised measuring was but a farce; it was but a means to get their hands upon our charms, a little opportunity Phillip didn't waste much time in doing with me, and it was Camilla's timely remark that saved me from asking Phillip to fuck me then and there.

She said: "Henri, dear, your clothes are so rough—"

"That's easily remedied," he cried, dragging Phillip

with him into the bedroom, from which they emerged as naked as ourselves!

A warm glow swept over me as I rested my eyes on Phillip's erect prick! And it was erect, if ever I saw one! Fully eight inches long and as large around as my wrist, it was, and I couldn't keep my hand from it! "Look," he whispered, nodding toward the opposite side of the room. I looked, and what I saw convinced me that Camilla had been right in her statement that this was to be a real party!

I had never met a man who wouldn't give me every sort of kiss and caress, but I had met but few who would allow another to see them in this strange position. Henri, however, seemed to have forgotten he had an audience; it was either that or he didn't care, for he was covering Camilla's body and legs with his warmest kisses, every moment or two burying his face between her widely parted thighs and madly kissing her slit!

"Like it?" came the whispered question in my ear.

My answer was a kiss, then: "I love it!"

That, my friend, was the beginning of one of the most naughty affairs I had ever attended. Like Ferry, Phillip and Henri cared not who knew or saw them. In utter abandon he buried his face into my willing crotch! Gazing across to the others, I saw Camilla take Phillip's crest between her lips and suck it in and out! Not to be out-done I followed suit, continuing the lovely operation till the handsome fellow went-off into my mouth! Roused, now, to the highest pitch I begged him to fuck me—

The following day being Sunday we continued the affair throughout the day. Naked save mules on our feet, Camilla and I flirted outrageously with the two men— and I had the pleasure of another night in the arms of the handsome man. They left us Monday morning, and

I was sorry indeed. I remained several days with Camilla.

The evening of the second day, Camilla was lying upon a couch her only covering being a short, lacy affair between the folds of which I could see the silky hairs on her lower belly. Settling down beside her, I said: "You told me a fib, dear. You told me how you had to pee-pee upon Henri before he could get an erection, but you didn't do it. Why?"

"I guess it was because you being naked with us—that wasn't the first party like that we've had, and its always the same; Henri always has a wonderful cockstand when he sees another nude."

"Nonsense," I scoffed, pulling her gown open all down the front, "Seeing you naked is enough to arouse any man."

"Just the same, I wish you remain with us forever, for then I'd get all the fucking I want, and I want it all the time."

"So I noticed," I said, laughing and sliding my hand up and down her splendid body which now lay bared before me. "I thought you would kill the poor fellow. I was on the verge of taking him off your hands."

"Why didn't you? Phillip hasn't a bad looking tool. If he were here now I believe I would ask him to fuck me, I'm that hot!"

"Then why not let's get ourselves a couple of men? They must be plenty about one can get, and I could stand a good poking myself."

She stared up at me for several seconds, then: "I could never bring myself to do that, but, well—if you'll promise never to give me away I'll let you into a secret."

Leaning over her and kissing her lips, I said: "Tell me what's on your mind, dear, and I'll promise in the most convincing manner!"

Another short silence, then: "I know a place where we can go, but oh! you must give me your faithful promise you'll never tell!"

I promised, and she went on to tell me of a place she knew of on a certain street. It was run by a woman she knew very well, and she catered to but the highest class men. The place, she said, was the naughtiest place she had ever seen. Ribbons of various colors hung in the front room. For every color there was a girl, and the men, wishing to enjoy the novelty of the thing as well as the woman, chose a ribbon and followed it through the halls and into the specific room to which it ran. There, she said, the girl, naked, waited for the man, and, since she had been there a number of times, she wanted to take me there.

I agreed, naturally. The thing held a certain amount of spice, and I wasn't at all sure but what I would take the first man that came along. Briefly, we went there. We were assigned two rooms, the following morning, just before daylight, we crept away; I, for one, having all the men I wanted for one evening.

From that day until I left Camilla, we had dozens of men, and I had the satisfaction of initiating Camilla into that little game known as "sixty-nine."

I had intended going to London, since I had business there, but I left a little sooner than I intended, and my decision to go earlier was brought about in a somewhat unusual manner.

One afternoon Camilla had a caller. This was a beautiful French girl. She, it seemed, was also an actress. She had been playing in Paris, but the show had been a "flop" to use the parlance of the stage, and was going to London where she had an offer to join another company. "Indeed," I said, smiling, "I am going to London, so why not make the trip with me?"

And she willingly agreed to this arrangement. I noted that she was unusually pretty, was well formed and sported a pair of the prettiest legs I have ever seen. Bidding adieu to Camilla and promising to spend more time with her, Yvonne (that being her name) and I left.

We sailed across the channel, and since we had embarked late in the afternoon, and because the weather outside was damp and foggy, we adjourned ot our cabin. It contained two beds, and I couldn't help but notice how elated she seemed at the prospect of being so near me.

As I have said, Yvonne was a very pretty girl, and as you might have guessed, I was looking forward to becoming better acquainted with her. I suggested having dinner in our room, since I was too tired to dress for dinner, and Yvonne readily agreed to this arrangement.

I said: "Slip out of your clothes, dear, and we'll enjoy our dinner in more comfortable attire. Being something of a nudist, I can't bear much clothing."

Darting into a tiny dressing-room, she gave a startled little laugh, and cried: "That's funny; so am I, but I hope I won't shock you."

I heard water running and knew Yvonne was taking a bath; a very considerate gesture I thought. Most actresses are more or less careless with the exposure of their body and limbs, and I'm sure the deck-steward got something of a shock at the gown I was wearing.

Dinner placed upon the table and the steward gone, Yvonne came into the room. The poor kid was a little low on cash and had little or nothing of extra clothing, but I had provided her with certain articles of apparel, and the radiant kid was wearing two of the garments now. A knee-length dressing-gown and a tiny under-vest

of black georgette, being her only covering beside mules
on her tiny, well-shaped feet.

After our dinner, she said: "I'm sorry I lied to you,
dear, but my name isn't Yvonne, but Sarolta. I had a
little trouble in Paris, and used the name Yvonne."

"Nothing serious, I hope."

"Just a board-bill, but in Paris that's serious," she answered.

"Then forget it," I said. "I have plenty of money
and you're welcome to it. What's more, when we get to
London I'll purchase you a whole new outfit, from head
to toe."

"You're awfully good," she said, "and I can't hold it
back; I'm not an actress, at least I haven't worked at it
for some time: I'm—well, I guess I'm just a little
whore."

"Forget all about it," I said, seeing a tear in each of
her eyes, "We've all made mistakes, and, well—if you
must know it, this little thing between my legs is almost screaming aloud for a stiff prick. Anyway," I continued, "I'm glad you told me that much about it, for
now I can feel ever so much more at home," and I
slipped the gown from my shoulders, it being the only
article of dress I was wearing. The cabin sported a broad
couch, and going to this I threw myself down, stretched
languidly, and said: "I can't bear a stitch of clothing
when I'm like I feel now."

"Then you should go with me to Mrs. Meredyth's
home; no one ever things of wearing a stitch of clothing
there," throwing herself down beside me after dropping
off her gown, but still retaining the tiny under-vest.

"Indeed," I said, patting a smooth, warm thigh, "You
interest me, my dear. Tell me about it," and I continued to stroke the warm flesh of her shapely leg. Sarolta,
however, didn't get to describing her friend, Mrs. Mere-

dyth. I had already taken note of the profuse, raven-black hair that almost buried her little slit, and wishing to hurry what was on my mind, I said: "Naughty, I thought you were a nudist. I feel silly lying without anything on and you all dressed up in a chemise."

"There," she said, throwing off the thing and turning about so I could view her splendid body, now completely nude. "Is that the way you want me?"

She moved to the couch again and settled down, raising her hands to toy with her hair on her head. Her knees, separated due to her position, gave me a view of her little cunt. I wanted it; I never wanted anything more, but I went slow. Placing my hand on her leg again, and feeling her, I said: "Really, dear, I had no idea your skin was so soft and velvety. And this hair . . . how lovely and black it is," running my fingers through it; it ran far up on her belly, and its feel quite thrilled me.

"Like it?" she asked, raising one leg, thus allowing me more freedom which I took by diving my fingers lower down. "It's lovely," I said. Turning, she glanced down at my hairy patch, then: "But it's not nearly as silky as yours; you must have taken good care of it," and the daring girl slid her hand into the patch, feeling and toying with it and running her fingers up and down through it.

"You like mine?" I asked, separating my legs a little and which she quickly took advantage of by sliding her fingers into my crotch and gently caressing my slit.

"It's beautiful," she said in a low voice.

"I'm glad you like it, dear, for your naughty fingers feel lovely, but if you keep it up I'll have to ask you to finish it for me."

"You really like it?" she asked, smiling into my eyes, and probing into the soft flesh, and when I told her I did, she said: "Then perhaps you'll like this better," and dropping to her knees beside me, she slipped her face between my thighs gave me one of the most delightful French parties I had ever had.

"Did you like that?" she asked, raising and leaning over me.

"How did you know I wanted that, little tribade?" and she said: "Camilla told me you loved to be sucked-off, and I love doing it."

She said this in the most matter-of-fact way. "And do you like having it done to you?" I asked.

"Sometimes," she answered, "but I'd rather do it any time than have it done, and that's why I'm going to London. There are any number of Mrs. Meredyths who delight in having it done, and that's why I'm going there."

Never in my short life had I ever heard anything like this. With the least possible insinuation she went-down on me, and afterward she tells me how she delights in doing it to women.

Using her own words, I said: "Do you like to suck my cunt, dear?"

"I love it. Shall I do it again?"

Nodding my approval, she quickly got her face between my legs and gave me another and far sweeter thrill than before.

A further description of what happened between us is useless here.

In London I found this Mrs. Meredyth a very charming woman. In her early thirties; she was wealthy; single, and lived for the pure love of living. I discovered, too, a very charming lady there whom I had previously met, and who turned out to be a sister-in-law of Ferry, my previous lover. Strangely enough this woman knew all about my affairs with Ferry, and then I discovered that she, like the other women and girls there, was a strict believer in "Free Love."

The place enchanted me. Mrs. Meredyth was one of the most charming women it has been my good fortune to meet, her home, besides being spacious, was beautiful and was frequented by the elite of London.

"We have no secrets," she smilingly told me. "Ferry's sister-in-law has told me all about you, and we welcome you as one of us, and we sincerely hope you will make my place of abode your home as long as it is possible for you to remain in London." With that she kissed me, told me she thought me beautiful, then: "Please do not think I presume, but I would keenly enjoy spending the night with you, if you haven't other plans."

"I could think of nothing more charming," I said. "I greatly delight in entertaining pretty women, and you are very pretty, indeed!"

My story is drawing to a close, my friend. There is little left to tell. I remained with Mrs. Meredyth for two years, and after an extended trip through Russia I returned there, and am there now.

I believe that woman knew everyone of importance in all London.

Every night a dinner party, and such parties! She kept the most beautiful girls in all London, and while it was a whore-house in every sense of the word, no one ever paid for the favors shown them by these women. In the rear of her palatial home was a great garden, and here one found tiny love-bowers, no one ever dreamed of wearing the slightest covering. Though one seldom ever heard a smutty word, the greatest freedom was enjoyed. Sarolta was a great favorite with the women and men alike and still here.

Would you like to hear a bit of scandal, my friend? Yes? Listen, then. Balls and parties were, as I have said, a frequent occurrence. Once the Prince of Wales (later King Edward) signified his intention to spend the weekend here. When Mrs. Meredyth made this known one very pretty and shapely girl said: "Really, dear! Then I must hurry and undress!"

Think of one undressing for the Prince of Wales! Yet, that is exactly what we *did* do. The night of his arrival, thirty girls sat at table with him. He was the only man, and every girl was stark naked, save slippers on their feet.

I had the pleasure of dancing with the Prince, and even though I was nude, the Prince proved himself a gentleman, and twice before his brief vacation was ended, I felt the weight of his nude body upon mine. I wonder what his Royal mother would say were she to know that? But then, perhaps she does. Who knows?

But our pleasures were not confined to the house and garden. We visited everywhere. Vauxhall Gardens— Piccadilly Salon — Holborn Casino — Portland Rooms —were some of the places we frequented, though we missed none of the lesser spots.

One night after a splendid dinner when Mrs. Meredyth was feeling in an unusual mood, she suggested that we walk in street as common whores. Several had already done this several times and boasted of the good times they had had. We did it. That night I had six sailors in the back room of a common saloon and nothing came of it.

Another time someone stole our purses. Mrs. Meredyth suggested taking a "hansom" home. "But how shall we pay?" I asked.

She simply smiled at this. "Wait and see," she said.

At our door we were obliged to tell the cabby of our plight.

He, good soul that he was, offered to take it out in

trade, and right there in his cab, Mrs. Meredyth and I allowed the cabby to fuck us. Some comedown for an opera singer, isn't it, my friend?

But remember, it was only a lark; either of us could have purchased a thousand hansom cabs.

I'll never forget his words as he adjusted his trousers. He said:

"Be jabbers I niver had a better put-in thin the two o' yer, and I'm treatin' yer ter the ride!"

But Mrs. Meredyth wasn't to be outdone by a cab driver. Telling him to wait there for her, she went into the house, returning with a well-filled purse. "Here," she said, handing it to him, "There is a hundred pounds in it, and it's worth it; you're the best fuck I've had in months!"

A nudist at heart, I've gone naked for days on end, as have many others here, and the longer I do it the greater the thrill.

Grove Press Victorian Library